To my Sanny
with
LOVE & Appreciation

SIGNALING

[signature]

May—30—2017

D0628746

SIGNALING

A MESSAGE FROM THE FUTURE

TILAK FERNANDO   ED STROUPE

ARCHWAY
PUBLISHING

Copyright © 2017 R. Edwin Stroupe and Tilak S. Fernando.

All rights reserved. No part of this book may be used or reproduced by
any means, graphic, electronic, or mechanical, including photocopying,
recording, taping or by any information storage retrieval system
without the written permission of the author except in the case of
brief quotations embodied in critical articles and reviews.

This is a work of fiction. All of the characters, names, incidents,
organizations, and dialogue in this novel are either the products
of the author's imagination or are used fictitiously.

Archway Publishing books may be ordered through booksellers or by contacting:

Archway Publishing
1663 Liberty Drive
Bloomington, IN 47403
www.archwaypublishing.com
1 (888) 242-5904

Because of the dynamic nature of the Internet, any web addresses or
links contained in this book may have changed since publication and
may no longer be valid. The views expressed in this work are solely those
of the author and do not necessarily reflect the views of the publisher,
and the publisher hereby disclaims any responsibility for them.

Any people depicted in stock imagery provided by Thinkstock are models,
and such images are being used for illustrative purposes only.
Certain stock imagery © Thinkstock.

ISBN: 978-1-4808-4435-3 (sc)
ISBN: 978-1-4808-4434-6 (hc)
ISBN: 978-1-4808-4436-0 (e)

Library of Congress Control Number: 2017905481

Print information available on the last page.

Archway Publishing rev. date: 4/13/2017

This book is dedicated to
Carol Angley and Mary Stroupe,
Our children,
and
Our children's, children's children

While the story depicted here is fictional, the
events that matter are mostly true.
If you recognize the events, you will be on
your way to the deepest of truths.

The truth, as always, will be far stranger.
—Arthur C. Clarke

PROLOGUE

Deep Space Adventurer, AD 4544

Something strange was happening on *Deep Space Adventurer*. Warning lights on the main navigation panel had begun to flash. Feeling a deep pit in her stomach, the astronaut realized at once that she had made a mistake. It was a big mistake, and a potentially fatal one. She was in command, and she was alone. She knew that operating her two-person craft without her navigator onboard violated basic ASA policy, as well as defied her academy training. Even in the forty-sixth century, strict safety laws governed travel. Nevertheless, as soon as she had heard the latest report of an unexplained time-space anomaly, dubbed A-421, she had decided that she had to be the first person to survey it. Some scientists were speculating that A-421 could be evidence of a possible black hole or a wormhole coursing through the solar system. Thus far, her biggest rival, a former classmate named Harris, had been the only team member to log a Notable Event Response Survey.

But it was not just a sense of competition that had driven her into acting rashly. It was also a burning wish to be the first at something, to leave her mark, to make herself known for all time as a great explorer, as her grandfather had been and her father and mother before her. These were the thoughts that had raced through her mind as she rushed to her ship. Two hours earlier, her navigator had reported ill and been grounded for the next day's watch. Knowing that she had to act now or else lose the opportunity—probably the last such opportunity of her career—she had immediately launched out on her own.

Now something strange was happening. Warning lights had begun to flash from the main navigation panel, and the cabin's hololights were alternately dimming and brightening. *Adventurer's* readings had all been normal until now. Something was coming. She could feel it. But what was it? This configuration of readings was completely new. She had never seen them before or learned about anything like them in the academy. They seemed to be indicating the approach of something from all directions at once, which made no sense. Likewise, she was seeing something completely new in her internal emotional registers. She instinctively shifted herself over into Zone Eight to heighten her sensitivity and cool her thinking. The panel indicated that she should be a safe distance from the targeted anomaly, and yet, at the same time, that a threatening, new presence was imminent.

She began signaling with her fingers and her breath, in order to bring herself and her ship into an integrated synchrony with Universal Intelligence. Within seconds she received a verbal warning from Alpha II. "DSA commander, change course at once. Set bearings for grid position 32-714-3500 immediately. A second anomaly has just been detected in your vicinity, and it appears to be on an intersection course with A-421. Situation dangerous, status unclear. Take evasive action at once." Had Sunanda been aboard, the two would have been able to respond in time. However, the astronaut was alone. Even in her state of self-generated serenity, she knew she was in grave danger.

Before she could take any action, the normally low hum of the *Adventurer's* command cabin was suddenly interrupted by a loud cracking sound. A violent explosion of sound and light erupted simultaneously as she saw her beloved ship fly apart at the seams. Within milliseconds, she found herself surrounded by the blackness and silence of space. Now engulfed in total silence, she was able only to watch helplessly as the remains of her former ship scattered in all directions. As she began to feel the severe cold pierce her thin nanoskin suit, she knew that she would be dead within thirty seconds in the ruthless vacuum of space.

The instant she realized that, however, she felt a hot sensation arise from within her second neuronexus, two inches below her navel. For the first and last time in her short life, she realized that the homing biocapsule implant had activated! She watched with fascination from inside her Zone Eight state as the membrane expanded first forward, then outward, like the opening of an umbrella, and finally blossomed, with a spherical movement, up, below, and all around her. The biocapsule sealed itself into an equilibrium state that resembled a glossy, transparent balloon ten feet in diameter. She could see that she was attached to one wall by a thin thread extending out from her navel. She was effectively dangling freely in its center. She immediately heard the rising whisper of air compression and was able to breathe again. Warmth permeated the new atmosphere. Feeling overwhelming relief, she almost laughed as she realized that the technology had actually worked!

She did not have much time to think about what had happened, however. Within a few seconds, she began to feel a sensation of acceleration. The feeling became more and more intense. Through the translucent membrane she could see the stars beginning to blur and streak, giving her the impression that she was moving faster and faster through space. Oddly, the stars seemed to be receding in all directions at once. She did not have time to ponder this either.

Time stopped as everything went black.

At some point, she became conscious. After briefly going through the ritual of taking stock of her body's internal state, she opened her eyes. She was lying on her back, on a firm surface that felt like earth. Above her was a blue sky filled with puffy clouds. Rising beside her was some kind of plant-like creature. An oak tree. She felt a warm breeze blowing across her face and through her hair. Placing her hands on the ground to either side, she felt grass. She was home again, on Earth! This was a miracle.

With great care, after assuring herself that her body was uninjured, she gently pulled herself into a seated position. She began to look out at her surroundings. She seemed to be alone. She was on top of a large hill, and she could see a city in the distance below. She heard humans talking behind her, and she turned her head to look over her shoulder. Two people—a man and a woman—were walking in her direction, looking at her inquisitively. They appeared to be middle-aged, probably in their seventies or eighties. Their dress was quaint and old-fashioned, like something she had seen before somewhere that she could not quite place. They sounded like they were talking to each other. No, they were talking to her. The language form sounded archaic. The word *English* popped into her mind. Without knowing how she knew this, she realized that she was listening to a form of English that dated from the ancient period that had called itself "modernity." How she knew this she did not know, although she did recognize that her understanding was cognihanced. Try as she might, she could not make out what they were saying to her.

The couple stopped a few paces from her—looks of both hesitation and concern showing on their faces. After several seconds, they looked at each other, turned around, and began to walk away. She suddenly realized she could not remember what had happened and had no idea where she was. All she could remember was her name, which seemed to cling to her consciousness like a bright light. She was now beginning to feel exhaustion creeping into her body and was becoming alarmed. She had to make a quick decision.

In a flash, she recognized that these people were friends. In the same instant, the words came to her. She called out: "My name is Samantha. Can you tell me where I am?"

PART ONE

LAUNCHINGS

Have no fear that the end is near.
Life is always and only in beginning.
                    —COMMANDER ZJON III

CHAPTER 1

Twenty-First Century New York City, Zero Hour

FLASHING LIGHTS? BLUE OR WHITE? WHAT WERE THEY? IF HE HAD BEEN FULLY AWAKE, Jonathan would have asked those questions. Instead, he gradually became aware of his body, and that he was waking up. As consciousness began to reveal itself from behind the shadows, he could tell he was in bed at home. The distant hum of the Manhattan traffic began to reach his ears. Judging from the hum's relative quiet, it must be the middle of the night. He opened his eyes, raised his hand, and clicked on his smartwatch. In the darkness he was just barely able to make out the time. It was 2:35 a.m.

Jonathan Robert Elliot had it made. By the age of thirty-five, he had achieved the position of chief science editor of *The New York Times*—the youngest in that illustrious newspaper's history. He had a fabulous penthouse apartment in midtown Manhattan. He had a gorgeous girlfriend and all the prestigious friends and influential colleagues a man could want. By the age of forty, he had won the Pulitzer Prize for feature writing—the first ever awarded to a science editor.

Under his leadership, the *Times* had produced groundbreaking stories on global warming, space exploration, oceanology, geology, microbiology, genetic research, and a host of other scientific subjects. With his dual PhDs in biology and physics from Duke University, he spoke the languages of both the human genome and string theory as well as any scientist alive. He had brought his news organization to a level of recognition in science that now rivaled the reputation of *Scientific American*. During his short tenure, he had fostered pioneering breakthroughs in medical reporting and space journalism, for which he had received accolades from both the White House and Congress. Many considered his contributions to have been a major factor in the surprising resurgence of print media in the United States.

Equally remarkable to Jonathan was that his work had earned respect across the American political spectrum—a virtually impossible feat in the twenty-first century. Whatever he turned his attention to, readers followed and leaders listened. He had the president's ear. He could write his own ticket anywhere in the world, with any news organization.

Simply put, Jonathan Elliot had become a man of stature and importance.

And Jonathan Elliot was bored. Now forty-five, he had come to harbor a persistent, nagging feeling that something was missing. As he fell asleep at night, he regularly encountered a single, repetitious thought: *There has to be something more.*

Occasionally Jonathan would pause from his busy work schedule and find himself reflecting on his life. He realized he had everything to be thankful for. Standing at just under six feet and weighing 165 pounds, he had a good, healthy body. Although his dark brown hair was beginning to thin on top, he still took pride in his appearance. Not particularly athletic, he nevertheless kept himself reasonably fit at the local gym. He loved his work and found it endlessly fascinating. By all normal standards, he had a very good life, one that most people would envy. Yet still, something seemed to be missing.

Jonathan had a satisfying relationship with his girlfriend, Diana Chadwick. In fact, they had talked about getting married and having children. Diana was an ideal partner in his mind. Beautiful, elegant, smart, sensitive, witty, and blond haired (Jonathan loved blondes), Diana, a well-respected fashion consultant, was ten years his junior. Recently, she had begun to hear the ticking of her biological clock. Perhaps having a family was the thing that was missing. She was not pressuring him, exactly, but had definitely sent him some signals. Yet somehow, he could not bring himself to commit to marrying her. The idea of having children seemed only like a burden, something that would tie him down and prevent him from achieving that one thing that would bring an answer to his spiritual unrest. Besides, why would he want to bring children into this crazy world at this crazy time in history?

When all was said and done, no matter what he had achieved, how many vacations he took, how many places in the world he explored, how many mountains he climbed, how many times he made love to Diana, this one question remained: Just what else was there?

Jonathan turned his body so that he was lying on his back. He could hear Diana's calm, steady breathing beside him. Always reassuring. Slowly, he began to reflect. Something had happened. Something was different. As he became fully awake, he noticed a strange feeling. Yes, something had happened. Flashing lights, blue or white—what were they? Was he remembering a dream?

No, it was more than a dream. He had seen something like a flashing light, but not that exactly. As he lay there thinking, Jonathan was startled to realize that the atmosphere in the bedroom had changed. He could see in the darkness! At Diana's request, the couple had always slept in total darkness. They never left the TV on, never had a nightlight, not even a luminescent electric clock. Light somehow had always kept Diana from being able to sleep, so long ago, early in their relationship, Jonathan had agreed to total darkness. He had even begun to prefer sleeping that way himself.

But now, something was different. No, something was happening. Their bedroom was slowly becoming, not luminescent exactly, but somehow lit—dimly, with a slight sheen of blue. It was almost as if the atmosphere in the room had grown a texture, like a kind of mist—a mild blue, shimmering mist. He held up both hands, and he could clearly see them in this almost-but-not-quite light. There seemed to be no moisture, no dampness like one would expect to feel from a mist. Could he actually see the light waves, or was he imagining it? *This is really weird*, he thought.

A strange feeling crept into his body. It was a vague, yet distinct physical sense of lightness, starting in his chest. It was a very pleasant feeling that began to expand until it seemed to fill his entire body completely. What was this feeling? As he tried to identify it, the word *joy* popped into his head. Why would he be feeling this way? *Now this is really, really weird!* his inner voice said, beginning to grow louder in his head. He felt like something was about to appear in the room, about to take a form. His body began to feel excitement, an anticipation of something about to happen. He was not sure if he was sleeping or not, so he touched his eyes to make sure they were fully open. The verdict was in. This was actually happening. This was real.

Just as Jonathan was about to wake up Diana, he caught a glimpse of something down by the foot of the bed. Fascinated, Jonathan watched as some kind of figure began to take shape. His attention was riveted. Over several moments, the figure gradually morphed and began to congeal into something that resembled a man. As he watched with astonishment, the full figure of a man crystallized, standing near the foot of the bed. The man was dressed in unusual clothing. Startled, Jonathan instinctively lashed out with his left foot to kick the intruder in the stomach. To his surprise, his foot seemed to go right through the stranger's body, without touching anything. The kick threw Jonathan so off balance that he almost fell out of bed.

Just as quickly as he had reacted in alarm the moment before, Jonathan suddenly felt strangely calm. He felt no fear. Instead, the strange sense of well-being or joy that he had felt when he first woke up continued to glow inside of him. The thoughts, *Shouldn't I be frightened? Shouldn't I be worried? What the hell is going on?* flowed through this otherwise calm sense of presence. *Is this a ghost? Or else, this must be a dream.*

As Jonathan pondered these thoughts, the man quietly moved closer until he was standing beside Jonathan's left shoulder, looking down at him. The man's face was calmly reassuring as he stood in silence. Jonathan quickly glanced to his right to see if Diana was still asleep. He desperately wanted to awaken her at that moment but for some reason sensed it would be better to let her sleep.

He tentatively pulled himself up to a sitting position, and after mustering up the courage to speak at last, he asked, "Who are you?"

The stranger just stood there, smiling.

"I asked you," said Jonathan, "who are you? How did you get in?"

The man remained standing there in silence.

Jonathan continued, "What do you want? Do you want money?"

After a few seconds, the stranger spoke. "I do not want anything from you, Jonathan."

"How do you know my name? And why are you here?"

"I just want to talk to you." As the man spoke, his voice felt so soothing to Jonathan that any feeling of alarm or fear completely dissolved. This man, whoever he was, was no danger. Something else was going on—something that was starting to be very intriguing.

Nevertheless, Jonathan's mind continued to try to understand what was happening. *I must be having a nervous breakdown. This is crazy. I have an intruder in my room, yet I am feeling warmth and affection for him.*

Feeling he needed to do something, Jonathan turned toward his girlfriend and said, "Diana, wake up, wake up!"

"Do not touch her, Jonathan. She is in a deep sleep."

Suddenly incensed, Jonathan exclaimed, "Who the hell are you to tell me that! This is my woman." The instant he realized what he had said, he felt embarrassed. How chauvinistic!

"No, Jonathan," the man spoke soothingly, "I have put her into a very deep, restful sleep. She will not wake up until I leave."

"You've got some nerve coming in here like this!" Jonathan told him. "You owe me an explanation, or I'm going to call the police."

"I do not wish to disturb your bedroom space. Can we go down into your kitchen and talk?"

Jonathan's mind continued to reel. "I'll ask you once again. How did you get in here?" Jonathan was almost shouting now.

The stranger spoke to him, again quietly and soothingly. "How is not important. I know all of your house. I just feel it. Just like I know who you are. Jonathan, you also know me, but you do not know me."

Jonathan retorted, "Oh come on. You're talking nonsense."

But at the same time, he was experiencing another feeling, a surprising affection for this guy. It was incredible! He was now becoming fascinated by his unlikely feelings despite this seemingly dangerous situation. Deep within his consciousness, Jonathan began to recognize that something very important was happening. He also sensed instinctively that whatever was happening was good. So at last he agreed. "Okay, I'll come with you."

"Please lead the way."

Jonathan got out of the bed and pulled on his robe, and the two of them left the bedroom and went downstairs to the first floor of the penthouse. As he walked into the kitchen and turned on the lights, his mind became riveted by the unreality of this situation. Where on earth did this person come from? If he even came from Earth! No. There had to be a rational explanation for all this. Otherwise, he must be going crazy!

Jonathan had paused when they entered the kitchen and turned around to face this stranger. The man looked normal enough. He was athletically built, well proportioned, probably in his thirties, with handsome yet unusual facial features, and a tannish complexion that could signify a mixed racial origin. There was something about his face that was striking. Also, his clear, yet intense, brown eyes had a strangely warm glow. The man seemed surprisingly serene. His clothes were unusual, but Jonathan could not put his finger on exactly how. They were well tailored, perhaps some new kind of Italian style? They definitely did not look American. Everything about this man seemed perfectly harmless, yet the situation was impossible. This just did not make any sense.

"Would you like me to get you a drink, some water perhaps, or something stronger?"

The man smiled and said, "Thank you, Jonathan. I would love a glass of Oban, on the rocks. Would you join me?"

Totally taken aback, but no longer surprised by anything, Jonathan blurted out, "And how the hell did you know I like Oban? It's my favorite Scotch. Never mind, do not answer that; I know that you just felt it." At that moment, both men began to laugh.

Jonathan could not believe that he was now laughing with this man, this strange intruder in his home whom he had never seen before in his life, until just a few minutes ago. He motioned to the stranger to take a seat at the breakfast table, walked over to the liquor cabinet, and pulled out a bottle of Oban. Retrieving two crystal glasses, he pulled out the ice bucket from the freezer and made two large Scotches on the rocks. "I think I am going to need this."

CHAPTER 2

New York City, Zero Hour

JONATHAN SAT DOWN, AND THE TWO MEN CLINKED THEIR GLASSES LIKE THEY WERE OLD friends. As they sat at the table and swirled and sniffed the fine liquor before taking their first sips, Jonathan could only marvel at what was suddenly unfolding in his life. Diana would never believe this. He was not sure he believed it himself. After a short pause, he said, "I feel like I know you. How do I know you?"

The unlikely companions eyed each other intently, the stranger with a slightly amused yet gentle expression on his face, and Jonathan with keen anticipation, yet also complete ease. Jonathan had the feeling that it was time for him to listen, so he waited without asking any more questions.

After what seemed to Jonathan like a very long time, the clear-eyed man broke the silence. "You do not know me yet, Jonathan. However, we are related in a very bizarre way. Allow me to introduce myself. My name is Zjon."

"How do you spell that, J-E-A-N or J-O-N?"

"Neither. My name is spelled Z-J-O-N." After a short pause, Zjon continued. "I am going to explain to you why I am here. I want you to do me a favor."

"You said you didn't want anything."

"I do not want anything material. I want you to write an article."

"About what?"

"The article is to be called 'Something Is Coming.'"

"But that title means nothing to me. What is this article supposed to be about?" Jonathan's interest was piqued, but at the same time, he felt suspicious. It was a very presumptuous request.

"I will get to that in a minute. But first I need to explain a little bit more about why I chose you. I know that you do not believe in UFOs, aliens, extraterrestrials, or things like that. The people who read your work know that you are a rational man who has an excellent scientific mind. That is why I selected you, Jonathan. You are the best man for this: a well-known and respected person. There is a very critical situation taking place in the world right now, one that could affect the future of human civilization. It is very important that people get a certain message, and you are someone who can help get that message to the right people. Also, when I verified that you are related to me through, let us say, a long, long genetic calling, I knew you were the right one."

"What are you talking about, our being related and a 'genetic calling'? Do you mean we are related?" Jonathan challenged.

"Listen to me very carefully. In years to come, many years from now, your great, great, great—actually one hundredth generation—grandson will lead a space expedition. I knew him. He was my grandfather."

"Are you kidding me? That's impossible!" exclaimed Jonathan, calculating in his head. "You are talking about two thousand years from now. That cannot be. You're telling me you are from the future, but time travel is impossible. Besides, I don't even have children."

"Two thousand five hundred years in the future, to be more precise. I know it seems preposterous, but it is true. I am here because my girlfriend, my sweetheart Samantha, was in an accident. Because of what happened, she is here now. She was pushed back through time, for reasons that I cannot explain to you. But it happened, and I am here to take her back to her own time. We have to rescue her within nine days. Right now she has no memory of who she is. On the ninth day, however, she will remember. If she remembers and we have failed to evacuate her, it will pose a great potential threat for the evolution of humankind. If she remembers, she will not hesitate to tell some of the things she knows. We cannot let that happen, Jonathan. I have a plan, and I need you to write this article. Noninterference from the future is an integral principle of the science that you call physics. Even my being here with you is a very tricky thing. However, you have a vitally important role to play for the future of humankind because of who you are in your own time, and in relation to me."

Jonathan pondered Zjon's statements, while Zjon waited. At last, Jonathan challenged him. "If you are so smart and so brilliant in the future, how could such an accident happen?"

"That is because of the nature of unpredictability that we cannot change, the natural unpredictability of the infinite fabric of time-space. I believe you call it 'space-time.' Unpredictability you cannot change. It is part of the very nature of the universe. This is one of the things we have learned as we have evolved as human beings."

Jonathan took another sip of his drink. Somehow, the Oban tasted better to him than it ever had before. It seemed to blend perfectly with the newfound feelings of well-being in his body. In spite of his strong emotions, his mind seemed sharper than ever. He asked, "Exactly why do you want me to write this article?"

"Because we have to come here, rescue Samantha, and go home, leaving no ripples. Your article is necessary for our success in the next nine days. Things are happening over which we have no control, and we need the right people lined up to facilitate us—people who will be attracted through your article. We have come just to rescue her and go back. But there is always the possibility of failure, of imperfection, however well we plan and act. We might not get her back. So it is a very interesting situation."

"Interesting sounds like an understatement! And what do you mean by 'us'?"

"That I will reveal to you at the right time. For now, you must be patient."

"Okay. Even if I buy this, and I am not saying I do, what do you want me to write?"

"Do not worry about that at this moment. Just mention that something is coming. And mention the possibility of a space accident that could happen and that could actually cause the world of today and the world of the future to be linked together. I know that you are aware of the abundance of theories that have cropped up in the last century about the possibility of time travel: the bending of space-time, wormholes, and exotic notions like tachyons and string theory. There are in reality aspects of time and space which lie just outside your current capacities for measurement, and 'now' has special qualities that are only beginning to be recognized in your time. Something is coming for all of humankind. You will discover what to write once you get into action. The important thing is for you to write this article. It needs to appear as the science cover article in this Sunday's *New York Times*, two days from now."

Jonathan was stunned. This Sunday! Two days from now! The idea was preposterous.

Zjon paused for a moment to take another sip of Scotch. He then said, "The world of today is actually moving very slowly for human beings. I know that you are in the very powerful, what you call 'computer age' or 'information age.' I know that things seem to be moving faster than ever before. You have seen many technological advancements. But at the same time, your emotions and energy are very, very sluggish and very crude. I am speaking about human beings in general, nothing personal about you. Writing this article can help you. You see, no accident is an accident. Everything has meaning and purpose."

"How can you be so certain?" Jonathan asked. A feeling that this was the right thing to do was beginning to take over, in spite of his scientifically trained skepticism. "I mean, you just spoke of unpredictability. If everything is so unpredictable, how can you be so certain?"

"Nothing is ever certain, Jonathan. But the universe has a fundamental Intelligence at the basis of all things. The wisest people in history, those rare beings like the Buddha and Christ, knew that everything is connected and that human beings are connected to everything in the universe. Even many of the scientists and thinkers of your time have had some sense of this. We humans tend to forget and become distracted by our need for survival. But the universe wants human beings to evolve and remember. Our wisdom lives at a cellular level. You just have to trust your heart and allow Intelligence to work in you."

Finally surrendering to his feelings, Jonathan said, "Okay, I admit I am intrigued by your story. I don't know if it's the alcohol, or if you are telling the truth. However, I will do it. People will think I'm crazy, but I will write this article."

"Is that a promise? I want you to promise me."

"I promise," Jonathan resolved.

"Good," concluded Zjon. "You have just moved the universe. It is time for me to go for now, and for you to go back upstairs and get some sleep."

Jonathan looked up at the clock on the kitchen wall. Seeing it was 3:30 a.m., he realized they had been talking for almost an hour. Both men finished their drinks and stood up. This time Zjon led the way back upstairs to the bedroom. Once in the room, he turned to Jonathan and said, "You are going to sleep now, and when you awake, this will seem like a dream to you. But you will remember what you have promised tonight, and tomorrow you will write the article. Meanwhile, have a good rest."

As Jonathan lay down on the bed, he asked, "When will I see you again?"

"Soon, I am very sure."

Jonathan joked, "I guess you know your way out."

Zjon chuckled and said, "I believe I can find my way. Now, close your eyes and remember, 'Impossible is possible.'" As Jonathan closed his eyes, thinking about Zjon's quaint grammatical constructions, Zjon started gently tapping Jonathan's right and left temples with the forefinger and middle finger of each hand. "Do not be alarmed. I am giving you a signal."

Before he could ask what this meant, Jonathan fell into a deep, relaxing sleep.

CHAPTER 3

New York City, Day One, 7:00 a.m.

THE NEXT MORNING, JONATHAN WOKE UP FEELING REFRESHED AND ENLIVENED. AS HE was getting dressed, he said to Diana, "I had the weirdest dream last night." He briefly recounted to her what he remembered. As he did so, he began to have doubts. He did not know whether he had had a powerful, delusional dream or whether the strange encounter had really happened. After he finished telling her the story, he decided it had only been a very weird, vivid dream.

"That's interesting," Diana commented. "Perhaps your subconscious mind is trying to tell you something."

"You must be right," he agreed, feeling anything but confident.

The couple kissed and headed downstairs to the kitchen for their morning routine of coffee and breakfast before leaving for work. As they entered the kitchen, Diana saw the empty glasses sitting on the breakfast table, next to the bottle of Oban. "What's that?" she asked.

"Oh, my God!" exclaimed Jonathan.

They looked at each other with amazement.

Jonathan said to himself under his breath, "What in the world have I gotten myself into?"

CHAPTER 4

New York City, Day One, Noon

MORNINGS AT WORK OFTEN FLEW BY FOR JONATHAN ELLIOT. IT WAS ALWAYS EXHILArating to think that he was a key person working for the most prestigious news organization in the United States. Each day, he felt he was at the center of the universe. People all over the world were waiting to read the next great discovery that his team would cover. He loved bringing the world of science to life for those who were leading ordinary lives. Secretly, he had harbored, since back in his college days, an unspoken dream that science could bring about a transformation for human lives everywhere, perhaps even world peace. And he loved the feeling that he was in a unique position to make a real difference in the world.

This was an ordinary morning for Jonathan, yet it was not ordinary at all. Something had happened last night, and it was gnawing at him. All the while that he was going through his routine editorial team meeting, huddling with his team of science writers and sitting at his desk thinking about his own writing, he was engaged in an internal struggle. Something had happened—something wonderful, yet not possible. Surely last night had been a dream. But it was so vivid! It all seemed so real. But that was ridiculous! Still, what if the things this person (what was his name?), whether imaginary or real, had said were in fact true? Well, that would simply be too good to be true! What if they were not true? Was he willing to make a fool of himself by writing such an article? But he had made a promise.

Or had he? His memory of the night's events seemed to be quickly receding. Just what had that man told him?

As he sat at his desk in a kind of stupor, he heard the usual sounds of the newsroom. From the international desk, he could hear that the Russians and Chinese were still causing trouble in central Asia, rogue cyberterrorists were once again attacking the global energy grid, insurgents were wreaking havoc in Aldiwan, the recently formed Israel-Palestine confederacy, and the African Union was still haggling with the ever-problematic economy and sporadic uprisings. Locally, the city was still in the midst of a heat wave. Nationally, there was another sports figure scandal, California might be coming out of the latest drought, and some strange hubbub was brewing in Las Vegas. Of course, most conversations were about the upcoming elections. Indeed, it was just another ordinary Friday news morning, with everyone scrambling to meet the Sunday deadline.

Noon seemed to come earlier than usual. When he realized what time it was, he decided he would go for a long walk to clear his head. He texted his secretary, telling him that he would be out for a long lunch break, and headed out of the office. When he reached the street, he suddenly felt a pleasant surge of energy. He flipped a mental coin and headed north on Eighth Avenue.

The combination of the bright, uplifting sunshine and the bluest July sky he had ever seen immediately calmed all of Jonathan's worries as he drifted through the streets of the city. Before he knew it, he had reached Broadway and Central Park South. He had stopped along the way in a deli and bought a pastrami sandwich. Finding an empty park bench, he sat for a while and devoured his sandwich, which had to be the most delicious sandwich he had ever eaten. What a strange night last night had been.

As his rational mind kicked in and he thought about it, he said to himself, *Don't write this article. Why risk your career? Besides, if this man's story is true, why doesn't he just come out and prove it? Better yet, why not just rescue the girl and take her back? Why come to me?* Finally, Jonathan came to the conclusion that Diana was right. His subconscious mind must have been sending him some kind of message. Maybe he was experiencing a midlife crisis. Maybe he needed a vacation. Whatever the reason, he now decided that he would be crazy to write this article. He just would not do it. Relieved at last to have resolved the issue, he stood and began to head back to the office, turning right on Fifth Avenue.

Nearly halfway back to his office, Jonathan stopped with a jolt. He heard a sound inside his head. It was the voice of the man from his dream, and the voice was saying, "Jonathan, you need to write the article. You promised me that you would write it."

"Yes, but I was dreaming last night, and I am dreaming now." Jonathan realized that he was talking to himself.

"No, you are hearing my voice, and you are not delusional."

"Then prove it!" Jonathan found himself so frustrated, he was almost yelling. People nearby began to look at him in a funny way, unnerved by the street crazy and moving away to avoid him. Realizing what was happening, Jonathan quickly got himself under control and muttered an embarrassed "sorry" to those around him. He cleared his throat and tried to look normal.

The man's voice resumed in Jonathan's head. "Continue on the way you were headed to your office. After you walk for three more blocks, there will be a girl dressed in red coming toward you. You are going to kiss her."

"Oh, no, I am not going to kiss anybody," Jonathan responded with a low voice. "This is crazy. Besides, there are so many girls dressed in red, not to mention that I would never go up and kiss a complete stranger."

"Go ahead and see for yourself." Then the man's voice disappeared, and the normal sounds of the city took over.

Jonathan waited for a few moments to regain his composure. *I cannot believe I am talking to myself like this,* he thought. He then began walking again, feeling more puzzled than ever, yet once again also feeling that strange, overwhelming sense of well-being and joy. Just as he had passed the third block and crossed the street, he spotted three different young women wearing red clothes, all approaching him from different directions. He kept walking, pretending to ignore them. Two of them passed him. However, as the third young woman walked past him, Jonathan suddenly whirled around, grabbed her, and kissed her. Immediately, he let go of her and exclaimed, "Whoa!" Shocked by his own actions, Jonathan shouted out internally to the phantom voice, *Okay, okay, I will write the article!*

Across from him stood a gorgeous, clearly surprised young woman. She asked, "Who are you? Why did you kiss me?"

Feeling as if he had entered into another world, Jonathan stammered, "I am so sorry. This is not like me. I truly hope I have not disturbed you. Something just came over me."

The girl in red replied, "By all means, thank you. You made my day." She then gave him a beautiful smile, turned north, and walked across the street.

At the end of day one on his new journey, Jonathan Elliot did not leave his office to go home for the night. Instead, the moment he sat down at his desk, the words flowed from his fingers, and they kept flowing. The visitor from last night had been right; Jonathan knew exactly what to write. The article wrote itself with an illumination and clarity he had never before experienced in his career. At last, he ended the article with the words, "I am preparing the world to meet tomorrow's sunrise." Looking at his finished work, he recognized that indeed, something was coming. At four in the morning, he caught a taxi home, and as he collapsed into a deep sleep, all memories of his encounter with the strange nighttime visitor were laid to rest.

That day the article, "Something Is Coming," would sail through the editorial review meetings without a hitch. He had expected resistance at the worst, and controversy at the very least. Instead, as the publication of Sunday's edition approached, everyone in the office who had read the article would come up to him and congratulate him on his new vision, the total plausibility of what he had written, in fact, the absolute indisputability of the whole scenario. No one had ever written such a bold article before, they lauded. He was likely to land another Pulitzer, people assured him. The article was unbelievably visionary.

To a dazed and surprised Jonathan Elliot, life seemed to have taken a miraculous turn. As he went to bed Saturday night, little did he suspect how events in his life would unfold over the next seven days.

CHAPTER 5

Washington, D.C., Day Two, 5:30 a.m.

FEDERAL SPECIAL INVESTIGATOR DAN HAMILTON WAS STARTLED OUT OF HIS SLEEP BY the harsh ringing of his bedside telephone. As he fumbled for the handset, he glanced at the clock, which displayed the ungodly hour of five thirty. "Hamilton here," he barked into the phone, without trying to hide his annoyance

"Did I spoil your beauty sleep?" a sarcastic voice asked.

"What do you want at this hour?" Dan calmed down, realizing his anger would do him no good. The man at the other end of the phone was, unfortunately, his boss, the Chief.

"We need you in Las Vegas, pronto. There is a situation there that calls for your personal attention. Actually, we need you to find out if there really is a situation at all. Our office has been getting questions from the White House, at the highest level, and we want you there to see whether or not something needs to be dealt with. Personally, I don't like wasting our resources on this, knowing as little as we do. The FBI is already on site, along with local police, and theoretically, they should be able to handle it. But apparently, they haven't. Anyway, as you well know, when POTUS calls, we listen." Dan knew POTUS was an acronym for president of the United States.

Actually, Federal Special Investigator Dan Hamilton's full title was federal special investigator of potential threats and borderline events. It was a job title specially crafted to suit his unique talents. As a graduate student in psychology and behavioral sciences twenty years earlier, Dan came to realize that he had an unusual level of rapport with people as well as a keen aptitude for logical investigation. He ended up being recruited by both the CIA and the FBI, eventually choosing the latter to be trained in profiling. This took place during the decade that foreign terrorism had reached the shores of America and everything familiar had turned topsy-turvy.

In his first job with the FBI, Dan had distinguished himself in helping to prevent what would have been the largest and most devastating terrorist attack on American soil since 9/11—his analysis of intercepted cyber-chatter had foiled a plot to set off a dirty bomb near the Washington Monument. His natural calmness during this intense event had soon led to his being recognized as a significant talent. In less than a decade, he had risen to a special position in an unrecognized government agency that only the president of the United States and a few top members of Congress knew existed.

Dan Hamilton stood six foot three, had sandy blond hair cut in a long crew, moved with the prowess of a basketball player, talked with a charming Southern California accent, and was known among his coworkers for being unflappable, scrupulously ethical, charming, and—most of all—very, very smart. Anyone who did not know him professionally would have guessed Dan to be either a salesman for a pharmaceutical firm or a California surfer dude. Sometimes he enjoyed actually playing one of those roles when he was with strangers. It was easier for him that way, or at least helped make the intensity of his work manageable. But his greatest strength in his own mind was that to everyone who met him, he was naturally able to exude calmness and charm. He was effective, and he knew it.

Dan's naturally calm manner was not present at this moment, however. "Just what's going on?" Dan asked, doing his best to keep from yelling, "Some kind of attack?"

"That's just it, Hamilton. Nothing seems to have happened. Or at least, nothing that makes any sense. That's why we need you there personally to get to the bottom of this. When POTUS calls …"

"I know, I know, we listen. Tell me where to be and when."

"Las Vegas. Yesterday. You'll get a full briefing when you get on site. The regional FBI division liaison's name is David Newman. Second generation Irish or Scottish or some such. He's been there since yesterday pulling together as much information as he can. Meanwhile, we have a flight booked for you on United out of Dulles at 10:45 a.m. You'll be picked up at McCarran by one of Newman's agents. We have a room booked for you at the Hampton Inn. You can call me after getting settled in. Meanwhile, Newman's getting statements from potential witnesses and hopefully, will have everything ready for you to take over. First thing in the morning, you'll be picked up to with meet him. As you know, by then everything could have blown over."

"Doesn't sound exactly like nothing's happened, Chief."

"Well, nothing seems to have, at least not exactly. A confluence of patterns and reports of strange anomalies, some things apparently picked up by our supercomputers. Probably nothing in the end, but it's important enough for us to be called in. Call me when you get to the hotel. I'll have more background information for you by then." With that, the line abruptly went dead.

"Wonderful, just wonderful," Dan muttered.

This was just where he wanted to go in the middle of summer—the desert—to deal with another black hole event, no doubt. A black hole event was department slang for a wild goose chase. The last three assignments Dan Hamilton had participated in had all turned out to be black holes. It seemed to Dan that the past few years had become crazy that way. Everyone was so fearful everywhere that a dog barking in the wrong part of the road could set off a full-scale terror alert. Lately, Dan had begun to wonder whether he was in the right job. What had started out for him as an exciting career in which he naively believed he could make a difference for his country over time had resulted in despondency, bordering on cynicism.

Dan sat upright and put his feet on the floor. Yes, it probably was just another black hole. On the other hand, the Chief had sounded a little more reticent than usual. There was something he wasn't telling him. This might be something after all.

As he started toward the kitchen to brew some coffee, he suddenly remembered what day it was, and the plans he now had to cancel. This was to have been his third day off in as many months, and he had really been looking forward to hooking up with Emily at last. She had to be one of the sexiest women he had ever met.

"Oh well," he said, sighing to himself. "I guess I'll give Emily a call to let her know I have to cancel. Damn!" For the third time in a row, Dan had to cancel his date with his new girlfriend. Or was it a new date with his third girlfriend?

Hell, at this point he could not even remember anymore.

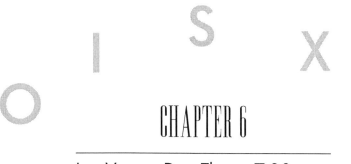

CHAPTER 6

Las Vegas, Day Three, 7:00 a.m.

"So what do you make of it?" Dan asked Special Agent David Newman.

It was Sunday morning, and they were meeting in a makeshift private room that had been cordoned off from public view. The room was carved out of a small, open-air park shelter that Dan had been told the FBI had "borrowed" to use for its headquarters in Sunset Park. When Sunset Park was originally set aside as a wildlife reserve and public recreation area, it had been on the far eastern outskirts of the city. Then came the great population explosion of the 1990s and early 2000s, and the park was now a 350-acre enclave surrounded by a gigantic urban sprawl. Still, Clark County had managed to turn a piece of sparse desert into a sweet little haven where families of people and animals could enjoy a harmonious coexistence among trees, carefully watered plants, ponds, grassy fields, and native shrubs.

In the northwestern corner of the park was the Clark County Police precinct building. At the center of the park was a small lake, surrounded by cultivated grass and large shade trees, and dotted with various structures like the picnic shelter he was now standing in. As he looked south, Dan observed a network of walking and jogging trails winding among a number of shrub-covered dunes. From looking at a map, he could see that the southern section terminated at a set of railroad tracks.

David Newman pointed across the street toward an ordinary-looking section of tract homes built on the other side of a six- to eight-foot-tall, painted, cinderblock wall that Dan assumed served as a sound buffer from the traffic rather than any type of security barrier.

"That cluster of houses over there seems to be the center of what's been goin' on," David explained. "The housing community goes by the name of Avalon Village, like in King Arthur's tale."

David spoke with traces of what to Dan seemed to be a mild Scottish or Irish brogue, like he probably came from one of those countries. Clearly, however, he was a long-term American citizen, or else he would not have this job. He also seemed to know some mythology. Dan was not in a position to tell, since he did not know much about mythology himself. What Dan did know was that he was becoming impatient and wanted to get to the bottom of this situation quickly.

David had explained that on a normal morning people would be scattered on the banks of the lake quietly fishing and joggers would be taking their morning run before going to work or in the case of Sunday, to church. This morning was anything but normal, however. Dan could see that a section of Eastern had been blocked off from the intersection at Maule Street down to the railroad tracks by barricades and orange cones. Signs had been erected reading "men at work" and "local traffic only," but the presence of patrol cars with lights silently flashing gave away the truth. Any idiot could see that something was going on. Along Maule there was a patrol car at each of the four northern street entrances leading into Avalon Village, and men and women in uniforms were scattered around the park.

"So." Dan spoke, this time more emphatically. "Agent Newman, please give me the rundown once again. Imagine that I was just now coming onto the scene and knew nothing about what has been happening, and that I was your boss and you were giving me a full report." In fact, the assistant director had made it clear to David the night before that until further notice, David was to treat Dan as if Dan were his boss.

David was jarred by the abruptness of this newcomer's tone.

However, he did his best to hide his reaction. This was an automatic response that had become second nature to him. Born in Edinburgh, he had lived there until the age of nine, when his parents had immigrated to the United States. His real name was David Ainsley, but he had changed it. As the only child of a former dock worker and a reformed prostitute, he had spent his early childhood feeling smothered by his insecure mother, while his father dragged the family from place to place across the United States, searching fruitlessly for the ever-elusive immigrant's version of the American Dream. When David turned twelve, his father finally succumbed to alcoholism, leaving him alone with his mother in Seattle. As soon as he was able, he had run away. Eventually, he had found his way down to San Diego.

It was there that he had his first break in life, being taken in by a kindly old couple whose only son had recently died in the first Gulf War. For once in his life, David experienced unconditional love, and he lapped it up. He took his newly adopted parents' family name of Newman. With the support of his adoptive father, a retired congressman, David enrolled in school, made his way into college, joined the sailing team and Kappa Alpha fraternity, and eventually graduated near the top of his class. Today, David Newman was a tall and lanky man of thirty, with fair hair, hazel eyes, and a permanent tan. Always accomplished, always dependable, always excelling among his peers, he had achieved what his Scottish father and mother could never have imagined. He was a decorated special agent with the FBI.

But in his heart of hearts, David Newman had a closely held secret. No matter what he accomplished, however much he excelled, he had never overcome a conviction that he did not fit in. The secret life for David Newman was the struggle to belong. In the beginning, it had been his shame for his poverty. So he had run away. For a long time after that, he had thought it was his accent, so he had tried to get rid of it. After a while, even his excellence in school and sports had only come to accentuate, rather than alleviate, this sense of himself. No matter how much he accomplished, David Newman always felt he had to prove something. He was always the odd man out.

He believed that he finally had these feelings under control. It was his little secret, and he was determined to keep it that way. Only occasionally, he would notice others looking at him strangely, casting a questioning glance when he laughed too exaggeratedly at a joke or made an offhand comment that he had first thought completely appropriate, but then thought not. This only spurred him to work harder to fit in. Yet somehow, he was always the last to know what was going on around him. A school counselor had once used the term *tactless* to describe him.

"Did you understand my request, Agent Newman?" Dan's voice penetrated David's distracted reverie. David felt his face flush with embarrassment.

"Fair enough," David said. "I don't know who you are or what you represent, but I do understand that you are in charge now, and I will respect that. Please understand, though, tha' I really have no idea right now what the heck is happenin' here. Up until two or three days ago, everything was normal. And it still looks normal on the surface. Then, people started reporting some strange things. It seems that some kind of invisible shield appeared surrounding that community. What makes it really weird is that anyone who lives inside doesn't seem to notice it or to be affected. The same with the postal service, UPS, and others who come in for their normal business deliveries. But for anyone who is an outsider, the shield won't let them inside."

"That's impossible, you know." Dan was stating the obvious.

"Yeah, tell me about it. We've been interviewing as many of the people who reported this as we could find. A number of them were winos or junkies, and who can trust what they have to say? But some of them were business people, and some of them were cops. After a while, all the stories jived. You can't deny that somethin' strange is happenin' over there. Finally, I decided to go over there myself." David pointed to an opening in the wall where there was a street entrance. To the right on the wall was a sign that appeared to have once had a decorative emblem, and was now apparently missing due to vandalism. The sign read "Avalon" in big letters, with "Village" below in small letters. "I walked over there late yesterday afternoon to try it myself, and sure enough, I couldn't get through. I mean, man, it's a regular street, and people who live there seem to be able to walk or drive in and out freely. But when I went over there, as soon as I stepped on the sidewalk right next to the wall, I got stopped in my tracks."

"What stopped you?" asked Dan.

"Well, it felt like a current of electricity running through my body. And it felt so strong that I didn't want to go any further. Like really uncomfortable! I know this sounds fantastic, but it's true! I tried it a couple of times, and then got clear real fast I wasn't gonna try it again! This is the same thing other people have told me: in almost all cases they suddenly realized it was a bad idea to go in there."

"You said, 'almost.' What do you mean by that?"

"Well, here is the wildest thing of all—there is this one cop ... But you will need to hear it from him in his own words."

"Is he here?"

"Yes, we have him sitting over on that bench. I knew you would need to see him."

"Thanks," said Dan, appreciating that Agent Newman was appearing to be fully cooperative and not like some agents who get territorial about their own turf. "Before I speak to him, I would like for you to show me on the map the area that has been affected."

"That's easy; we have it completely mapped out." He spread the map on the shelter's picnic table and pointed. "As you can see, this is a six-block subdivision, completely surrounded by walls similar to the one you see over there. The street I just pointed to where I tried to go through is called Sierra Stone, and it's the only direct entrance from Eastern. Then, as you can see to the north, there is another street, Maule, which runs along the northern boundary of the community for four or five blocks, ending at Luminary, right there." He ran his finger along the map again. "There are no street entrances from the south or west, just walls dividing it off from neighboring subdivisions. From what we can tell, the walls surrounding the whole six-block area make up the exact boundary of this shield, or whatever it is. It felt like some kind of electrically charged field to me, but what do I know about science?"

"Sounds like as good a description as any at this point," Dan replied. "Let's call it the 'Avalon Charged Field' for now. Have you talked with any of the people who live there?"

"Yes, as well as a local postman and a UPS delivery man. And we are still gathering as much information about all of the residents as we can, including names from the local tax database and photos from the DMV. We hope to have that information by this evening at the latest. Of course, what makes this especially tricky is that we can't go into the community to knock on doors to talk to the residents ourselves, and we don't wanna create a panic by calling for an evacuation. So we've taken the tactic of quietly intercepting traffic as it leaves and enters the area, under the guise of a routine license check. This won't work for long. On top of that, it's a weekend, and many appear to be out of town. But we have talked to some, and you know what's the strangest thin'?"

"What?"

"Well, to them everything seems just hunky dory!"

"Hunky dory? I haven't heard that expression in a long time."

"I know, but actually it fits exactly. Things are good inside. Nothing has been going on in there. They haven't even noticed anything strange at all. On the contrary, things are so good that each resident, to a person, reports feeling really good!"

"What's so weird about that?"

"I mean, really, *really* good!" David replied. "Have you ever interviewed any witness anywhere, or any person on the street, who says everything seems just great? These people all report feeling really happy. To a person. No complaints at all."

"That seems impossible," acknowledged Dan.

"My thoughts exactly. And after hearing this same story about ten or twenty times, I checked with the local police. In the past, the statistics for this area have been the same as any other middle- to working-class neighborhood in the city. They've had their burglaries from time to time, the occasional complaints against neighbors or strangers, and problems with noisy kids or late-night parties. And of course, the occasional drug bust. But in the past year or so, the frequency of those kinds of events has dropped steadily here. In fact, in the last three months the crime rate was exactly zero! Not even a traffic ticket. You're lookin' skeptical, man, but it's absolutely true. You can check our reports and see for yourself."

Actually, Dan did not need to check David's reports. The night before, the Chief had included these facts during his telephone briefing. There were, in fact, other anomalies that the Chief had told him about but that Agent Newman did not know yet. For example, the weather had changed. When Dan had arrived, he was shocked at how cool the temperature was for the middle of July. Dan did not live in Las Vegas, but he had been there to see some shows in the summer in the past, and he always recalled it being at least a hundred degrees in the late afternoon. Last night, it had been around sixty, and he felt like he was back home on the California coast. For the last several days, temperatures had hovered between fifty degrees at night and a perfect seventy-two degrees at midafternoon.

These were not the only unusual phenomena Dan knew were taking place. Both this temperature anomaly and a lowered crime rate appeared to be centered right at this particular community, spreading out from this point in a concentric circle for thirty-five to forty miles. The farther away one moved from Avalon Village, the higher the crime rate and temperature. The measures for all of these, and other seemingly unrelated phenomena, had been checked and rechecked by all of the computers in the National Weather Service, the FBI, the DOD, and the NSA. These changes had begun to appear gradually and steadily over a one-year period. When the evidence had become unshakably convincing, it had reached the White House.

There was one other thing that Dan was not going to tell David. Scientists studying cosmic radiation had also observed a strange pattern of radiation that appeared to be emanating from the same location, radiation that normally would be detected as a result of sunspots or other celestial phenomena, but never from a location on Earth. This had appeared abruptly ten days before. There seemed to be no danger, as the frequencies involved were known not to be harmful. Coincidentally, someone had coined the term "charged field" to describe it, and the investigation project's working title was now "Operation Avalon Charged Field." This had been the phenomenon that had caused the red flag in the first place, setting the supercomputers into action.

"Good work, Agent Newman," Dan told him. "I'd like to speak to that officer now, if I could."

"Just call me David."

"And you can call me Dan. However, we need to be careful when in earshot of others, and it's important that you don't forget who's in charge of this project."

"Understood. Clear as a bell."

"I think we're going to get along just fine on this project—whatever this project is."

CHAPTER 7

Las Vegas, Day Three, 10:33 a.m.

"OFFICER ROB CANTRELL, THIS IS SPECIAL AGENT DAN HAMILTON."
Dan motioned the uniformed officer from the Las Vegas Metropolitan Police Department to take a seat. "Thank you for coming down here on a Sunday morning, Officer Cantrell."

"No problem. I work most Sundays, anyway." Officer Cantrell was a young, robust man, with clear eyes and an open, unassuming face.

"How long have you been with the department?" Dan inquired.

"I've been on the force for six months, since completing my training."

"You look very fit. Have you done weight training?"

"Actually, quite a bit," Cantrell replied. "Before joining, I worked for several years in physical therapy, and before that was a serious body-building competitor in school, until I blew out my shoulder. As a physical therapist, I got to know a number of people in the police department, and so I decided to apply. I was lucky." The man seemed to Dan to be both straightforward and modest, without the kind of defensiveness a federal agent often encountered when talking to the police.

"So, Agent Newman tells me you had an interesting experience recently. Would you please relate to me exactly what happened?"

"Can you keep this confidential? I mean, if what I say gets out, it could come back around to cause me trouble. I could lose my job if my superiors thought I was mentally unbalanced."

"What you tell me will not be confidential because this is an official investigation," Dan told him. "However, I will assure you that your name will be kept out of the picture. I promise, and Agent Newman also promises you. Right, Agent Newman?" David nodded. "So, tell me what happened, from beginning to end. Don't leave out any details; every little thing that you remember could be very important."

Cantrell visibly relaxed and took a deep breath, and his eyes turned up to the right, as if gazing into the distance. Clearly, he was concentrating carefully on recalling the events he was about to relate. Dan liked to see that. This man appeared to be a careful observer.

After a few moments, he started. "It was this past Thursday afternoon, around three o'clock. I had just finished taking a break. My partner Maria was off sick that day, so I was patrolling alone. I often cruise the whole area of Paradise, so I was coming down Eastern Avenue from Starbucks, where I took my break. As I was approaching the Warm Springs intersection, I decided on impulse to take a drive through the Avalon Village residential area. Nothing had happened there; in fact, nothing had happened there for quite some time. That in itself was unusual. Everyone in the department had been talking about how that was too good to be true. So anyway, just like I said, I decided to turn up Sierra Stone and do a drive through." He paused for a few seconds.

"Please go on," said Dan.

"Well, I had been hearing some rumors for the last day or two that some people had said they had been turned away from going into Avalon Village."

"What do you mean by 'turned away'?" Dan asked.

"I mean, two or three different people had reported to the precinct that they had tried to go into the street and gotten stopped. One woman said she had received an electric shock. Of course, this did not make any sense. When I drove by there earlier in the morning on Eastern, I could see there weren't any electric lines down or anything. But since a couple of people had said something similar, I just got very curious."

"So, you decided you would check just to make sure, right?" Dan asked.

"Exactly. I just wanted to do my job thoroughly," Cantrell replied.

"Perfectly right. Go on."

"Okay. So, I started to drive onto Sierra Stone. I happened to glance at my clock, my customary habit, and the time was 3:05 p.m. As soon as my car came up to the Avalon sign, I suddenly got this weird sensation. It felt kind of like a tingling down my spine, all the way down to my toes. It was really strong. My immediate impulse was to put on the brake, but I think instead I accidentally hit the gas. Then I blacked out. The next thing I knew, I was sitting in my car in the middle of Maule Street, just outside the intersection at Luminary. That's about five blocks from where I started. It's probably more than a mile away from where I'd entered."

"Was your car still moving?"

"No, it was just sitting there, idling."

"Did you see anyone around there?"

"Nope. The street was pretty empty."

"And you have no memory of getting there?" Dan asked.

"Well, everything was black, as if my eyes were closed. But I remember hearing a high-pitched buzzing sound. And along with it, I felt a vibration, as if the car were vibrating back and forth really fast. It lasted for several seconds."

"That's interesting," acknowledged Dan. "Did you happen to see what time it was then?"

"Yes. The clock still read exactly 3:05 p.m. It was as if no time had passed at all. How could I possibly have gone from one place to the other in no time?" The shock was still registering on Officer Cantrell's face. Sweat had begun to appear, and his body was shaking. "I swear to God, this is the truth. I didn't tell anyone at the station because I knew they would think I was nuts. Then, when I heard about Eastern Avenue being shut down and saw the Feds here yesterday, I decided to come and tell my story. I was really hoping somebody could tell me what was happening. It looks like something really big is going down."

After Officer Cantrell had finished talking, David turned to Dan and said, "That's exactly what he told us yesterday. Other people have corroborated the part of the story about feeling some kind of shock and being stopped from entering Avalon Village. At least a half dozen."

Dan turned to the officer. "Thank you very much for your honesty and your sense of duty. As I said before, you should have no concerns about negative repercussions."

Just as he was about to dismiss the officer, Dan caught a motion out of the corner of his eye. He turned and saw a white news van turn off Eastern onto Maule and pull over to stop, catty-cornered from the roadblock. If he was surprised, it was by the fact that he had not seen any evidence of the press up until now. But where there was one news organization, there would soon be many more.

Dan turned back to Officer Cantrell. "Listen very carefully. This could turn out to be a matter of national security. It is very important that you do not talk to the press, or to any of your friends, your coworkers, or even to your family about this. We must get the matter cleared up, without interference from anyone or panic among the public. You understand?"

"Yes sir. You can count on me."

"I am sure we can. Before you go, is there anything else you can remember at all?"

"Well, actually there is. The one thing I didn't mention to you was that, for several hours after I woke up, my body felt as if it had been in some kind of shock."

"That's not surprising, I suppose. Are you okay now?"

"Yes, but that's part I don't understand. You would think I would have felt bad or something. But just the opposite. I felt incredibly good! Like I was walking around for the rest of the day completely happy, almost giddy. And it was almost like being pumped up with endorphins after having a super exercise session. But hundreds of times beyond that. I was full of energy, and at the same time, I was very relaxed!"

"Thank you. You can go now."

"Just one more thing. You know I told you I had blown out my shoulder back in college? Well, since Thursday, I haven't felt any pain at all."

Dan and David looked at each other. The whole thing was getting stranger by the moment.

After the police officer had left, Dan said, "I have to try to go in there and find out for myself. Right now, though, I think I need a cup of coffee."

"My feelin' exactly."

"Where is that Starbucks?"

"Starbucks is a few blocks north of here on Eastern. But we should go in the other direction, away from the press," David said. "There's an Einstein's Bagels around the corner on Warm Springs."

The two men left word with David's next in charge to take any messages, headed over to the parking lot, and got into David's car. As they were about to pass the Sierra Stone entrance to Avalon Village, Dan barked, "Stop!" The two men looked at each other. David said, "Are you thinkin' what I'm thinkin'?"

Dan looked around. The surrounding area was deserted, typical for a Sunday. Turning back to David, he said, "Let's do it!"

With that, David turned the wheel to the right and stepped on the gas. The car screeched off as it accelerated through the gateway into Avalon Village.

Everything in Dan Hamilton's field of vision went white, as if he had stared into the flash of a camera. After the momentary flash of white light, everything went black. Time felt like it had stopped, and thoughts completely stopped running through his mind. There were no sounds; and then there was one sound, the sound of a faint, high-pitched buzzing. Suddenly, there was the feeling of vibration. Everything seemed to shimmy back and forth. All of this was happening instantaneously, yet completely out of time. For the moment, there was no Dan Hamilton. All there was, was one sound.

Dan opened his eyes and heard himself wailing. He stopped, but the wailing sound was still there. Then he realized the sound was coming from David Newman. It was the sound of an elongated, never-ending "ohhhhhh." Dan turned in his seat, put his hand on David's shoulder, and shouted, "David, wake up!" David opened his eyes and closed his mouth, and all sound abruptly stopped. The two men sat in the car without moving or talking for what seemed like several minutes.

After a while, they heard a sound like knocking: knock, knock, knock, knock. Dan and David could only look at each other with puzzled expressions. "Sir!" came a voice. "I said, open the car door!" The voice was emphatic. David and Dan both turned to look at the source of the sound. They realized they were sitting in the front seat of David's car. Outside, knocking on the David's window stood a police officer.

David and Dan both raised their hands where the officer could see them. David shouted through his window, "Yes sir, officer. We are with the FBI, and we are getting out of the car." Metro police officer Jared Hanes stepped back to allow the door to open, placing his hand on his belt. David and Dan opened their doors and stepped out, keeping their hands in full view. As soon as he was standing in the street, David said, "Officer, let me show you my identification."

Officer Hanes nodded, and they both reached into their breast pockets to retrieve and display their badges. Seeing their IDs, Hanes relaxed and asked, "What are you doing here? How did you get here?"

Dan saw that David's car was idling in the middle of a street, pointed toward an office building and away from a street whose sign read "Luminary." He realized they were in the middle of Maule Street. The officer's Metro Police car was parked about fifty feet away. The officer must have been posted at this entrance and seen their car suddenly appear.

Realizing it was important not to divulge the truth outside of his team, David replied, "We were just cruising past. I was taking Federal Special Investigator Hamilton here on a tour of the area to orient him to our joint operation."

"I heard a loud crack, like a gunshot," Hanes explained, looking dubious. "When I looked around your car was right there, where it is now."

Dan jumped in. "Why yes, officer, our car backfired. Agent Newman, who was driving, thought for a second we had a flat tire, and he started turning left." *Weak explanation*, Dan thought to himself.

"Oh, I see. Is everything all right?" The two men nodded.

"Do you need any assistance?" The two men shook their heads.

"Have a good day, then, and be safe." The policeman turned and walked back to his car. Reaching into the front seat, he retrieved a cup of coffee, took a sip, replaced his cup, and then got into car.

David turned to Dan and asked, "Do you think he believed us?"

Dan said, "What choice does he have? Even if he saw us appear there, the truth about what happened would be impossible for him to handle. We gave him an alternative that he can live with."

"I guess you're right."

"Let's go get that coffee."

CHAPTER 8

Something Is Coming

Dan and David sat quietly, sipping their Starbucks coffees. Each was lost in his own world, trying to digest what he had just experienced. The two men had driven around the area in a dreamlike state after leaving the scene with the police. Finally, David had snapped awake enough to turn into the parking lot of a strip mall whose anchor store was none other than Starbucks. Dan and David had both fumbled with their wallets as they attempted to buy each other a cup of coffee. Eventually, Dan had won.

Sitting there now, surrounded by adults with their wireless tablets and teenagers with their smartphones, the whole experience they had just shared simply seemed completely unreal. What puzzled Dan the most was the physical feeling he had. It was almost as if waves of joy or well-being were cruising through his system. He felt profoundly happy, in fact, almost giddy and childlike. Looking at David, he could not read his face. He was not going to bring up what he was feeling. However, he could see that David also seemed to be changed. His face looked lighter, younger somehow, almost shining. *This is very strange*, thought Dan.

After a few minutes of fruitless contemplation, Dan got up to get a newspaper. He picked up a copy of *The New York Times* and noticed immediately that on the front page was a banner announcing a cover story in the Science Section. As he turned to the article, he saw that the article's author was Jonathan Elliot. Not only was Dan a fan of

Jonathan's writing, but he also happened to have a personal connection with him. The two had been in a class together for one semester while they were undergraduates back at Stanford. The class was in creative writing, which Dan had learned very quickly was not his forte, while Jonathan, who had obviously been a natural writer, ended up majoring in journalism, and had done his graduate work at one of the Ivy League schools. The two had never been close friends, but they had shared a meal or two and gotten along pretty well. Dan had followed his former acquaintance's career from a distance ever since.

As Dan read the title of the article, "Something Is Coming," a sudden flash of intuition jolted him out of his foggy state of mind. Noticing, David asked, "What is it, Dan?" But Dan was completely absorbed and didn't answer. Curious, David walked over and picked up his own copy. Turning to the same section, he too began to read.

Something Is Coming
By Jonathan Elliot, Chief Science Editor

This weekend I have decided to deviate from my methodology of asserting a knowledge of "facts" and take a speculative approach. I realize that in the past I have remained steadfastly scientific, and I have preached that to be scientific one must only deal with what can be empirically tested and proven. This is the foundation of our modern worldview, and it has been the source of all progress humankind has made for the past four hundred years. Our societies, Eastern as well as Western, have taken centuries to build upon a scientific framework, a framework that goes back to the time of Aristotle. With our ever-accelerating breakthroughs in the past century, we have managed to build an amazing world in the process. You have read about many of these breakthroughs in this publication's weekly articles.

And yet, we all know, and we are reminded every day, that our human world remains an imperfect one. Our societies continue to be caught in the grips of prejudice. Our nations have never learned how to move beyond using warfare to try to settle our differences. We live in a world where scarcity is the prevalent norm, in spite of a plethora of evidence that the human race has all that it needs for everyone to live a fully satisfying life. If there is one thing that science has not been able to handle for us, it has been its failure to transform the most important part of ourselves—call it our collective "soul" or "spirit." To compensate, masses of people continue to hold to religion in the hopes that God, or some larger spirit, will rescue us from ourselves. In its higher forms, religion can be a good thing. In its baser forms, it has only added to superstition and fear. Others, myself included, have held that science will ultimately provide the answer. Despite all good intentions, both of these belief systems seem to be driving our entire human family toward the brink of possible extinction. We bring ourselves again and again to the question of existence versus nonexistence.

Last night I had an experience that I want to share with you. It came as a realization, in the form of a dream. I know that many of you will consider a dream revelation to be silly, perhaps even nonsensical. However, I ask you to consider what I am saying today as possibility, even if it falls into what you consider pure speculation.

Let me just say that last night a visitor came to me, as if he were a visitor from the future. I am not saying this was a real person from the future. What I am saying is that I had a visitor who managed to awaken in me a long-lost sense of the possible, of the beautiful, of the wonder that I had once had as a child. In this most unlikely dream, I received the message that "something is coming."

Of course, it is obvious that something is always coming. Everybody knows that. We all orient ourselves toward the future, and we spend most of our time anticipating or predicting or scheming or planning. We want to engineer a future that will be better for ourselves and for our families. Oddly enough, however, I realized that we never stop to look at the wonder of Future itself. Consider for one moment what Future is.

Time is divided into past, present, and future, each of which is supposed to be made up of consecutive moments of "now," a bunch of "nows" strung together, each one following last one in some kind of a logical progression. This notion, too, goes back to Aristotle. In the twentieth century, it was Einstein's discoveries and the work of quantum physicists that have taken these commonsense notions to the extreme, positing time as another dimension that, along with space, can be bent and shaped, but never violated.

Last night I had a completely new experience. I felt touched by the Future. My night visitor opened my eyes to consider the distinct possibility that maybe, just maybe, we have a closer connection to the Future than we think. I was startled into facing the probability that I do not know everything, that we all do not know everything, and in fact, that we probably know nothing. In a fundamental way, we are still primitive people trying to find our ways through a strange world. We are adolescents who play with the toys of our technologies, thinking that those toys somehow give us understanding of our world. All the while, we walk around failing to see practically everything that is right in front of our eyes, anything outside of what we are preoccupied with in the current moment. All the while, the Future may be beckoning to us like a sunrise, the Future that we cannot imagine because we are blinded by our personal "pasts," our personal "presents," and our personal "futures."

What if the Future is calling to each of us right now? What if you and I are each being beckoned by signals emanating from something that is coming? I am convinced that until last night I had never considered such a possibility. I invite each of you to think outside of your normal boundaries of thought. As you go through your day-to-day living, try to look at the world as if you do not have any idea what it is all about and what the Future will bring to you. Consider the possibility that "something is coming" could be the mantra for your own life, and that perhaps if you look closely enough with the openness to receive whatever that "something" may be, you will engage in a whole new Future of which you previously could never have dreamt.

Speaking personally, from this point forward I commit myself to preparing the world to meet tomorrow's sunrise.

"I know this guy," said Dan after the two of them had both finished reading. "We had a class together back in college. I've never seen him write something like this—so speculative, and yet at the same time, so sure of what he is saying. I have this feeling that the timing of this article is no coincidence. David, I think this article may somehow be connected to what's going on here in Vegas, and I need to check this out."

"Well dammit, Dan. If your gut tells you somethin', I say listen to it."

"Let's finish our coffee and get back to our base. On the way back, I'm going to go ahead and try to walk through the entrance. Then, I'll get on the phone and make something happen. Chief Science Editor Jonathan Elliot is going to be our guest tonight, and Uncle Sam is picking up the tab."

CHAPTER 9

Las Vegas, Day Four, 7:00 a.m.

"HELLO, JONATHAN. I'M DAN HAMILTON, FEDERAL SPECIAL INVESTIGATOR IN CHARGE OF this investigation." He held out his hand. "I don't know if you remember me or not."

"I remember you very well," replied Jonathan, shaking his hand. "Good to see you again, although the circumstances are most peculiar. It is not every day that you are met at your front door by two Secret Service agents announcing to you that the president expects you to fly to Las Vegas in a private jet. But then again, it's been an unusual week for me all around."

"Believe me, I understand. By the way, I think you've met Special Agent David Newman?"

"Yes, we met late last night at the airport."

"Good. Would you like some water?"

"No, I'm fine, thanks." The three of them took a seat. It was eight o'clock Monday morning, and they were in a conference room in a building located directly across from the branch office of the Metro Police at Sunset Park. The sign in front of the building read "Park Administration." Several agents were located in the hallway just outside the conference room, but the three men had plenty of privacy.

The police continued to block off the one section of Eastern Avenue that abutted both the Avalon Village community and Sunset Park. Overnight, however, people had begun to assemble on the sidewalks along the avenue and in the parking lot of the park. At first they were mostly curiosity seekers who had heard rumors, but now there were several news vans parked on Maule. It would not be too long before this became a national story. Dan knew he only had so much time to get the mystery solved.

"You understand that we are dealing with a very confidential matter, I assume?" Dan asked.

"Yes. The only message I received was that I am to keep everything completely under wraps, and we are possibly dealing with some incident that could involve national security. I have given my vow of secrecy, although I stated that I may not be willing to go along with just anything. I made it clear to the president that if things go against my conscience, I will draw the line."

"Fair enough. Let me explain why you're here." Dan began to recap the events he had been dealing with for the previous two days. Over the next half hour, he explained the call he had received, what he had learned from David the day before, the interview with Officer Cantrell, and his own personal experience when he attempted to enter the community. He also included the data regarding anomalies in the weather patterns and crime statistics, including the information he had received from the other agencies and his chief regarding the results of the supercomputing. By the end of the conversation, he had told him everything. Dan's boss had agreed on full disclosure, given Jonathan Elliot's reputation. Besides, the president had insisted on full transparency. He obviously trusted Jonathan.

At last, after giving Jonathan time to digest what he had said, Dan asked the question that had brought Jonathan there: "Please tell us how you came to write your article in this Sunday's *Times*. Just what do you believe is coming?"

"I truly don't know if what I have to say will make any sense to you," Jonathan responded after a few moments.

"After yesterday, Agent Newman and I won't be surprised by anything."

"I wouldn't be so sure, once you hear what I have to say. You see, last Thursday night I had this dream ..."

As Dan and David listened with rapt attention, Jonathan told them the few pieces he could remember from the incident of his mysterious night visitor. He then described in detail what was going through his mind the next day, the voice he heard while walking in Manhattan, and how he eventually wrote the article. The only part he left out was about the woman in red. That was one part he did not want to confide in these relative strangers. He then recounted how the article seemed to breeze through the editorial process, almost as if everyone had agreed to publish it untouched and unedited.

"That in itself was unprecedented," said Jonathan. "It seemed almost as if everyone in the office was participating in the same dream. Nobody questioned what I had written. They all acted like I had received some brilliant or privileged information from the future. I found the whole thing disconcerting. But then again, it all seemed so real! To be honest, I am actually glad that someone is questioning me about this. I cannot be the only person who thinks what I have written is fantastical at best and crazy at worst."

"Well," Dan replied with a grin, "I wouldn't be so sure that Agent Newman or I are thinking that at all, given what we've personally witnessed. You may be the only person with a real clue about what is actually going on."

"I fear you may be barking up the wrong tree. I don't really see how I could help."

"I think," chimed in David, "there has to be some logical explanation for what's happening. After Dan told me about who you are, I felt I would be very happy, relieved even, for us to have a scientific genius working with us."

Dan had begun to think that Special Agent David Newman had a tendency to be overly dramatic. *Must be his Scottish blood"* he thought, *or is it Irish?*

Jonathan asked, "Just how do you think *I* could be of help to you?"

Several moments of awkward silence descended upon the threesome. Worried that they were at risk of coming to a complete impasse, Dan suddenly had an idea. "Agent Newman, did you receive all the names and photographs from the DMV?"

"Yes, they were delivered this morning. I have them here."

"Good. Let's start by sifting through them to see if we get any ideas. It's logical to suspect that since this community appears to be at the center of this mystery, there could be something unusual about someone who lives here. Let's divide the portfolios into three groups, and each of us go through one group to see if anyone stands out. If a person does stand out, set the picture aside for us all to look at when we're done. Then, we'll rotate to the next group and do the same, and then again, until each of us has looked at every one of the residents. Hopefully, a photo of somebody in this community will trigger something, and that could lead to an insight."

"Excellent idea!" Jonathan exclaimed.

"Sounds good to me," David agreed.

There were more than 250 photo portfolios, not counting children and teenagers. Each was organized into folders grouping families and households together. Each man took one-third of the folders and spread them out around the conference room table.

After about an hour, Dan, David, and Jonathan were finished reviewing their first group of folders. It was somewhat disappointing that no one had set a single picture in the center part of the table to be reviewed. The men took a break and then each came back to a different section of the table with a different group of folders. After another hour or so, each came to the end of his group of portfolios. Again, the results were the same. "This might not have been such a great idea after all," grumbled David.

Nevertheless, after another brief break, the three reconvened for their last grouping. This time it only took five minutes before something extraordinary happened.

"Oh my God!" Jonathan's outburst startled the other men.

"What the *hell* was *that*!" asked David.

Dan, being slightly more poised, asked, "What the hell *was* that?"

"I think I found something!" said Jonathan.

David said, "You look like you've seen a ghost!"

"What have you found?" Dan asked.

Jonathan handed him the picture of a woman. "I need a cup of coffee. Then, I need to tell you a story."

CHAPTER 10

The Woman on the Tube

"I MET HER ABOUT A YEAR AGO. IT WAS A VERY ODD MOMENT IN MY LIFE, AND I THOUGHT I had put it all behind me. Now I feel strange because when this guy appeared in my room—I wish I could remember his name—I thought it was a dream or hallucination. But seeing this picture, I know it wasn't. I strongly feel that the man I met in my dream is connected to this woman, and I don't know how or why. But I know her name; Samantha. I met her and had a remarkable experience."

"What happened?" David and Dan.

"Last year I was in London on leave for the summer, doing social science research at a place called The Tavistock Institute. My girlfriend Diana and I were staying with a couple of friends who lived in Ilford. Late one afternoon after leaving the clinic, I got onto the tube to go to Ilford. Tube is the name Londoners use for the underground railway system, or subway. I found a seat in the back of the car and began dozing off. Suddenly, I felt a tapping on my knee. It startled me. When I opened my eyes, there was a beautiful woman sitting across from me. That was the woman in your picture.

"The moment I opened my eyes, she said, 'Excuse me, sir, who are you?' I said, 'Well, I'm a journalist from New York City on an assignment.' She then said the strangest thing to me: 'No, I mean, who are you?' I said, 'I don't know what you mean.' She said, 'Do you know what I'm feeling right now?' I said, 'No, I have no idea what you're feeling.' She said, 'This is the strangest thing. The moment I sat down and looked at you, I suddenly got this powerful feeling. It was like my entire body was on fire.' I said, 'Oh, really?' That's all I could think of to say at the moment. I was looking at this beautiful young woman. She had deep-blue eyes and long, blond hair almost down to her waist—the most gorgeous person I had ever seen.

"She then said, 'My name is Samantha. I'm suffering from some kind of unexplainable memory loss. I don't remember much about myself, just my name. It has been going on for two years. But when you came and sat down across from me, I suddenly felt something. I felt a charge like a lightning bolt. I am on my way to fly back home to the United States, where I have been staying with friends. But I feel right now that I have some kind of bizarre connection with you, Jonathan. I feel like I should get off this train. And if you said to me right now, 'Samantha, get off the subway and come with me,' I would. We could get out at the next station. I would leave everything in my life and go with you!'

"This was such a shocking statement that all my senses came alive, and my heart began pounding. Everybody in the car who had been talking suddenly stopped, and I could feel that they were listening to us. It was a palpable, physical sensation!

"Then she said to me, 'Do you know what deep feelings I am having for you?' When she said this to me, I felt totally shocked and embarrassed. I could only stammer out the words, 'No, I have no idea. But that's very flattering.' She said 'It's not flattering. It's very disturbing, the way I feel about you.' Then she said to me, 'I have never felt such a connection to another human being.'

"I looked at her for a moment and then realized something. I said to her, 'So, your name is Samantha. How did you know my name is Jonathan?'

"She looked at me with an innocent look on her beautiful face. She ignored my question and repeated, 'I feel this bizarre connection with you. I feel like I should get off this train and go with you.' Once again, I felt we were the center of everybody's attention. Everybody

SIGNALING

was looking at us. I could almost sense that everyone in the subway car was thinking, 'Get out of the car and go with her, you fool! Get out. Go!'"

"So, what happened next?" David interrupted. Dan could see the romantic in him.

"Well, as you can imagine, I was very tempted. Part of me was saying, 'Go with her; just do it!' The other part was saying, 'No, I can't do it.' Finally I said, 'Samantha, I have a girlfriend in New York, and I'm very happy with her and committed to her.' Then Samantha said to me, 'It doesn't matter to me that you have a girlfriend. I'm telling you that I will go anywhere in the world with you, anywhere. I don't even know why I'm saying this. But I feel like I've known you forever, like I was meant to meet you. I can only remember the last two years of my life. I've been living with a couple from San Francisco who have taken care of me. They've been visiting London this summer, and they brought me with them. Tomorrow we are scheduled to fly back home. But I will drop everything if you say to and will come with you, anywhere.'

"So, I said to her, 'The truth is, Samantha, I'm also feeling something. I feel I know you. Like you are connected to something so powerful in my world. But at the same time, I feel that whatever you are connected to is too strange for me to understand. It doesn't feel right to me.' My mind was saying, 'Don't be a fool; get out right now! Take her hand and go.' But something was holding me back.

"Then, I said to her, 'Come here a little closer, Samantha.' She came closer. 'All these people are telling me to get off the train, to take your hand, and go with you. This is a one in a million chance. But Samantha, I can't go with you. The time is not right.'

"Then this amazing woman asked me something very interesting, as if she were reading my mind. 'Do you think we knew each other in another lifetime? Maybe you were with me in a past life.' I said, 'For some reason I know it is definitely not the past, and I don't believe in reincarnation.' Then these words just came out of my mouth without thinking. I said, 'I just feel that I have a tremendous and deep feeling, like love, for you.' You have to understand, gentlemen, I never talk like this.

"Right then the train started slowing down for my stop at Ilford. I said, 'I'm sorry; I can't go with you now. Please let me have your number and address in San Francisco, and maybe after thinking about it, I might call you.' Samantha said, 'All right, Jonathan.' She reached into her bag and took out a piece of paper and a pen. When she finished, she told me, 'Please don't lose it.'

"She held out the paper toward me. I took it with my left hand and enclosed it in my fist. Then she grabbed my fist in both her hands and looked into my eyes. Everything was happening in slow motion. I said to her, 'Thank you, I will never lose this. I will keep in touch with you.' She said, 'Promise me.' And I said, 'I promise.'

"The train came to a stop. I stood up, and we gave each other a hug. Time seemed to stand still. The door opened, and I stepped out onto the platform. But she wouldn't let me go. She kept holding onto my left hand with her right hand. She wouldn't release my hand! She was on the train, and I was now on the platform. Then the doors started to shut, but our hands prevented the doors from closing. After two times, the conductor jumped off the train onto the platform and shouted to us: 'You're holding up the train!' I tried to release my hand, but still she wouldn't let go. Then she began to cry.

"I now felt as if my body was on fire. This time, when the doors closed, the doors went right through our hands as if they weren't even there. The instant the doors shut, a white light exploded in front of my eyes. At the same moment, I was overwhelmed by a loud sound. The sound came like some kind of roar from the people on the platform and on the train. I heard someone scream out 'Bloody hell!' The train started pulling away. The people around me looked terrified, as if they thought there had been a bombing. As the train accelerated down the track, I started crying like a baby."

While talking to Dan and David, Jonathan teared up. Dan and David were stunned. After a moment, when he had pulled himself together, Jonathan continued. "Every tube station has a pub, so I ran upstairs from the platform, went to the pub, and ordered a Guinness. Eventually, I settled down enough to call my friends to come and get me. I couldn't stop crying.

"Then my friends, Tony and Mary, brought Diana to the pub to pick me up. I couldn't say why I was crying, but I couldn't keep the story inside me, either. Fortunately, Diana isn't the jealous kind. After I told them all the story, Mary said, 'Let me see the address.'

"I realized I had been clutching the piece of paper in my left hand the whole time. When I opened my hand, however, there was nothing in it but ashes! We were all shocked. The paper had apparently burned when the subway doors had shut, when there had been a flash. There must have been a tremendous heat of some kind. I took the fact that it was destroyed to mean that we were destined not to be together.

"For a while I kept dreaming about her," Jonathan continued. "I dreamed that she would come to see me and talk to me. Eventually, I kind of erased the whole experience from my memory. Now I can't believe that she lives here. That's very strange because she told me she was from San Francisco. I guess I was somehow destined to meet her again, after all."

David asked Dan for the picture, then looked closely at it and said, "The caption says her name is Samantha Hunter, and her driver's license is from Nevada, just issued this March. It says she lives at 4544 Indigo Way. Indigo Way is the third street over from Eastern in Avalon Village."

Doing a quick calculation in his head, Jonathan remarked, "That's an eight."

"What?" asked Dan.

"My mind automatically takes any number and performs a numerological calculation. It's kind of an automatic reflex. You add all the digits of a number together, and then keep adding the digits of the resulting number until you get to just one digit. In this case, four plus five plus four plus four makes seventeen, which is one plus seven, which makes eight. Her address is an eight in numerology. I always associate eight with infinity. You know, the sign for infinity is eight turned sideways. I don't put any stock into it, of course."

"Some scientist you are," chuckled Dan.

"Yes, I know. It's a strange habit."

Dan looked through the folder, pulling out four other images of drivers' licenses. "It looks like she's staying with two other couples, a younger couple named Edward and Clare Hunter, and a more elderly couple named Henry and Hazel White. The elderly couple appears to have a strong resemblance to Clare and is shown to be living at the same address as Samantha. However, the Hunter couple each has a California license with a street address in San Francisco. Another coincidence, maybe? Incidentally, how is it we would have the out-of-state licenses, David?"

"The police and our men have been stopping and interviewing everyone who has either walked or driven in or out of the residential area for the past two days. They must have come out or gone in at some point; so, we got their licenses."

"Well, Jonathan," Dan said after a pause. "It sounds like the next step is for you to meet Miss Samantha Hunter."

Unbeknownst to the three men, someone was listening to this conversation from the hallway, with keen interest.

CHAPTER 11

Avalon Village, Day Four, 11:00 a.m.

"DO YOU REALLY THINK THIS IS GOING TO WORK?" ASKED JONATHAN.

"Piece of cake," David assured him.

Ignoring his new partner's nonchalance, Dan said to Jonathan, "I know this is just a hunch, but because of your emotional connection with this woman, I'm almost sure that this field, whatever it is, will allow you to enter the neighborhood. It's certainly worth a try. And the field has proven to be perfectly harmless so far, so it won't hurt you."

"'So far' is an expression that has always made me nervous," Jonathan muttered.

Dan continued. "Together we'll drive over to Maule and let you out at the entrance to Indigo Way. We should know immediately whether the field will let you pass. Assuming you're able to go in, you'll walk over to number 4544 and knock on the door. If Samantha is there, from what you told us, she'll surely let you into the house. All you have to do then is convince her to come out to meet us. We need to find out if she knows anything about what's happening. I'm convinced that she's a link, whether she realizes it or not. Who knows? By now she may have fully regained her memory."

"Actually," David chimed in, "I think it would be better if we drove down to the Sierra Stone intersection on Eastern. The TV and newspaper reporters are lined up all along Maule, and since Eastern is blocked off, they are less likely to cause trouble for us."

"Good thinking," agreed Dan. "Are you ready, Jonathan?"

Jonathan nodded. The three of them walked out to the administration building parking lot and got into David's car. As they drove, Jonathan watched the tops of the houses and occasional palm trees pass by behind the cinderblock wall of Avalon Village. The homes were single- or two-story, stucco constructions with uniformly pink-tiled roofs that looked like they belonged to a '50s or '60s housing development. David stopped the car at the intersection of Eastern and Sierra Stone.

"You know where to go from here?" Dan asked.

"Piece of cake," Jonathan said, and got out of the car. He walked into the middle of the intersection, and then turned so that he was facing down Sierra Stone.

Holding his breath, he took one step. Nothing happened. He took three more steps. Still nothing. He was now standing across from the entry sign to Avalon Village. *Here she goes,* Jonathan thought to himself, and without further hesitation, he began walking briskly up the street. After about ten steps, his body and mind still intact, he looked toward the FBI car and raised a fist in victory.

Dan and David gave each other a high five.

Jonathan turned back and continued walking until he reached Indigo Way. Turning right, he walked until he reached his destination. As he looked around, he observed that the street was completely deserted. The house numbered 4544 had a garage and a short walkway that led up to a front door. Garbage cans and recycling containers were awaiting pickup. The only thing he found interesting was that the home seemed to be nested behind a larger number of trees and bushes than the other homes on the block. The foliage appeared green and well watered, and there were lots of cheery, colorful flowers.

Jonathan texted his arrival to Dan's cell phone. After receiving a thumbs-up emoji, he headed up the driveway through the shaded archway created by the overhanging trees. As he walked to the front door, he suddenly felt a shiver of excitement. Holding himself steady, he rang the doorbell.

After a few seconds, Jonathan heard muffled voices and steps approaching. The memory of deep-blue eyes and long, blond hair overwhelmed him. His heart began to race. He suddenly lost track of time and forgot what he was going to say. Momentarily, he heard the unlatching of the lock, and the door opened.

"Can I help you?" Jonathan was shocked back into the moment. Standing in front of him was an older man with glasses and graying hair, probably in his seventies. Feeling let down, he recognized the man's face from the picture he had seen of the older couple that lived at this address. What was the couple's name? Oh, yes, White.

"I'm looking for Samantha."

"I'm sorry; she's not here right now. Can I ask who you are?"

"My name is Jonathan. I met Samantha last summer in London, where I was doing research. Actually, we met on a train, and she gave me her address and asked me to look her up the next time I was in town." It was only a small, white lie.

"Oh, I see. Well, unfortunately, she's traveling right now, and we don't expect her back for several days."

From the background came a woman's voice. "Henry, aren't you going to ask the young man in?" *That must be Hazel*, Jonathan thought.

"Oh, I'm so sorry. I'm being most impolite." The man stepped aside and held the door open for Jonathan. "I'm Henry White, and this is my wife, Hazel. We're friends of Samantha's. That is, Samantha has been living here with us and our daughter and son-in-law. It's too bad she isn't here. Hazel, this is, uh, I'm afraid I've already forgotten your name."

"Jonathan Elliot. Just call me Jonathan. Very pleased to meet you, Mr. White." Jonathan stepped through the front door into the living room and shook Henry's hand.

"Please call me Henry. 'Mister' makes me feel old."

"All right, Henry."

Hazel White motioned Jonathan over toward the couch. Taking a seat, Jonathan looked around, trying not to be obvious. The living room opened into a dining area in the back, and through the door to the left appeared to be a den or family room. "You have a lovely home, Mrs. White."

"Thank you. And please, call me Hazel. Can I offer you some iced tea or water?"

"No thank you. I can't stay very long. I was just hoping to get a chance to say hello to Samantha again."

Hazel and Henry White sat down across from Jonathan in two easy chairs.

"What do you do for a living, Jonathan?" Henry employed the standard conversation opener men used when meeting each other.

"I'm a writer," Jonathan replied. Immediately, he saw Henry tense up. "Actually, I'm a science editor, for *The New York Times*." At that, Henry seemed to relax again. "I specialize in bringing important scientific topics to the public. I believe that science can be a force of good for humanity, and I want people to be educated about that." Jonathan wondered what had made Henry tense up. What was he afraid of?

"An admirable enterprise!" exclaimed Hazel. "I think the world would be a better place all around if science were used to its full benefit."

"I heartily agree!" said Henry. "In fact, our daughter Clare is an anthropologist, and our son Edward, or rather our son-in-law, is a mathematician. He's pretty well known in academic circles, and so is Clare, for that matter."

"Really?" Jonathan asked with interest. "Might I have heard of them?"

"If you haven't, you can certainly Google them. Look up Professors Clare and Edward Hunter."

"Do they live here in Las Vegas?" Jonathan already knew the answer, but he was looking to discover more information about Samantha.

"Oh no, or at least not normally. They have been staying here for about a year, on sabbatical from their work. They both teach at the University of California."

"At Berkeley?"

"No, in San Francisco. UCSF. We've been very happy to have them with us again in our home, at least until they decide when to return. They brought Samantha here last year. She has become a good family friend," Hazel enthused. "And how did you say you met her?"

"We met each other on a train in London and hit it off. She gave me this address and invited me to look her up sometime. I happened to be here for a short trip and thought I would take the opportunity."

"We're so sorry you missed her," Hazel said. Jonathan noticed that both Henry and Hazel had traces of a southern accent.

"I get the sense that you might not be from either Las Vegas or San Francisco," Jonathan commented. "Are you from somewhere down south?"

"Why yes, actually," said Hazel. "Henry and I are both originally from North Carolina. I guess you never lose your accent, no matter how much you travel."

"I guess that's true. It doesn't take people long to tell I'm from New York. North Carolina is a beautiful state. I've been to the Outer Banks and the Great Smoky Mountains. Are Clare and Edward from there as well?"

Hazel answered, "No, they met when they were both in graduate school at Berkeley. I think they were very lucky to find each other, especially studying in different departments."

"It was love at first sight," interjected Henry.

"Yes," Hazel continued, "Clare had always been a very quiet and studious girl. She's our only child. From the beginning, Clare was always fascinated by science. She was always begging us to take her to see the dinosaur bones in Florissant Fossil Beds and in Dinosaur National Monument and Arches National Park. Then as she became a teenager, she became interested in Native American cultures. We spent many wonderful weekends touring Mesa Verde and visiting the pueblos near Colorado Springs. I think by the time she graduated from high school, she knew she wanted to be an anthropologist. She went to the University of Colorado in Boulder and graduated near the top of her class. Then it was on to Berkeley."

Once again, Henry took the conversation. "We were very happy when she met Edward. She seemed to blossom around him. And both are very smart."

"When I met Samantha, she didn't tell me much about the people she lives with. I see that she has the same last name. Is she Edward's sister or a cousin, perhaps?"

"Oh, no, she's just a good friend." Hazel glanced over at Henry with a slight questioning look, as if to ask whether it was all right to go further. Henry gave a subtle nod, and Hazel continued. "They met about three years ago, in San Francisco. Edward and Clare happened to meet her while on a late afternoon walk in a park. She looked dazed and confused, and Edward thought she might have been in some kind of accident."

Henry jumped in at this point. "The most amazing thing was that she had lost her memory. She knew her first name but couldn't remember anything else, even how she got there. They offered to take her to a hospital, but she refused. She didn't look hurt, so they took her back to their apartment to give her some dinner and let her regain her bearings."

Hazel then jumped back in to pick up the story. "Samantha ended up staying with them, and before long they became wonderful friends. They've been together ever since."

Jonathan asked, "And she still hasn't gotten her memory back?"

"Not so far," Henry said. "But she didn't match any reports of a missing person, so they just let her stay with them. After a time, they introduced her to a neurologist they knew from the university. He examined her and told them the best thing was for them to keep doing what they were doing, and eventually her memory would probably return."

Bad luck about her memory, Jonathan thought to himself. Out loud he said, "So Samantha just adopted their last name?"

"That's right," Hazel responded. "And Samantha has been our friend as well, ever since they joined us here. She's a remarkable young woman and seems to be very talented as well—you know, in the sense of being very intuitive in understanding other people. I always feel calm and safe around her. She's just a sweet and *very* refined girl."

"And she's always reading and learning about all kinds of things," Henry added. "She has a voracious appetite for knowledge. She's overall a very nice, smart young lady."

"I really feel bad that I missed her, but I'm glad to have had the chance to meet the two of you. Do you happen to know where I can find Samantha, or how I can reach her? I have some important things to talk about with her."

"You say you are from New York?" Henry asked. Jonathan nodded. "Well, that's quite a coincidence. The three of them flew to New York just a couple days ago."

"Oh, that's great. I'm planning to head back there tonight." It was just another little, white lie. "Do you know where I can find her?"

"Sure," said Hazel. "They're staying with a very dear friend of Clare's, a philosophy professor at New York University. Her name is Allison Russell. She lives in the East Village."

"Would you please give me her address or phone number?" Jonathan's heart was beginning to beat quickly again.

"Keep your seat, Hazel," Henry said. "I have it right here." He reached into his wallet, pulled out a business card, and handed it to Jonathan.

"Thanks so much, Henry. And thank you, Hazel. I really need to run, since I have a plane to catch this evening. I'll look them up as soon as I get home. Do you know how long they'll be there?"

"They'll be flying back this coming weekend. You should have no trouble finding Samantha at Allison's place. Allison also might be someone you should talk to for your scientific research, if you are ever interested in the philosophical side of things. Of course, the same goes for Clare and Edward. I'm sure you'll all hit it off nicely."

"Thank you for your hospitality," Jonathan spoke genuinely. "I very much appreciate your time." The three of them stood up, and Jonathan shook hands with the Whites and said good-bye. Henry held the front door open for him, and as he stepped outside, Jonathan heard the words, "What colors did *you* see?" The question was coming from Hazel.

A bit startled, Jonathan turned and asked, "Pardon me?"

Hazel joined Henry in the doorway and said, "I just asked what colors you saw—when you were with Samantha on the train. You can see lights and colors around her sometimes. I usually see blue, but sometimes red or white."

For a moment, Jonathan did not know what to say. Finally, he said as nonchalantly as he could, "Oh, that's right. It was white." He then abruptly turned and walked out onto the street. As he walked away from 4544 Indigo Way, he carefully searched his memory of the conversation with the Whites, but felt sure he had not mentioned the story of what he had really experienced on the train. Once he reached the corner of Sierra Stone, he turned and broke into a fast run to rejoin Dan and David.

When he reached the waiting car, he breathlessly exclaimed, "Yes!"

Back at the park administration building that had served as their makeshift office, Special Agent David Newman asked one of the police officers on duty to make copies of all the photos and documents. While he was gone, Dan, David, and Jonathan came up with a game plan for their next actions. They agreed that Dan and Jonathan would fly to New York immediately to bring Samantha in for questioning. David would resume responsibility for monitoring the status of operations at the Avalon Charged Field site. The greatest challenge for him now would be to create disinformation to keep press coverage from escalating. He would continue operating under Dan's instructions and report to Dan anything new that arose.

Within an hour, Federal Special Investigator Dan Hamilton and Chief Science Editor Jonathan Elliot were seated together on the private government jet that had brought Jonathan to Las Vegas the evening before. Once airborne, Dan quickly reported to the Chief that he and Jonathan were now working together and following a person of interest (a.k.a., Samantha Hunter), who apparently held the key to everything. Dan asked the Chief to get any background information on Samantha that he could. He faxed him all of the pictures and contents of the portfolio and outlined a plan for taking Samantha into protective custody as a key witness. He then requested special FBI and local police assistance to meet him upon landing.

The pilot estimated their arrival time in New York to be around six thirty in the evening. The first stop would be the home of Professor Allison Russell. With a little luck, Dan and Jonathan would have Samantha in their charge by seven thirty or eight o'clock.

Little did either of them know that the police officer who made the photocopies had kept one extra copy of each item. There was another interested party who was willing to pay him for the documents—and to pay him very well.

PART TWO

GATHERINGS

You, in your time, underestimate your presence
as human beings in the universe,
your power and your true nature.
We are custodians of the universe.
　　　　　　　—Commander Zjon III

CHAPTER 12

Edward and Clare, Three Years Earlier

"DO YOU THINK SHE'S ALL RIGHT?" CLARE HUNTER ASKED HER HUSBAND EDWARD. THEY were staring at a young woman sitting about a hundred feet away under a lone tree on one of the famous Twin Peaks, in San Francisco. It was 6:45 p.m. on Friday, July 12.

"Let's go over and ask her," Edward answered. Clare had already started walking in that direction before Edward had had time to answer her.

Edward, a bearded teddy-bear of a man, chuckled to himself as he saw that his wife once again was off on some kind of rescue mission. Whether it was an animal in distress or a homeless person on the street, Clare always seemed to find some way to give of herself. And animals and people always responded as if they instinctively trusted her. Sometimes he felt jealous. But then he would remember that he was once the object of one of those rescue missions. Edward knew he was a lucky man. Before meeting Clare, he had always considered himself to be nothing but a wonky guy. He had chosen mathematics because his sixth-grade teacher had seen something in him and sown the seed. In many ways, math had been his refuge from social awkwardness. He was good at it, true, but he had never felt that he had the ability to relate to people—until Clare came along, that is. Meeting her had changed everything.

Tonight Edward sensed that this was no normal rescue mission.

"Slow down, Seabiscuit. Wait for me." He began trotting to catch up to her.

Twin Peaks was a large pair of hills located roughly in the center of the stunning peninsula on which the city was built. From the peaks one has a 360-degree view of the city. Toward the north and east, one sees sprawling hills, dotted with old Victorian houses, gradually descending toward the Golden Gate Bridge to the north and the downtown financial district and Market Street to the east, eventually abutting the Bay. To the west and south, one sees Golden Gate Park, the Pacific Ocean, and down along the coast, the Santa Clara Valley reaching toward Monterey.

For decades the city had maintained a natural reserve around each of the peaks, managed by the San Francisco Recreation and Parks Department. Eureka Peak, the northern peak, was one of Edward and Clare's favorite places to stroll.

For several years since getting tenure at UCSF and buying their apartment in Noe Valley, Edward and Clare Hunter had established a pleasant routine of driving up to Twin Peaks on their way home from the campus after work. On Fridays they would often stop to purchase a bottle of Chardonnay or a nice Cabernet to take with them. They would sit on one of the many benches overlooking the city, sipping their wine as they shared their experiences of the day. Frequently they would follow one of the winding trails that wrapped around the hills, stopping only to watch as the sun began to set over the fog rolling in from the Pacific. At one of their favorite spots, a small cluster of evergreen, oak, and eucalyptus trees overlooked the city reservoir. To the north stood the iconic Sutro Tower, San Francisco's once controversial, red and white, three-pronged television antenna. At first the tower was hated, opposed, and mocked by local residents. Eventually, however, it had become another grand symbol of this great city.

One of the trees standing apart, but not far from this particular group of trees, had captured Edward and Clare's attention for the past several days. The tree itself was not remarkable. It was a typical

California live oak, probably sixty or seventy years old. Sitting under it this evening, however, was the most beautiful woman Edward had ever seen. As they moved closer, occasionally catching each other's eye with a questioning look, Edward and Clare realized they each were thinking the same thing. Something unusual was happening.

Four nights earlier, both Clare and Edward had had a dream about this tree. In Clare's dream, a magnificent condor had risen from the top of the tree and flown away in the direction of the Pacific. A ball of blue light had suddenly shot out of its wings, expanding to encompass both Clare and the tree, and then completely disappeared. The air was left filled with hundreds of Monarch butterflies. Then the dream had ended as abruptly as it had begun. Nevertheless, the dream's impact had been vivid and unforgettable. When she awoke in the morning, she recounted the details of the dream to Edward. Shocked, Edward had told Clare of his own dream that night. In his dream, he was walking toward this same tree, when an eagle appeared. Flying directly over his head, the eagle suddenly burst into a fiery, white ball of light, like another sun. Equally suddenly, the light and the eagle were both gone. In their place, however, thousands of jasmine flowers dropped from the sky, covering the ground and filling the air with the scent of jasmine. Just as mysteriously, his dream had come to an uneventful end but had left him in a state of wonder.

Both Edward and Clare knew they had dreamt about the same tree. Each evening following their dream, the two of them had made it a point to walk by the tree and stop for a few minutes during their evening ritual. Emotionally, they had both felt strangely drawn to this simple, old oak tree. They felt that something was coming.

Now, on this summer evening there was a lovely young woman sitting under their dream tree. Both of them simultaneously felt as if something wonderful had come. When they were within ten or fifteen feet from the woman, they stopped. "Do you need help?" Clare called.

The woman only looked at them with an expression of both

bewilderment and serenity. Her eyes were a deep blue and conveyed a beautiful clarity.

After a few moments, Clare tried again. "My name is Clare, and this is my husband, Edward. We saw you sitting over here under this tree and wondered if you were okay. Is there anything we can do?"

Again, the young woman looked at them, now with a hint of curiosity. She appeared to be in her late twenties or early thirties. Her clothes, a closely fitting blouse with matching pants, looked like they were made out of some unusual kind of material. They were stylish but plain at the same time, in a shade of color between light purple and blue. As her long blond hair cast shadows across her body, her clothing seemed to shimmer in alternating colors.

After another few seconds of silence, Clare and Edward looked at each other and decided they should leave her alone. Perhaps the woman wanted privacy.

As they turned to leave, the woman at last spoke: "My name is Samantha. Can you tell me where I am?"

At five o'clock the following afternoon, Edward and Clare sat together at the kitchen table pondering what had unexpectedly unfolded in their lives. The evening before, they had brought the woman who called herself "Samantha" back to their Noe Valley home. She had immediately fallen into a deep sleep in their guest room, without having spoken more than a dozen words. The woman had clearly been in a state of shock. Clare and Edward had kept an alternating vigil throughout the night and morning, and then into the afternoon, until she had awakened at last, just one hour before. Now, after having had a series of brief but remarkable conversations over dinner, she had gone back to sleep.

Who was this strange and enchanting young woman asleep in

their guestroom? She seemed to have no memory of who she was. On the one hand, she did not seem to even know where she was. When Edward had told her she was in San Francisco, he was only met with a blank stare. Yet, on the other hand, she seemed extremely intelligent. When Clare had suggested she must have amnesia, Samantha had offered up an explanation of the Greek etymology of the word *amnesia*.

At the same time, there was something endearing about her. Being around her had evoked in them an almost parental desire to protect her, as if she were their child. Indeed, she had walked around the house, looking with childlike wonder at everything, unabashedly fascinated by her surroundings. Edward wondered if she was from a foreign country. She spoke English, but in a formal way with a slight accent that he could not place. Perhaps she was Scandinavian? Just who was she?

"What did Andy say?" Edward asked. Earlier, while Edward and Samantha were eating their dinners, Clare had gone into the next room to call Andrew Chen, a good friend who happened to be chief neurologist and head of the neuroscience department at the university.

"He's going to stop by tomorrow afternoon. If he decides he needs to take Samantha into the lab for some testing after talking with her, he can do it then."

"That's perfect. I've always liked Andy, and I trust him." The two sat together for a few minutes in silence, once again lost in thought.

Eventually, Clare spoke up once more. "We need to talk about the feelings we are experiencing with this perfect stranger."

Edward knew exactly what Clare was referring to, and he too had been puzzling over the powerful, new feelings he had been experiencing. "Just what do you think we are feeling?" he asked.

"It's not a physical attraction, but I'm definitely feeling some kind of pull toward her—like a motherly instinct. I feel this powerful connection with her, in my whole body. Something I have never quite felt before."

"That's how I feel. It's not a physical attraction, but for me it's like what I imagine I would feel if I were a father and she were my daughter. But that doesn't say it, either."

"I'm going to say something that will sound ridiculous," Clare ventured.

"Go ahead."

"What we are feeling may not really be an attraction at all. It's more like a magnetic pull, and we have never had this with anybody, including each other. With Samantha, there is some kind of connection that seems like magnetism."

Edward said, "That says it beautifully. It's as if we were drawn to her. That's even what I was feeling for the last several days every time we walked by that tree, as if I were being pulled by some powerful force that I couldn't name."

"Exactly," agreed Clare. "This feels to me like a moment of destiny. Funny that she brought up the etymology of the word *amnesia* using Greek legends. The Greeks called a moment such as this 'Kairos,' a special moment in time. I've never been a believer in religion or mythology. But I think we're being called to something greater than ourselves, a special moment in time."

"I just wish I knew what that could be."

"Me too. But one thing feels for certain."

"What's that?"

"It's very important that we take good care of this person. She means something to us that we don't yet understand."

Edward pondered this for a moment and then added, "Yes, and I have this feeling that something much bigger is going on. Strange. I'm now finding myself driven by a part of me that I didn't even realize was important."

"Your heart?"

"Exactly! My heart. I think that, with this woman, you and I have stepped into some kind of mission. It's no accident. Let's call it 'Mission Heart.' We need to help Samantha find herself, and I suspect we'll be helping ourselves find new meaning in our own lives."

Clare agreed. "Yes, and we need to take care of her for as long as it takes, until she uncovers her history or ..."

"Or we uncover for ourselves why she landed in our lives. Also, we may have to create a cover story to explain to our friends and colleagues who she is. She has no driver's license or identification papers. All we have is her name."

"Let's call her Samantha!"

"How original!" he teased. "Here's what I propose. Until she remembers who she is, we'll say we found my missing cousin named Samantha Hunter. They'll say things like, 'You never told us you have a cousin who was missing.' So we have to create a story about how we didn't want to tell anybody she was missing, and then one day we accidentally met her on Twin Peaks. She was traveling around on her own and sightseeing. We'll have to get Samantha to go along with this story in order to avoid suspicion. At some point, we'll need to find a way to get her a driver's license, but we'll cross that bridge when we come to it. That is, assuming her memory never recovers."

"That's a distinct possibility."

"Unfortunately, you may be right. But first and foremost, we need to help her get oriented to us and our home."

"Her new home, that is."

"Right, her new home."

"One thing at a time. Right now, let's have a glass of port!" Clare enthused.

"You bet! Let's celebrate our good fortune." Edward stood up from the table and walked to the wine shelf in the pantry. He pulled out his favorite vintage, which he had been saving for a special occasion. He poured two generous glasses of port, then handed one to Clare.

Clare stood up, and the two clinked their glasses. Then she said, "No, I have a better idea. Not just our good fortune. Let's celebrate something else."

"What?" asked Edward.

"Let's toast the unknown!"

"Here, here! And to all the improbabilities that the unknown has in store for us."

"You are such a mathematician!" Clare said with a laugh. Edward smiled. This had always been a favorite tease of hers.

"To Mission Heart!"

Clare and Edward clinked their glasses again and savored their first sips.

CHAPTER 13

New York City, Day Four, 6:50 p.m.

SAMANTHA, CLARE, AND EDWARD SAT AT A POLISHED WOODEN TABLE IN THE BACK corner of a popular restaurant and bar called Raoul's. Each was sipping a glass of a fine California Pinot Noir. Across from Samantha sat Allison Russell, esteemed professor of philosophy at NYU, enjoying her martini. Happy hour had just wrapped up, and the four friends were eager for one of the restaurant's excellent meals. Raoul's was one of the hottest places to eat, drink, and be seen in the SoHo district of Manhattan. As usual, every table was occupied; the bar was filled, and there was a line beginning to form outside. It would soon be another standing-room-only evening at Raoul's.

Allison and Clare had been friends since their undergraduate days in Boulder. Their relationship was founded on an attraction of opposites. Clare, the soft-spoken, middle class, Southern white girl who was fascinated by Native American culture, was culturally about as far removed as possible from Allison, the brash, direct, Harlem-born black girl who had clawed her way up from the streets to become a master of philosophical dialectic. Emotionally, Clare was a lover; Allison was a fighter. Clare trusted every stranger; Allison trusted no one. For three years, the two kept finding themselves in the same dormitories and many of the same classes. The crowning moment of soul mate-hood had occurred one evening during a wine tasting at the commons room, when each simultaneously saw herself in the other. From that moment forward, the two were virtually inseparable throughout their last year in Boulder. Together they matriculated to Berkeley, each for advanced study in her own chosen field.

Edward had won Allison over the first night Clare introduced them in a Berkeley pub and they launched into an evening-long discussion of Bertrand Russell, Ludwig Wittgenstein, and Martin Heidegger. They argued about whether the nature of truth could be found primarily through mathematical logic, language games, or ontological phenomenology. The debate had waged for hours, coming to a draw, but having brought great pleasure to each of them. Their friendship had been a match made in cerebral heaven.

Once Samantha was introduced into the picture a couple of years back, it had not taken long for her and Allison to become good friends as well. Like Clare, Allison had found herself in the unexpected but thrilling role of surrogate mother. Whenever they had the opportunity to visit, life turned into an adventure.

As usual, once the four friends had begun imbibing their cocktails at Raoul's, it had not taken long for their conversation to turn inquisitive. "Is it really true," prompted Allison, "that you still have absolutely *no* memory of your past?"

"Yes, it's true. I have no idea who I was before the day I met Clare and Ed."

"Even after working with that neurologist, what was his name?"

"Dr. Andrew Chen. Yes, even after that. He has helped me enormously though in coaching me to handle fear of the unknown. He's a very dear friend, and I owe him much."

"I think Andy would like to be more than a friend," interjected Clare.

"I realize that," said Samantha, "and I'm sensitive to his feelings. I told him, though, that I just couldn't get involved with him. It doesn't feel right. Somehow I feel there is someone else with whom I was meant to be. I just either can't remember who that is."

"I do love your ability to trust your intuition, Samantha," Allison said. "I frankly don't know how I would cope if I lost my memory. But Ed and Clare are probably the best people you could have ever met."

"We agree completely," Edward said. "You are just so lucky to have us, Sam." With that they all laughed and clinked their glasses.

As her three friends sipped, Samantha moved her glass toward her lips, then hesitated. She stared down into her wine, as if searching for something. Inhaling deeply through her nose, she blew into her glass through pursed lips, gently and steadily. She repeated this ritual two more times before she took another sip. Edward and Clare didn't seem to pay attention, but Allison was fascinated. Once Samantha had put down her glass, Allison asked her, "What in the world are you doing?"

"What do you mean?" Samantha asked.

"I mean blowing into your glass of wine. What was that for?"

"Oh, that," she said. "I just do that sometimes to charge the wine."

"'Charge' the wine? What do you mean?"

"When I blow into a drink, it puts a kind of charge, like a kind of energy into the drink. It's very subtle, but sometimes I can see that it needs an extra charge. After doing that a couple times, I can see the energy change. Anyway, when you do that and then drink it, you feel really good."

Turning to Clare and Edward, Allison asked, "Do you know what she's talking about?"

"This is something that Samantha has done ever since we've known her," Edward said. "It seems to be some kind of innate talent she has. She's blown into our drinks many times. She's right; you do feel good after drinking it. It can even be just a glass of water. You should try it."

Allison, shaking her head, said, "You mean I should try blowing into my martini?"

"No," Clare interjected. "I mean, you can try it yourself. I have, but it doesn't seem to do anything. Edward means you should let

Samantha blow into your martini. Samantha, would you do that for Allison?"

"Of course," Samantha replied.

"Go ahead," Edward encouraged Allison.

"But what about germs?" Allison persisted.

"We've never gotten sick. Besides, the alcohol in your martini would probably kill any germs anyway." Edward and Clare both chuckled. Samantha just smiled.

At last, Allison gave in. "All right, but this feels foolish." She slid her martini glass across the table to Samantha. "Go ahead!"

Samantha nodded, picked up Allison's glass, and performed the ritual. Then she slid the glass back across the table.

Allison stared at the glass and said, "It doesn't look any different to me."

Samantha smiled and nodded toward the glass. "Have some. It's charged."

Allison picked up her glass and took a good swallow, almost causing herself to choke.

"Careful," Clare laughed. "No need to rush it."

Allison set her glass down. She looked around in turn at each of her three companions. "I honestly don't feel ..." She stopped in midsentence, her face suddenly softening. Allison felt a great swell of warmth rise through her body as she was wrapped in a cocoon of well-being. She could feel the blood pulsing through her face and scalp, and her cheeks felt tingly. She felt totally giddy, happy, and alive, like she was going to burst out singing or laughing.

"See what we mean?" Edward gave a chuckle.

"That's unbelievable!" was all Allison could muster.

"Please don't ask me how I can do that," Samantha said, heading off the obvious question. "It's just a connection I feel. The wine or water or whatever sometimes just seems to call me to breathe on it, so I do. When I do, it seems to make it happy."

"My God, Samantha," Allison said with true wonder. "Do you know what this reminds me of?"

Samantha shook her head.

"In studying philosophy over the years, I came to admire the ancient Greeks, not only Plato and Aristotle, but also especially the ones who preceded them—the original ones. They are referred to as the pre-Socratics. I admired their original way of seeing things. They were the first, at least in Western culture, to look at the world in an inquiring way. These people saw things twenty-five hundred years ago for the first time and managed to put them into written language. From them came our whole Western tradition that led to the science and technology that we take for granted today. We really do take the way we see and experience the world completely for granted. We have no idea that some remarkable people in the past not only saw the world freshly, but also laid the whole framework for what you and I understand reality to be."

Clare chimed in again. "And that was just in the Western world. In the East, around the same time, the Buddha and Zoroaster and Confucius and others were waking up to new realities as well. I learned in the one philosophy course I took that this period around twenty-five hundred years ago has been called the 'Axial Age.'"

"Yes, that was a term created by the twentieth-century philosopher Karl Jaspers. The point is that you just reminded me of those great people, only a few of whom we actually know by name. Watching you just now put me into a state of wonder. 'Wonder' is what Aristotle called the source of all philosophy." With that, Allison stopped talking and raised her glass.

As she did, Allison glanced up at the television above the bar. To her surprise and shock, she saw what looked like an exact picture of Samantha on CNN news. The picture looked like a driver's license photo. The caption below read: "Key Person of Interest Wanted."

"Oh my god!" gasped Allison. Edward and Clare turned sideways to look at the television, and they also gasped. Samantha, who was facing the back wall, had to turn all the way around to look. "Samantha, turn back toward the wall. Somebody might recognize you," Allison commanded in a quiet but firm voice. Samantha immediately obeyed. Edward and Clare turned back to the table. "Nobody's looking this way," Allison observed.

The other customers were all going about their business, lost in their own private conversations. Soon the picture was gone, and Anderson Cooper was interviewing some talking head.

After a few strained moments of silence, Allison asked, "Do any of you have any idea what that was about? 'Key person of interest'? What the hell do you think is going on? Did you witness anything, Samantha, like a crime?"

"No. Why would anybody be looking for me?"

Edward and Clare looked at each other for a moment. "Do you remember when we decided to move to Las Vegas a year ago?" Edward asked Samantha.

"Yes, of course. You and Clare told me you felt something strange was going on, and that you thought it would be a good idea for us to stay with Clare's parents."

"Yes, we did say that," Edward resumed. "However, it was something more than that. We couldn't be sure, but it felt like you might be in some kind of danger. So we decided to take a sabbatical, and that's why we drove out to Las Vegas."

"You didn't tell me any of this." A warning signal was going off in Samantha's body. It wasn't fear, but felt like a heightened alertness, an acute sense of presence.

"No, and I apologize for not telling you," said Clare, taking her hand. "We didn't want to scare you."

Allison continued to watch the television out of the corner of her eye. Samantha's picture flashed up several times. After a few minutes, the story changed to a commercial. When it resumed five minutes later, Anderson Cooper had moved on to another topic. With that, she breathed a sigh of relief. However, as soon as she had relaxed, Allison saw two men come in through the front door at the other end of the restaurant. What made them suspicious was that they appeared to have cut the line, and others standing outside the door were making irritated gestures.

"Samantha," Allison spoke commandingly. "Put your head down on the table so nobody can see your face." Samantha complied, pretending like she might be dozing. Edward and Clare just watched the men, feeling uncertain and anxious.

Within a few seconds, one of the men moved over to the bar and stood watching the door, while the other man made his way directly toward their table. He moved like he knew exactly where he was going. Allison watched with great intensity. As the man reached the table, Allison asked with defiance, "Who are you, and what are you doing here?"

The man, appearing to ignore her question, pulled up an empty chair from one of the other tables. He then sat down. "Do not be alarmed. I am a friend of Samantha's."

Edward then said, "I don't believe you. We know all of Samantha's friends, and we have never seen you before."

"I understand your concern," the stranger replied. "You are good friends. I also know that Samantha can hear me, and I know what she is feeling."

Samantha kept her head down on the table. Nevertheless, upon hearing this man's voice, she felt an unusual sense of comfort. As she listened to her heart, she began to feel something very familiar. It felt like an emotional cool breeze. She noticed a distinct lightness in her body. Keeping her head on the table, she said to Allison and Clare, "Girls, let the gentleman stay here."

Without hesitation Edward turned to Samantha and said, "Honey, this man is an intruder. You are wanted; you could be in great danger. I don't trust him."

Samantha responded quietly and calmly, "That doesn't matter. I can feel him. Let's hear what he has to say." At the same time, she continued to keep her head down. Her concern now was purely about other people recognizing her.

Edward said, "Okay, I'll trust your intuition." Turning to the stranger, he then added, "But if you try anything ..."

Their mysterious table guest said, "Samantha, I know you are recognizing a certain familiarity and comfort. I know what you are feeling. This is not a time to explain anything. You are in utter, deep danger right now. I need to protect you. We need to get you out of here, and quickly. Otherwise, you will be taken by the government and the police, and I will not be able to help you."

"Tell me what I should do," Samantha said, still keeping her head down.

"In three minutes, when I stop talking, the FBI and the police are going to raid Raoul's restaurant. There will be a big commotion. Before that commotion, I want you four to get up and leave through the kitchen. There is a back staircase outside that leads to an alley. Go down the staircase, then get out onto the street and find your way to a safe place in the city where nobody will look for you. You cannot go to Allison's home because the authorities are there right now. Do you know a good place?"

"They're at my house?" Allison became visibly upset.

The mystery man answered, "Do not worry. They have not invaded your house. But that is how they know to come here. Your neighbors told them you are here. Again, do you know a good place to go?"

"We can go to the Roger Hotel, just a couple blocks from the Empire State Building," Allison responded. "I know the management." She then added, "But it still pisses me off about the police coming to my house." Allison was naturally sensitive to racial tensions. She felt she had been fighting discrimination all her life, and this occurred for her as just one more example.

"That will be perfect. Once you get there, stay put and wait for me to contact you again."

"Just who the hell are you?" Edward asked. "And what is this all about?"

"My name is Zjon. However, my friends, there is no more time. Please, take her now and get out."

Hearing Zjon's name sent a bolt of electricity through Samantha's entire being. Without understanding why, she felt the strongest urge to say to him, "I have been waiting for you." Somehow, she knew he was telling the truth and that she should trust him. A single phrase surfaced in her mind: "heart trust." Instead, Samantha proclaimed, "Okay, let's go!"

The man who called himself Zjon rose up from his chair and began to walk to the front of the restaurant to join his companion. Simultaneously, Samantha and her three friends got up quietly and proceeded through the back hallway in the direction of the kitchen. As they left the restaurant through the back entrance, Samantha wondered, "I know this man. I know him so well. But I don't even have a memory of who I am. How do I know him?" She told herself, "He must be someone I was close to in my past. Why can I not remember my past?" The frustrations that she thought she had conquered since living with Edward and Clare began to resurface.

Upon reaching the end of the bar and joining his companion, Zjon made an ostentatious show of paying for the drinks for his "good old friends" at the back table. He then asked loudly for the location of the restroom. The bartender pointed up a spiral staircase near the front door, and Zjon and his friend turned around and headed toward it, inconsiderately bumping into one or two customers in the process. By the time the two men had disappeared up the staircase, the other customers muttered epithets about the two men. Obviously, they were tourists who felt self-important and were probably drunk to boot. Then everyone resumed the conversations they had been having before they were so rudely interrupted!

CHAPTER 14

Rainbow Rain

At exactly half past seven, thirty seconds after Zjon and his companion had gone up to the men's room, the front door to Raoul's swung open with a crash, banging against the wall. Four men in dark suits and uniforms rushed in, their hands buried inside the breasts of their suit jackets or at their hips. Following closely behind was a tall, athletic-looking man, holding up a badge that clearly identified him as a member of the FBI. Outside two squad cars with flashing lights were positioned perfectly to intercept anyone who tried to make a getaway.

The man with the badge walked to the front of his fellow officers and said, "Relax, everyone, and please stay where you are. This is the FBI." Everyone stayed exactly where he or she was. As the customers waited in quiet anticipation, continuing to sip their cocktails, a sixth man walked into the room. This man looked vaguely familiar to some of the guests. Joining the leader, the two conferred with each other as they scanned the room with their eyes. Meanwhile, the hostess tentatively walked up to the two men and asked, "Can I help you?"

When it had become apparent that the person he was looking for was not in the room, Federal Special Investigator Dan Hamilton turned to her and said, "Have you seen this woman tonight?" He held up a picture of Samantha Hunter.

"Yes, she was here with her friends."

"Are these the people she was with?" Dan held up pictures of Edward and Clare.

"Yes, along with another woman who comes here fairly often. They were sitting at their favorite table over there, back in the corner." She pointed to the now-empty table.

"And where are they now?" Dan pressed her with obvious urgency.

"I don't know; they must have left," the hostess responded. She had the guilty look of someone who knew she should be aware of the whereabouts of all her customers.

From the bar, sitting just a few feet away, another woman chimed in. "They're gone. And there were two other guys here with them who just paid for their drinks. One seemed very drunk and almost knocked me out of my chair."

Jonathan Elliot, the man with Dan, suddenly had a strange feeling. "Did you see where these men went?" he asked

Dan turned to him and said, "You need to let me do the talking, please."

Dan turned back to face the woman at the bar. "Those two just went upstairs to the men's room," she told him, pointing up the staircase.

"Thank you," Dan said to her. "Please stay here." He then faced the room of customers and projected with authority: "Everyone, please remain where you are for the next few minutes. Thank you for your cooperation."

Looking around at the faces in the room, Jonathan could see that people were beginning to enjoy the drama. *I love New York,* he thought to himself.

Dan turned to the other men. He motioned for the uniformed officers to stay and guard the front door and for the two FBI men to follow him up the stairs. As the three climbed the spiral staircase, Jonathan decided to follow. Once at the top of the stairs, Dan motioned for one of his agents to stay outside the men's room door with Jonathan and for the other to follow him in. They drew their weapons and held them pointed upward. Upon Dan's whispered command of "Now!" the two of them pushed through the door. Jonathan maneuvered his body next to the other agent so he could see into the room.

Across the room on the opposite wall were four urinals, three of which were occupied by men who were eliminating their latest drinks. To the right were two stalls, doors open and unoccupied. Dan shouted at the three men, "This is the FBI! Raise your hands immediately, and put them on your heads!" Without protest, all three men quickly zipped up their pants, raised their hands, and put them on the backs of their heads. Dan then instructed, "Now, stay still and do not move. We are going to come behind each of you one at a time to handcuff you. You are not under arrest, but we need to ask each of you some questions. Everybody got it?"

The word *yes* echoed off the tiled back wall. Keeping his gun trained on the suspects, Dan called out for the agent who had remained outside to come in. Dan then signaled by a nod to both his men to move forward, keeping his gun in a position of readiness. The two agents nodded, reached into their pockets, and pulled out their handcuffs. As the two agents moved forward, everyone heard a sudden, loud crack from above. Instinctively, they all looked toward the ceiling. Another loud crack sounded, then echoed through the restroom.

The startled men watched as a large crack appeared in the ceiling. At the same instant, a bright flash of blue light emanated from the crack, followed by another loud rumble, sounding like thunder.

The two agents who were stepping forward with handcuffs stopped dead in their tracks. Jonathan saw Dan open his mouth and start to say, "What the f—" but at just that moment a huge sheet of water suddenly poured out of the crack in the ceiling, causing him to jump back. It was a veritable deluge. The water crashed to the floor in a constant, unbroken sheet, separating the men at the urinals from himself and Dan, and pouring directly on top of the two agents who had moved forward. As Jonathan stood staring at the spectacle, his mouth wide open, he thought he could make out strobe-like flashes of colors, dancing randomly about inside the otherwise impenetrable wall of water.

After what seemed like a full thirty seconds of this spectacle, the cascade ceased, just as abruptly as it had started. Everyone in the room was frozen in place. Stunned like everyone else, Jonathan looked up to see that there was now no trace of the opening in the ceiling. Just as strange, there was very little water on the floor. Dan and Jonathan both saw that now standing at the urinals was just one of the three men who had been there before. His clothes and hair were completely soaked, as were those of the two agents.

The other two men had vanished into thin air.

The two soaked agents looked at each other. One of them said, "That was the weirdest experience. Did you see that?"

The other agent replied, "I don't know about you, but when I was standing there in the pouring water, what did I see? A rainbow! It was like being in a rainbow rain."

Dan and Jonathan looked at each other. Jonathan hunched up his shoulders in the universal expression for "beats me!"

"I guess that's as good a description as any for what we just witnessed," Dan said. He turned to his agents. "Stand down, gentlemen. Chuck and Charlie, why don't you go get dry clothes? And don't talk about this to anyone until we've had a chance to debrief." The two agents nodded and left. "And sir," Dan said, addressing the remaining customer who was still facing the urinal was sobbing, "please tell me everything you just witnessed. We're with the FBI."

The customer, a short, bald-headed man probably in his fifties, turned around and answered, "I've never seen anything like that in Nebraska, where I come from. I saw two rainbows, one on either side of me, where the other two men had been peeing."

"Had you seen either of the other two gentlemen before?"

"No, sir. This is my first time in the city."

Dan concluded, "You should get dried off. I hope you enjoy your stay in New York."

CHAPTER 15

The Roger Hotel, Day Four, 9:15 p.m.

SAMANTHA AND CLARE RELAXED TOGETHER IN A FAR CORNER OF THE ROGER HOTEL lobby, while Allison and Edward arranged for two adjoining rooms. The Roger was a nicely modernized, four-star, boutique hotel on Madison Avenue in midtown Manhattan. Fortunately, two adjoining rooms were available on the sixth floor. Once Edward and Allison had entered their rooms and tipped the bellman, Edward went back downstairs and retrieved the women.

From one of their rooms they could easily see the sidewalk in front of the hotel entrance. All agreed that Edward would take the first watch. While they knew they had little chance of escaping should the police show up, at least they would have some warning. Clare stepped into the adjoining room to call her parents, while Allison left the hotel and went across the street to pick up some Thai food. By now the four were very hungry. Samantha sat quietly on the edge of the bed and waited.

An hour later they finished eating a satisfying meal, and each of them sat quietly reflecting on the mystery surrounding that evening's events at Raoul's.

Clare opened up the conversation. "I spoke with my parents back in Las Vegas. They told me that this afternoon they were grocery shopping and saw Samantha's picture on the front page of the *Celebrity Observer* at the checkout stand. The headline said something like 'Have You Seen this Alien?' The article talked about strange things that had been happening around our neighborhood—cars disappearing and then reappearing, people getting electrocuted trying to climb over the walls—totally crazy stuff. But to cap it off, somebody got the idea that Samantha is an alien, and they somehow got a picture from her driver's license."

"That's outrageous!" Edward cried out.

"Tell me about it. Then, they turned on CNN news and caught the story that Allison spotted when we were in the restaurant. According to my parents, CNN was reporting the search for Samantha, and they had her name. The FBI has set up a special task force to find her and bring her in for questioning. Anderson Cooper didn't talk about aliens. He just called her a 'person of interest.'"

"'Key person of interest,'" Allison corrected. "That's what was displayed on the headline bar that I read."

"Mom and Dad called me, but it must have been while we were scrambling to get out of Raoul's after that man, Zjon, came to warn us," Clare continued. "I told them we would figure out a way to get home as soon as we could. They send their love and told us to be careful. They also wanted me to tell you they know that you haven't done anything wrong." Clare took Samantha's hand and held it. Samantha clearly looked distressed.

"I called my neighbor while waiting to pick up our dinner," Allison added. "She confirmed that the police and the FBI went to my apartment while we were at Raoul's. Apparently one of my other neighbors told them we were probably at Raoul's. I can't really blame him. But it's clear that we can't go back there tonight." Inside Allison continued to seethe with indignation.

"I'm really sorry," said Samantha. "I understand how you must feel. And, I can't imagine why anyone would be after me. I haven't committed any crimes. I didn't witness anything. I hate putting you through this." She appeared to be on the verge of tears.

Clare immediately hugged her. "Nonsense, dear. We are all in this together. Isn't that right, Edward?"

"Damn straight! The police have no business coming after you."

Clare broke in again. "Oh, I forgot there was one other thing my parents said. Yesterday a man came to their home looking for you. He said he was a science reporter with *The New York Times*. He said he had met you on a train in London. I think his name is Jonathan. Do you remember him?"

Samantha looked shocked. "Oh my God! Yes, I remember that man. I met him a year ago, just before we all came back home from our trip. It was the strangest experience I have ever had. I felt this incredibly deep and strong love for him, like we were soul mates. I gave him my phone number and address, and he said he would call me. Then I never heard from him again. I thought he had forgotten me." Samantha went silent.

"All of this makes me think that this is something much more than a simple kind of crime investigation," Clare said. "Think about it, Ed and Allison. The government wouldn't have any reason to call in the FBI and the New York police and have Samantha's name plastered on national news, unless something extraordinary is going on. And on top of this, a science reporter from *The New York Times*? What could this mean? Apply some of that mathematical reasoning, Ed."

"Okay. So, what do we know? One: Samantha is a wanted person. Two: Samantha has no memory of her past before we found her and took her in. Three: Samantha has been with us almost daily for the past three years, and our lives have all been completely normal—well, almost normal. Four: the FBI raids Allison's apartment and subsequently Raoul's. Five: a science writer named Jonathan comes looking for her in Las Vegas. If I am not mistaken, that could be Jonathan Elliot, a very prestigious person with very important connections."

"Six," jumped in Allison, "a complete stranger comes into a restaurant, seems to know everything about Samantha—and about me, and probably both of you—and claims to be her friend. Seven: this strange man saved Samantha from what he called imminent danger. He can't be a cop or a part of the government!"

"Eight: he's a friend." This came from Samantha. All heads

turned her way. "I don't know who he is. That is, I can't remember who he is, but I just know I know him from somewhere. He must be from my past, part of my lost past. And when he said his name, he triggered my heart spectrum."

"Your what?" Allison and Clare asked simultaneously.

"You know, my heart spectrum."

"Honey, we have no idea what you're talking about," Clare said gently, as if Samantha had turned into a delusional person. "You know, sometimes you just come out with strange expressions that nobody else understands."

"Like that time you told us you didn't think you were from 'nowhere,'" Edward jumped in.

Samantha, looking truly surprised, said, "Oh, I thought everybody knew what 'heart spectrum' is. Your heart spectrum is an experience. How can I describe it? It is a form of brilliance that connects people, not at an emotional level, but directly connects their emotional intelligence in a very different way—beyond any attraction." Samantha was speaking about this as if this were common sense.

The three of them were at a loss about what she was saying. At last Clare spoke. "You know, in different cultures I've studied, there are many differing ways a people may have collectively of experiencing emotions. The Japanese, for example, are known to have much more emotional subtlety and to have words and expressions that we Americans can't relate to. This is a well-documented phenomenon among anthropologists for many cultures. Perhaps, Samantha, you grew up in a culture where this 'heart spectrum' is a common expression. I just have never heard of it before now."

Samantha smiled, feeling slightly embarrassed at once again having become the center of attention. Still, deep down she was very clear about what she had just spoken about. How could the others not know about heart spectrum?

Clare's cell phone rang, startling everyone. Clare saw it was an unknown number. She picked it up and said, "Hello."

"This is Zjon," said the same soothing voice they had heard in the restaurant. "Please let me talk to Samantha."

Without speaking, Clare put the phone on speakerphone and handed the phone to Samantha, who said, "Hello."

"Honey, this is Zjon. You know me. I love you."

As soon as he said that, sensations exploded throughout Samantha's body. Everyone else in the room witnessed a visible change in her. Samantha had suddenly come alive. An overpowering feeling of love seemed to radiate from her, infecting each of them.

As he observed her from his window seat across the room, Edward's intuition began to kick in. His mind started racing. A wild thought crossed his mind: *It's possible that Samantha may not be from our time, or from our solar system.* But as soon as he had this thought, he shook his head to clear his mind: *Don't be ridiculous! No, that's way too improbable. It has to be something else.*

Meanwhile, on the phone, Zjon continued. "I am going to send somebody to your room, someone other than me, but who will be very familiar to you. He is going to carry some clothes in a bag. I want you to put them on. This person also is going to put some kind of makeup on you, so that you will look totally different and people will not recognize you. And he will give you false identification documents." With that, he hung up.

Everyone in the room had heard the brief conversation. Clare immediately said, "No, we can't disguise you. It's too dangerous."

"I need to do this," Samantha argued. "Otherwise, when I go through airport security, they're going to recognize and identify me. We have to leave here and go back home, where I'll be safer. He's not just going to put makeup on me; he's going to change something about me so they won't recognize me."

Edward and Clare both realized there was no use resisting. They were overwhelmed by the whole situation. But at the same time, they were aware that they were sensing something else, and it was disturbing. For three years they had been living with this woman, and now suddenly they were going to lose her. Their imaginations began to run wild. Maybe she had committed some crime or belonged to some powerful group of criminals, or maybe she was a spy. But as soon as they had these thoughts, they pushed them aside.

Clare broke the silence, saying to Samantha, "We're with you all the way."

Edward nodded in agreement. "We'll support you in whatever you choose to do. You can count on us."

"I agree wholeheartedly," Allison concurred. "I don't know you as well as my good friends Clare and Ed, but I trust their judgment. This may sound strange for a philosopher who lives on reasons and logic! But even logically speaking, something must be very wrong for them to be coming after you. You are anything but a dangerous person."

"Thank you," Samantha said.

Soon there was a knock at the door. Edward looked at Allison and asked, "How did this man, Zjon, know which room to come to? He didn't even ask our room number!" He motioned the other three to go into the adjoining room and close the door. Once they had, he went over and opened the door.

Standing there was a young man, the one they had seen come into the restaurant with Zjon earlier that evening. Edward ushered him into the room and closed the door. "What is your name?"

"My name is Neal," said the man.

"Neal what? What is your last name?"

"Just Neal."

"Neal, where are you from?" Edward hoped to elicit anything that would clarify what was going on.

"I am from here."

"Where is here? Manhattan, Brooklyn, Queens?"

"Let us just say, right now I am here. That is enough for now. We have not much time. I need to see Samantha."

Edward called through the adjoining room door that it was safe to come out. "This is Neal," he told them.

Neal nodded to each of them in turn and gave Samantha a big smile. Samantha felt her heart warming and returned the gesture.

Again, she knew that she knew him but could not remember from where or when.

Seeing the bag in his hand, Allison asked, "What have you brought with you?"

Neal only responded, "Let me take Samantha into the bedroom, and I will apply some makeup and redress her. Then she will be ready to go with you."

Clare stepped forward as if protecting her child. "You can't take her into the room by yourself!"

Right away Samantha reached out and touched her shoulder. "Clare, it will be fine. I'm safe with this person. Follow your heart trust."

Samantha's three companions, once again unsettled by her unusual turn of phrase, looked at each other. This time it was Allison who broke the awkwardness with a touch of humor. "Well, darlin', I guess we're not in Kansas anymore."

Everyone laughed, including Neal, who without further hesitation disappeared through the door into the next room. Samantha turned and followed him, closing the door behind her.

After what seemed like a very long time, but had really been only twenty minutes, Samantha and the man who called himself Neal emerged from the other bedroom. That is, a woman emerged whom Ed, Clare, and Allison could only assume was Samantha. The woman who now stood in the room before them did not look like Samantha at all. Instead of having long, blond, glamorous hair, she now had short, red hair that was cut in a chic style. Was it a wig, the two women wondered? Likewise, her face was now somewhat similar, yet totally different. The nose was different, and the cheekbones and chin were more rounded. The only way the others could be sure it was Samantha was because of her eyes. Their color was now green, but it was clearly Samantha shining through them.

Out loud, Edward exclaimed, "Oh, wow!"

Samantha, reading their thoughts, said, "Yes, it's really me."

As soon as Samantha had spoken, they all knew it, indeed, was really her. Clare asked, "What did he do to you?"

It was Neal who answered for her. "Do not worry. This will only last until you go back to Las Vegas. After she arrives there, this will all be taken off."

"What will be taken off?" Allison asked.

Samantha replied, "This is like a costume. I'm in it. You don't see it?"

Neal turned to Samantha and spoke again. "The whole world is looking for and expecting Samantha. If they see a woman who looks like you, they are going to check your fingerprints. For now your fingerprints will not register. Also, they will recognize you from your driver's license. So, here is a passport with a new name for you to use." Turning to Edward, Neal asked, "May I use your cell phone?" Edward handed the phone to Neal, who dialed a number. When an answer came from the other end, Neal clicked the speakerphone button and handed the phone back to Edward.

"This is Edward," he said after a moment's hesitation.

It was Zjon on the line. "Hello, Edward. Please listen carefully. You need to book a flight to Las Vegas for tomorrow morning for the four of you. Use Samantha's new name from her passport. The rest of you can use your own names. Make sure the tickets are first class, not economy. Call me back at this number when you have reservations." With that the call abruptly disconnected.

Edward spent the next thirty minutes futilely trying to arrange airline tickets through his smartphone's travel assistance apps. After trying Expedia, Travelocity, and Orbitz, he gave up at last in exasperation. He redialed Zjon's number. When Zjon answered, Edward announced, "All flights are fully booked for tomorrow morning, except not in first class but in economy."

Zjon answered, "Just give me five minutes, and I will call you back." Again the phone disconnected.

Five minutes later Edward's phone rang again, this time from an 800 number. When he picked up the line, he heard, "This is Robert McPherson from United Airlines. I understand you've been trying to book a first-class flight for four to Las Vegas. We've had a cancellation and now have four seats in first class, behind each other in the second and third rows."

"I'll take them," Edward replied, bewildered. He spent the next few minutes completing the reservation and paying with his credit card. When finished, he said, "Just out of curiosity, how did you get my name and number?"

The representative answered, "Well, your names were first on our VIP standby list, with this number as the contact number."

Edward disconnected the call with a powerful sense of gratitude. "You won't believe what just happened," he said to the others in the room. "We were on a VIP standby list. I never heard of such ..." Before he finished his sentence, his phone rang again, this time from the number Zjon had used earlier.

Before Edward could speak, Zjon said, "Edward, would you please give the phone to Samantha?"

Edward complied, without hesitation this time.

Samantha took the phone and heard Zjon say, "Honey, I love you, and I will see you in Las Vegas. Have no worries. All is right."

Samantha, feeling deep emotion once again at hearing Zjon's voice, replied, "I still don't know who you are, but I feel very right. Very, very right. And I love you, too." Samantha found herself in an overwhelming, incredible emotional space.

"Good night," Zjon said, "and sweet dreams, my darling."

When the call had disconnected, Samantha handed the phone back to Edward. The four of them stood for a few minutes looking at each other with nothing to say. At last, it was Allison who said, "Wait a minute! Where is Neal?"

Neal had completely vanished, as if he had never been there.

CHAPTER 16

Jonathan's Apartment, Day Four, 10:30 p.m.

"GOD, THAT'S GOOD SCOTCH! MIND IF I HAVE ANOTHER?" DAN HAMILTON WAS SITTING at the kitchen table with Jonathan and Diana in Jonathan's New York apartment. "What's this called again?"

"Oban."

Jonathan had retrieved the same bottle that he had shared with his mysterious visitor four nights before. Only four nights ago, he realized with some amazement. Who could have believed what had transpired since last Thursday evening when he had been awakened in what still seemed to him like a surrealistic dream? Even now, it felt like a dream, though he had become convinced that whatever had happened that night had been real, even if he could not recall many of the details. Like, for instance, what was that man's name? It was an unusual one. And he now remembered the visitor mentioning someone named Samantha. In a flash he made the connection for the first time that this was the same Samantha he had met on the London train—the Samantha they were chasing now. How could he have missed that? And now, what just happened this evening topped everything. It was all coming together in his mind. His thoughts continued to stream at light speed as he poured them both a second drink and handed one to Dan.

"Thanks. And thank you for hosting me this evening. It was kind of you both to offer me the spare bedroom in your apartment. Sure you won't join us in a drink, Diana?"

"No, but you are most welcome. It sounds like the two of you have gotten involved in wild and unknown territory. What's that old saying: 'I think we're not in Kansas anymore?'" she teased, and Dan smiled in return.

"That's an understatement," Dan said. "And no, this is not my usual turf. Normally, I get called in to handle special situations involving security or potential threats to security."

Jonathan said, "It doesn't seem to fit anything I've ever encountered before, and it surely doesn't feel dangerous. Quite the contrary; I feel strangely safe."

Diana jumped in again. "Detective Hamilton, just what does your government agency think is happening? The news is reporting a national manhunt, but without saying what has actually happened."

"It's Investigator, not Detective, but please call me Dan."

"Okay, Dan. The *Celebrity Observer* and other rags are talking about aliens from outer space. Can you tell me really what's going on here? Jonathan doesn't believe in aliens." She glanced at Jonathan and gave him a wink.

"I'm sorry, Diana, but I can't really talk about specifics. This is an ongoing federal investigation. There has been no crime, there are no criminals, and it would be unwise for us to be jumping to conclusions about aliens. Incidentally, I apologize for having to take Jonathan away from you so mysteriously. It just happens that he has met this person in the past, and with his knowledge and experience in reporting we felt he would be an asset to our investigation team. So far he's proven to be most helpful."

"Fair enough," Diana let it go without further questions. "Thank you. For now, I think I'll retire so that you gents can discuss the case more freely." With that she gave Jonathan a kiss and went upstairs.

"Good night, and thanks again," said Dan.

"Good night, dear," Jonathan called after her. Turning back to Dan, Jonathan returned to the events of the evening. "So, what's next?"

"First, and obviously a problem, we had a leak."

"Do you think it was David Newman?"

"No. I talked with him briefly while you were preparing Diana for my visit here. The only thing he can think of is that someone overheard us in the park administration office. He thinks that either the officer he sent to make copies of the documents, or the secretary who made the copies for him, or perhaps the two in collusion gave them to that gossip magazine. Probably made a few hundred bucks. Either way, David was swearing on the phone that he would have their heads in the morning."

"Regardless, that doesn't help us."

"You're right. Just another variable that we have to juggle, and we don't have a lot of hands to juggle with at the moment."

Jonathan took another sip of his Scotch, then ventured, "And your boss. How did that go?"

"He wasn't happy at all. In fact, I've never heard him so angry. He's now feeling some real pressure from above. We don't have a lot of time to find Samantha Hunter and get some real answers. Otherwise, the president may have to call in the National Guard or the military. The last thing anybody wants is a public panic. So now we've got demands on the airlines and other public transportation to let us know the minute any of the four known people surface. Allison Russell hasn't returned home yet, and police have her apartment under surveillance. And as you know, there are at least two other mystery players."

"The two men in the restroom."

"Exactly. Bloody good magicians, if you ask me." Dan withheld his real thoughts for the moment because they sounded too crazy even to him. Both men quietly took another sip of their drinks.

Jonathan probed further. "Were the witnesses you interviewed any help?"

"Not really. They only added more to the mystery. Everybody saw something, but nobody saw the same thing. People only tend to notice what they're interested in. Especially in a situation like this, where nothing seems unusual."

"You mean, nothing unusual happened until we arrived with the police."

"Yes, precisely. A few people remembered seeing three women and a man sitting at the back table. Nothing unusual there. The waiter noticed how beautiful the blonde was. Nothing strange there; she's quite striking."

"No kidding."

"What was funny was how the manager, the owner's son, said he noticed them all blowing into their glasses at one point. Peculiar, but nothing that would have a special meaning, at least not one I can think of. It's really funny what people notice, and what they don't."

"What about the woman at the bar who said she recognized the face?" Jonathan asked.

"Again, nothing useful. She's a forty-five-year-old banker from Citibank. She confirmed that she saw Samantha's face on TV and realized that woman was in the restaurant. When I asked her how she realized this was the same person who was on TV, she said when Samantha entered the restaurant, she had felt some kind of 'excitement in her body.' This woman Samantha has a strong effect on people. The one other thing that a couple of people noticed was an aroma, like the scent of jasmine in the room. Several people mentioned this. Beyond that, we couldn't find any witnesses who noticed the two other men before they made a big deal about paying the bill and going upstairs to the restroom. As it turned out, this must have been some kind of diversion tactic to let the others get away."

"An effective one, too. And nobody saw either of them after that?"

"Right. The only significant thing anyone reported was seeing two soaking wet agents coming back down the stairs and looking like they'd seen a ghost. Those guys will probably never live that down."

The two newfound friends chuckled.

Changing his tack, Jonathan asked, "Do you think it was a good idea to put out the all-points bulletin for her?"

"We had no choice. Once the *Celebrity Observer* had put out its special edition and the local Vegas press starting making a ruckus, we had to put in some fast control. The Chief made the call after talking to the White House. CNN was most happy to cooperate."

"I understand, but it certainly makes things more difficult," Jonathan said with a sigh.

"No kidding. I work much better under the radar. Have you cleared your next few days to work with me?"

"I called my editor-in-chief and let him know I might be out for a while. He agreed to have my assistant editor Harold cover the next week's issue. He didn't ask any questions, which makes me think he understands the importance of what I'm dealing with."

"Thanks," acknowledged Dan. "I think you're still the key to our being able to make a connection, and now you may be key to avoiding a dangerous situation."

"My pleasure. The only caveat is that I get the first crack at revealing the scientific truth, whenever that time comes." Jonathan withheld revealing his deeper desire to meet the woman who had captured his heart the year before in London.

"Agreed."

Jonathan and Dan finished their drinks and set their glasses down on the table. At last, Jonathan put forward the real question that had been on his mind. "Dan, you saw what I saw, and I've told you about my past interaction with Samantha and the events that led to my article as well. I want to know where you're at. Are you just being an investigator, or do you have something else at stake?"

"My mind is going full throttle right now, Jonathan. Everything I've witnessed argues that there has to be a rational explanation behind all this. But I also can't ignore what I have been feeling. If you tell anybody else this, I will deny it."

Dan continued, "I feel almost like I'm in love, and I haven't even met this woman Samantha. Since the incident in the car two days ago, my whole body has been feeling some kind of vibration. I've been feeling more alive than ever before in my life. Jonathan, we have to find this woman. We can't let her fall into the wrong hands. We're up against something much bigger than anyone knows right now. I'm convinced."

Jonathan let out a deep sigh of relief. He had not even realized he had been holding his breath. "You and I are on exactly the same page, Dan. Before these past four days, I feel as if I've never truly been alive. Meeting Samantha on the train last year jarred me to my very core. Now this has just reawakened me. We must find her and meet with her, whatever it takes. And I agree that we must protect her at all costs. I think, Dan, the future may be resting on our shoulders right now, perhaps even the future of all humankind."

With that, the two men stood up and shook hands.

CHAPTER 17

Flight 107, Day Five, 10:30 a.m.

SAMANTHA SETTLED INTO HER WINDOW SEAT, 2F, ON FLIGHT 107, FROM NEWARK TO Las Vegas. Next to her was Allison, and in the row behind them sat Edward and Clare. As the other passengers slowly filed past them, occasionally banging their luggage against the sides of the seats, Samantha could only feel a powerful sense of calm. All was right with the world. She was going home, and soon she would solve the great mystery she had been living in for the past three years. She just knew that Zjon held the keys to unraveling her past. Her heart quickened at the thought.

Behind her Edward was lost in his own reverie. The morning so far had been almost surreal. They had arrived by taxi and immediately been able to pick up their e-tickets at curbside check-in. Everything was proceeding without a hitch. Not having to check luggage, they easily navigated their way to the TSA section. Surprisingly, all of them had the "TSA Pre" stamp on their boarding passes, so they were able to go through the expedited security lane without having to take off their shoes and belts or empty their pockets. Edward did notice, however, that there were well-dressed men and women, wearing sunglasses and shiny black shoes, their hands empty of hand luggage but invariably holding newspapers, scattered around the airport. Everything about them screamed "FBI agents." *This scene could be from an Alfred Hitchcock movie,* he thought with amusement. Nevertheless, he felt nervous.

As they were about to go through the security lane, Edward was suddenly hit with the realization that he had overlooked one obvious fact. The FBI and police would surely be looking for them as well! At the very least, they knew who Allison was because they had raided her flat. And they must know about him and Clare because her parents had received that unexpected visitor looking for Samantha. How could he have overlooked that?

Dread overwhelmed him as Edward, first in line of their group, stepped up to the TSA examining agent and handed her his boarding pass and driver's license. Amazingly, the TSA agent stamped his boarding pass and said, "Have a nice flight, Mr. Masters." Barely maintaining his composure, Edward had looked down at his license and read the name Brian Masters below his picture. The same thing had happened to Clare, who was now Henrietta Masters. Likewise, Allison's ID now read Janet Johnson. They had all miraculously gotten through security.

By the time they boarded the plane, they found themselves laughing. Whatever was happening was beyond all belief and logical explanation. The air was becoming magical.

The four covert adventurers sat back and relaxed as the plane took off. The flight was only twenty-five minutes behind schedule. One by one, Allison, Clare, and Edward each drifted off to sleep, exhausted from the excitement of the past sixteen hours.

Samantha continued to engage in pleasant fantasies until she at last began to drift off as well. At some point, she became aware of an announcement that they were flying over the Grand Canyon, but she immediately drifted back into a deep sleep. She then began to dream. In her dream she saw a man stepping out from behind a blue curtain and coming toward her. He was a very handsome man with dark hair and deep-blue eyes. The face was somehow very familiar, yet at the same time unknown. Yet, she knew that she knew him. After a few seconds, a name came to her, *Zjon*. It was the face behind the voice she had heard in the restaurant and on the phone! The man in her dream smiled and nodded.

Zjon said to her, "Everything is going to be fine. Right now you need to know one thing. There are two FBI agents in the opposite aisle seats in rows three and four. They are pretending to read. After you all boarded the plane, there was a sudden alert. The FBI realized that your friends have fake IDs. So after you got on the plane, they decided to substitute two agents for two of the passengers. The moment the plane lands, there will be a team of agents waiting to arrest you. Before you land, the two agents are planning to handcuff you and Edward. So, when you wake up, I want you to stand up and gently tap the thumb and forefinger of your right hand together." The man in her dream demonstrated. "When you do this, you will feel an electric feeling, like a tingling, between your fingertips. Get up as if you are stretching your legs and stroll back toward the economy-class seating. As you go by the agents, very gently tap their foreheads, using your forefinger and middle finger together. They will sleep for the next three hours. Then after you land, leave the plane and head directly to the airport limousine area. A car will be there to meet you."

Samantha snapped awake, surprised. Her body continued to resonate with feeling. Without waking Allison, she stood up and glanced around casually, pretending to stretch her arms and yawn. She saw a man with glasses reading the *Times,* and another man behind him also pretending to read. She touched her thumb and forefinger together, and the moment she did, she felt a remembrance from far away. With that, she experienced a burst of energy. She stepped out into the aisle, and as she walked past the men, she quietly and casually tapped each man's forehead with her middle and forefingers, saying to each of them, "Oh, excuse me, sir." As Zjon had predicted, each man's head fell forward as if he had fallen into a deep sleep. Samantha slowly turned around and returned to her seat. After she sat down, she gently awakened Allison and explained the situation. Allison in turn stood up, stepped out into the aisle, and casually woke up Clare, who then quietly told the game plan to Edward.

When the plane landed in Las Vegas and taxied to the gate, Samantha and Edward both looked out their windows and saw flashing lights in the distance. They realized there was a large police presence at the airport. Suddenly each of them saw that something was happening to their clothes, as if a shimmering light had passed over them. They grabbed their hand luggage and got off the plane, along with the other passengers in first class. As they passed through the gate, they saw several men in suits waiting in the gate area. The men did not seem to notice them. Samantha and her friends walked briskly through the terminal, went down the escalator, and got onto the shuttle to the main terminal.

The flight attendants alerted the airport emergency team that they had found two passengers on board who would not wake up and appeared to be in some kind of coma. When the men waiting at the gate saw emergency first-aid personnel hurrying onto the plane, they showed their FBI badges and rushed in behind them, only to find their colleagues unconscious.

Once the four travelers reached the main terminal, Edward's phone rang. It was Zjon. "You have a car waiting that will take you to the Bellagio hotel, where you have VIP reservations," Zjon told him. "Go outside to the passenger pickup area and look for a purple limousine with the sign, 'Elvis Presley's Limousine Service.' That limo has been prepaid and will take you to the hotel. Once you arrive, go to the nearest VIP lounge and show your identification. They are expecting a party of four under the name Brian Masters. When you get to your room, I will contact you. Get some rest, and then we will have a nice dinner tonight, where I will explain everything."

Edward led the way to passenger pickup, where they found the car. The limousine took off, and within minutes they reached the Bellagio.

As they pulled up to the front entrance, they were greeted by the eruption of the giant fountains in front of the hotel and by a VIP representative at the door: "Welcome, Mr. Masters. We've been expecting you." The representative named Franz, who introduced himself as the Bellagio vice president of international marketing, led them to the VIP lounge for check-in. From there the four of them were quickly escorted through a maze of corridors and high-stakes baccarat game rooms, down the lobby hallway to the exclusive VIP elevators, and up to their penthouse suite. Upon entering, each of them collapsed gratefully onto their luxurious beds and fell into a deep sleep.

CHAPTER 18

Day Five, 5:45 p.m. Eastern, 2:45 p.m. Pacific

"THANK YOU FOR THE UPDATE, DAVID. I'LL CALL YOU AS SOON AS I LAND. MEANWHILE I remember, don't touch them! Just watch, and let me know the minute anything changes. Nobody goes near them but me." After receiving a final acknowledgment, Dan ended the call on his cell phone and leaned back in his seat. Once again, he and Jonathan were in flight on their government jet, heading back to Las Vegas.

"Unbelievable, huh?" Jonathan remarked wryly.

"No kidding. I guess you heard everything."

Jonathan nodded. "Pretty much. I take it our FBI team had them and then lost them. For ordinary, law-abiding citizens, these people seem to have quite a bag of tricks."

"I've dealt with a lot of very cunning people in my time. Criminals, terrorists, spies. But this group takes the cake. They managed to make plane reservations right under our noses. Using their real names, no less, except for Samantha's. Apparently Samantha had a disguise and a false passport. Somehow, somebody got into the system and changed the names on the reservations to Janet Johnson and Brian and Henrietta Masters. Then they slipped right through security with false identifications. In spite of that, our team managed to get two good men on the plane before it took off. We had everything lined up to take them upon landing."

"And they still got away."

"They still got away! We don't know yet if they somehow drugged our men or what, but by the time the passengers had deplaned, our guys were found dead asleep. The good news is that one of David's agents at the airport recognized Edward Hunter from his photograph. He was getting into a limousine called, believe it or not, 'Elvis Presley's Limo Service.' David traced that limousine to the Bellagio. The group was then given a VIP check-in."

"I would call that pretty audacious."

"Audacious as hell!"

"At least they have good taste. The Bellagio is spectacular." Jonathan remembered a trip he had made there with Diana two years earlier. He recalled being dazzled by the fine art, the lush carpeting, the five-star restaurants, the ever-changing indoor garden, the Chihuly flowers, and especially the geyser-like eruptions of the Fountains of Bellagio—all orchestrated to music. He considered the Bellagio to be a modern work of art, an astonishing show for all the senses. "Why would they go to such a public place?"

"Sometimes the best hiding place is right in the open," Dan said. "Besides, it's very easy to get lost in the crowd in a resort hotel the size of the Bellagio. Not to mention the hotel's extremely high level of security."

"You know, that also might work in our favor, making it easier for us to meet with them."

"That's exactly what I was thinking. A place like the Bellagio, filled with celebrities and money and all the distractions, could provide us with the perfect cover for having a discreet meeting, unobtrusive and unobserved."

"Safe for them, and a chance for us to get to the bottom of all this, as well. Assuming they are still in the hotel when we get there, I can arrange for them to meet us at a restaurant I know well. Unobtrusive, as you say."

Dan smiled at Jonathan, then summoned the flight attendant. "What is our ETA?"

"Sir, we have been cleared for landing in about thirty minutes, at three twenty-five p.m., local time."

"Thank you." Dan turned back to Jonathan. "Let's make it dinner at seven thirty. You pick the place. Meanwhile, I'm going to report to the Chief and give him an update. I'd like for you to listen in with me, in case you have something to add. I think it's most important that we connect personally with Samantha and her friends, but privately. I'm going to need the Chief's help making sure our guys don't go off half-cocked and arrest them. There's too much at stake in this whole thing, and POTUS is clamoring for answers. Some of his aides are even harping about a possible alien invasion!"

Jonathan rolled his eyes. "Makes complete sense. If necessary, I can use my connections to talk with the president myself."

"We'll see. Oh, I don't think you heard, but David told me one other thing."

"What's that?"

"You know the Avalon Charged Field?"

"Yes."

"It's gone."

"Gone?"

"Yes, just gone. It was there yesterday, and apparently sometime this morning it was no longer there. People can get in and out of there just like normal. It's as if the phenomenon never happened. Evidently even the press has given up and is now leaving. No longer news."

"It keeps getting weirder and weirder, doesn't it?"

Dan nodded, then picked up his cell phone and scrolled to the number he needed. After a few seconds, he spoke into the phone, "Get me the Chief."

CHAPTER 19

Bellagio Prime, Day Five, 7:15 p.m.

JONATHAN ARRIVED AT THE BELLAGIO PRIME STEAKHOUSE A FEW MINUTES EARLY IN order to make sure that the table he had reserved in the private dining room was ready. As an added precaution, he had reserved all five tables in that room to make sure they could speak privately. Indeed, the room was clear of all guests.

The room Jonathan had reserved was a small, hexagonal-shaped room, partitioned on three sides from the main dining areas by a set of glass windows and two glass-paneled doors. The room reminded him of an indoor gazebo. It featured a set of large windows looking out onto the Fountains of Bellagio, the world-famous, man-made lake that erupted every twenty or thirty minutes into spectacular water shows set to popular or classical music. In the center of the cozy room was a circular table that was set for six.

After generously tipping the maître d', a dignified gentleman wearing a Brioni suit and introducing himself as Josef, Jonathan explained the importance of discretion and that he would personally signal the wait staff when service was needed. Josef bowed smartly and positioned himself strategically outside of the room, poised to receive the expected guests. Unbeknownst to Jonathan, Josef had already been informed by the vice president of international marketing, of the importance of this meeting. Earlier in the day, the Chief had personally contacted Franz, who happened to be an old friend.

Jonathan and Dan had agreed that afternoon that the Prime was the perfect place to host a get-to-know-each-other meeting with Samantha and her three friends. The restaurant was quiet, and their private room guaranteed nearly complete seclusion. In addition, Jonathan and Dan would have an excellent view of people coming in and out of the restaurant. This was about as safe and discreet a place as they could want. The most important things tonight were for Samantha and her three friends to be comfortable enough first of all to stay; second, to talk freely; and finally, to agree to further interviews.

For Jonathan, this evening promised to bring the answers to what had become the greatest mystery of both his personal and professional life. For Dan, the upcoming meeting held the possibility of clearing up what he quietly prayed now to be just a black-hole case. He also hoped with every fiber in his being that these people were anything but a national security threat.

As Jonathan sat down at the table and waited, Dan stationed himself at the bar in the far corner of the main dining room and pretended to be nursing a Scotch. He had agreed to wait for a signal from Jonathan before joining the group. Meanwhile, Dan had arranged for Special Agent David Newman and his team to keep a security watch throughout the lobby and casino areas. David's job was to ensure that the special guests were kept free from the "observing minds" of the *Celebrity Observer*, the press in general, Bellagio security, the police, or any other intruders. He had positioned himself on the balcony of the Bellagio Spa, overlooking the Conservatory and Botanical Gardens and the lobby. From there he could watch the flow of the crowd and could direct the movements of his men.

At precisely seven thirty, Jonathan saw Edward and Clare descending the escalator from the main level toward the restaurant entrance. Two other women whom he did not immediately recognize accompanied them. He quickly made eye contact with Josef and nodded toward the group as they entered the restaurant. Josef smartly greeted the foursome and then led the way into the private dining room.

Jonathan stood to greet his guests. He smiled and said, "Welcome, and thank you for coming. My name is Jonathan Elliot."

"Don't you recognize me, Jonathan?" asked the chic and alluring redhead. Before him stood a beautiful and radiant woman. Jonathan's heart practically leapt out of his chest at the sound of her voice, a voice he could never forget.

"Samantha!"

"Yes, it's me. I was afraid you had forgotten."

"Are you kidding?" exclaimed Jonathan. "I could never forget you. And I want you to know that I never have forgotten you. As soon as I got off the train, I lost your address. Or rather, it disappeared into ashes ..." Jonathan was flustered.

"That's all right, Jonathan. I understand. We need to catch up." Jonathan felt taken aback at Samantha's apparent aloofness. Was this really the same woman he had met the year before on the train? Could that experience have been nothing more than his imagination?

"First," interrupted Allison, the fourth woman, "I think we should all introduce ourselves."

"Yes, of course." Jonathan quickly regained his composure. "I assume you are Allison Russell."

"Yes, I am Professor Allison Russell." Jonathan suspected that her feathers had been ruffled these past couple of days.

"It's an honor to meet you." Turning to Edward and Clare, he continued. "And I assume you are Clare and Edward Hunter. I had the pleasure of meeting your parents, Clare—if I may call you Clare."

"By all means. My parents told me about your meeting. They were quite charmed, although quite concerned after hearing about what happened in New York last night."

"I understand," Jonathan assured her. Then he spoke to all of them. "I am committed that our evening together will completely clear all that up. But I apologize for any stress it might have caused."

"You can call me Ed," put in Edward. The two men stepped forward and shook hands.

"Please sit down." They all settled into their seats. Samantha positioned herself in a chair next to Jonathan that commanded a view of both the fountains outside and the glass doors leading into the main dining room. Jonathan signaled a waiter. "Would you all like a cocktail or a glass of wine?"

The response was unanimous. Jonathan could feel Allison beginning to relax. Edward and Clare seemed completely at ease, which he felt was a good sign. If anyone had cause to be concerned, it was the couple that had befriended and sheltered Samantha for the last three years. Jonathan asked the waiter, "Do you have Oban Scotch?"

The waiter answered, "Of course, sir."

"Excellent!" Jonathan nodded toward Allison first. The waiter looked at her expectantly. She quickly responded, "I would like a Bombay martini, straight up with olives." The waiter nodded and made a note. He then turned to Clare.

"I would like a glass of Chardonnay."

"Any particular kind?"

"Your house wine will be just fine, thank you."

Edward deferred to Samantha, who said, "I'll have the same." Again the waiter nodded and made a note.

"Make it three," Edward followed.

"And you would like an Oban, sir?"

"Yes, neat, with a glass of ice on the side," Jonathan replied.

"Very well. Would you like some appetizers?"

"Not yet, thank you. I'll call you when we're ready. Meanwhile, why don't you bring a bottle of your finest Chardonnay for my three friends?"

"Very well. Thank you, sir." The waiter turned and left through the glass doors.

As the waiter disappeared in the direction of the bar, Jonathan made eye contact with Dan and shook his head, indicating he should wait a few minutes. He then turned his attention back to the table, finding all eyes upon him. For a moment he found himself not knowing what to say. He could only smile and nod his head, once again saying, "I'm so glad you agreed to meet me."

After a few awkward moments, it was Samantha who broke the silence. "Jonathan, I'm so happy to see you again. I thought you had forgotten me."

Samantha's voice put Jonathan completely at ease. "I could never forget you, Samantha. It may seem strange to say this, but I could not get our meeting on the train in London out of my mind. I'm so happy to be able to reconnect again."

"So am I. I felt like I had met a soul mate, and then you just disappeared. I'm so happy to hear that you just lost my address."

Jonathan then turned to Clare. "And Clare, I'm so sorry that your parents had to go through that worry. When I went to meet with them, I was genuine about wanting to reconnect with Samantha. On the other hand, I wasn't there for just that reason."

"We suspected as much," Edward said. "Did you know about Samantha being a wanted person?"

"No, I mean, not exactly. When I went to Clare's parents' house, she wasn't at that point. As you know, I'm the chief science editor for *The New York Times*. I went at the request of someone who works for an agency directly accountable to the president of the United States because of an article that I wrote for last Sunday's *Times*."

"We read that article," Clare said. "'Something Is Coming' was certainly an unusual title, and what you had to say was intriguing."

"Yes, well, it's a long story—and a strange one. But to answer your question, Ed, Samantha did end up on the wanted list because I identified her to the federal investigator I was working with as 'a person of interest.' There have been a lot of strange, unsolved occurrences that caught the president's attention, which led to the investigation team, which, in turn, led them to bring me to Las Vegas after they saw my article. The fact is, it was a total surprise and a thrill to find out Samantha was here."

Turning to Samantha, Jonathan said, "I just had to find you

again. Forgive me if I have caused you any trouble. And I ask all of you to forgive me for these disruptions."

Allison spoke up next. "I do have to say that, while it was quite an insult to have my home invaded by police, this has become something of an adventure." Allison surprised herself with how quickly she was beginning to let go of the initial indignation and turn it into a sense of excitement.

"I'll second that," Edward burst out.

The waiter entered the room with their drinks. All waited as he went through the usual motion of displaying the wine bottle for Edward's approval. Allison and Clare looked at each other and rolled their eyes in a reaction to the standard gender presumption the waiter had made. Jonathan politely waited until the waiter was finished pouring the wine. Jonathan then said, "Thank you, we'll let you know when we're ready for appetizers." The waiter bowed and left the room.

Edward raised his glass and said, "I propose a toast to all of us, and"—turning to Jonathan—"to your promise to clear up the mystery of the last twenty-four hours."

"And to Samantha's freedom," added Clare.

All raised their glasses and took a sip.

As he set his glass down, Jonathan turned to Samantha and said, "I want you to trust me, Samantha. I *am* on your side."

"I know that, Jonathan. I feel it."

With that Jonathan felt a weight lift from his being. *Who is this remarkable woman?* he wondered to himself. For the first time in a long time, Jonathan Elliot felt in touch with his own natural innocence. Something *is coming*, he thought. *Hell, something incredible is here, happening right now!* His eyes were beginning to tear up. "My God, I'm completely moved," he said out loud.

Clare, who was sitting to Jonathan's left, reached over and took his left hand. "Edward and I have gotten to know Samantha very well over the last three years. One thing I've learned is that Samantha has a way of reading people. If she trusts you, then so do I. I can see that you mean to be her friend, and if you are her friend, then you are ours as well." Edward nodded his agreement.

"Thank you," was all Jonathan could muster.

"Okay, I'm with the three of you," Allison chuckled, taking another sip, and everyone followed suit. The table was already beginning to resonate with a slight alcohol buzz.

Jonathan announced, "I haven't told you quite everything about this evening. I wanted to wait until you all knew where I'm coming from. You may have noticed that there is a sixth place setting at the table. To get everything out in the open, I need to introduce you to another friend."

Jonathan looked over in the direction of the bar and nodded to Dan. Everyone turned to look as Dan stood up, picked up his untouched drink, and began to walk toward the room. As he approached, Josef shot Jonathan a questioning look, and Jonathan nodded his assurance. Dan pulled open the glass doors, and entered the room. Jonathan stood up and said, "Everyone, please don't be alarmed. Allow me to introduce to you Federal Special Investigator Dan Hamilton."

All at once there arose from outside the sound of a gigantic whoosh! Startled, everyone turned toward the windows. Dozens of water spouts shot hundreds of feet into the air, swirling and twirling, like swords in unison crossing in battle, with beams of light cutting through each spout and producing tiny rainbows as the waters crisscrossed in time to the music of Ravel's "Bolero."

The evening's show was just beginning.

CHAPTER 20

Bellagio Prime, Day Five, 8:00 p.m.

"Y͏OU'RE THE MAN WHO HAS BEEN CHASING ME." SAMANTHA BROKE THE SPELL THAT HAD been cast by the water show. Everyone at the table turned back toward Dan, who remained standing inside the doorway as if awaiting permission to join them.

In the background the sounds of the water show came to an end, and clapping could be heard coming from the main dining room and outdoor terrace. Moments later, the muffled sounds of a busy restaurant resumed, with people chatting and silverware clinking against plates.

"Yes, I guess that would be me," Dan answered her, keeping his eyes in contact with Samantha's.

"Please sit down and join us," Samantha said. Edward and Clare looked at each other with bewilderment. Allison inhaled loudly and stared at Samantha with wide, questioning eyes. Jonathan sat back down in his chair and said nothing. It was time for him to listen, he thought to himself.

Samantha repeated, "Please join us."

Dan cleared his throat, nodded his head, and said, "Thank you." He stepped forward and took a seat at the empty place setting next to Allison. As he set his glass down, he ventured, "You must be Samantha."

"Yes, I guess that would be me," Samantha mocked him with a gentle smile. Dan noticed that his natural "cop" skepticism was completely dissipated by the sound of her voice. He felt that he was present to a great mystery. He realized that the room had become completely silent, yet was full of expectation.

"I owe you all an explanation. But first, I need to ask, Samantha, who are you and where do you come from?"

Samantha responded, "I was hoping you could tell me. I have no idea."

Dan nodded. "Okay, I hope that I can help you figure that out. Do I understand correctly that you have no memory?"

"Not from before three years ago, when I met Clare and Edward in San Francisco. I have complete memory of everything since then, but no memory of my life before."

"Why, exactly, are you here, Dan?" Allison demanded, focusing her gaze on him. "And what gave you the right to come to my home in New York and harass my neighbors? I am seriously considering a discrimination lawsuit."

"I apologize and will tell you everything I can."

"First," Jonathan said, stepping in to break the rising tension, "I suggest we order some appetizers. May I order for the table?"

"Sure," Edward said, "and let's have another drink." The others nodded.

"Great," Jonathan motioned to the waiter, who instantly appeared through the doors. Jonathan said, "Another martini for the lady"—nodding toward Allison—"and then, I would like to order appetizers."

"Of course, sir." The waiter pulled out his pad.

"We'll have two orders of the steak tartare, two shrimp cocktails, two Dungeness crab cakes, and two large beet salads for the table. Please bring extra plates."

"Thank you." The waiter smiled and exited the room.

Once the doors had clicked shut again, Allison repeated, "So, Detective?"

"Please just call me Dan. I'm not a detective, but a special investigator for the federal government."

"Okay, Dan. Why are you investigating Samantha; and why was her face plastered all over the news?"

"Can you hold any questions until I finish telling you?"

All the people gathered nodded their agreement. Allison said, "Only if you tell us the whole truth."

"Fair enough. I will tell you everything I know. I represent a US government organization that reports directly to the president. We are a special team charged with investigating potential threats that appear to fall outside the normal domain of law enforcement agencies, as well as the National Security Agency and the CIA. In short, we are a top-secret agency that comes in when something happens and nobody else is properly equipped to deal with it.

"In this case, we were called in by the president after receiving information from the FBI about strange events taking place here in Las Vegas. I came to investigate, and the regional FBI office and local police have been put under my umbrella command until I can get everything cleared up."

"But what does this have to do with Samantha?" Clare asked.

"Last week mysterious things began to happen, and they appeared to be centered in your neighborhood, Avalon Village. The most shocking event was the appearance of an invisible force field that functioned as a shield. This shield, which we called a 'charged field,' prevented anyone who did not live or have business inside of your neighborhood from being able to enter it. Believe me, I know this sounds crazy. But the only people who could come in and out were the residents, their guests, and people like postal carriers. Anyone else who tried to come in was immediately repelled. My partner and I confirmed it by personal experience. There were also other phenomena being reported, mostly related to weather patterns and crime statistics in that area. Nobody has been hurt, but we needed answers as to what was happening. That is why I was called in this past Saturday.

"Then on Sunday, after experiencing the effects of this field myself, I came across an article that Jonathan had written for *The New York Times.* I had a hunch this article might be connected to the charged field somehow. Since I already knew Jonathan, I brought him to Las Vegas, as much to get his scientific opinions on the matter as to see what he might know himself. He discovered a driver's license photo of Samantha from the files we had compiled and told me about meeting her in London."

Jonathan stepped in to corroborate. "When I saw your picture, Samantha, it was like being hit with a bolt of lightning. I agreed with Dan that I should try to meet you at the home of Clare's parents, which was the address listed on the license."

Dan continued. "Unlike myself and my partner, Jonathan was able to walk right into the community and up to their house, Clare. It was as if the charged field knew that he belonged, and let him enter. That's when he met your folks."

"Yes," Jonathan said. "When I met them and they told me how they had met you three years ago, Samantha, I knew you were the key to the entire mystery. Or at least I thought and felt so. They gave me Allison's address in New York, and Dan and I headed there to find you."

"But why the national news?" Edward persisted.

Dan continued. "That was unfortunate. While we were investigating, somebody in the county administration office leaked Samantha's photo to the *Celebrity Observer*. Before we knew it, Samantha was reported as being some kind of an alien from another country or even another planet. We had to create a diversionary story of a manhunt that would not put the public into a panic. In addition, we thought it might actually help us find you. From the events that have ensued, everyone is now convinced that you hold the key to the mystery, Samantha. And it appears to be locked somewhere deep inside your memory, or lost memory, that is."

"But I'm just an ordinary person," Samantha objected, wishing that were true but recognizing deep down that it was not.

"Samantha, you are anything but ordinary," Jonathan retorted. "You have some special talent, or some special knowledge, that we think is tied to what's been going on."

Clare asked, "Are my parents in any danger?"

"Absolutely not," Dan replied, "and they will not be bothered anymore by any of our people. Oddly enough, the mysterious charged field disappeared this morning. Vanished just as unexpectedly as it appeared. Everything has returned to normal."

"Except," Jonathan corrected, "the weather patterns seem to continue unabated. Doesn't it occur to you all as strange, Edward and Clare, that you have consistently had such moderate weather this summer?"

Edward nodded. "Las Vegas has been like a paradise."

"That in itself should be enough of a mystery," said Jonathan.

"That is why we were so desperate to talk with you, Samantha," Dan went on. "The president needs assurance his country and people are safe, and we need answers to resolve what has happened. I was hoping you would agree to meet some experts who could interview you and help you recover your memory."

Samantha was lost in thought.

"The last thing we want to do is hurt you," Dan tried to reassure her. "In fact, Jonathan and I made a pact to protect you at all costs. Whoever you are, we both feel some kind of affection or even love for you, not like romantic love, but more like you are a part of our family." Jonathan nodded. So did Edward, Clare, and Allison.

"Ever since we first met you, Samantha, we have all loved you like you were one of our own." Clare told her. "Maybe we are family in some way."

With that, tears welled up in Samantha's eyes. "I'm sorry I'm causing so much trouble. If I could only remember who I am! I've been spending the last three years reading everything I could about psychology and brain science, but nothing has helped. I just don't understand how other people think, and especially how the world can be so full of conflict! This floods my heart with compassion. What can you do to help me?" The last question was directed to both Dan and Jonathan.

At that moment a stream of waiters appeared, delivering the

appetizers, replacing Allison's martini, and refilling the wine glasses. Everyone at the table showed visible signs of relief from the heaviness of the conversation. Once again a sense of celebration returned to the table. Jonathan and Dan watched with curiosity as Samantha picked up her glass of wine and began to blow gently into the glass. The others were behaving as if nothing unusual was going on at all.

After a few minutes of silence as each person was eating, Samantha put down her fork and said, "Something is coming."

Taken aback, Jonathan asked, "What do you mean?"

"I mean someone is coming."

"Who?" Dan asked.

Samantha did not answer his question. "I smell something. I know this smell. But the smell doesn't belong here."

Clare said, "Honey, what are you talking about? What are you smelling?"

"There's a very distinct smell. It's the smell of the Future."

Dan turned to Samantha. "What are you talking about?"

"I can't say exactly what I'm talking about. It sounds like gibberish, but the smell is coming from the element Air."

Allison, her professional curiosity suddenly piqued, asked, "Are you talking about elements like the ancient civilizations used to talk about the elements, like earth, fire, air, and water?"

Before Samantha could reply, the Fountains of Bellagio erupted for a second time with another magnificent show of water, light, and sound. Once again, everyone's attention turned to appreciate the magnificent display. This time Jonathan was delighted to recognize the theme song from *Titanic*. The music touched something deep within his soul.

CHAPTER 21

Bellagio Prime, Day Five, 8:20 p.m.

A S THE OUTDOOR SOUND AND LIGHT WATER SHOW CAME TO AN END, THE GROUP SHIFTED their attention back into the room, to the table, and to each other. "I love that show," Jonathan remarked. Just as he was about to resume the conversation, he suddenly noticed a coolness in the room. It was not like the coolness from an air conditioner, but more like a subtle, cool breeze. He wondered if the others felt it too.

Before he was able to remark on this, Samantha's voice cried out, "Zjon!"

Jonathan quickly looked over toward the door. Startled by Jonathan's reaction, Dan spun around to look behind him. The others looked too. Standing inside the room were two men, one in his twenties and the other perhaps around forty. Their dress was appropriate: sport jackets and blue shirts, without ties. However, Jonathan noticed that both of their shirts seemed to shimmer in some way. It had a very pleasing effect on the eyes. "Those are shirts I would like to own," Jonathan said to himself, surprised by having such a trivial thought at this impactful moment.

"Hello, Samantha," responded the older man. The sound of his voice sent an electric shock up and down Jonathan's spine: he recognized this man to be his mysterious visitor from five nights before.

Josef rushed into the room immediately behind the intruders, looking visibly distressed. He apologized profusely to Jonathan, "I am so sorry, sir! I did not see them come in. Would you like me to ask them to leave?"

"No, not at all, Josef. Thank you. These gentlemen will be joining us. Would you bring over two more chairs and place settings, please?"

Josef released a sigh of relief. "By all means, sir." He motioned to two of his staff, who quickly brought the chairs while the four adjusted their settings to make room for the unexpected guests. Within a few moments, the room was cleared of staff, and the two new arrivals moved to take their seats.

The man, whom Jonathan had recognized from his dream and Samantha had addressed as Zjon, gracefully walked around the table to take the chair beside her. Before he could sit down, Samantha leapt up and gave him a long hug. Seeing this, Jonathan suddenly recognized that Samantha had a special connection with this man. The two looked natural together, and he sensed this was more than just friendship. Jonathan was surprised to find that instead of jealousy, he felt a sense of relief.

When he at last sat down, Zjon turned toward Jonathan and smiled. "It's good to see you again, Jonathan."

"Same here. Would you like a glass of Oban?" he responded wryly. The events of that first night were now crystalized in his memory, released from the cloud that had been concealing them. Jonathan again began to feel joy and well-being.

"Yes, that would be perfect."

Jonathan signaled the waiter. "Another Oban for my friend here. One for you, as well?" he asked Neal.

"Perfect," Neal said, smiling. The waiter departed with haste. "I am called Neal, and Zjon has told me a lot about you."

"All good, I hope," Jonathan said. Neal smiled.

"Neal is the man who did the incredible job of changing Samantha's appearance," Edward told Jonathan.

"Stunning!" was all Jonathan could think to say. Again Neal smiled.

The waiter returned with Zjon and Neal's drinks. Zjon raised his glass. "Allow me to toast our newfound friends." Everyone raised their glasses and drank.

Dan now turned his attention to everyone at the table and remarked, "Well, everyone seems to know each other here. I guess I'm the lone exception." Clearly, the situation had gotten away from him. He lifted his drink to take a careful sip, while desperately thinking about how he could regain control.

Zjon immediately responded, "On the contrary, Inspector Hamilton, we have all met. I believe you recall meeting us in the men's restroom at Raoul's."

Flabbergasted, Dan almost choked on his drink. "That was you?" He then realized that of course, these had to be the same men, kicking himself for missing the obvious.

Zjon smiled and said, "Please forgive our bad manners. We could not reveal our identities at that moment. It was most important that Samantha and her friends escape the situation and make their way back to Las Vegas, where we could provide safety. Hopefully, you will agree, 'No harm ...'"

"No foul." Dan, regaining his composure, continued to stare at Zjon with both disbelief and admiration. "But don't you think it would have been easier for you to talk with us, instead of resorting to magic tricks?"

"With all due respect, Inspector ..."

"Call me Dan."

"First, Dan, let me say that what you experienced had nothing to do with magic. Second, I put it right back to you: How would you have responded if we had tried to talk with you? Were you not really obligated to arrest us or detain us? I think you will have to admit that our course of action turned out to be much better. After all, we are all here sharing a wonderful meal together."

Jonathan said to him, "Dan, this *is* the man who appeared in my dream the other night. I now realize that I wasn't dreaming at all."

Dan asked Zjon, "Were you also behind the charged field that was preventing people from entering Samantha's neighborhood?"

"Yes. It was a signal."

"A signal?" Jonathan, Dan, and Edward all asked in unison.

Zjon quickly responded, "I think we are all ready for our dinner. Shall we order before resuming the conversation? I, for one, would like to have a bite to eat before we talk. I think Neal would also appreciate that." Neal nodded. "Once we order, I will be happy to address the questions that I'm sure you have. At least, we can get started. The conversation we start tonight will take several days. Please know that I intend for each of you to learn what you need to know before we take our leave."

Jonathan motioned to the waiter, who quickly stepped into the room. "Let me recommend that I place orders for all of us again," Jonathan suggested to the group. "I know this menu and have some suggestions. We can do family style."

"Makes it easy," Edward concurred.

With everyone's agreement, Jonathan ordered four bone-in, rib-eye steaks and four Dover sole dishes, with generous sides of Brussels sprouts, green beans, and the famous Prime garlic mashed potatoes. When the waiter had left, Jonathan turned his attention back to Dan and said, "Well now, where were we?"

Dan nodded and repeated, "Please tell us who are you, and why you are here."

All eyes turned toward Zjon.

CHAPTER 22

In the Presence

SPEAKING SOFTLY, ZJON SAID, "WE ARE FROM ANOTHER PLACE." HE LET HIS STATEMENT sink in.

Dan said, "I think that is obvious to everyone here. What do you mean, 'another place'? Do you mean another country?"

"Not another country—another place."

After a long pause, Dan asked what everybody else was wondering. "Zjon, are you telling us you are from another planet?"

Zjon spoke with great patience. "What is happening right now is very good for the whole world. We never expected anything like this to happen. We are all witnessing what we call the three primary openings in life—Imperfection, Unpredictability, and Impermanence."

"What does that mean?" Dan was beginning to lose patience. "Who are you, and where do you come from?"

"A long time ago in the history of humankind, great teachers came, like Buddha, Christ, and others whom you may never have heard about. These great teachers all taught the three principles to people. This is what we call, in our time, an 'organic truth.' Inorganic truths can change. Organic truths you cannot change; they are the very fiber of life. For you to realize this at this time will be very challenging, but very, very important."

Dan looked at everyone around the table. "Are you getting this?"

he asked. Nobody said a word. When he looked at Jonathan, Jonathan gave him a nod of encouragement.

"Okay. So, you say you are not from here. Just where exactly are you from?"

Zjon took a deep breath, as if pondering his next words. Finally, he said, "Actually, Samantha and I are not from any other country, and we are not aliens from another planet. We are from the future."

Edward could not restrain himself at this point. "Come on! Einstein proved years ago that to travel in time you would have to exceed the speed of light, and that light is the upper limit that nothing with any mass can ever exceed. Time travel is impossible!"

"You are absolutely correct. Time travel is impossible—even theoretically. And yet, here we are."

"You are going to have to say a lot more about this to convince me." Edward turned to his wife and said, "Don't you agree, honey?" Clare looked bewildered, but she nodded. "Allison?"

Allison only raised her shoulders in a gesture of "Don't ask me." She smiled, now starting to enjoy the situation.

Turning to Jonathan and Dan, Edward said, "Guys, do you buy this? How about you, Samantha? What ..."

When he saw the look on Samantha's face, Edward abruptly stopped talking. Samantha's face radiated a look of childlike wonder. "Oh, wow!" she exclaimed. Samantha was catching glimpses of memory, coming in flashes like lightning. Among the images was a flash of Zjon's face. Something was coming, and it was a very good thing. She knew it.

Dan turned back to Zjon, who was looking deeply into Samantha's eyes as he held her hand. "Zjon, as impossible as what you're saying might be, I actually think I do believe you." He looked at Jonathan, who now was nodding. Dan continued, "I'm just a cop. I'm no scientist. But the experiences I've had over the last four days have convinced me that we're dealing with something outside of our ordinary experiences in life. At least mine. And I can't explain the strong feelings I've been having. I feel as if I can completely trust you, Zjon. There is nothing about you that indicates to me that you're dangerous. In fact, the feeling I get from you is—the only word I can come up with—love. My God, this is not a cop-like thing for me to say!" With that, Dan shut up, embarrassed. His face was feeling flushed.

"Thank you for telling the truth, and for speaking for the group," said Zjon. "I would not be telling you if it were not absolutely necessary. You are right that you can trust me, and I want you all to know that I trust you, as well. We all have a special connection with each other, a connection that spans across timespace. I need your help, and so does Samantha. She and I need your help right now, more than ever."

At that moment, Jonathan spied the waiters bringing their dinner. "Hold that thought, please. We have company."

Four waiters stationed themselves around the table, making great fanfare. Jonathan chuckled to himself. *If these guys only knew what was going on here.* The waiters carefully placed the covered dishes in front of each person. On cue, each of the waiters reached down to remove the covers from two of the plates, unveiling that they had alternated the meat and fish dishes. Two waiters neatly placed an additional steak knife at each place setting, while the other two placed the vegetables and side dishes on a circular serving board in the center of the table.

A sound of "aah" arose in unison from everyone at the table. Just as swiftly as they had entered the room, the waiters bowed and retreated.

"I love this restaurant!" Jonathan exclaimed.

"Let's dig in and continue our conversation in a few minutes," Dan suggested.

"Fine idea!" agreed Allison.

Zjon nodded to the group, smiled, and plunged into his meal.

Over the next several minutes, the group focused on the plates in front of them, eating with gusto. Everyone's attention turned back to Zjon when he picked up his glass of water and began inspecting it.

His expression was like that of a child who had never seen anything like it before. At last, he inhaled deeply through his nostrils and then blew through pursed lips, sending patterns of dancing ripples across the surface of the water. He repeated this action two more times.

"I can see where you got that from," Allison remarked to Samantha with a trace of irony in her voice. Samantha watched the scene with delight.

Zjon, unruffled by Allison's sarcasm, explained, "In our time we learn as children how to interact with the elements. The element Water is one of the most powerful forces in life, and I am paying homage to it by sending the water in this glass a signal."

"A signal?" Jonathan repeated.

"Yes, Jonathan, a signal. Human beings are equipped by Nature to be able to send signals with their bodies. If trained, we can do this with our hands or with our breath, and sometimes even with our eyes. These signals interact with the Universal Intelligence. In this case, my signal rearranged the molecular structure of the water, causing it to carry a special charge—a charge that is beneficial to life. Here, each of you take a taste from my glass and pass it around. It does not have to be a large gulp, just a swallow." He handed the glass to Allison.

Allison, after a moment's hesitation, said, "Oh, well, when in Rome ..." She took a swig of water, swished it around in her mouth, and swallowed. She passed it on to Dan, who raised the glass toward Jonathan, smiled, and took a swallow. Around the table each, in turn, took a drink from the glass of water, until the last portion came to Samantha. Before taking her drink, Samantha closed her eyes for a moment and blew on the remaining water three times. She then gulped the last of it.

Within a minute, every person around the table began to laugh. When Allison, who was laughing the loudest, tried to stop, she looked across the table at Clare and, catching her eyes, was immediately thrown back into a deeper fit of laughing. The same thing kept happening to Jonathan, Dan, and Edward, as each in turn tried fruitlessly to bring his laughter under control, only to lose it altogether the moment one of them looked into the eyes of another. The merriment continued for several minutes unabated. Zjon, Samantha, and Neal were the first to recover, followed slowly by Jonathan, then Dan, then Edward and Clare, and finally Allison, who ended the session as spontaneously as it had begun with a simple exclamation of "I feel giddy! Is that what you meant by a charge?" Zjon nodded his head.

Becoming suddenly self-conscious, Jonathan looked through the glass and saw that everyone in the main dining room was looking at them, some showing amusement and others disgust. Josef was gazing at them with a look of mild concern. Jonathan gave him a wink, and he immediately averted his gaze.

After everyone had settled down, Dan turned back to Zjon and said, "Now, where were we? Where in the future do you come from?"

CHAPTER 23

Of the Future

"WE HAVE COME FROM TWENTY-FIVE HUNDRED YEARS IN YOUR FUTURE. THE YEAR IS 4544 by your standard calendar, what you call the 'Common Era.' When I say 'we,' I mean Samantha, Neal, myself, and one other who is not here in this room."

"So, I am from the future?" Samantha asked.

"Yes."

"Why can't I remember it?"

"Do not be alarmed. That was actually for your protection. You had an accident, and your memory loss was necessary to protect your system from shock. You will be fine soon and will remember everything."

Samantha pressed him, "I am so ready! Can I quickly get my memory?"

"No, no, no. It takes three days and must be done right, every night. Do not worry, dear Samantha, it will be painless, and we will be there with you to guide you all the way."

"I'm totally with you, Zjon."

Dan asked, "Is that why the rest of you are here, to help Samantha recover her memory?"

"Not entirely. We have come to rescue Samantha and bring her back home, to her own time."

"What do you mean by 'rescue'?" Edward demanded. "She has been safe and happy living with us for the last three years."

"Yes, what do you mean?" echoed Clare. "She's been like family to us. And Samantha, I can't believe you're talking to a stranger this way and are considering going off with him."

Zjon responded, "Please do not be offended. I used the word *rescue* as a reference to protection from physical and psychological harm. Actually, we have come to return Samantha to her own time, her own home, and this is just as important not only for Samantha, but for the entire human race."

Turning to Clare and Edward, he continued, "We are eternally grateful that you came upon Samantha and took her into your home and your lives. It no doubt seemed to you to be something accidental. But in reality it was not. You knew her and are related to her. I do not want you to start thinking about past lives. That is not what I am talking about. However, there is a certain way that you know Samantha. In a few more days you will come to understand. For right now, let me say that you knew Samantha was coming. You did not know who it would be. That is why you were drawn to the tree where you found her. While you were drawn to the tree for three days before you found her, Samantha was falling from a different time. Now it is important that she return to her own time."

"Why? What will happen if she stays?" Allison asked.

"Let me back up and explain from the beginning. Samantha is an astronaut. In the year 4544 she was conducting a survey in space in a territory where it was unwise to go. She took a risk because she was very daring, and she believed she was right to do so. In the forty-sixth century, the world is in a very sweet space. We have a very different kind of governing. The Advanced Solar Administration (ASA) is one of our most honored and respected institutions. The ASA is a world body, not a government, consisting of all the nations of humankind. One of the reasons it was formed was that the human race had put so much junk into space that we had to clear it away. Only once you put trash into space, it stays there unless you clean it out. You treated the Earth's environment in much the same way in your age. There was a lot of cleaning to be done, and it took many centuries. You underestimate your presence as human beings in the universe—your power and your true nature. We are custodians of the universe. When I say 'we,' I mean humankind. When I say 'the universe,' I mean our universe, which really means our solar system, our sun. There are many stars in the known universe. But among them our sun is a prince. You need to realize and appreciate this.

"In regard to Samantha, the ASA gave Samantha authority to go into a certain territory in space. But she went beyond that authority and ventured into another territory beyond that. This was a very dangerous situation. She encountered something unexpected; her spaceship could not bear the pressure, and it exploded. In your time when space accidents happen, astronauts die. In our time, fortunately, we have advanced science and technology that prevents a total disaster. I am only telling you this to give you a sense of how advanced we have become. So, to put it in layman's language, she had an accident. Her spaceship exploded, causing her to fall, in accordance with the seventh principle of gravity, which governs the actions of gravity waves. This falling, because of where she had ventured, effectively took her back in time. That is what brought her two thousand five hundred years into our past, into the Earth of your time. We call what happened a 'timespace phase shift,' or, more formally, a 'timespace appropriation event.' That is the seventh principle I referred to."

Zjon turned again to Edward and Clare. "While she was falling, you were drawn to that particular tree. That is because the signals went through the phase shift into you to let you know she was coming. You received an emotional signal, which is what you were feeling. You went to the tree because you had already received the signals through your emotional spectrum. We are all connected, but actually the most immediate connections are the direct connections among people. Samantha and I are directly connected. And then, Samantha is also connected to you."

He turned back to Jonathan. "Also, Jonathan is connected to

me. That is how Jonathan recognized me, and also how Samantha recognized Jonathan on the train, though he did not know anything about Samantha. These connections are all at a cellular level, cellular remembrances sending neuronal impulses to the memory saying, 'Remember?' So all the emotions that you felt on that train, including the love and affection for Samantha, were real. They were real for a very different reason than just emotional or physical attraction. We are all connected. Jonathan. One day I will be a distant grandson of yours, just as Samantha one day will be a distant granddaughter of Clare and Edward's. It is a cellular tie that transcends even the distance of time."

When Zjon finished, the entire room was silent. Jonathan was dumbfounded. Edward and Clare were in a deep state of wonder. Dan and Allison each were deeply shocked.

Samantha broke the silence. "Zjon, can you tell me more about my time and where I came from?"

Zjon reached over and took her hand. "In due time, honey. Trust me, it will all come together. The fact that you are here, and that we are here together, is actually a great thing. We are here for the whole human race at this moment. In a very fascinating way, your accident has been a wake-up call for the human race existing in the twenty-first century. And for you and me, this is a special form of grace. Time travel is forbidden for a good reason. The ASA has made this one exception, also for a special reason. We have a vital mission for the entire human race. So, we consider this accident a good event in human history."

"So, wait a minute," Allison challenged. "If all this happened and you are from the future, how can you be here? You say time travel is impossible, and the universe has to keep its equilibrium."

"As wise ones say, 'there are no accidents.' I believe that this accident with Samantha is an event for all humankind. A time warp occurred for us to come and experience your time right now. And in the last few days, we have experienced everything. We are so thrilled. All our friends are so envious. In fact, when the accident happened it was the High Council that determined whether to rescue Samantha or not. The High Council is the closest thing we have to a governing body within the ASA, only it is actually a group of people who take care of all others. The council decided to send us to rescue Samantha because they recognized that otherwise Samantha would divulge things that should not be revealed at this time. That is why we were sent, as a one-time exception to the rule. We were granted the passage by the High Council, and we must follow their plan."

"But you previously acknowledged that time travel is impossible!" Allison insisted again.

"Yes, it is impossible. I am going to say something that you will just have to take my word for: 'Impossible is possible.'" With that nonexplanation, Allison decided to let it go. However, she was anything but satisfied.

"So what happens next?" Dan asked.

"First, we need to restore Samantha's memory to bring her back to her full self. This will take three nights, in sessions lasting six hours a night. Then, we will need to take her back to our time. Unless and until we do this, our shared universe is in a sense out of equilibrium. Disequilibrium, like a vacuum, cannot be tolerated indefinitely. If we do not restore that equilibrium, Samantha will probably die, and we who came to retrieve her will probably be destroyed as well. So, we need your help."

"How can we help?" Jonathan asked.

Edward jumped in before Zjon could answer. "Wait, I have a question. Haven't you already caused some kind of irreversible warp or cosmic interference? Isn't this the opposite of the general principle of Noninterference you referred to earlier? Hasn't the damage already been done?"

"A question from a true mathematician's mind. The answer is yes and no. Assuming we succeed in our mission, we cannot leave you with any special knowledge or technology, or anything physical at all that you do not already possess. In fact, everything I have been saying right now—like the recordings Jonathan and Dan are secretly making right now—will disappear and be erased."

Dan and Jonathan looked sheepish, realizing they had been found out.

Zjon continued, "We are going to have several meetings with you before we leave. But when we leave, what we say will only exist in your memories. You will not have any records, physical or electronic. This must be so, in order not to interfere with human evolution. I know that if they have the opportunity, your press will try to take pictures and make recordings. But if they do, those pictures and recordings will be erased. Your children's children's children will not believe you when you tell them what happened. You will not have any evidence. Your memories will even seem like a dream to you. Evolution requires that the human race as it moves forward will need to learn everything for itself."

"Then why," Allison jumped in, "do you say this is a momentous event for humanity?"

"Life is unpredictable, imperfect, and impermanent. No matter how well we may plan, even in the timespace from where Samantha and I come, there will always be surprises. This accident itself was a great surprise for us all. In the end, the nature of life is that life is. Life grows. Life lives and loves."

Zjon paused, then continued. "Think about it. We are here with you now, in the twenty-first century, and we were born twenty-five hundred years from now. The fact that we human beings are alive in the forty-sixth century should give you confidence that everything will work out in your time."

Suddenly, everybody began laughing again. As weird as this idea was, it had the ring of truth.

"I'll ask you again," insisted Jonathan. "How can we help?"

"You and your friends can help Samantha to escape."

"How do we do that?"

"You can give us the time we need to bring back her memory."

CHAPTER 24

A Prime Escape

DAN AND JONATHAN LOOKED AT EACH OTHER. EACH MAN REALIZED THAT HE HAD MADE a pact with the other that could not be broken. This was the right thing to do. Jonathan saw that Clare had begun to weep, a gentle stream of tears trickling down her cheeks. "How are you with all this?" Jonathan asked her.

Edward took his wife's left hand into both of his and grasped it. He returned Jonathan's gaze and said, "I think I can speak for both Clare and me. The last three years, having Samantha with us, has given our lives new meaning." Samantha looked at them both with love. "It's intolerable to think about losing her now."

Clare managed to speak. "We never thought this day would come. She's become a daughter to us. I knew something was special about you, Samantha. I knew you were from somewhere else, but I figured someday you would remember and then take us to see your home. I've assumed we would be lifelong friends."

"We are lifelong friends, Clare," Samantha assured her. "That will never change. I'm forever grateful that you and Edward took care of me. You will always be family to me."

Clare reached her hand up to cover her mouth. "Thank you."

"You know that I need to go with Zjon. This is the only way I can recover who I am and what my life is supposed to be about. Will you please help me with this? I need you both now more than ever."

"Of course, we will," Edward assured her, with forced bravado. Clare nodded her head and gave her a smile.

Allison took the opportunity to speak: "Count me in. Frankly, I was beginning to think that my field of philosophy had reached a dead end. This changes everything. And I surprise myself in saying that I buy your story, Zjon. Who knows, this may be the beginning of a second Axial Age—meaning an age that will change the course of human development—and I am not going to be left out of it." She lifted her glass and downed the remains of her martini.

"Good," Zjon said with pleasure. "We have a common mission. I believe you already have called it 'Mission Heart,' Edward." Zjon said these last words while casting a look to Clare and Edward. Clare and Edward looked at each other with surprise.

Zjon continued. "Tonight Neal and I will take Samantha to our ship, where we can begin the process, which will take three nights to complete. However, during the next two days we can all meet, at which times I can provide you with all that you need to understand, and we can decide on our exit strategy. We will not be out of the woods, as your expression goes, until we succeed in taking Samantha back to our time. There is still a danger that we could be intercepted between now and four days from now. If that happens, and the ninth day passes, the timespace phase shift window will close. That could be disastrous."

Clare could not contain herself any longer. "Can we come too?" she pleaded.

"Do you mean to our ship?" Zjon asked.

"Yes, and even to your time."

"Unfortunately no, to both questions. You cannot come aboard our ship because it would contaminate the energy, in the sense of time-contamination. Our ship is tuned to our future time. We cannot allow any matter from your time to enter within. Nor can we take you with us. You all belong in your own time, as do we. We are here with you right now, for these nine days, only on 'borrowed time.'"

"Okay," Jonathan spoke up. "How do we go about this?"

"I will contact Jonathan in the morning to arrange the first meeting. Will you be staying here at the hotel?"

Jonathan nodded. "Yes, Dan and I have already gotten a room on the same floor as the rest of them."

Zjon said, "Good. This means that all we need to do is get out of here quickly and quietly." Zjon turned and nodded to Neal, who got up from the table, left the restaurant, and quickly disappeared up the escalator.

Dan observed how catlike Neal's motions were. Turning to Zjon, he said, "So, what you really need now is my part."

Zjon smiled at Dan. "Yes, exactly."

"As you probably already know, our plan has been to take Samantha with us tonight so we could interview her. My boss—and his boss, the president—wants her in safe government hands in order to control the situation. My temporary FBI partner is upstairs awaiting my call about where to meet us. He has men scattered throughout the Bellagio prepared to act upon my signal. We were going to escort her to our jet and fly back to Washington. Obviously, this is a change of plans."

"Yes."

"And in addition, the press is sniffing around to get the first scoop. If the word gets out that Samantha is who you say she is, there will be a media feeding frenzy."

"I realize this. In fact, I predict that the word will get out somehow. I know that we will not be able to hold off your government agents indefinitely."

"That's the tricky part for me. I have a sworn responsibility to the president to inform him of everything I know. At the same time, I know that I must protect Samantha, and my heart tells me that this is a higher responsibility."

"I am grateful you see it this way. Thank you." Zjon bowed his head slightly.

Jonathan stepped in with, "Not only that, guys. The United States is not the only government that we need to be concerned with here. I would not be surprised if China, Russia, and other governments are working on this as well. And due to the fiasco of a leak, Samantha herself is no longer an unknown person. We could end up with a race to grab her."

"We also have arrived at the same conclusion," Zjon replied. "This could actually work in our favor, if you think about it."

"How so?" Allison and Edward asked, almost simultaneously.

"It has become clear to me that our mission is no accident. Samantha would not be here with you otherwise. Let me put it another way. You would not have been the ones who found her, who were attracted to her, and who have helped her. Not only you personally at this table, but the entire human race in your time, must be poised for this event. Another 'Axial Age,' as Allison said. In our time some of us have called this epoch the 'Age of Unfolding.' I prefer calling it the 'Flowering.' This contact across timespace belongs to the entire planet of human beings, not just one nation. In the next two days, you must come up with the right way to make this connection possible."

Dan and Jonathan each began thinking hard.

"Edward, Allison, Jonathan, just think about this," Clare said. "We have sufficient connections to the greatest scientific and academic minds. We could call a spontaneous global scientific conference here in Las Vegas. Scientists from around the world could attend, and those who couldn't come in person could be connected online. I know people who could coordinate such a gathering on short notice."

"That could possibly work," Jonathan said.

"Do you think you could pull this off?" Dan asked.

"Why not!" Edward exclaimed.

Zjon responded, "That is a possibility. But I am not agreeing to the suggestion that Clare and Edward are making right now. We have a much higher priority: Samantha's memory must be recovered without causing a shock that could have repercussions throughout all time!"

Edward said, "Yes, protecting Samantha is paramount. We need to keep our government from getting control. Dan, can you pull that off?"

Dan answered, "Are you kidding me? As my partner David likes to say, 'piece of cake.' I'll call David when we're finished here and tell him that everyone is going over to the VIP elevators. I'll ask him to intercept three of you—Edward and Clare and Allison—as you head to your rooms. I'll direct him to hold you for me. I won't tell him that Samantha won't be with them. I'll let him think that she's with me. Then, by the time we're all together, Zjon and Samantha will already be gone. Do you need me to get a car, Zjon?"

"No, we have already made that arrangement."

Dan answered, "Great. Then, let's settle the dinner bill. Meanwhile, I'll call David and get the ball rolling on getting Samantha out of here safely." Everyone nodded, and Dan reached into his jacket pocket for his cell phone.

Jonathan caught Josef's attention and asked for the bill. Within a few seconds, Josef came into the room and announced, "Franz has instructed me that your dinner tonight is on the house."

"What? We've been given a comp?" Jonathan was surprised.

"Yes, and I have no idea why. Franz must consider you very important people."

"Please give him our wholehearted thanks." Jonathan reached into his wallet and extracted three one hundred dollar bills. He stood up, walked over to Josef, and handed him the bills. "We have to leave quickly, but please see to it that your staff get good tips, and include yourself."

Josef was clearly touched by the rare event of receiving two tips from one party. "Thank you, sir. It has been a pleasure having you here tonight. Might I also say that everyone has found it most entertaining." Josef, head held high, strode out of the room.

Dan hung up the phone and said, "It's all set. Just to be safe, do you think we should create some sort of diversion? David says there are a lot of press people out there."

Zjon said, "By all means." Standing up, he turned to Samantha. "Samantha, please stand up for a moment." She complied. "Incidentally, this is good timing. I see that the next water show is just starting. Give me your right hand, and hold up your left hand like this." Zjon raised his left palm to demonstrate for Samantha, holding his left hand up, palm forward, as if he were taking a pledge or an oath. Samantha mimicked his left hand position and held out her right hand to Zjon. He took her right hand between his two hands and spread her fingers so that the thumb and pinky finger were apart, and the other three fingers were close together, clasped between his own. Holding her three fingers up close to his lips, Zjon took a deep inhalation and then blew air out through pursed lips onto the tips of her three fingers. Immediately, a flash of blue-green light shot out of the palm of her left hand.

Suddenly in the background arose sounds of screaming from outside. Everyone in the restaurant turned to see a water show blazing in multiple alternating colors, like an old-fashioned Technicolor movie. Splashes of water sprayed back and forth high above the fountain's lake, creating mesmerizing patterns of rainbows. Voices outside on Las Vegas Boulevard were screaming in amazement and wonder, as people rushed across the street get a better view. All traffic on the street had suddenly come to a halt. Everyone in Prime's main dining room left their tables and rushed over to the outside balcony. This time the light show was accompanied by Beethoven's "Ode to Joy."

"Well, I'll be damned," Allison said, hardly believing her eyes.

Laughing, Dan turned to everyone and said, "Okay then, let's go!"

"Can I speak with you for a moment, in private?" David Newman glared at Dan with fury in his eyes. The two were standing at the elevator bank inside the VIP lounge at the Bellagio. It was 10:30 p.m.

"Sure," Dan said. He turned to Jonathan, Edward, Clare, and Allison, who had been surrounded by four other men in suits for the last half hour. Speaking to the four men, Dan said, "Let them go upstairs. These are innocent bystanders." The men stepped aside and moved out into the corridor to await further instructions. "Jonathan, why don't you go with the other three up to your suite, and I'll join you all in a little while. Special Agent Newman and I need to tie up some loose ends."

Jonathan nodded, and the four of them got into an elevator.

"You and I need to have a serious conversation," David continued, glaring at Dan. David had been absolutely furious when he found out that Samantha was gone. "I'm supposed to be your partner here."

"I had to make a quick judgment call," Dan explained.

"That's no excuse for leavin' me out," David retorted.

"I know, but if I had told you what we were doing, would you have let her go?"

"Probably not."

"You're damned right you wouldn't have. Our job was to capture this woman and bring her to Washington for questioning. If you had disobeyed your orders, you would have wrecked your career."

"But what about you? Now you're in deep trouble, my friend."

"Yes, but I'll figure out how to set this right with the Chief. Let's go over to the piano bar, and I'll buy you a drink. But first, send your guys home and tell them the alert is over. Everyone can rest easy—crisis averted. Then, I'll explain everything that's going on. We have some interesting work cut out for us, and you have a vital part to play."

"Now you're talkin'. That's much more like it. But you need to promise me one thing."

"What's that?"

"You'll never leave me out again."

"I promise."

"Well, all right then." David turned, walked over to his men and gave them instructions for standing down. He then sent them to tell the rest of the team to go off duty, but to be ready to return at a moment's notice at any time.

When he came back, Dan commented with humor, "You know, David, your brogue comes out when you're pissed off."

"That's what my ex-wife says." The two men laughed and headed for the piano bar.

CHAPTER 25

Las Vegas, Day Five, 10:30 p.m.

*Z*JON STEPPED UP TO THE BLACK LIMOUSINE THAT WAS WAITING IN FRONT OF THE NORTH entrance to Bellagio. He opened the back door and held it for Samantha. He then walked around to the opposite door and got in himself. Seated in the driver's seat was Neal, who greeted them cheerfully. Neal looked amusing to Samantha in his chauffer's cap. The disguise was simple, but effective. None of the security guards or valet parking staff had attempted to approach the car or asked him to "move along."

Neal navigated the limousine out of the driveway. Within seconds he had reached Interstate 15 and pulled onto the freeway heading south. Ten minutes later the three were heading west on I-215.

"Welcome back, Samantha," a female voice announced from the front of the car.

Samantha looked to see where the voice was coming from, but the passenger seat was empty. "Who said that?"

"Do you not recognize me?" the voice asked. "It is me, Melissa."

"Melissa? Where are you? I can't see you."

Neal laughed and said, "Do not worry, Melissa. She does not remember anything yet. She will remember you when we restore her memory." Neal then explained to Samantha, "Melissa is your personal escort vehicle. She was a gift from your parents, and she has accompanied you on many missions."

Zjon and Neal laughed as Samantha said, "Oh, my God!"

Zjon explained, "Melissa agreed to disguise herself to look like a twenty-first century automobile. She will unmorph herself when we get back to the ship, as soon as we are off the road. We should be at the ship in less than an hour."

"Where exactly is the ship?" Samantha asked.

"I would prefer not to say at this point. For now, I suggest you sit back, relax, and have a catnap. You have had a long day."

Samantha suddenly realized how tired she was. It had indeed been a very long day, and now she was feeling exhausted. "Good idea. I think I'll lie back and close my eyes for a few minutes." Thirty seconds later she was sound asleep.

The limousine that called herself Melissa cruised softly down the freeway, carrying her precious party from the future away from the fantastic sound and light show that had become the signature of twenty-first century Las Vegas. Overhead, the belt of Orion stretched out across the deep blue-black night sky, as if pointing the wayward group back home, toward the Future.

CHAPTER 26

Bellagio, Day Five, 11:55 p.m.

FEDERAL SPECIAL INVESTIGATOR DAN HAMILTON AND FBI SPECIAL AGENT DAVID Newman stepped out of VIP elevator number three onto the forty-eighth floor of the Bellagio Tower. A sign posted in the alcove indicated that penthouse suite number 4801 was around the corner and down the hall. The two men quickly located the double doors labeled "Royal Suite 1" and knocked on the door. Within a few seconds both doors swung open, revealing a haggard-looking Edward Hunter. Edward stepped aside and motioned them to enter. Dan introduced David and Edward, who shook hands.

It was clear to Dan that the Bellagio had spared no expense in decorating the suite. The walls were hung with original watercolors and oils. Across the room a set of French doors opened onto a large balcony that looked down on the Fountains of Bellagio below and across at the gaudy replica known as the Eiffel Tower Las Vegas, home to one of the finest restaurants on the Strip. To the far left and far right sides of the living room were sets of double doors leading into luxurious bedrooms. The center of the room was occupied by two sets of Renaissance-styled sofas and four matching chairs, facing each other around two rococo coffee tables. The far sofa was occupied by Clare Hunter and Allison Russell, each cradling a cup of coffee. Seated and facing the French doors to the balcony was Jonathan Elliot. All heads turned toward Dan and David.

"Nice digs!" David commented.

Ignoring the remark, Dan began by saying, "Everyone, I would like you to meet Special Agent David Newman from the FBI. He's the man who provided security this evening and helped protect our friends from the future as they made their getaway. You can consider David a friend."

Jonathan stood to shake David's hand and introduced himself.

David blurted, "I read your article on Sunday, though I didn' have any idea what you were talking about at the time."

"Neither did I," Jonathan jokingly confessed.

Edward walked around and took the chair near Clare, who nodded to them while Allison teased him gently. "I'm sure you know our names already, Agent Newman."

David nodded and smiled. "Call me David. I heard you had somethin' of a bite, Professor."

To David's relief, Allison just chuckled. "Call me Allison. We all seem to be newfound friends, sharing a common mission. Edward and Clare were just telling Jonathan how they came to call it 'Mission Heart.' Our Samantha has certainly come to be the center of a big surprise for all of us tonight."

Dan and David took the sofa opposite the two women. Edward poured Dan and David cups of coffee. "It's freshly brewed." Dan and David each accepted his cup with a nod of thanks.

Edward began to catch Dan and David up on the ongoing conversation. "Clare and I were just telling Jonathan the story about how we came to meet Samantha three years ago, the story we had to invent because of her lost memory, and how we ended up coming to Las Vegas."

"Ironically, your long-lost cousin has apparently turned out to be lost for *twenty-five hundred years*!" Jonathan tossed in.

Edward let out a laugh. "Yes, whoever heard of losing someone in the future?" This remark made them all join the laughter.

"Mind bending!" said Dan.

Things settled down once again. Dan took the opportunity to

satisfy his curiosity: "So why did you end up moving to Las Vegas? I realize your parents live here, but why did you leave San Francisco?"

Clare decided to answer him. "Well, there were really two reasons. Three actually. First, a dear friend and colleague of ours is a neurologist and neuroscientist from UCSF. He ran a series of tests to help Samantha recover her memory from her amnesia and gave a substantial amount of his time. In the end, unfortunately, his efforts were completely unsuccessful. And then, uh ..."

"What Clare is trying to say," assisted Edward, "is that this friend fell in love with Samantha. His feelings were not reciprocated. Samantha was kind and understanding with him, but after a while he became so obsessed, we decided it would be better for him not to see her at all. He just couldn't take no for an answer, and it became a problem for all of us, especially Samantha. She felt terrible that she didn't love him."

Clare came back in turn. "Yes, that was our first reason to move. The second reason was that people were beginning to get very suspicious about Samantha. You have to admit that once you meet her, you realize that she is not a normal young woman. It all started with our neurologist friend's colleagues. She aced all of the tests, and the other scientists and lab assistants decided she must be hiding something. To make matters worse, she had no documentation. People began to speculate that she must be some kind of criminal or spy. After a year and a half or two years, Edward and I decided we had to get her away, for her own safety."

Edward continued, "What capped it all off was that one day we spotted a man who seemed to be following her wherever she went. This continued for several days. I finally got one of our colleagues to admit that he had hired a private investigator to find out who she was. So, I told Clare that we had to get Samantha away from San Francisco before things got too dangerous."

Edward looked back to Clare. "I called my parents, and they were happy to help," she said. "So, Edward and I quietly notified the university that we were taking a leave of absence. The school was fine with that, thinking one of us must have some kind of illness." Clare chuckled to herself.

"You said there were three reasons," David pointed out.

Clare hesitated. "Well, the other thing was that Samantha was slowly beginning to change. It started out with a few small things that Edward and I just chalked up to her being eccentric. Every now and then she said strange things that didn't make any sense."

"Like what sorts of things?" Dan asked.

Edward answered, "For example, one time she started talking about her lover on her ship. At first we thought maybe she was talking about an ocean cruise. But then she said, 'No, no, the ring surveyor.' Then when I pressed her about this, she completely denied talking about any of it at all. Looking back, I now interpret this as some kind of momentary memory leak. But at the time I was afraid she might be breaking under the stress of not knowing who she was. There were numerous other slips that started happening after she had been with us for about a year. Gradually, they became more and more frequent, and we became afraid she was breaking under the pressure, like from our friend who was trying to force her to talk about herself. So, we got into our car and drove to Las Vegas. Then we took a diversionary trip to London just to get away from it all for a few weeks."

Dan said, "Thank you for telling us all of this. I'm sure this must have been quite stressful."

"Yes, it was," Clare admitted.

"Was there anything else?"

"Well, we had a nagging sense that Samantha might not be from our planet. She adapted incredibly well, knowing what we know now. Yet she often acted like a foreigner. Finally, she has all of these talents, like what she calls 'signaling,' a couple of which you witnessed tonight."

"Like blowing into the glass and the light coming out of her hand."

"Exactly," Edward put in. "So, there you have it; that's basically our story. Pretty wild, wouldn't you say?"

"Man, I missed some excitement," David said, a bit miffed.

Jonathan broke in. "I think we need to get on the same page about where we are and where we are going from here."

"You're right," agreed Dan. "We are obviously in a very, to say the least, delicate situation. Let's talk about that. Why don't you start, Jonathan?"

"We have a hell of a lot of brains in this room. And it's really pretty amazing that this group of people has been gathered together by Samantha and her two friends, Zjon and Neal. Clearly, these three people have some remarkable gifts. We have to agree whether we can believe, or at least accept, that they are human beings from twenty-five hundred years in the future."

Jonathan stopped talking. Dan nodded but patiently waited for the next person to speak.

Edward spoke up next. "As wild as the idea seems, Zjon's explanation that they come from the future at least seems to explain all that Clare and I have witnessed. Don't you agree, Allison?"

"I honestly don't know what to think, Ed. My life has always seemed to be a fairly logical progression. I grew up, went to school, got interested in philosophy, studied hard, and worked my way up to being a professor. Until I met Samantha, I didn't realize how much I had been living in an ivory tower. I think that meeting Samantha may have been the first time I became familiar with someone who actually looks at the world differently. The words that come out of her mouth are a demonstration of the most originary thinking. By 'originary,' I mean thinking that is grounded in some profound level of experience that I've never encountered before—in anyone. It makes me wonder, is everyone in the future like her? If that is so, it is truly great news for humankind. It would mean that somewhere along the way human beings managed to crawl out of our narrow, predefined views of the world, and that is the true philosopher's dream.

"It would also mean that we somehow managed not to wipe ourselves out," Jonathan said. "I have worried for many years about whether humans would ever be mature enough to use science for some purpose beyond gaining an economic advantage over others."

"Unlike my friends Clare and Edward, I have pressing work responsibilities that I need to deal with. And I have concerns for my safety. Do I need to be concerned, Special Investigator Dan?" Allison asked.

"No, I promise. You are free to go, and you won't be harassed by any government agents. You're strictly an innocent bystander. I can vouch for that fact. Guilt by association is not a criminal offense in the eyes of the law."

"Thank you, Dan. Then, Clare, if you'll forgive me, tomorrow morning I'm going to get the earliest flight back to New York that I can. I don't want to be left out, but I have to get back."

"We completely understand," Clare said. "Thank you for all your help. You're a very dear friend."

The group stood up. Allison hugged Clare and Edward, shook the other men's hands, then exited the room, closing one of the bedroom doors behind her.

"I hate losing her right now," Jonathan said. "We need good thinking about all of this."

"She is a lioness," Edward said. Clare only nodded.

After a moment's pause, Dan said, "I suggest we meet back here early in the morning for breakfast. Jonathan and I are sharing a room down the hall, room 4812, in case you need to reach us. Edward, would you place an order for a room service breakfast, say around seven o'clock?"

"Certainly, that would be perfect. Good for you, dear?"

"Of course."

"Good. David, would you also be able to join us for a breakfast strategy session?"

"Wouldn't miss it for the world."

"Great, I'll give you one of our keys to get up the VIP elevator. Any other urgent business that we need to talk about tonight?"

Jonathan said, "I just have one thing to say. This whole thing is simply amazing! This is the most important story of our generation and our lifetime. And we are part of it."

Everyone sat in silence. They could feel the tingling excitement pulsating up and down their spines. Something had come, and more was coming.

Dan wrapped it up. "All right then, silence will be interpreted as satisfaction."

The two men walked down the hallway to their room, each lost in his separate thoughts. Dan was trying to figure out how he was going manage David, keep the Chief and the president from coming down on Samantha and her cohorts, and keep his job. He thought to himself, *I know they are going to try to capture Samantha; this is what I'd do if I were in their shoes.* Equally importantly, if not more so, Dan was wondering how he could handle what now seemed to him a sacred mission of protecting these people.

Jonathan shared Dan's last concern. But he had another: "How can we make the most of this situation for the people of our time?" He found it interesting that he, the most skeptical of the skeptical, had fully accepted that these people were indeed from another time.

Finally, Jonathan said, "Dan, we need to convince Zjon and Samantha to agree to an interview. I know they are going to refuse at first, but we have to convince them to have a discussion with some of our best scientists. We have to give whatever is necessary for them to succeed in their mission, but we also need something in return.

This event is potentially a huge opportunity for science, and for the betterment of the human race."

"That gives me an idea that could also solve one of the problems I've been wrestling with," Dan concurred. "But if I don't manage this situation right, everything could backfire and create a lot of chaos. The next few days are going to be very interesting. As David would say, 'We ain't seen nothin' yet!'"

PART THREE
CONNECTIONS

Space is the ultimate boundary of infinity.
It is in the space within you that everything happens.
What is space? Space is light.
What is light? Light is love.
                                   —Commander Zjon III

CHAPTER 27

San Francisco, Three Years Earlier

SLOWLY SHE ROSE INTO CONSCIOUSNESS FROM A DEEP SLEEP. HER MIND WAS BLANK, although she was becoming aware of her body. Her consciousness drifted down to her heartbeat. She noted it to be the normal fifty-eight beats per minute. Eyes still closed, she began scanning from the bottoms of her feet, up through her legs and torso to her shoulders and down to her fingertips. She found no points of pain, and her energy felt very good. Her self-reflectors seemed fully intact, both in the heart and head regions. Most importantly, her emotions and feelings were in deep harmony. She further noticed that the life energy was flowing in an uninterrupted circular motion, from the base of her spine up through the top of her head, out and around and back down to her pelvic floor. Even though her eyes remained closed, she saw the internal rainbow colors, emanating from inside the center of her forehead. She was now awake. All was right. Her name was Samantha.

"I think she's waking up," a woman's voice said, penetrating her awareness. It was a gentle, friendly voice.

Samantha opened her eyes. She looked around and saw that she was lying on some sort of soft cushion in a brightly colored room. Around her was what looked to be antique furniture. One piece was apparently a table. One might be a kind of desk. A taller one in the corner appeared to have several section panels with handles, a chest of drawers. The words came to her without effort. Oddly, she seemed

EH STROUPE AND TILAK FERNANDO

to be unable to recall the past or where she had seen these things before. After a few moments of taking stock of her surroundings, Samantha realized she was lying in a bed, her head resting on a soft pillow.

Turning in the direction from which she had heard the voice moments before, she saw a woman sitting in a chair, leaning toward her with kind eyes and a smile. Samantha smiled in return. There was a slight rustling sound as a man walked through the door, stood by the seated woman, and said, "Oh, good. She's been completely gone since yesterday. I was beginning to get worried." Looking down at Samantha, the man smiled and said, "Hello, and welcome."

This must be a greeting. "Hello," Samantha said. She surmised she must be a guest in this couple's dwelling place.

The woman spoke first, "My name is Clare Hunter, and this is my husband Edward."

Husband, she noted. They must be married. An eccentric, but not unheard of, kind of relationship still practiced mostly in the southern regions. "My name is Samantha. Where am I?"

"You are in the guest room in our home, in Noe Valley," Clare answered.

The name was not a familiar one, and the man named Edward elaborated, "In San Francisco." Still there was no recognition. Feeling somewhat helpless, Samantha continued to look at the two of them without speaking. "You know, the great state of California, in the good old USA?" He chuckled awkwardly, raising his eyebrows as if asking for some kind of response.

Clare turned to him and said, "Ed, I think Samantha might like a glass of water."

"Of course," he answered his wife. "Would you?" he asked Samantha.

Samantha said, "Yes, I would very much like a drink of water. I have much thirst."

"I'll be right back," Edward said. He stepped out of the room briskly.

Once he had left the room, Clare said, "Now, honey, you just relax and make yourself at home. You have been asleep since we found you on Twin Peaks yesterday. We brought you here to our home. You're safe with us, and we're happy to have you as our guest. Do you feel strong enough to get up?"

Samantha ran another quick scan of her internal physical state, stepping through each of the nine opening centers one by one. She nodded. "Yes."

Clare stood up. "Let me show you around our house." Samantha jumped up, apparently surprising Clare with her spryness. "Oh, you do seem to be feeling good. That's a relief. Please come with me." Clare turned and Samantha followed her out of the room.

Within a minute Edward rejoined them and handed Samantha a glass. She downed the water greedily, and followed it with an enthusiastic exclamation. "Oh, that was wonderful! May I have some more?"

"Certainly," Edward took the glass and headed back to the kitchen.

For the next few minutes Samantha followed Clare and Edward through their house, enjoying being given a tour by these new friends. Feeling happy and at ease now, she was delighted when they entered a room that she immediately recognized as being a place for preparing food. Clare turned to her, smiled, and said, "Why don't you and Ed have a seat and talk, while I fix us some dinner?" Following Edward's lead, Samantha pulled out a chair and sat down at the kitchen table.

Once Samantha had asked questions about the coffeepot, the Arrowhead water dispenser, and the refrigerator, Edward resumed the introductions. "Clare and I are professors at UCSF, the University of California here in San Francisco. I'm a mathematician, and she's an anthropologist. We have lived here for more than twenty years, and this is our home. We would like to know about you and where you came from."

"My name is Samantha."

"Just Samantha? Do you have a last name?"

"Just Samantha. It means 'bird of light.'"

"How sweet!" Clare chimed in from across the room where she was preparing a salad.

"Thank you." Samantha found that she very much intuited these nice people and felt warm toward them.

"And can you tell us a little about yourself, like where you are from and what you do?" Edward prodded gently.

Samantha turned her attention back to her self-reflectors, her heart center, and her memory repository. To her consternation, her neuronal cellular systems emitted no information. All that was present was blankness. It was as if there was a blank wall between her and her recollection, or perhaps some kind of door with a lock for which she did not have a key. In exasperation, she declared, "I do not remember who I am or where I came from!"

"You mean you can't remember anything?" Clare asked.

"Nothing at all. What day is this?"

"It's July 13. A Wednesday."

After pondering Clare's answer, Samantha said, "I have no past."

"Everyone has a past, Samantha."

Searching for the right words, Samantha ventured, "I cannot remember who I am."

"It sounds like you may be suffering from some kind of amnesia."

"'Amnesia,' loss of memory, derived from ancient Greek, the condition of forgetfulness and oblivion that came from drinking from the river Lethe, the river of oblivion. Adopted into medical terminology during the early industrial age. Yes, that must be what is happening."

Edward and Clare both looked taken aback. Clare stopped what she was doing and turned around to face her. "You clearly have some faculties intact, Samantha. And you seem well educated. Is it just that you can't remember your personal history?"

"Yes, I cannot remember anything about my past life. I do not know where I came from. I do not know who are my friends or my family. I only know my name. My name is my password."

"Whoa, Samantha," Edward stopped her. "Just what does that mean, your name is your password?"

With Edward's question, Samantha found herself once again confused. "I do not know. The words just slipped out. I need to find my Mnemosyne."

"You are talking about the mythical Greek river that would restore memory," Clare conjectured. "Is that what you meant by 'password'?"

Samantha was beginning to feel on the verge of tears. "I do not know. Can you help me?"

Clare came over to the table and took Samantha's hands in her own. "Take it easy, my dear. I suspect that you had some kind of accident up there on the hill at Twin Peaks. Perhaps you slipped and fell and hit your head, or something. I'm sure your memory will come back."

Samantha looked into Clare's eyes with gratitude. "I trust you, Clare. And I trust you, Edward. Thank you."

Turning to Edward, Clare said, "I think we should give Andy a call. I'm sure he'll be happy to come over to talk with Samantha." Turning back to Samantha, she explained, "Dr. Andrew Chen is a colleague and friend of ours at UCSF. He's the perfect person to be able to get to the bottom of whatever your amnesia is. He's one of the top neurologists and neuroscientists in the world." Samantha found Clare's faith and confidence most reassuring.

Clare stood up. "I'll go right now and give him a call. Meanwhile, Samantha, why don't you have some salad?" She handed Samantha and Edward salad bowls, then turned and left the room.

Samantha watched Edward intently as he picked up a fork and began to eat his salad. She imitated his actions and smiled as the first bite of a cherry tomato burst against her teeth and the taste exploded on her tongue. "They are organic," Edward informed her, observing her pleasure.

"Of course, they are." *Everybody knows that,* she thought to herself.

"Really good, aren't they?"

Samantha nodded enthusiastically and plunged her fork into the salad bowl to get another mouthful. Samantha and Edward ate in silence until both had finished.

"You were clearly hungry," Edward observed.

"Yes, thank you. And now I am feeling sleepy again."

Edward got up and said, "Why don't you go back into the guest room and get some more sleep? Consider that your room." The two got up, and Edward called out to Clare. Clare took her back down the hallway to her room and told her to make herself at home. Handing her an extra set of pajamas and a robe, she finished with, "Good night, and sleep well. We'll see you in the morning."

Samantha lay down on her back on the bed, with her head cradled between two feather pillows. She closed her eyes, raised her hands to the sides of her head, and placed her fingers so that they were touching both temples. Slowly and gently she began humming, and at the same time rhythmically tapped the forefinger and middle finger of each hand against her temples in an alternating pattern. Within seconds she had fallen into a deep and restful sleep.

CHAPTER 28

Mojave Desert, Day Six, 12:30 a.m.

SAMANTHA WAS GENTLY AWAKENED BY A TAP FROM ZJON AND BY MELISSA'S VOICE. "Wake up, Samantha." She realized she had been asleep in the vehicle, dreaming about her first meeting with Edward and Clare. Looking around, she saw that all was dark, except for the sparkling of stars in the clear night sky. She could make out in the darkness that they were surrounded by mountainous terrain with very sparse vegetation. The night was moonless. "Where are we?"

Zjon said, "You are in a very safe place, in a desert, near the ship."

Samantha's body instinctively shifted into timespace attunement. Without straining her eyes, she could now see that they were sitting inside some kind of canyon, partly surrounded by the half-moon shape of enormous rock walls. She also could see the outline of something else rising out of the desert floor, silhouetted against the twilight. It had looked at first like one of the many big rocks that jutted up from the desert floor. Instinctively, she knew this was their ship. Indeed, in this place, it was perfectly camouflaged.

"Follow me, and be careful where you step. There are cactus plants that really hurt when you step on them," said Zjon.

The three visitors from another time eased their way out of the car. As they emerged, Samantha looked up to see the great white swath of the Milky Way, like paintbrush strokes across the desert sky. This had never failed to move her deeply. Somehow she knew that she would always be touched when she came into contact with the continuum of the eternal. She felt a deep, profound sense of appreciation. It was beautiful.

Zjon interrupted her reverie. "Yes, it is, is it not? It will not be long before you will remember everything. Let us go into the ship now."

From behind them, Melissa spoke. "You forgot about me. Please allow me to help." Instantaneously the vehicle morphed into another shape and began to hover about one foot above the ground. Now appearing like some kind of shelled creature, resembling a giant conch shell, Melissa extended a platform in their direction. Following Zjon and Neal, Samantha stepped up onto Melissa's platform. The foursome then glided into an opening that had appeared in the side of the ship.

As they stepped out of the vehicle, the ship's walls resealed themselves behind them. Looking around, Samantha noticed they were standing inside a cavernous room that had several other rooms stemming from it, like the spokes of a wheel. The vehicle that called itself "Melissa" now blended into the wall behind her, like just another one of the spokes. Samantha spotted another woman standing across from them in the center of the main room. This woman had jet-black hair and appeared to be in her late twenties or early thirties, about the same age as Samantha. "Sunanda!" she burst out with glee. Zjon and Neal laughed as the two women rushed to give each other a big hug.

"Wow," the new woman marveled. "Neal really did a masterful job on you. I hardly recognized you. And I was afraid you would not recognize me."

Zjon interrupted the happy reunion. "The disguise is no longer necessary, and Samantha will return to her normal shape before morning. Samantha, do you really remember Sunanda?"

"I have no memory at all of who she is, but her name jumped out of my mouth without thinking about it," Samantha replied. "I know that I know you. You are like a sister."

"That is close enough for now," Sunanda responded. "You are with family again. In the next three days, it will all come back to you. I am simply thrilled that you recalled my name."

Neal busied himself with some routine ship business, walking around and alternately talking to and touching various control mechanisms. Colored lights blinked in response, followed by automated verbal responses. Meanwhile, Zjon and Sunanda guided Samantha into the main room. "Do you remember any of this?" Zjon asked.

"I think so. I mean, I feel it. Everything is so familiar to me. It feels like I am at home here."

"That is a good sign, indeed."

For the next several minutes, the others watched in amusement as Samantha wandered around, closely inspecting the various mechanisms. She looked at it, touched it, and even smelled it. She closed her eyes for several seconds and listened carefully to the pulsating hums that surrounded them. These sounded to her like her own heartbeat, so familiar and yet in a way so foreign. She knew the ship was talking to her through all of her eight senses. Everything was becoming very, very right. She felt her presence more fully and clearly than she had in what seemed like a long, long time. Her name was Samantha, and this was her password.

When Neal gave Zjon the signal that all was ready, Zjon shifted into command mode, and turning to Sunanda, ordered, "Sunanda, escort Samantha to the gathering chamber. We have no time to waste." His tone had turned to business.

"Right, Commander." Sunanda walked over to Samantha and took her by the hand. "Come with me. We have no time to waste."

"Aren't you going to take me yourself, Zjon?" Samantha asked with a puzzled expression.

"No, Samantha. Neal and Sunanda are going to manage everything from here. I am too close to you, and I do not want to interfere in the process. But have no worry, they will take very good care of you tonight."

Before leaving the room, Samantha turned to Sunanda and said, "Wait just a minute." Then Samantha walked over to Zjon and gave him a warm embrace. She then turned back to Sunanda and said, "Okay, I am ready."

The two women followed Neal as he led the way to one of the small rooms in a corner of the ship's main cavity. Inside the room, Samantha saw some kind of horizontal chamber connected to a number of tubes, which in turn joined with several other devices that she did not recognize, each attached to a wall with a bank of blinking, colored lights. If she unfocused her eyes, she noticed that the lights created the impression of rainbows. The chamber was enclosed in some kind of transparent membrane and rested about one foot above the floor. It was open at the top but appeared to have a lid that could be closed. To Samantha it looked like what twenty-first-century people referred to as a coffin.

"So this is it," she said.

"Yes, this is it." Neal was standing next to the head end of the chamber. That end was several inches wider than the foot of the chamber. Sunanda guided her over to the chamber and stood beside her, and Neal began to explain. "The process is completely painless, and you will be in a suspended sleep-like state the whole time. Each session takes about six hours, and we will conduct one session per night. These tubes will circulate a liquid-like mixture of nutrients and intelligent nanoparticles through the chamber. It will be like taking a bath, except you will have no problem breathing. You may from time to time experience lights, as light bathing is part of the process. That will all be familiar to you, since it is not unlike what you experience as a backfire when you do hand-and-breath signaling sessions. Do you have any questions?"

"Just one. Will I remember everything from my past life all at once?"

"Good question. What takes place will be both chronological and holographic. We have known for centuries that memory is both holographic and time sequenced. This process works from the inside out, so to speak. Your recollections will be restored following an associative pattern, starting with the earliest and proceeding to the most recent. That is the chronological part. However, it is also holographic in the sense that everything is being restored at once, but in stages or layers. Everything in your life will start out kind of faint, but gradually over the three nights will become clearer and clearer, until the last morning when you wake up, you will have full access to all of it. The other thing that will happen in the final stages is an 'integrating' of your memories from your previous life in our time with your most recent three years spent here in this time. This is vitally important, and it is why we needed to keep you safe so that you can go through the whole process. Your brain, neurons, and cellular memory must be fully integrated. Without this last piece, it could be such a shock that it fractures your personality."

"What happens between sessions?"

"You will feel completely 'normal' but will experience your recollections gradually coming back. Your body will be digesting your past, in a sense. I understand that overall this is a pleasant process."

"Okay! I'm ready. Let's get started!"

Neal laughed. "Your dialect sounds like the way people talk in this time."

"I guess I have picked up some of those traits of speech when I get excited. Verbal contractions are quite useful at times, really."

Sunanda interjected, "I have no idea what you are talking about, but I look forward to learning more these next few days. You should realize, Samantha, this has all been a very foreign experience for the three of us. We are still trying to navigate through this culture and some of its strange customs. We actually have a very unclear picture of what this time is like, since we have only been here a few days. Out of everyone, you are the only one who carries all of the sense of connections between this time and ours. But enough of that. Go ahead and step into the chamber, then lie down on your back with your head at Neal's end."

Samantha did as she instructed.

"Now, place your right hand across your chest, covering your heart, and cross your left arm over it so that the hand rests over your right breast. Just like that. Perfect."

Neal leaned over Samantha and performed a signal with his hands, first holding them together above her face and then quickly allowing them to fly apart, as if clearing the air away along with any particles of negativity. Samantha's mind cleared instantly. He then blew three short breaths onto her forehead, and Samantha plunged immediately into a restful sleep as her sense of time came to a stop.

Sunanda drew the lid closed, sealing the chamber. Neal signaled the rear wall panels, and a deep blue liquid shot through the tubes, filling the chamber. Samantha's body floated inside the chamber, equidistant from the top, bottom, and sides. A few moments later, there appeared waves of light, shimmering in all the colors of the rainbow in every direction around her body. These gave the illusion at times of multicolored butterflies fluttering around and enveloping her.

The process had begun.

CHAPTER 29

In the Ship, Day Six, 1:00 a.m.

"I REMEMBER SO CLEARLY THE FIRST TIME I SAW SAMANTHA." ZJON WAS WITH NEAL AND Sunanda in the main room of the ship. They were all sipping their forty-sixth-century meal-replacement protein drinks and had just settled back to wait while Samantha went through the first phase of her process. "It was as if my heart just exploded. I thought to myself, 'Who is this remarkable woman?' I sensed we belonged together forever."

Sunanda nodded her head. "I know what you mean. It was like that in many ways when we met as roommates the first day of academy. It felt like we had been sisters forever."

"Tell us again about your out-of-time experience with her," Neal encouraged Zjon.

"That happened the same day, shortly after we first met. We were in a restaurant eating together, when suddenly I saw that she was in a different time. It was a very strange sensation. I thought, 'Oh my God, what is she doing there?' It occurred suddenly in a flash, like a purple light. But of course, I never thought of this as being about her space accident a dozen years later. How could I?"

"Yes, but you knew it was the past from the color?"

"Right. As you know, the purple horizon indicates the past, while the blue horizon is the horizon of the future. I thought I was just imagining what I saw. It felt very confusing to me. I had the sensation that she had emerged directly from the past into the present.

Of course, there is no way to do that, so I just dismissed it. It did not register until this timespace appropriation event. Actually, at the time I was just enamored with this woman!"

"She is, indeed, one of a kind," agreed Sunanda.

"Hey," Neal chimed in. "Remember that time, Sunanda, in our third year of academy when we sneaked off the campus and went swimming in the lake?" The three of them were contemporaries from the same class in the Space Academy. The Space Academy in the forty-sixth century was located in the northern section of the California region, on the peninsula that rested in the location south of the ancient city that we now call Golden Gate.

"I remember very well."

"Remind me of this story," Zjon requested. Zjon did not remember being there on that occasion.

"Well, eight of us went down to Santa Clara Lake and stripped off our clothes. Then we all held hands to jump into the lake at the place where the bank is about five feet above the water. The water is about fifteen feet deep there. You must remember this, Zjon, because you arrived just as we were about to jump in."

"Oh, yes, how could I forget?"

"We all jumped in together. But somehow when Samantha landed in the water, she dislocated her shoulder. Samantha told me later that she was writhing in pain and began to sink to the bottom. Then, all at once it was as if a platform of solid water, like ice but not cold, formed below her and lifted her up so she broke the surface. The rest of us in the water were completely amazed to see her pushed up out of the water and shoot across through the air above our heads, back toward the bank."

"Right into my arms." Zjon was remembering the incident clearly now. How could he have forgotten that experience? "I will never forget the look on Samantha's face as we both realized I had caught her. I saw what had happened to her shoulder and quickly put it back into place. It was another of those unbelievable moments in life that you cannot explain logically. One of those things that clued me into how special Samantha is."

"It was not long after that you proposed a contract relationship, if I recall," said Sunanda.

"That is correct. We soon initiated our first mutual-consent love cohabitation contract, which we have continued to renew every three years since." Zjon smiled as he looked back over the ensuing years.

The three astronauts from the future spent the next hour having a great time recalling the wild events they had experienced together. They found themselves filled with enormous energy and joy, knowing that Samantha was safely back with them at last. They were full of confidence that the four of them would be able to return home within the allotted timespace window, which was set to expire in just four days.

This thought brought Zjon's attention back to the present situation. He looked at the ship's space chronometer and saw that the time was approaching zero two thirty local. Samantha had been in the chamber for ninety minutes, leaving four and one-half hours until she would complete her first night's session. Zjon realized that, in spite of their adrenalin, he and his cohorts were all very tired. They had a lot to do and needed to be at full attention capacity for the next three days, so he said, "I hate to break this up, but we need to get some rest. We have an important job to do over the next three days. We are going to take rest shifts of ninety minutes each."

Neal asked, "Zjon, why do we not imbibe the wake potion again?"

The crew had carried a specially formulated potion that, when ingested, would keep a person awake and alert for seventy-two hours at a time. It was a combined synthetic–organic compound in serum form that scientists had genetically engineered a little more than a thousand years before, when the Global Federation University Network had cracked the timespace code that made possible true interstellar, timespace travel.

Zjon said, "No, we need some authentic sleep rest. Since we each took one dose of wake potion for the first seventy-two hours after arriving here, followed by another, it would be a bad idea to go for another three days without true sleep regeneration. We should do this in shifts, so that two of us are available to handle any situation that might arise. Who wants to go first?"

Sunanda told Zjon, "You should go first, as our commander. You have exerted yourself more than we have. We can wait."

"Very well, then. Neal, would you give me a signaling?"

He turned and walked over to a blank wall on one side of the ship. As if responding to his presence, the wall unfolded itself into a formation that resembled a bed. Zjon lay down on his back, folded his arms across his chest, and closed his eyes. His body appeared to be hovering a few inches above the mattress. In reality, he was suspended by a finely controlled cushion of air, which made for the most comfortable sleeping. In response to his request, Neal walked across the room and administered the standard sleep signal.

CHAPTER 30

Some Time-Where, Unlocking Session One

WHILE THE OTHERS SLEPT, SAMANTHA WAS ENJOYING HER OWN PERSONAL HALF-DREAM, half-real light show. It was like Aurora Borealis, but inside her head instead of in the northern sky. Blue, green, yellow, and red fireballs danced across her internal horizons. Occasionally, one would explode, filling her head with white, blue, or golden light. She could feel the light expanding behind her eyeballs, filling her skull cavity, and spilling down through her body to her fingertips and toes. Interspersed among the lights, she felt her body buffeted by a gentle, cool breeze. During those moments, she recognized her body to be in Zone Eight.

As the sense of timeless time unfolded through her nervous system and cellular membranes, she began to experience moments of recognition. All was in a state of temporality, but seemingly void of time. Time was unencumbered by the boundaries of counting. Thoughts roamed free from the constraints of wording. Then, for an unbounded eternity, her present world ceased its worlding. All that was present in her consciousness was that her name was Samantha, and this was her password.

Showing themselves bit by bit, there began to arise flashes of images, images constructed in light, in sound, in sensation, in emotion, in words, in timespace.

A door appeared before her inner eyes. The door flew open, revealing a scene from her childhood. She was two years old. Daddy was now a governor. His face was warm and loving. He smoked a pipe and laughed with Mommy. They took her into the sunlight on a picnic. She felt the energy of nature. There were sparkles all around. They told her this was the Intelligence. Intelligence was playing with her. Just as quickly as it had appeared, the scene disappeared.

In an instant a second door appeared and swung open. She was now four years old. Her parents had left her room, and she was playing with some kind of a computer device. It made things appear in her room, holographic things. Mommy and Daddy told her these were her toys. When she touched them, sounds and lights jumped out and stood around her in her room. They played with her and talked with her. They were her new friends. Dogs and cats, and horses and cows, and goats and birds, and flowers in rainbow colors.

In a flash she became aware of her family. Her mother was a teacher of world history. She had one other sister and two brothers. They must have lived in a place of luxury because they had gardens. Many people did not have gardens. Most people lived in high rises. Her family was special. They lived in their own house with a garden.

They were rich. Samantha now remembered that while growing up she always had the sense of feeling very excited about something. Then one day in third grade she realized she was excited about the Unknown.

The next door opened, and a new scene replaced the last one. Samantha remembered that when she was a little girl she had the ability to play with the flower gardens and the trees by using her hands. Her hands could call forth the Intelligence in everything around her. Then she would spin and spin and spin, and she never fell down. She and her friends would play the spinning game together. She never lost her balance. She never felt dizzy. She and her friends wanted to see who could spin the longest.

Another scene appeared to her as the last one dissolved. She was seven years old. She kept being attracted to one particular flower in the garden. It was a sweet-smelling flower, a little bigger than a jasmine blossom. She knew she had been going to visit the flower every day for weeks, attracted to its wonderful sweet smell. Then one day while she was smelling this flower, it slowly began to withdraw and contract. As she watched in rapt attention, the flower grew smaller and smaller, until it completely disappeared. When it disappeared, she cried her heart out. Her parents came and consoled her. They said, "Do not worry." She said, "No, I want it." She was inconsolable. That night when she went to sleep, she dreamed the flower was like a fan twirling above her head. She dreamed it came down from the ceiling toward her forehead. Finally, it entered her forehead, and the image was gone. When she woke up in the morning, she smelled so good. She was happy. When she went to school, everybody asked her, "What is that smell? You smell like jasmine."

Again a door opened into another time. She saw herself as a young girl of twelve. One day she was standing in the schoolyard when she suddenly felt a sensation. She turned around, left the schoolyard, and ran toward the town center. After she got there, she saw a hover taxi. Without thinking, she ran over and jumped into the backseat. She told the driver to take her to a place whose name she happened to remember. It turned out that the place was six hours away. All the way she talked to the driver and sang to him. Not knowing how she knew, she gave the driver directions as they appeared in her mind. Then at a certain point, she got an urge to do some movements with her hands. Something like an invisible cloak appeared out of her hands and surrounded the car. Everybody who was watching could see the car become completely transparent. She told the driver to stop, and then she got out. To her utter surprise, standing there in front of her was one of her aunts, Auntie Jill.

Auntie Jill said, "What are you doing here? How did you come?"

"Well, I came in a hover cab."

"You need to go home. Why did you come?"

"Oh, I just wanted to come." She knew she was being very pure, very clean, and clear.

Auntie Jill led her to her own car and flew her back home. When Samantha arrived, it caused a huge commotion. Her father and mother laughed when Auntie Jill told them the story. They pretended to be mad at Samantha but could not hide their smiles.

A connected door flew open in her mind. The picture had jumped to years later, when she was at the Space Academy. One day there was a knock at the door. She opened it and standing in front of her was the cab driver. He was holding some flowers and handed them to her. He said to her, "You touched my life. After I drove you, my life changed. Now I own an entire fleet of hover taxis. My whole life is blessed. Thank you."

In the chamber, Samantha continued on and on in her conscious dreaming. She was experiencing moments of prime awakenings of the heart. Each memory was like the push of the button of Innocence. With each push of the button, a key memory was unlocked from her neurons and cells. Each moment was like a hologram slowly coming alive, starting out like a hazy cloud and crystalizing itself into full-dimensional existence. The feelings were intensely pleasurable as Samantha recognized herself emerging as a unique human being, gradually and gently becoming complete.

At six in the morning, she awoke to see herself surrounded by the smiling faces of her three friends. One of them was holding out a glass of orange juice. While she still could not place these people from her past, she knew in her bones that they were her best friends. She reached up and accepted the juice. "I am Samantha, and I was born on Earth and came here from the forty-sixth century. How did I get here?"

Neal and Sunanda looked at Zjon. Zjon said, "Patience, my love. All will come in good time."

CHAPTER 31

Mount Charleston, Day Six, 11:30 a.m.

THE SLIGHTLY BEAT UP, WHITE, 1994 DODGE CARAVAN ES ROLLED ALONG NEVADA State Route 157, heading west. Its destination was Mount Charleston. At the wheel sat Dan Hamilton. To his right was Jonathan, and in the backseat were Edward and Clare. A short while before they had passed north of Red Rock Canyon National Conservation Area, known by locals as "Red Rock." Soon they would be approaching the intersection with SR 158, which would mean they were near the place where Zjon had instructed them to pull off the road and begin their hike. Dan had received precise instructions by phone from Zjon that morning as the group was finishing their breakfast in the Bellagio Buffet. The four of them were to drive to a remote location in the wilderness area near Mount Charleston. There had been no explanations, and no questions allowed.

Dan listened as David Newman grumbled into the cell phone. "I still don't know why they picked such a remote location for meetin' you. Do you realize the trouble I'm havin' to go through to keep my guys scattered around to make sure you are safe?"

"I know, I know, David," Dan commiserated, at the same time rolling his eyes as he looked over to Jonathan.

Jonathan just smiled. He, too, was beginning to understand and recognize David's histrionics. Jonathan had learned from Dan over the past several days how important a role David Newman had played in helping them with Mission Heart. *Still,* Jonathan thought, *give us a break. This isn't your ordinary assignment. We're all having to make some sacrifices here.*

"It really pisses me off that I can't be there with you. You gotta tell me every last detail!"

"I will, David. I'll be in touch as soon as we get done. Thanks for handling everything. We need to sign off now. I think we're getting near the trail."

At last Dan ended the call. To the group he said, "David assures us there's no one following us, and that nobody can trace our car." David had met them at the Bellagio with the car, which he claimed he had picked up from a pawnshop that morning. While not a modern SUV, the ES was a well-built sports model of the classic Dodge Caravan line. It would have no problem handling whatever rugged terrain they had to drive through to reach the trailhead. And best of all, they could ditch it if they had to. Dan went on to share, "You know, I had one of these twenty years ago. Drove it with a bunch of friends to a ranch in the Grand Tetons."

"What are you talking about?" Jonathan asked.

"Oh, sorry. I was thinking out loud. Guess I'm going to sleep very well when this mission is finished."

"I know what you mean."

From the backseat, Clare said, "I brought plenty of water. Let's take it on our hike. You can get really dehydrated up here."

"Good thinking," Jonathan said.

"Here we are." Dan pointed to a half-covered road sign marking a dirt road on the right. He made the turn and gunned the engine to get started up the incline of the well-rutted road.

Fifteen minutes later they came to a dead end in front of a rickety old sign announcing, "The Charleston Trail. Founded 1936. Beware of wildlife." There were no other cars around, and the trail looked like it might not have been used since the Depression Era. It appeared to be the perfect spot for a remote and private rendezvous. Jonathan thought it was interesting that their visitors from the future would know about this place.

"Well, let's get started," Dan shut off the engine, and they all got out of the car. Edward pulled out a backpack, and Clare put four Fuji water bottles inside and zipped it up.

Without further conversation, Dan took the lead and started walking up the trail. The trail meandered gently at first through some open, green fields, then turned abruptly into a series of switchbacks that wound up a hillside. Ahead the climbers could see that the trail disappeared from view among the underbrush and finally reappeared at the edge of a dense pine forest. Above the tree line, they could see a series of gray, craggy rocks. At times they could catch a view of Charleston Peak several miles away. They were now deep in the pine forest, and the air was fragrant and fresh. Everything was quiet, the silence broken only occasionally by the sound of a woodpecker.

The group walked among the pines as the trail seemed to meander in a random fashion. Dan was just about to decide they had gone too far and suggest they turn back, when all at once they came upon a wide clearing in the woods. On one side of the clearing a green, algae-covered boulder poked up about five feet above the ground.

"This is it," Dan announced. "That's the rock they told me to look for, and this must be the clearing."

The place was empty. Jonathan looked around and said, "So, where are they?"

"Good question," Dan replied.

Edward said, "Don't worry, friends. If Samantha told you they would be here, they will be. We should just be patient and wait. Anybody want water?"

"Thanks, I'll have some," Dan said.

Clare took the four bottles out of Edward's pack and handed them out. The four hikers moseyed over to inspect the rock. Just as Jonathan was about to take a drink, he heard the sound of laughter. "Listen." Everybody's ears perked up as the sound of Samantha's and Zjon's laughing voices reached them, seemingly from all directions at once. They all looked around, disoriented and somewhat confused.

Samantha and Zjon suddenly appeared in the center of the clearing. "You guys are so impatient!" Zjon hailed them. The two stood hand in hand with smiles on their faces.

The four hikers stood up to greet them. "Good afternoon to you, as well," Jonathan answered. All six members of the happy reunion began to laugh for no reason. "We're happy to see you again."

"So are we," said Samantha.

"Seriously," Dan said. There was annoyance in his voice. "Why the big production? It surely would have been easier to meet us in town and could have been just as secure."

Zjon answered, "We have something to show you, and we needed a place where absolute seclusion was guaranteed. I surveyed the area and saw that this would be the best location for us to meet in complete privacy."

"Wait a minute!" It was Clare. "There's something different, and I almost didn't notice it. You're back to your old self!"

Indeed, no one had noticed before this moment that Samantha's face and hair had been transformed back to their original appearance. She was now once again a long-haired blonde with Scandinavian facial features and deep blue eyes.

"Yes," Zjon answered. "During the memory-gathering process last night, her disguise was discarded. It is no longer necessary, since we will not be exposing Samantha to public view again."

"Actually, we want to talk with you about that, Zjon." Jonathan decided to take the opportunity to bring up what he and Dan had been plotting the night before.

"We will have time to talk later. I know what you are going to ask me. At this moment, however, we have other things to attend to. Between now and two nights from now when Samantha has her memories fully restored and integrated, this is the opportunity for us to become more connected. Whether you are fully aware of it or not, the four of you have played very special roles in what is happening. Edward and Clare, you have adopted Samantha as if she were your own daughter. Jonathan and Dan, the two of you have become our trusted friends and put your careers on the line for her. You have made it possible for us to come to Samantha at this critical time. We both hold all of you in our highest esteem and trust. In return, we want to share with you some things that will be good and helpful as well."

"There's not much one can say to that," Jonathan said.

Dan pointed out, "But there's not even a good place to sit right here. Couldn't we go to the restaurant? Surely you can work your magic to keep people from eavesdropping."

"Do not worry about a place to sit." With that, Zjon reached into his jacket pocket and pulled out a small cube. The cube appeared to be about one inch in each dimension, with color on its faces. Zjon said, "Watch closely." He then turned and tossed the cube to the ground, so that it landed about ten feet from the opposite side of the clearing. In an instant there sprang up in its place a large, dome-shaped, tent-like object. They could see it was not a tent, however. The structure seemed to have a shiny, intricate texture. Its walls were solid, and there was no entrance. It was hexagonal in shape, with each face being six or seven feet tall.

Zjon turned to the group and said, "Come on in, everyone." He took Samantha by the hand, and the two of them walked up to the nearest wall. Just as they were about to collide with it, the wall opened, and they walked inside. The wall closed immediately behind them.

Edward laughed and said, "Well, Clare, what are we waiting for?" He took her hand, and the two of them followed. Just as before, the wall appeared to open up for them to enter, and as soon as they had gone through, it closed again. This left Dan and Jonathan standing outside, shocked.

Dan turned to Jonathan and joked, "Well, don't expect me to hold your hand." The two then followed the others, side-by-side, and were also immediately swallowed by the structure.

CHAPTER 32

Nothing and Everything

THE SIX UNLIKELY COMPANIONS STOOD INSIDE WHAT APPEARED TO BE A LARGE, EMPTY room. The space seemed much larger from the inside than it had from the outside. In fact, it looked cavernous. The walls were completely white. There was no sign of lights, but the dome-shaped room was well lit, and it was completely empty except for the people themselves.

Clare was the first to speak. "Wow, what is this place?"

Zjon answered, "This is where we are going to have our first private conversation together."

"But there's nothing in here."

Zjon then said cryptically, "'Nothing' is actually what we need because nothing is already filled with whatever we wish. But we cannot see this because we live in doubt and distraction. There is nothing that, as such, exists in here. But for the time being, for good or bad, Samantha had her accident, and we are here-now together. That is not exactly nothing."

Zjon paused to allow Jonathan, Dan, Edward, and Clare to let his words sink in. Jonathan noticed that for himself this made absolutely no sense, but it seemed to be pointing to something. At last he admitted, "Zjon, this makes no sense to me. I can't understand it."

"Precisely. You need to look somewhere other than your verbal, intellectual understanding to see it. When you look at your lives, you already know that many things in life lie outside the grasp of your understanding. The best things, in fact."

Edward said, "So, where should we look?"

"Rather than answer your question, let me show you something. Everyone, close your eyes."

The four of them closed their eyes. Dan said, "Okay, now what?"

"I am going to give a signal. Samantha will explain to you fully about signaling the day after tomorrow. For now, just keep your eyes closed until I tell you to open them."

Zjon held out both of his hands toward the group, his palms facing forward with his fingers pointing upward. He nodded to Samantha to do the same. He then spread his fingers apart and began to move them in the air, as if they were drying them when they were wet. Samantha did the same. Samantha and Zjon looked as if they were possibly casting some kind of magic spell on the other four. After about ten seconds, the two of them stopped and Zjon commanded, "Open your eyes."

To their astonishment, when they opened their eyes, they saw that there were twenty or thirty metallic boxes of different sizes scattered around the room. Then they noticed that behind them were four stools, like barstools, which were made of hardwood and had soft black cushions on top. Zjon motioned to them to take a seat.

As he sat down, Jonathan felt as if his stool was floating rather than resting on a solid floor. The others noticed the same thing. Clare exclaimed, "Wow! This is really cool! How did you do that?"

"Who says I did anything?"

"But you made these things appear. How?"

Samantha answered her, "Clare, they were already here. Zjon did not do anything except send a signal to Intelligence, and you found yourself able to see what was always there."

"This is too much!" Jonathan laughed. "This is the wildest thing I have seen since back in my old drug days in college. It even beats the last few days, which were already far wilder than I could explain."

Edward pointed to the various box-like items scattered around the room. "What are these things?"

"Would you like something sweet?" Zjon asked. "Like hot chocolate?"

"Why not!" Dan exclaimed.

Zjon held out his two forefingers in the direction of one of the boxes that sat against a wall and drew his two fingers apart, as if making a straight line in the air. Instantaneously, the box transformed into what appeared to be a modern refrigerator. But it was not a refrigerator because it had no door on the front. Inside there were what looked like containers on a series of shelves. On the top shelf was a row of drinking cups. Zjon walked over, reached in, and pulled out one of the containers. He then took a cup and poured a dark liquid from the container into it. He turned around and handed it to Dan. The cup was steaming in Dan's hands.

Dan bent down to take a whiff of the contents. He then took a tentative sip. "Wow! This is delicious!" he said. The others witnessed this event unfold in wonder.

Zjon then said to the group, "You live in the twenty-first century. Samantha and I are from twenty-five hundred years in the future. By then, you have to realize, if we could not manifest things with our fingertips, we would never have been able to travel through time. I am not going to try to explain this any further." Zjon continued, "The human race will learn about this and many other things in future centuries. As I said last night at dinner, it is not for us to interfere in your time. I did this as a demonstration to eliminate any remaining doubts you might have. It is important that you understand the crucial role you are playing in what must happen over the next three days."

The four looked very serious.

Samantha laughed. "And you do not have to be serious, either! Anybody else want hot chocolate?" With that the mood lightened. Samantha proceeded to pour them all cups of hot chocolate. The six sat together enjoying their drinks.

After a few minutes, Jonathan asked, "Can you please teach us how to bring this technology to our world today? Compared to you, we live like barbarians. It seems as if you have mastered science and used it to create the world humankind has always dreamed about. Your time sounds like it must be a kind of paradise."

Zjon thought for several seconds and then answered, "No, Jonathan, I am afraid I cannot. We are talking about human evolution here, and you are asking me to interfere with that. Think of it this way. We, as the human race, always lived facing the unknown. At each moment in history we have learned from what was needed for that time. A good example is the wheel. You could say this was perhaps the first invention that launched the long process of coevolution between human and machine that would eventually produce the world in which you dwell today, which you call the 'technological age.' The wheel provided a stepping-stone for all of us to reach the next level.

"In your time, in comparison to us in our time, the human race is in an evolutionary stage called 'adolescence.' As a metaphor, the hormones are kicking for the whole human race right now. The wrong technology, that is, a new technology that is wrong for your time, could be very destructive. Let me put it another way: The unknown you are facing today is calling for an evolution of the whole spirit. I am not talking at all about religion; I am talking about something much more fundamental."

"But please, could you give at least some of this advanced technology to our doctors?" Clare asked. "People in our world are suffering unnecessarily, and many are dying. Surely there are some things that you could share that would genuinely help humanity."

"Again, that would be interfering with the evolution of humankind. You need to go through the steps to learn these things for yourselves. But at least consider the possibility that the next step for the people of your time will not be found in science and technology, but within yourselves. You have innate capacities that you can develop. Besides, no matter how great the science and technology we have developed may be, as you have witnessed, Samantha's accident shows that even the highest form of technological prowess is still subject to the principles of Unpredictability, Impermanence, and Imperfection."

After a short pause, Zjon continued. "I will say this much to you. Most of the diseases you are suffering from right now will be eradicated within the next three hundred years. Also, it is actually around your current time when millions of children of genius will be born. You are rapidly approaching the time of a great opening."

Once again the tone of the group had become serious. Sensing this, Dan asked, "Are we really drinking hot chocolate? Or is it an illusion?"

Laughing, Zjon said, "All the things you have been experiencing are absolutely real, I assure you." He looked at Samantha and then at each of the others and continued. "Now, it is time for us to go. We will speak about more, but later." With that, he stood up. Taking Samantha by the hand, the two walked back toward the wall through which they had entered. As before, the wall seemed to part as if making way for them. The others followed.

Once they had all exited, Zjon turned back toward the tent-like structure and made a rapid motion with his right fist. The motion resembled a violent brush stroke that an artist might make to splash paint onto a canvas for a modern abstract painting. Immediately, the structure collapsed back into the small cube.

"How did you do that?" Edward asked. "How did you bring that about, just with your hand and this little, crazy cube? Can I borrow that cube?"

Zjon laughed once again. "I am sure you already know the answer to that question." After a pause, he concluded, "I think we have had enough for one day. Now it is time for you to return to the hotel. I will contact you again in the morning to arrange our next meeting." He started to turn to leave, taking Samantha by the hand.

"Wait!" Dan called.

Zjon turned back to face him. "Yes?"

"You must be aware that I'm an agent of the US government. They know about Samantha and are expecting me to bring her to them. They aren't going to accept any more failure from me. These are very powerful people, and they're rapidly losing their patience. You've told us why you're here, and why you need to take Samantha back to your time. You can trust me that I believe you, even if I don't fully understand. But I have a problem. I can't stall them much longer."

"This is what you were going to ask me about earlier?"

"Yes."

"And if you keep stalling them?"

"They will take extreme measures, which could include sending in the military. Think about it, Zjon. No matter how good you guys are, with your magic technology, this could cause a huge mess. You said you didn't want to interfere. However, in a big way you already have."

"I can feel that you have a solution to propose."

Dan relaxed at this point, realizing that Zjon was already on the same page. He nodded to Jonathan to take it from here.

Jonathan took the cue, "Yes, Dan is completely right, and we have an idea. We tell them the truth. That is, we tell them part of the truth. We tell them that Samantha is from the future and that she wants to meet them to tell them something very important. She wants to give them an interview, but it has to be here in Las Vegas. Why Vegas? Because she has something to show them. Maybe the ship or something."

Dan picked up, saying, "Top members of the president's advisers, as well as selected top scientists and scholars, and perhaps Jonathan representing the press, will be the only people invited. You will name the time and place for the meeting."

Jonathan jumped back in. "You've been telling us that Samantha has to return with you three days from now. This is the one thing that we withhold from them. Samantha can give them the interview, and then you all can escape. I assume that you can do that without a problem, using the element of surprise."

"Don't leave us out," Edward jumped in. "Clare and I also know a lot of good people to include in that interview."

Samantha turned to Zjon and urged him, "Zjon, I trust these people. I can feel what is in their hearts."

Zjon replied, "Then, so be it." Turning to Dan, he said, "Arrange the meeting for noon, three days from today. You decide the right place. You decide the right people. Samantha and I will be there. Neal and Sunanda will have the ship ready and positioned for us to make a successful exit. We will take off at 3:33 p.m."

"David and I were talking about this last night. The best place would be somewhere near McCarran Airport. We will obtain authority to have the FAA close the airport that day. You could use the airport to take off with your ship. I assume that would work for you?"

"That would work perfectly. It also would enable us to provide a parting gift."

"What kind of gift?"

"You will see, and you will like it. You should let others witness our departure, including your news agencies."

"Sounds good. As for the interview, David and I will figure out the best place, probably one of the local hotels with a conference room."

Edward put in, "Jonathan, you and Clare and I should put our heads together and come up with a list of people to invite."

"Great. Then Dan can present all of this to his chief, and we can get the ball rolling."

"Sounds like a plan, then." Dan said to Zjon, "We're good."

"Thank you." Zjon started to turn to go once again.

"Wait!" It was Jonathan this time.

"Yes?" Zjon turned back.

"Is there any way we can go back to our hotel from here, without all that walking and driving?"

Zjon grinned. "This one time, I will give you a treat so that you do not have to spend two hours getting back. But, you will have to send somebody back for your car. Close your eyes, and do not open them until I tell you. Closing your eyes actually changes your perception and your nervous system. I need you to do that, for purposes of something like anesthesia." The four of them closed their eyes. Zjon continued, "Now, count from one to ten."

By the count of three, Jonathan sneaked a peak, and exclaimed, "Dan, open your eyes!" The four opened their eyes and saw to their astonishment that they were in Edward and Clare's suite at the Bellagio.

Dan laughed. "Unbelievable! David's going to just love my next phone call."

CHAPTER 33

The Situation Room, Day Six, 10:00 p.m.

"ALL RISE FOR THE PRESIDENT."

The highest-level officials of the US government, the intelligence communities, and the military stood to greet the president of the United States. With quiet determination, the president walked to the seat at the head of the table, nodded to the group, and sat down. His chief of staff closed the door behind him.

The president immediately spoke. "Thank you for coming on such short notice. I trust that each of you has had time enough to review the briefing papers for this meeting. Clearly, this is not a normal situation, and I made the call that it warrants our being careful and thoughtful, at the highest levels. This is a situation unlike any we have ever faced before.

"I know that some of you have been in this room on several occasions, and that for a couple of you this is the first time. Let me make the rules clear. You are here as an official representing the people of the United States. We will address each other by title, rather than by name. Understood?"

"Yes, Mr. President."

"Good. Also, be aware that each of you has signed the pledge of confidentiality that you found in your briefing book. Any leak or any failure to maintain strictest confidentiality, even with your spouses and your staff, will be considered an act of treason. Do I make myself clear?"

"Yes, Mr. President."

"Thank you. Last, tonight I want to hear what each of you has to say. But I only want to hear it one time. All decisions in this matter rest with me. Understood?"

"Yes, Mr. President."

"I realize that what you have read in your briefing materials may sound farfetched, and even wild. Ordinarily the claims made there would be considered a hoax, but we need to take them seriously. The truth is that we do not know what we are facing."

With that, the president took a deep breath. "Okay. You have undoubtedly noticed that the vice president is absent. He would normally be here, but as you know, he is at a meeting in India. Instead, due to the unusual and important nature of this particular situation, I have invited the two highest-ranking members of Congress. First, our esteemed Speaker of the House." The president nodded to the Speaker, who returned a dignified nod in acknowledgment. "And also the senate majority leader." The president and majority leader exchanged nods. "I have a commitment that we must keep this situation from becoming politicized, and I trust that you both share that commitment." The two congressional leaders nodded in unison.

"We appreciate that, Mr. President," acknowledged the senate majority leader.

"Good. A second point: we do not appear to be facing any kind of military threat at this time. For this reason, I have included only the chairman of the joint chiefs, but have not invited any other members of the military or military advisers. Also, you will notice that I have not included other members of my cabinet, with the exception of the secretary of homeland security. The only other people I want in on this conversation for now are the director of central intelligence—to whom I have given permission to update the director of national intelligence under strictest secrecy—the director of the FBI, my national security adviser, the attorney general, and someone whom most of you have never met and never heard of. Allow me to introduce Wallace Wade. Mr. Wade is the chief of a special unit and has been reporting directly to me on this matter." Each person in the room nodded to acknowledge one another.

"Wallace, who is the only person I will address by first name tonight because he does not have an official title, is actually the person responsible for uncovering and collecting most of the information contained in your briefing. He is a long-standing, trusted friend, and he has the great quality of entertaining absolutely no political ambitions." The two men nodded to each other in keeping with the evening's newly established tradition. "You can call him 'Chief Wade.' By the way, this is not his real name. I better not read the name 'Wallace Wade' anywhere in the papers. Got it?"

"Yes, Mr. President." They all nodded their assurances.

"All right, then. Chief?"

"Good evening, everyone. As you have all read and presumably understood by now, seven days ago the president asked me to investigate some reported anomalies that appeared to be either occurring in or emanating from the Las Vegas area. These included several strange statistical phenomena that had been picked up by one of our supercomputers. It is not really that rare an occasion that strange things get reported and require investigation. Almost invariably in the past, scientists or investigators have managed eventually to account for them, admittedly not to everyone's satisfaction, as the history of UFO sightings and the infamous Area 51 have demonstrated."

With that last comment, the president interrupted. "There is no way that we are going to allow this situation to turn into another Red Scare, or alien invasion, or other similar public outburst. We will not have a national panic on my watch. Please continue."

"Thank you, Mr. President. Things came to a head when people began to report that some kind of barrier was preventing some people, but not others, from entering a neighborhood known as Avalon Village, near the Las Vegas McCarran Airport. We received reports that this invisible barrier was acting like some kind of charged field. One rumor was that a policeman had actually been teleported in his car from one end of the neighborhood to the other. Wisely

acting under the FBI director's oversight through his regional office"—Wallace nodded to the FBI director—"they sent one of their
top agents, Special Agent David Newman, to set up an observation
post in a local park adjoining the neighborhood. The president then
asked me to dispatch one of my top men, Special Investigator Dan
Hamilton. We dubbed this investigation 'Operation Avalon Charged
Field.' Investigator Hamilton and Agent Newman both confirmed the
existence of this field."

"Again, if I may," the president interrupted, "I personally requested Investigator Hamilton for his intelligence and track record
of public service. Please continue."

"After confirming the situation, Hamilton and Newman together
initiated a full investigation at the site. On Sunday, Investigator
Hamilton called in a former acquaintance, based upon an editorial
the man had published in *The New York Times*."

"Excuse me again," the president interjected. "Jonathan Elliot
is a Pulitzer Prize-winning journalist and a trained scientist, not to
mention a personal friend of mine." The president nodded to Wallace
to continue.

"The three managed to pinpoint a key person of interest, one
Samantha Hunter. This started the manhunt that led to New York
City and then back to Las Vegas. At least two other men, one of whom
we understand goes by the name of Zjon, appeared to be connected.
There is no indication thus far that we are dealing with foreign na-
tionals, although we have been unable to confirm Samantha's or the
other men's origins.

"Earlier today Dan Hamilton and Jonathan Elliot succeeded in
having a meeting with the subjects of the manhunt, in a rural area
in the mountains outside of Las Vegas. Their report is shocking, to
say the least. The men claim to be here from twenty-five hundred
years in the future. They claim that Samantha is also from the future, but has been living in the United States for the past three years.
Apparently an accident caused her to have amnesia. Hamilton and
Elliot are both convinced of the veracity of their claims. The three

have demonstrated that they are in possession of a technology that is far ahead of any that we know of today. Ms. Hunter has asked to meet with top leaders in America, as well as a selected group of top scientists and religious leaders from 'our time.' They have requested a meeting on this Saturday afternoon in Las Vegas, at a place to be announced. Questions?"

"Why didn't your agents apprehend Ms. Hunter and the other two men?" This challenge came from the Speaker.

"They managed to elude us. They have some technology at their disposal that allowed them to escape. You saw the incidents described in the briefing. I know Dan Hamilton, and you all know Jonathan Elliot. There were many witnesses who corroborated what Agent Newman reported to his boss and what Hamilton reported to me. These strangers have unusual powers."

"What has happened to the charged field?" This came from the senate majority leader.

"It appears to have vanished, as of a couple of days ago. It disappeared as mysteriously as it appeared. It is also worth noting that not a single person has received any injury during this entire series of episodes. There is no evidence of a hostile intention."

The national security adviser spoke up. "Mr. President, I have a concern that even if these people are telling the truth, it could be very dangerous for you to meet with them. If they really have these powers, they could assassinate you. This is a huge risk. We need to have some way of controlling the situation. And what if they are really terrorists? Or what if they are space aliens masquerading as human beings? We need to consider all the possible risks."

"And," the Speaker added, "what if our agents and that newspaperman are in on this with them? Or what if they're brainwashed? It's hard to believe they have not been able to apprehend them."

The president thought quietly for a few moments. "Let us think this through logically. To begin with, if these were hostile aliens from some other planet, especially having such powers as have been reported, why would they bother trying to set up a meeting with us? Why wouldn't they just attack us without warning? Why would they broadcast their existence to begin with? I think the alien angle is an extremely low probability. We do not seem to be facing that kind of threat.

"Likewise, as to some kind of foreign terrorists, there is nobody in the world who has technological capabilities like those that have been reported. These tactics are frankly above the intellectual level of any extremists that we know. And we have not picked up on the kinds of Internet chatter that indicate an imminent attack. This is just way above their pay grade.

"I actually think we need to employ the principle of Occam's razor. The simplest explanation is probably the one that they are telling us. We should take this as our working hypothesis. We do not have to believe it as absolutely being true, unless and until they prove it to us. But I think it is the right place to start.

"Finally, let us look at the full picture: First, for whatever reason these people are here and have made contact. They have not harmed anyone, and they are building trust with people who we all know to be skeptics. They have successfully escaped our pursuits but still have done no harm to anyone. Second, they have made an offer to meet with us. We are the logical country for them to meet with, due to our democratic principles and our commitment to freedom. Third, they seem to think they have something very important to tell us. Perhaps they are going to share their advanced technology with us. It is certainly worth the risk of having a meeting. Do I hear any objections?"

The room was silent. Everyone was at a loss for a better idea.

"Good, then we are going to agree to a meeting. I will have the chairman of the joint chiefs contact the FAA to shut down McCarran Airport from Friday night through Saturday night. My press secretary will work with me to concoct a cover story. All of us in this room will secretly fly to Nellis Air Force Base, from where we will be transported undercover to a secure location in Las Vegas. Meanwhile, Wallace, your report indicated a request to include several people in particular, right?"

"Yes," Wallace answered. "They have asked to include the pope and the Dalai Lama, as well as high-level American leaders from the Jewish, Muslim, and Hindu faiths, which do not have a single global leader or figurehead."

"The first two will be quite a challenge, but let's see what happens. I know the pope is in Mexico right now, so there is a good chance he will make it. Any other questions?"

"Yes," the director of the FBI said. "Are we to call off the search? What about apprehending them?"

"The first thing your men need to provide is security for the meeting. That is the top priority right now. By the way, I understand congratulations are in order for the fine demonstration of cooperation your men have made so far. Next, it is important that we *not* create a big military presence. However, we need to have some special forces on call in the area, as well as all forces in the proximity on standby in the event of problems. I personally will call all the shots, however. Third, I will deputize Jonathan Elliot with the responsibility for controlling the press. On second thought, I am *not* going to invite the press for this first meeting. That would doubtless backfire on us; we absolutely cannot have this initial meeting become a public event.

Turning to face the FBI director, he said, "Finally, in answer to the last question, after this meeting I want you and Wallace to stay behind to talk about options for dealing with our guests after Saturday's interview. We cannot allow things to get out of our control and cause a panic. Does everyone understand?"

"Yes, Mr. President."

"Any other questions?"

"Yes, Mr. President." The chairman of the joint chiefs was speaking. "It puzzles me how these people arrived without our detecting them. We've investigated UFO sightings, our own radar records, and satellite footage. So far, we have nothing to indicate the existence of any kind of spacecraft, ship, aircraft, or anything. Should we be searching for a mysterious craft, and if so, where?"

"Excellent question." The president nodded. "Wallace and I talked about that a bit this afternoon. If these people truly have come here from the future, it would be foolish for us to presume they needed to arrive in some kind of ship. Who knows, they may be able to teleport directly and do not need one. I think that searching for a ship could be a wasted effort, until we have had a chance to meet with these people and learn more. Meanwhile, from your end, raise the DEFCON level to green, under the guise of a defense system test. You can use your imagination and come up with what kinds of phenomena to be on the alert for. I will expect you to present me with a plan for this tomorrow. Can you get one to me by noon?"

"I will do my best, sir," the chairman responded. "We can do this fairly readily and explain it away to the press, given the recent climate of terrorism threats. For example, we could create a scenario of conducting a military response test for a fictitious dirty bomb or a chemical threat of some kind. I definitely will have what you asked for in place by Saturday."

"Thank you. Let us adjourn for now. But be ready to meet again tomorrow night, and be prepared for Friday's excursion. And remember, everyone. You are to keep everything as far under the radar as possible. We may be involved in something that is potentially huge for our country's future. One last thing, by the way." The president smiled mischievously. "I would not plan on seeing any shows in Las Vegas this time around."

CHAPTER 34

The Situation Room, Day Six, 11:05 p.m.

THE PRESIDENT, THE DIRECTOR OF THE FBI, AND WALLACE WADE REMAINED SEATED IN the Situation Room as the others filed out the door. When they had all exited the room, the president instructed his chief of staff to meet him first thing in the morning for a planning session and to close the door behind him.

"Okay, gentlemen, I want to talk about some contingencies," the president said when the chief of staff was gone. "First, Wallace, are you sure Dan Hamilton is completely trustworthy?"

"That's a good question. I don't doubt his loyalty. But, as I shared briefly with you before, the events that have transpired have seemed questionable in some ways. I *have* been wondering if maybe he hasn't become too close to these people. The thing is, you vouch so strongly for Jonathan Elliot, and it would be difficult for the two of them to conspire with Agent Newman. That would be too huge a coincidence."

"Yes, I ..." The mention of a coincidence immediately reminded the president of something that he had experienced three summers before. For the fourth time in as many days—the first time being when he had read Jonathan's article in the Sunday *Times*—he recalled a particular night in July. That night he had awakened with a start.

"What's going on?" he had practically shouted as he sat up in bed. He was shivering and covered in sweat, and his heart was racing. He looked around the room to see if he could identify the source of his panic. He reached over to his bedside table and switched on the lamp. No, no one was in the room. It must have been a dream. He looked at the clock. It was 3:15 a.m.

"Take a deep breath," he told himself. Did he have a dream? He must have, but he could not for the life of him remember. He reached over and took a drink from the water glass. His heart was slowing back down to its normal rate, and he felt his body emptying itself of the excess adrenalin.

Becoming calmer at last, he allowed his rational mind to take charge once again, and he decided that he might as well go back to sleep. He reached over, switched off the light, and lay back down.

"Something is coming."

Instantly, the president bolted upright and switched the light back on. "Who said that?" he demanded. The room was silent, just as before. He furiously tried to place the voice. Was it in his head? As he sat there, an image quickly flashed into his mind. A face. It was a face from a man in his dream. Yes, that was it. The face of a man had appeared in a dream while he was sleeping and said that something was coming. But what?

Although now the image of the face was fading again, he felt that this was someone he had never met. The man appeared to be in his thirties, maybe. That man in his dreams had told him that something was coming. The face had seemed concerned, perhaps giving him a warning.

The president shook his head, took another drink of water, and switched off the light. He decided that there was nothing for him to do but shake it off. Dreams were only dreams. He laid his head back down on the pillow and drifted back to sleep.

"Sir?" Wallace's voice brought him back into the room.

"Oh, uh, yes, I agree," the president responded. "However, one must always be leery of the possibility of coincidences. I have known Jonathan for a long time. But, you have to admit that last week's editorial was unusual for him. Also, he seems to have become enchanted with this Samantha Hunter. Perhaps too enchanted. He may be losing his objectivity." Turning to the FBI director, the president asked, "How about this Agent Newman? Can you vouch for him?"

"I have reviewed his personnel file. He has been a consistently high performer in the past. In fact, he is obsessed with perfection. Also, it was he who first compiled the data that led to identifying Samantha Hunter. In my book, he was very efficient and effective. I think he can be counted on."

"That's good." The president suppressed a yawn. "Pardon me, gentlemen. It's getting late. I, too, think these men are to be trusted and would be shocked if it turned out otherwise. However, the stakes are very high. I want the two of you to come up with a contingency plan in the event that we encounter a breakdown. Perhaps one more independent person who can be fully trusted should be brought on board to help us monitor the situation."

"Yes, Mr. President."

"And one other thing. Obviously we must get everything we can from these people from the future. Even if that means finding a way to keep them in our custody—with or without their consent."

CHAPTER 35

Unlocking Session Two, Day Seven, 1:00 a.m.

NEAL AND SUNANDA ONCE AGAIN SEALED THE CHAMBER FOR SAMANTHA TO BEGIN HER second cellular and nervous-system unlocking session. Just as on the night before, the blue fluid filled the chamber, and light streams began to pulsate. Samantha rested in a state of deep waking sleep, as multisensory images from her past life began to flash in and out of her consciousness once again. With each event of remembrance, her recollections were assimilated and resealed into her mind and body, naturally and painlessly.

In this session, her memories began resurfacing from her years as a teenager and young adult. Her feeling was that her memory was like a jigsaw puzzle whose pieces were beginning to fill in what had previously been holes in empty space. Samantha was no longer just a password, but was quickly and steadily becoming a whole human being once again. It all felt very, very good and very, very satisfying.

In the next room Zjon was also feeling very good and very satisfied.

Neal, on the other hand, was not feeling quite so sure. "Zjon, I think the three of us should talk about the next three days."

Zjon, Neal, and Sunanda were once again sitting together and sipping their protein drinks. In addition, Zjon was savoring a glass of Scotch. In his short stay in the twenty-first century, he had been surprised to learn how much he enjoyed this ancient concoction, owing to Jonathan. Jonathan had slipped a bottle to him as a token gift after dinner the night before.

Zjon turned to Neal, and said, "What is on your mind, Neal?"

"I am a bit worried about this interview you have agreed to for Samantha and the rest of us. It was one thing putting up the time-space protection hole before they knew about us. We had to activate that through Samantha to be able to attune to her timespace–moment–point from our own. But now we are dealing with another demand entirely. I do not know if I can provide us with the full-scale level of security needed when we are so exposed to the public view. Also, humans are unpredictable, especially in this war-torn age so long before they make their evolutionary leap in consciousness."

"Neal is right, Zjon," said Sunanda. "We are taking an enormous risk, and I question whether this is a wise one. We have succeeded in finding Samantha. By tomorrow night we will have completed the unlocking process. Perhaps we should just leave with her then."

"You must not forget that our timespace window will not be opened until Saturday at midafternoon on the ninth day. That was the plan that was programmed, and we set it that way because we thought we would need all of that time to accomplish our mission here. We cannot change that." Zjon paused and sat for a few minutes to gather his thoughts. The other two knew Zjon well enough to wait for him to continue.

"I made a judgment call after talking with Samantha before we departed for our Mount Charleston meeting. You see, you and I do not have the experience with the people here that she has. To us, these people seem strange, confused, and even barbaric in many ways. They lack the most basic sense of their Presence as human beings. But it is clear to me from what Samantha shared with me about the people she has met in this time that many of these people do have heart drive. They certainly have heart thrust, even if they do not have heart trust. The ones who have been closest to her and have helped her, Edward and Clare, and also Allison, have demonstrated unconditional love and compassion. That says something to me that could not have been predicted based upon what we knew of human history.

"Remember also, when we first arrived here, I took the risk of reaching out to Jonathan because of my personal genetic connection with him. It was fortuitous that he had already connected with Samantha before. In addition, he had the standing, credentials, and resources in this time to be able to be of service to us in fulfilling our mission successfully. That has proved to be a risk worth taking, would you not agree?"

"Indeed," Neal immediately concurred. "He actually saved us twenty-four hours."

"I would say more than that, not to mention the surprise factor that Dan has brought. And that is just looking from a practical perspective, Neal. Look at this from the larger picture. In the whole recorded history of humankind, never was there any record that people from our time, or any other time for that matter, visited the earth in the past. We may have been blindly assuming that the principle of Noninterference was inviolate. We *have* been assuming that!"

Sunanda jumped in. "We may have been missing something all along."

"Exactly, Sunanda. That is what I am seeing now. We have all learned that everything is impermanent. That life is unpredictable. What we have failed to recognize is that this may include the principles of Impermanence and Unpredictability themselves! Just because our history did not report that human beings from the future came back to the twenty-first century, and that we in fact find ourselves here now, does not mean that we did not interfere."

"Zjon, are you proposing that we interfere in this time by showing them our technology?" Neal asked, incredulous. "That is incredibly dangerous. It could rip apart the whole fabric of timespace!"

"Not at all, Neal. But think about it. What did we learn from history?"

Sunanda answered, "One thing we learned was that starting

around this time, and in the next couple of hundred years, an amazing level of transformation took place in human cultures."

"Yes!" Neal said. "This time came to be called the 'Age of First Awakening,' the 'Flowering.' It was a kind of quantum leap in human consciousness, It also represented a shift in the relationship human beings had to technology, a shift toward unity with nature."

"And," Sunanda joined in, "it was a time of reconciliations among the classic religions and the sciences. Some textbooks have called it the 'Age of Reconciliation.'"

"Exactly. It was the first great step toward the discovery of full Presence. But our history never tried to explain how or why that happened. There are interventions of necessity and of luck—the unpredictable. I am proposing to both of you right now, Neal and Sunanda, that we, I mean our visit here, just might be, or have been, one such unpredictable intervention."

"So, just what would you call that intervention that you think we might be bringing through our timespace travel here?" Sunanda's tone was one of challenge.

Zjon's eyes began to radiate a new light. "How about 'unconditional love'?" Instantaneously, all of the rooms and chambers in the timespace craft were filled with and reflected a lightness of being that was rare, even among future beings. In her chamber, a smile appeared on Samantha's face as she now remembered who Zjon was. She continued to cycle through her process, deep into the night.

CHAPTER 36

Red Rock, Day Seven, 11:00 a.m.

The white Dodge Caravan ES pulled into a parking space in front of the Visitor Center at the Red Rock Canyon National Conservation Area. Driving the van this time, at his personal insistence, was Special Agent David Newman. Sitting shotgun was Dan, and in the backseats rode Jonathan, Clare, and Edward.

"Okay, we are here," said David. "Now what?"

Dan saw that David was still miffed following yesterday's "fiasco," as David had characterized it. There was no point in arguing with him. After all, David had a valid point. It was he who had been required to pick up the abandoned vehicle at the Old Charleston Trailhead. He then had to hotwire the car because Dan had kept the car keys with him. "I would have been pissed myself, if I were in your shoes," he told David over dinner that evening.

For the past eighteen hours, Dan had been forced to balance both David and his team in Las Vegas and the Chief back in Washington. Fortunately, he was skilled enough to pull it off, and at the moment was feeling rather proud of how well things had turned out. So far, at least. "Skeptical Dan" was not yet ready to declare victory.

Dan turned around so that he could address David as well as the others in the backseats. "So, let's go over the game plan." The call had come once again from Zjon that morning, while the group was having breakfast together at the Bellagio buffet. "Zjon was very specific about our meeting him here promptly at eleven this morning.

He promised to give us an update on Samantha's progress and said he wanted to share some more background to give us a better understanding, whatever that means. So far, Zjon has proven to be good to his word, and so here we are. Let's make the most of it."

"Agreed. More than agreed!" Jonathan said, hoping to help break the tension. "By the way, thanks again, David, for all you have done to cover security and make this work. We're all glad you could join us for this meeting."

"Here, here," Edward and Clare echoed together.

"Thanks, guys." To everyone's relief, David seemed to be letting go of his anger. "I had a job to do yesterday, and I guess I took it a bit too personally. I won't let that happen again."

"That's great," Dan said. "No hard feelings?"

"No hard feelings." Then David added, "But don't let that happen again, okay?"

"You got it. We're all on the same team." The excitement began to rise once again, as the group waited with building anticipation for Zjon to arrive.

Clare said, "I wonder what kind of appearance they will make today."

Edward said, "Maybe they'll ride in on a magic carpet."

Within a few seconds, two black vehicles pulled into the parking lot. Everyone watched as the cars turned in their direction and pulled into the parking spaces on either side of the van. "Relax. Those are my guys," David announced. "I told them when we would be arriving. They've actually been cruising around for the last hour or so, just to make sure nobody who looked suspicious would be in the area. Hang on a second." David opened his car door as two men in dark suits got out of the other cars and began to walk around behind the van.

"David, tell them to ditch the jackets and ties," Dan said. "We're in a public recreation area."

David gave Dan a thumbs-up. He then shut the door and walked around to meet his men.

Dan turned to the others and said, "In many ways that's a thankless job: having to be on full alert all the time and most of the time just sitting and waiting for something to happen. Federal agents have to be masters of boredom. Then they get to deal with hostile people from both sides—the cops and the criminals. Luckily, at least it's another beautiful day, and we are still having unseasonably good weather. There really could be worse gigs."

"Let's get out of the car and have a look around while we're waiting," Edward suggested. "This is a very interesting place, particularly if you haven't seen it before."

"Great idea!" Jonathan had already opened the side door. "I've heard about this place, but this is my first time actually seeing it." The others followed as Jonathan led the way toward the Visitor Center building. Dotting the sidewalk leading up to the main entrance were a number of information signs, spaced every twenty or thirty feet apart. The group paused at each sign to read about the history of the canyon, its geology, and its wildlife.

For the first time, Dan took full notice of his surroundings. "Wow, this is truly amazing!" Jonathan and the others looked up to take in the breathtaking panorama of the sprawling red cliffs that rose thousands of feet above them. They looked like they had been standing there since prehistoric times. Each rock protrusion stood on its own yet was connected to the adjacent rock structures by horizontal striations of different colors and shades that looked like someone had taken a giant paintbrush and made swaths of red, orange, purple, brown, and tan streaks in a random pattern. Clearly the artist was Mother Nature herself. No human being could have created such a stunning sight.

Edward interjected, "We are just inside the easternmost boundary of the Mojave Desert. The desert extends that way"—he pointed toward the mountains rising nearby—"and continues deep into California. The Mojave is one of the most rugged wilderness areas in the United States and contains some of the hottest land in the world, including Death Valley. This place, however, is one of my favorites."

Just as he finished speaking, David announced, "I'm back," as he walked up to rejoin them. "My men have reported seeing around fifty or so people, mostly dressed in outdoor hiking gear, all clearly tourists. They'll alert me if they see anything fishy. And I got them to dress down like you asked, Dan. That made them very happy."

"Thanks, and good work," said Dan.

Clare asked, "Do you think Zjon wants to take us on a hike up there?" Clare knew that the recreation area had a vast network of hiking trails that would take anywhere from twenty minutes to many hours for a person to cover on foot. "I forgot to bring water this time."

Jonathan answered, "Who knows what Zjon is thinking? But somehow I suspect not. He sounded like he was interested in show-ing us something. At least, he didn't ask us to hike somewhere to meet him."

"Right," Edward said. "He asked us to meet him here at the Visitor Center."

"Look at this." Jonathan brought everyone's attention back to one of the signs. "These signs are arranged around the theme of the four elements: earth, fire, water, and air. Isn't that a coincidence?"

"I never noticed that before," said Clare, "but you're right. Samantha and Zjon both talked about the elements at our dinner. And Samantha's mentioned them before."

Edward said, "Yes, but they mentioned five. What was the fifth element?"

"Space." The voice came from about twenty feet behind them. The group turned around and was surprised to see Zjon standing at the edge of the parking lot.

Jonathan exclaimed, "Zjon, you startled us!"

Zjon smiled and said, "Good morning, everyone. You are right on time." Zjon was dressed casually, like a tourist.

"How did you get here?" This came from Dan.

"Nothing exciting this time." Zjon laughed. He turned and ges-tured toward the parking lot, where a nondescript car was parked at the end of one of the parking rows. At that moment, Neal stepped out from the driver's side and waved hello, clearly pleased that they had succeeded in surprising their friends. "We apologize for the delay. We chose to wait until David's men had dispersed before making our appearance."

"No problem," Jonathan said. "I think we are getting used to your surprise appearances. By the way, you remember David, I assume."

"Why yes. I am very happy you could join us."

"So am I, thanks." David looked somewhat sheepish. "I'd hate to miss out on any more fun."

"I trust our meeting today will be fun. I have a place I want to show you, just past the far western end of the Red Rock formations. If you will get in your van, Neal and I will lead you there. We will follow the scenic loop to the parking lot I have in mind. Then we will take a short walk. There is a special place that is off the beaten track, away from other tourists. David, would you please radio your men to let them know where we are going and ask that they make sure we are not disturbed?" Without waiting for a reply, Zjon turned and walked over to the car where Neal was standing. David pulled out his cell phone and with the others walked back to the parking lot and climbed into the van.

CHAPTER 37

Presence

A S THE GROUP OF SEVEN STROLLED DOWN THE PATH THAT LED AWAY FROM THE PARKING lot toward the trailhead at the end of the Red Rock formations, David asked Zjon, "So, where did you get your car?"

Without missing a beat, Zjon answered, "Her name is Melissa."

"She?"

"Yes, she came with us."

"From where?"

"From the future."

"Oh," was all David could say. "She looks like about an old Audi. You have cars like this in the future?"

"She is very adaptable."

"You're pulling my leg, right?"

"Not at all. Does your leg feel like it is being pulled?" Zjon was smiling now.

"No, I mean, you're joking, right? You must have picked up that car in the city."

Dan and Jonathan, who were bringing up the rear, looked at each other and shook their heads. Edward and Clare, who were walking behind Zjon and David in the middle of the group, also looked at each other and smiled. Neal, who had remained back by the car, about a hundred feet behind them, laughed.

Dan called up to the front, "Hey, David. You can stop being an investigator now."

"I was just interested. I happen to like Audis and just wanted to know where he got it."

Zjon said, "Just imagine for yourself how technology could evolve in the future, and how the relationship between human beings and technology could be different. The relationship people have to technology today is very different from what will be possible in the future. To you, cars are just tools. For us, there is a living relationship."

"You know, I've always given my cars names. My first car was called 'Jezebel,' and she was a 1970, gold, Buick Skylark."

"I am sure you had a great relationship."

David laughed. "She was a real sweetheart of a car."

Zjon stopped and pointed toward a huge boulder about a hundred yards from the path. "That is where we are going today. Come this way." He left the path. The group followed, stepping their way through hardscrabble and small thickets leading up to the rock. As they approached, it appeared larger and larger, until they could see that this rock had to be more than fifty feet high. Zjon then turned and began walking clockwise around to the far side of the rock, out of view from the Red Rock formations and the path they had just followed. When they had all reached the opposite side, he stopped. "This is the place I want to show you."

Edward and Jonathan stepped up close to the base of the boulder to examine it more closely. Unlike the main formation of Red Rock, this boulder was mostly tan and gray and appeared to be solid granite. Edward guessed, "The circumference must be around two hundred fifty to three hundred feet."

Jonathan felt it with his fingers and said, "Granite, I would say, with lots of fine particles of mica."

"Yep," Edward agreed.

Just below eye level there was a ridge, about two or three inches thick, that appeared to wrap around the rock in both directions. It looked like a belt holding up a pair of trousers. Below this protrusion the rock curved gradually downward and then inward. Above eye level, the rock wall rose several feet, tapering to a peak that was out of their sight. Parts of the wall were speckled with moss or lichen, light green or grayish in color. All in all, Jonathan surmised, this looked like a mighty fine rock.

"Looks like a mighty fine rock," Dan said, as if reading Jonathan's mind.

"Yep," Edward agreed.

"I am glad you all approve," Zjon said with a wry grin. Everyone in the group was beginning to see that this man from the future had a sense of humor.

Clare said, "Zjon, you should go on the stage."

"What do you mean, Clare?"

"I mean, you could do stand-up comedy at a club."

"Well, I will give that some thought when we return home. You know, in our time we have a very thriving art and drama scene. People still love performances, and we even have a theater where artists perform ancient dramas and comedies. Also, we have the future equivalent of your movie theaters. Some of them periodically show ancient classics in entertainment, like *Star Wars* and *Star Trek*."

"Really? Are you kidding?" David said.

"Not at all. These classics are important for teaching our kids about cultures of the ancient past. By that I include the wildness of human imagination. The human spirit reveals itself most clearly through the timelessness of art."

"Well, I'll be damned," David proclaimed.

"I doubt that, David," Zjon quipped. "Now, I brought you to this place to give you a couple of treats. But first, I wanted to convey greetings from Samantha. She is doing very well and has successfully completed her second session of memory restoration, what we call 'unlocking.' She is staying with our other crewmember, Sunanda, while her body's neurological system reintegrates itself. For her right now, consciousness is occurring as a kind of dream-like state. It is a sensitive point in the process. However, she will be ready to see you all again tomorrow."

"That's great," Clare said. "Please give her our love."

"I will do that. Now, as I said, I have two treats for you. The first thing I want to do is what we call a 'session.'"

"A session?" Jonathan inquired.

"Yes. I want to share with you a special connection to Intelligence, and I brought you to this rock because of its special properties. Rather than try to explain, I will demonstrate. Each of you find a place that feels comfortable to you, step forward to the rock, and place both of your hands along the top of that ridge-like formation. Take a moment to make sure you feel good about the place you have chosen. That is most important."

Edward and Jonathan returned to stand where they had been examining the rock moments before. The other three stepped up and positioned themselves near the rock as well. On Zjon's cue, each placed both hands on the rock as he had described. "Everybody good?" he asked.

"Yes," everyone answered in unison.

"Now, close your eyes and gently begin vibrating the fingertips of both hands against the rock, as if you were lightly playing a piano. That is good. Let your fingers relax and move in a way that feels right to you. Keeping your eyes closed and your fingers moving, begin making a humming sound under your breath."

The five all began making their own sounds. As they did this, Jonathan felt a tingling sensation begin to creep up his spine, and the hairs on his arms stood on end. Each of the others began to have similar sensations. After thirty seconds or so, it seemed that time began to slow down and their thoughts and inner voices began to quiet down. Then they heard Zjon say, "Now, keep your eyes closed. When I give you the signal, I want you to open your eyes, but not until I say so." Everyone nodded as they continued to tap their fingers against the rock and hum. After several more seconds, they heard Zjon take several deep breaths, and suddenly, as if in a rush, they heard a loud "swoosh" of an exhale, followed by the command, "Open your eyes."

All five were dazzled by what they saw when they opened their eyes. Lights sparkled and vibrated in front of their eyes, dancing in gold and white patterns all across the rock above their hands. As they continued to tap their fingers, the boulder seemed to come to life right before their eyes. Jonathan saw that his fingers were now vibrating on their own, seemingly no longer under his volition. Some kind of force seemed to be radiating from the rock and entering through his eyes and fingers, down into his body, causing a most wonderful sensation, a sensation of pure wonder and light and joy and ...

"Too much!"

Nobody was sure whose voice had spoken. It did not really matter anyway. Each person was totally gripped by the awe and the mystery of what they were witnessing. They all recognized that what stood before them was no longer just a boulder. It was a living, breathing force. Jonathan placed his forehead against the rock wall, overcome by the softness of its texture. Clare and Edward gave each other a hug. David and Dan just stood there in awe and wonder. This was just too much.

"Yes, it is; is it not?" Zjon echoed their thoughts, bringing them back into their bodies. "From this point forward, you should know that this rock knows you and will remember your presence. Whenever you come here, it will recognize you."

Each of the five removed their hands from the rock and turned to face Zjon. "You should see your faces." Zjon smiled. "Come over here and take a seat. I have one more thing to show you. But first, let us take a break. Neal will bring you some water. You just had an experience of the elements Fire and Air. Consider yourselves initiated."

Each of the five initiates walked over to where Zjon was standing some distance from the rock. Together they looked around until one of them located a clearing in the underbrush. Clare pointed to a flat spot that was shaded by a small piñon pine, and she and Edward sat down with their backs to the tree. Jonathan, Dan, and David did the same after finding their respective spots. Zjon observed that they had naturally formed a half circle twelve feet in diameter, so he took a seat in a place equidistant from the other five. Within a few seconds, Neal approached them from behind the rock, carrying a small backpack. Without speaking, he walked around the inner circle and gave each person a bottle of water. He then took a seat a few feet behind Zjon. Dan noticed that the backpack did not appear to be empty.

The group sat in a state of peaceful reflection for the next fifteen minutes. Jonathan realized that his mind was remarkably quiet. He also felt a powerful sense of connection with the other members of his group. Looking around at each person, he was suddenly struck by the transformation he saw in everyone's face. They each appeared ten years younger than they had looked before. Everyone was smiling—even Dan and David—and their smiles seemed totally natural and effortless. Something remarkable had happened, and they had all shared this experience. He felt as if he had known these people all of his life, and he knew in that instant that this feeling was mutual.

Eventually Jonathan could contain himself no longer. "How on earth did you do that?" he asked Zjon.

Zjon smiled. "Who said I did anything?"

David jumped in. "Come on. You know you did something. How did you make that happen?"

"No, *you* did that. I merely facilitated it. What you experienced was your own natural connection. You got a taste of your own Presence. I just helped coax it along by sensing and signaling Intelligence. We human beings have this as a natural capacity. The only difference between you and us—that is, Samantha, Sunanda, Neal, and me—is that we come from a time when the majority of human beings live in the awareness of their Presence and their connection with Universal Intelligence."

"Zjon, we have seen Samantha do what seemed like strange things at times over the last three years," Edward said. "Is this related?"

"Perhaps. I cannot speak for Samantha's actions. However, she is an advanced master of the domain of sensing, tapping, and signaling."

"Can you teach us how to do these things ourselves?" Edward looked so eager that Zjon was touched.

"Humankind eventually will need to discover these things on its own. There is a time for everything, and that time has not yet come. The whole of evolution is based on Innocence. Out of Innocence you get fascination. Out of fascination you then begin to discover various things. That is the very nature of development, and the nature of evolution. We cannot just accelerate it by sharing information you cannot yet digest.

"We four are bound to you, however, in a bond of gratitude. We wanted to give you a taste, as a gift. It is our wish that each of you will live rich and happy lives. Who knows what the future might hold? No one can know what the future holds, and no one can even know the past, really. What is always available is available now, in the present moment. The greatest knowledge one can achieve is to know one's own Presence. We human beings are blessed by Intelligence to have that capacity. It is up to each one of us individually to learn and find that for ourselves." Zjon paused to allow the others to reflect upon what he had said.

Jonathan asked, "Would you explain more about what you mean by 'Presence'?"

"I can say this. In our time, people are attracted to each other through their Presence, not their stories. In the short time we have been here, we have observed that people in your time are basically attracted sensuously. Then you get to know about each other's families, jobs, hobbies, interests, and all that. But all of this really comes from your past. In our time, we do not ask about one's past. When we meet somebody, we do not ask, 'Who are you? Who is your family? What do you do?' Instead, we are attracted by each other's Presence.

"Your Presence is different from your story. Presence is actually who you are, created and designed out of pure Intelligence, containing all the forces and the elements. Basically, five great forces are moving through you, creating emotional waves and wonder, and creating the Presence within you. Presence lies at the heart of your very experience of existence. Right now, that is to say in your time, you mostly experience your world in terms of your circumstances, and your attention gets absorbed by worries, desires, fears, thoughts, and anxieties. In short, you are infatuated with the immediately given appearances of the world around you, and you are distracted from what is possible. There is, instead, another way to be, a way you can expand your heart into the very nature of existence. Look for yourself and see what I am talking about."

Everyone sat quietly and pondered Zjon's words.

Zjon then continued. "But enough about Presence. You had a direct taste of it, and that is more important than understanding it. I will ask Samantha to speak with you tomorrow about sensing, tapping, and signaling. We will get together for breakfast, and she will share more with you then. As I said before, we cannot give you any specifics about our science and our technology. What I can do right now, however, is have another conversation I think you will find interesting and fun."

"What is that?" Dan asked.

"Let us begin a conversation about time and space."

CHAPTER 38

Timespace

Jonathan asked, "I'm very curious about that. Have you been to other times in the past?"

Edward jumped in, "Yes, like the Age of Dinosaurs?"

Zjon smiled. "We do not travel in time. Samantha's accident brought us here, and it is the only accident of this nature that has ever happened, not only to your time, but also in our time. In answer to your question, no, we do not travel in time, although we clearly are capable of doing it. As I mentioned before, time travel would become a violation, and not only a violation of our federation agreements but also a violation of Sacred Space. Such an action could create an enormous interference in human evolution. We dare not risk this."

Jonathan persisted. "But you are here now. Isn't that a contradiction?"

"I understand how it seems. This time, however, we were receiving a signal through timespace, something like a homing signal. Our experts realized when-where she was, and we knew from the intensities, frequencies, vibrations, and other aspects of the signal what was going to happen if we did not come here. It was truly a unique situation for us. It also is critical that we return with her at the right time."

Zjon saw that Edward was about to ask another question, but he interrupted him. "Before you ask anything else, I am going to give you a little treat. Neal, would you hand me the sonic-templifier please?" Neal reached into his backpack and took out a device that looked to Edward and Jonathan like the same kind of box they had seen the day before on Mount Charleston. However, its color, patterns, and insignias were different. Zjon made a motion in Neal's direction with both hands and said to him, "You show them, please."

Neal nodded, then stood up and walked over beside the rock. He set the device against an indentation in the stone and did something with his hands. Nothing happened for several seconds. Then suddenly, the group was surprised to hear a strange sound, like an animal's roar. This was followed a few seconds later by another roaring sound that seemed to answer the first one. Jonathan noticed it sounded like two large animals making mating calls. "Is that what I think it might be?"

"What's that?" David asked. Dan, Edward, and Clare sat still, as if mesmerized by the sounds they were hearing. From the rock came other, more distant sounds that reminded them of the sounds of a jungle. When the sounds came, everybody experienced a cold chill running throughout their bodies. The sounds caused an immediate change in their state of consciousness, a shift in their level of alertness. Everyone had an intuitive awareness that they were hearing vibrations from the past. "Dinosaurs!" David answered his own question.

"Perhaps," Zjon answered him.

To everyone's disappointment, Neal broke the spell by reaching down, making another motion with his hands, and placing the device back into his backpack. All the animal sounds ceased immediately.

Zjon spoke again. "Red Rock is one of the greatest places on earth. It stands as a timeless witness to life. Red Rock will always be Red Rock. Las Vegas will be remembered for its flashing lights but in the end will have been here only for a few seconds in the eons of time.

"There are a number of great places that are vortices in the Earth's matrix by which we can sometimes listen back through time. Machu Picchu, the Buddhist holy sites in Sri Lanka, the land under the Jerusalem wall, and many others are such spots on the planet. People go there and feel the energy. But people do not realize that these places also contain condensed gratitude—the force of gratitude."

Clare said, "What you are saying is very true, Zjon. Gratitude is something you feel when you are in one of those places. Please say more."

"Yes, but what you feel as gratitude is actually appreciation and love for all that is. But even that is only the tip of the iceberg. Great human beings of the past who became inspired in these places contributed to the world in unbelievable ways. They are the ones who laid the foundations for our understanding. Their profound realizations were not just doctrines or philosophies. These realizations were truly mathematics, and at that time human awareness had not yet developed to a high enough resolution for people to understand the greatness that was behind the teachings. So, out of these places and from these great beings, people became inspired in poetical and philosophical ways and created many amazing things: great buildings, works of art, and scientific breakthroughs. I am talking about concepts like the Ten Commandments, the Four Noble Truths, the Dharma Chakra, the Kabbala, the I Ching, the Tao Te Ching, and for example, the astronomical observations of the Greeks, the Mayans, and others. These contributions to human knowledge were actually a form of mathematics. They were showing us diagrams for how to live our lives in the most amazing ways. But even into your time, people could not appreciate what they were being shown, because they were restless. You are like excited kids in big bodies; you are excited by discovering various toys. You have yet to discover for yourselves the grace that is here all the time in the patterns and connections of Intelligence."

Zjon sensed that the group had absorbed all they could for the moment. "Please do not ask me anything more right now. You have been very good to us. You are very kind, loving human beings. We have become friends, and we will remember you forever. Tomorrow we will get back together once again with Samantha. We will continue our conversation about timespace and signaling then."

As they reached the parking lot, Dan and David both noticed that the Audi was gone. Parked in its place was a gold Buick Skylark. "Is that what I think it is?" David turned to Dan. He looked like an excited, little child.

Zjon and Neal both laughed. "*That is Melissa!* Would you like to take her for a spin, David?"

"Are you kidding me?" David was enthralled.

"Neal, how would you like to go with David once around the scenic loop, while I have a short conversation with Jonathan?"

As David was walking around to the passenger side of the Skylark, Neal insisted, "No, David, you drive."

"Oh, wow!" David laughed as he went around to the other side of the car and opened the door. As he settled into the driver's seat, David could smell the familiar aroma of leather that he remembered so fondly from his college days. The interior was identical to what he remembered—the soft, ridged seat cushions, the instrument panel, the clock. He saw that the clock read 7:30. "Oh, my God. This is just like my car, even down to the clock. Jezebel's clock never told the correct time. My best friend Conner and I used to joke about how her clock carried the true time, the 'enlightened time' we called it. Where are the keys?"

Neal was totally amused as he listened to David's enthusiasm. "We do not need keys, David. I would like to introduce Melissa to you."

"Hello, David," a woman's voice came from the front panel. "I thought you would enjoy an excursion into your past."

"This is too much. Your name is Melissa?"

"Yes. Jezebel could not make it today, so I came in her place. She sends fond greetings, though."

"I must be going crazy."

Neal said, "You are not, and do not be alarmed. You can trust Melissa. Just put the car in gear and start driving."

David did as he was told. The Skylark purred gently and smoothly as they pulled out of the parking lot and turned right onto the scenic loop. As he accelerated, David's grin became wider and wider, until finally he shoved the gas pedal toward the floor.

"Be mindful," Neal cautioned him, gripping his own seat belt. "There is a speed limit."

"Don't worry, I know how to handle this baby." Melissa's wheels squealed as they rounded the first curve. David felt like the king of the world as he heard Melissa's voice saying, "Way to go, David!"

"What the hell was that? Charlie, did you see what I saw?" One of the two FBI men, who had parked their car on a shoulder in the road, almost spilled his water bottle when he saw the golden flash of the car fly by.

Charlie answered, "Just a couple teenagers out for a joy ride."

"You must be right. But the driver looked like Agent Newman."

"No. That's not possible."

"You must be right. I sure hope they don't crash. They're really burning rubber."

"Not our problem, Harry. Not our problem."

The gold Skylark disappeared down the road, leaving a trail of dust behind.

Standing in the parking lot beside the Dodge Caravan, Zjon turned to the remaining group and said, "Dan, would you and Edward and Clare please excuse me and Jonathan for one moment? I have a couple things that I need to talk with him about privately. We will be just a couple of minutes."

"You bet." Clare took Edward's hand.

"No problem," Dan answered. He had to be careful not to know too much, so he would not be in the position of withholding any more than was absolutely necessary from the Chief and the president. Maintaining their trust was imperative right now. He climbed into the passenger seat of the van.

Jonathan and Zjon strolled over to the other side of the parking lot, looking like a couple of regular tourists stretching their legs after a hike.

"You are feeling good, Jonathan, are you not?"

"I'm feeling wonderful. More alive than ever."

"That is good. You and I have a deep, genetic connection, Jonathan, and I feel a most powerful heart connection with you."

"I feel the same about you, Zjon."

"I want to talk briefly about the day after tomorrow. It is important that Dan and David not know what we are talking about."

"I understand."

"Good. You know, our visit here cannot be just for the benefit of one country. Countries and nations are a temporary concept of history. Humankind is universal. Our visit has to be for everyone."

"My feelings exactly. I'm so glad you feel that way."

"After we leave here, our visit will seem to the world like it occurred in a dream. All electronic records will automatically be erased, leaving no trace of our visit. This is necessary to ensure we have not violated the laws of conscious evolution."

"Yes."

"At the same time, I want as many people in the world as possible to hear what we have to say and to witness our departure. I understand you have the connections in your field to help make that happen."

"Yes, I know many important people in the press, as does my boss, the executive editor of *The New York Times*."

"Then I will leave it to you. Just be sure that the invited people come quickly, before your government closes the airport."

"Edward and Clare will help. But how will David's men be able to handle the crowds? Things could get terribly out of control."

"Do not worry about that. You remember the charged field?"

"How could I forget?"

"What I did not explain to you is that the field was part of the homing mechanism that arose and made our connection with Samantha possible through timespace. Just as it was present for our arrival, it will be there again for our departure. This will protect us from intruders and also will safely take care of anyone who inadvertently comes too close. It has the added benefit of repelling weapons of any strength, although I do not think that will be a real danger."

"I certainly hope not. I'll get right on it this afternoon, when we return to town."

"Excellent."

At that moment the two men were distracted by the sound of tires squealing as David and Neal and Melissa whipped back into the parking lot and screeched to a halt in a parking space nearby. "Well, my ride is back," Zjon quipped. "She looks sound and healthy."

David jumped out of the driver's seat and exclaimed, "That was great! Thank you, Melissa!"

"You are welcome, David. It was very nice to meet you."

Zjon walked over and put his right hand on David's shoulder. "Thank you for your friendship. You and Dan have a very important role to play two days from now. I know that you will be very busy tomorrow arranging for security. I want you to know we will not forget you."

"It is an honor for me, Zjon. You have made me feel like a new man."

"Your last name represents you perfectly, David. Farewell." With that, Zjon got into the Skylark and said, "Let us go, Melissa." David Newman watched as the car that replicated his fondest memories coasted out of the parking lot. Was it just his imagination, or did he see the car fade away and disappear into thin air?

CHAPTER 39

Unlocked, Day Eight, 5:00 a.m.

THE INTENSITY WAS CHANGING. EVEN IN HER SLEEP STATE, SAMANTHA EXPERIENCED A difference in pulsation frequency and coloration patterns. Everything was feeling lighter now. If she could have seen what was going on from the outside looking in, she would have seen that what for the past two nights had been a deep blue color in the chamber's nanoparticle liquids had now turned into a clear, light, sky-blue color.

Samantha's consciousness of herself as a temporal being was gradually emerging into fullness, into wholeness, into completeness. Her past life in the future was inching its way forward as if to touch her present life in the past. It was now clear that she had lived two lives in two times. But it was not yet one life. She felt herself on the verge of coming into an integrated awareness of all of it. An inner sensation was urging her to wake up. Yet, it was not time to wake up. There was just one important memory missing. That memory held the answer to the most important question.

With a sudden flash of white light, Samantha saw herself sitting at the main control panel of her craft, the *Deep Space Adventurer*. The memories of Space Station Alpha II and the A-421 anomaly mission rushed in. She watched with an awed clarity as the space accident unfolded. She witnessed herself falling through timespace, passing into unconsciousness, and awakening to blue sky and clouds on the hill at Twin Peaks, under the stately oak tree.

Samantha was back, and life was whole again.

CHAPTER 40

On the Ship, Day Eight, 6:00 a.m.

O N THE MORNING OF THE EIGHTH DAY, SAMANTHA WOKE UP INTO A NEW LIFE. THE GATH-ering chamber had retracted into the wall of the ship. She found herself sitting up, surrounded by the smiling faces of her best friends in the world. She looked with total serenity into the face of Sunanda, her sister in adventure, then at Neal, her mischievous brother, and last at Zjon, the true love of her life. "Oh, my God!" she exclaimed.

The three comrades began to laugh and celebrate together. Zjon took Samantha's hand and pulled her into his arms, as Sunanda and Neal gave each other a high five. Even in the forty-sixth century, the high five remained a universal acknowledgment of victory.

Zjon confessed to her, "I was so afraid we would lose you."

The full impact and shock of everything she had gone through suddenly rushed into Samantha's body. She began to cry, spilling tears of joy. Zjon caressed her back. Neal and Sunanda stepped up to her from either side and did the same. Samantha felt comforted as she allowed her emotions to flow freely, safe in her own timespace.

When at last she regained her full Presence in the now-here, she saw what she needed to do next. "I really want to show my gratitude to Edward and Clare for taking me in and protecting me for these past three years."

Zjon said, "You will have that chance at breakfast this morning. Have a shower and change into fresh clothing. Meanwhile, Neal, please get Melissa ready."

PART FOUR
ASCENDANCE

You are not this and not that.
Out of the space of the nothing that you are
arises All Things.
Let it rise!

—Samantha

CHAPTER 41

Air Force One, Day Eight, 9:00 a.m.

"WHY ARE WE BEING SO SNEAKY?"

The first lady was sitting across from the president in his private quarters aboard Air Force One. The two were comfortably relaxed as they enjoyed a cup of coffee together. At the moment they were cruising 38,500 feet above the Rocky Mountains of Colorado. It was a stunning day, and a few minutes previously they had passed over the top of Pike's Peak, still flaunting a few patches of snow in the face of all the recent evidence of global warming. Seeing the snow had briefly cheered the president's heart. Nature really did want to win this battle. How arrogant could we be to think we had nothing to do with what was happening? The problem of negotiating with his people, and especially Congress, to somehow come to grips with this looming phenomenon lay at the forefront of his concerns.

Today, of course, he was occupied with a more immediate situation—the biggest one he, or perhaps any other president, had ever faced.

He answered his wife, "Because this is one cat that we cannot afford to let out of the bag. At least until we really know what kind of cat it is."

"But don't you feel that this is something that can benefit the whole world, and not just America? If others find out that we are keeping these people a secret, don't you think that will cause problems?"

"Ultimately it will, for sure. If these people turn out to be who they say they are, we will definitely need to introduce them to the greater world community. You know that once again I have to walk a political tightrope here."

"How do you envision the first steps of this walk?"

"After landing at Nellis, we will caravan together with a small military escort to a suburb of Las Vegas called Summerlin. You and I, as well as the Speaker and majority leader, will spend the night at the home of one of our loyal supporters. The senate minority leader has arranged this for us, discreetly. Meanwhile, Wallace's people and the FBI have arranged a secure location for our meeting tomorrow morning. No press allowed, just my press secretary. When the time for our meeting approaches, the five of us will ride there with our FBI liaison, a man named David Newman. The Secret Service is already on the ground working with him to secure the location. Just in case anything goes wrong, which I am sure it will not"—the president knocked on wood—"the chairman of the joint chiefs is standing by with any military assistance that might be required."

"And what happens after the meeting?" the first lady asked.

"A Secret Service detail will escort us and our guests back to Air Force One. The plan is to be in the air by five o'clock and back home around midnight. From Andrews, we will all take a ride to Camp David. As far as the public is concerned, we will have been there the entire time, since this morning."

"What about the religious representatives, especially the Dalai Lama and the pope?"

"I decided after all not to try and include them for this first gathering. Way too much publicity and way too much of a risk. For this first meeting, we will only have twenty-five hand-selected scientists and scholars present at the meeting. Jonathan Elliot will be moderating. We will secretly be in an adjoining room, listening. Nobody will know we are there but us."

"And our visitors."

"No, not even our visitors. They were very specific that they wanted only a small group of scientists and scholars to be there. No politicians and no press. I can understand that. In many ways, it makes it better for all of us, especially during election season."

Satisfied, the first lady leaned back in her chair and sipped her coffee. Then, "How are you going to handle the press when the right time comes?"

"That's always the question, isn't it? But first things first."

"Yes, first things first." The first lady paused, then continued. "Well, my dear, when I agreed to be your first lady, I never dreamed we would be meeting with someone from the future."

"Neither did I!" The president smiled.

"And if this whole thing turns out to be some kind of hoax?"

The president thought for a moment before answering. "That's a real possibility, of course. Naturally, we will have no alternative but to see what kind of legal action may be appropriate and whom to hold responsible. The best news is that I am not running for another term. If necessary, I can take the fall. This will just end up being another item in a long list for the other party to add to its arsenal. But they will not be able to use it against our candidates, because our candidates know nothing about it. And in this case, the Speaker of the House and the majority leader are also both on the hook here. They personally have a lot more to lose than I do politically. I would say that this is a risk that can be mitigated and is well worth taking.

"The much more difficult question will be how to handle everything if these folks turn out to be who they say they are. Then I will keep them under guard in order to delay any revelations until after the elections. Then I will ask them to work with us to titrate information to other world leaders and ultimately, to the public."

"The elections are a long way away."

"Yes. But do you have any better suggestions?"

"No. That's what the American people elected you for, to make the important calls."

The president reached for his coffee. As he finished it, the thought crossed his mind that he knew, deep down, that these people were for real. With a reawakened sense of wonder, he reflected once again on that dreamlike interlude from the middle of the night three years before, the voice in the night and an unknown face. He had been unable to shake this incident from his mind. Now he understood clearly why he had to meet these people himself. This whole thing carried an uncanny feeling of destiny.

CHAPTER 42

Four Seasons, Las Vegas, Day Eight, 9:30 a.m.

JONATHAN ELLIOT STROLLED THROUGH THE LOBBY OF THE FOUR SEASONS HOTEL, STOP-ping at the information desk to ask directions to the Veranda, a restaurant with an outdoor patio. Earlier that morning Edward had called his room and told him they were to meet Zjon and Samantha there. Edward and Clare had headed to the restaurant an hour earlier, in order to meet Samantha in privacy. Jonathan had honored their wish.

As he made his way through the restaurant, he spotted his four friends through a set of glass doors. They were seated at a circular table at the far edge of the patio, several yards away from the nearest guests. "Good morning," he called as he crossed the patio. Zjon and Edward both stood to greet him as he approached. "Am I interrupting?"

"Not at all," Edward assured him. "Samantha just finished telling us about her last two days, and we were waiting for you and Dan to arrive." The two men shook Jonathan's hand, and he took one of the empty seats.

Jonathan noticed that Clare had been crying. "Are you sure I'm not too early? I can wait inside until you're finished."

Clare spoke up. "No, no, Jonathan. I was just feeling sad, realizing that Samantha won't be with us much longer. You aren't interrupting."

"Okay, thanks." Looking around he observed, "Wow, this is a lovely place."

"Yes it is," Zjon responded.

Edward asked, "Is Dan coming separately?"

"Dan won't be with us this morning. He decided he needed to get some work done with David in preparation for tomorrow. I think he also sensed we could use some time for any planning that probably should not reach his ears. He's in a sensitive position, you know."

"Indeed," Zjon said. "I think Dan is very wise."

Jonathan said, "Before we talk about anything else, I think it would be good for us to review the situation that is shaping up for tomorrow. But first, Samantha, you look radiant!"

Samantha beamed at him, her azure eyes alight in a way that he had not seen before. There was a new strength behind her smile. The only word that came to Jonathan's mind was *gumption*. Whatever loss of confidence he had sensed in her before was gone. It made Jonathan feel really happy to see this.

"Thank you, Jonathan. You are looking at a new woman. The process was a complete success. You could say that I have my whole life back now, and it feels *so good*."

"I'm really glad to hear that."

"I want you to know that it would not have happened that way if not for you, as well as my two dearest friends who are my twenty-first century family. I am very grateful."

Jonathan could only nod. He was beginning to feel like he was on the verge of tears himself. He could not quite tell if they were tears of joy, of relief, or of sadness, recognizing that he, like Clare, would probably never see Samantha again. "Thanks," he said.

After a moment's pause, Zjon reopened the conversation. "Please share with us the status of things from your end."

Jonathan looked at Edward and Clare, who both gave him a nod. "Well, as of late last night, I think that, between Clare and Edward and myself, we have confirmed somewhere around twenty-five to thirty people. These are a mixture of people representing all the major fields of science, as well as professors in history and the humanities. We even have one renowned scientist who could not travel, because he is bound to a wheelchair, but we are hoping we can connect him through Skype."

"Guess what!" Clare jumped in. "Allison is flying back to join us again. She said she just couldn't stay away."

"I'm so glad!" Samantha exclaimed.

"Yes, that is great," Jonathan agreed. "I hope you told her to get here before the FAA closes the airport at midnight tonight."

"Yes, she is arriving in time to join us for dinner."

Jonathan picked up where he had left off: "Good. Now, Dan and David are working to arrange the final location for the meeting. They will tell me the location tomorrow morning by nine o'clock. Meanwhile, everyone will check into one of the hotels that we recommended. David will arrange for his men to pick up everyone and take them to the meeting site. I have some of my contacts working through the university to set up closed-circuit audio video, so that the president's people can have discreet access. Zjon, can you spare Neal to help with this?"

"Absolutely, Jonathan."

"Perfect. Ask him to contact Dan. Now, remember, we also will have limited representation from the US government, although they will not be physically present in the meeting room. While I do not have confirmation, I predict that the president himself will be there. Dan's boss is handling all that from his end. If the president does come, he will have his own contingency of Secret Service. Also, remember, as far as our government is concerned, this entire meeting is restricted and top secret. They have no idea of our true intentions for making this a global event. Neal has to be very careful as he works with the technical crew not to spill the beans."

"Spill the beans?" Zjon asked. "What does that mean?"

Samantha answered for him. "He means tell the secret."

"Rest assured, Neal will be totally discreet. No beans will spill."

"Good." Jonathan paused. "Now I want to be totally straight with you."

"Straight?"

"That means honest and forthright. Once the meeting is concluded, a signal will have been established to alert the president's people to take you into custody. If they judge by the end of the meeting that you are legitimate, then they will try to take you both with them. This means you two, Zjon and Samantha. They will call it 'protective custody,' but it will be custody nonetheless. They know there is one other man with you, but they don't know who he is. And they know nothing about Sunanda. She should stay out of sight altogether.

"In the event that they decide you are not legitimate, they will send the police and the FBI to arrest you. I am not worried about that. I am sure you will prove to them who you are."

Clare broke in again. "I must underscore everything that Jonathan has been saying. Allison and I have spoken many times about the forces that have been at play since the dawn of modernity. Prime among them has been the idea of 'security.' Governments are obsessed with this idea. At the same time, oppositional forces, like terrorists and anarchists, consider themselves dedicated to destroying it. All of them are chasing a grand illusion, caught up in the same dream."

Samantha said, "That is most perceptive, Clare. I have read about this phenomenon." Motioning toward Zjon, she explained further, "We all have. But having lived among you all, I've been able to see that what is chiefly behind this illusion is the lack of experience of your true Presence. Your lives are dedicated to survival, and underneath this battle around security is nothing more than bundled fear. This condition of fear is not 'evil.' But it will take time for it to change. Believe me, we understand what we are dealing with here."

Jonathan had been listening to this exchange with interest. Seeing that Samantha had finished, he continued. "If all goes according to plan, we will be secretly broadcasting the meeting globally. Then it will be much more difficult for the feds to grab you. They will have to act carefully, finding themselves under public scrutiny.

That factor, which they have not planned for, should give us the advantage of figuring out how to whisk you away to safety before they can reach you. I am hoping that you do not need to resort to more magic tricks, I mean advanced technology. Any questions?"

Zjon smiled. "No, Jonathan, you have been very thorough."

"Then so much for logistics for now."

Edward said, "Let's take a short break and allow Jonathan to get some breakfast."

"Thanks, Ed, I forgot that I haven't eaten."

Jonathan stood up to head to the buffet, while Edward motioned a waiter over to bring everyone more coffee and juices.

CHAPTER 43

Time and Space

WHILE HE WAS EATING HIS BREAKFAST, JONATHAN LISTENED AS SAMANTHA RECOUNTED the story of her accident, and her experience of waking up under the tree on Twin Peaks three years earlier. Jonathan could not help noticing that a number of people in the restaurant had been casting side glances at Samantha. Who could blame them, given how attractive she was. Nevertheless, he could not help wondering if some may have recognized her from the publicity she had received several days before. A couple of the customers had puzzled expressions, as if possibly thinking she looked familiar. He filed this away to serve as a continuing reminder that they all needed to be vigilant until this thing was over.

When she finished her account, Zjon explained, "I want to clarify things, since I can see from reading your faces that you find her story mysterious. Samantha described her experience of a kind of capsule that enveloped her before she lost consciousness and subsequently awakened back on Earth. Allow me to risk explaining a small part of our science, since she has opened that 'can of worms,' as you say.

"As humankind ventured further and further into space exploration, accidents happened, and many good people died from those accidents. To prevent these deaths, scientists eventually invented a biological microcapsule that could be surgically embedded, in embryonic form, into an astronaut's body, just behind the navel.

This biocapsule was nanoprogrammed to be highly charged and intelligent. It was made of cellular material that, upon the devastating impact such as occurs in a space accident, in conjunction with the dramatic depressurization of space, would activate itself. The biocapsule would eject itself through the navel and then essentially explode into a kind of protective cocoon completely surrounding the person's body. That is what Samantha witnessed before she lost consciousness.

"What took place after the capsule self-activated consisted of three primary directives. First directive: keep the astronaut alive. Remaining connected to the body through a link to the navel, the capsule would supply the bloodstream with oxygen. Second directive: chart a course toward a safe environment. In this particular instance, Samantha's capsule ended up following a kind of wormhole that took her back in time. She essentially 'fell' into 'now.' Third directive: protect until rescued. This consisted of a network of functions, which included intelligent deflecting of extraneous matter, shock absorbing and heat deflecting upon reentry through an atmosphere, and sending a homing signal back to the source monitoring station. Also, the capsule provided camouflage from alien discovery. And finally, it provided memory encapsulation. This last you all have personally witnessed.

"The short-term functions can last up to seventy-two hours. At that point, the capsule was designed to dissolve itself. Samantha's capsule had actually landed on Earth and kept her invisible until she was ready to awaken, at which time Clare and Edward found her. However, the long-term functions—that is, the memory encapsulation—scientists designed to last for three years. I trust this short explanation gives you a better sense of what Samantha was sharing with you."

Jonathan, Edward, and Clare nodded their heads.

Turning back to Samantha, Zjon continued. "So, honey, all that vanity about having to make a name for yourself as a great explorer certainly created an enormous amount of trouble for us."

Samantha laughed. "Look at the bright side. We all get to do something no one has ever done before in human history. We are directly experiencing human life in another time."

Zjon agreed. "You are right. However, we are still not out of danger yet, and our good friends are very important to the success of this mission."

"Speaking of your mission," Edward cut in, "can you elaborate more on why Samantha fell through time?"

Zjon shook his head as he answered. "The truth is we do not know ourselves. Our scientists have speculated about this. The only hypothesis they came up with was that the timespace anomaly that Samantha was investigating was the most likely culprit. Perhaps she encountered something like what you call a wormhole, and this caused the phase shift. Perhaps not. We may never know. The fortunate thing about this accident was that Samantha's homing signal remained intact, so that we were able to track her location in the fabric of timespace."

"Come on, Zjon," Edward said. "Tell us more about time and space."

"I will try to explain in the best way that I can. But I warn you, my explanation will not satisfy you." The listeners at the table nodded their heads.

"Fair enough," conceded Edward. "We will appreciate whatever you can tell us."

Zjon began. "Since the dawn of human science, or as you speak about it in your time, since the dawn of Western civilization, all of Western culture latched onto several notions. These notions actually directed that culture to proceed down certain paths. Perhaps above all else was the path of attempting to interpret everything and understand everything through language. In the discourse that became known as *physics*, everyone attempted to use the language called *mathematics*. Mathematics from the beginning was held to be some kind of eternal, inviolable truth. There was nothing wrong with that in itself. It was extremely useful and succeeded in bringing your society into a state of super-survival."

Clare asked, "Super-survival?"

Samantha jumped in to clarify. "That is what we refer to as the innate propensity from Intelligence that allows for human beings to survive successfully, and in fact, go way beyond survival. Zjon is exactly right in that in your time most of you have achieved a level of super-survival. Just look around at the wealthy people who come to Las Vegas. They are the perfect demonstration of super-survival in action. But survival is not everything."

Zjon continued, "Exactly, survival is not everything. You live like you are masters and like you just want to control. But life is a force. You have not yet learned this truth. You are here not just to control or balance life, but to touch Intelligence and play with Intelligence like a musical instrument, so that you can bring about a melody of brilliance in your life at any time. Of course, we have mastered these things over thousands of years, and you are not yet ready. But even our coming and telling you these things may have an impact on your personal life. The place for you to begin is by cultivating appreciation and reverence in living.

"Some people around your time have asked the question, 'What else is there?' At this time things are on the verge of erupting, but nothing has completely come about yet. People are doing different kinds of things to answer these questions, things such as mind control and meditation practices. In the end these things are still in the service of super-survival. Yes, they have provided exciting, intelligent, and even brilliant revelations, but that is all you can actually have at the moment.

"Until now human beings could not have a different kind of brilliance. That would be too much to handle. As an analogy, just because you like electricity, you do not send a thousand-watt current into your light bulbs. You are in a process of evolution, which is the way it must and should be. But you can perhaps get some sense of what I call 'emotional combustions.' Emotional combustions are ways that you can actually ignite the fire inside you that will emanate out of you as a light, so that you can see things that other people do not see.

"To get back to what I was saying about time and space ... as Samantha pointed out, you have compiled enormous amounts of knowledge. But knowledge, no matter how useful, gives you no access to your Presence. In fact, it gives you no access to the *present*, not to mention the *future*. You can only engage the present and Presence, by being present! This is not a function of knowledge, nor is it a function of language. There were many great philosophers who looked to language as the key to solving the great mysteries of life. Some even claimed that language was the key to the future. Perhaps this is so, but perhaps not.

"What is for certain is that in the past, philosophers and scientists latched onto mathematics as the language for dealing with time and space. They developed a conception of time as a series of linear, successive points of now. In this way, they could *measure* time. Likewise, they did something similar with respect to space. They conceived of space as a huge mass of points of extension and they developed the idea of three dimensions. With three dimensions and points, they arrived at a similar way of *measuring* and *using* space, again to aid in survival.

"I can see from the expressions on your faces that you are thinking, 'Of course, this is common sense.' It did, indeed, become common knowledge. It became so fundamental, in fact, that the notions of matter, energy, space, and time could in theory, through the language of mathematics, enable marvelous technologies for effective traveling into outer space. But there was a big catch."

Jonathan ventured, "The speed of light."

"Yes, very good Jonathan, the speed of light. Einstein proved that nothing having mass can travel faster than the speed of light, and along with that, time and space are bent by mass, through gravity. There were many implications of this, including the one that time travel is impossible. We are stuck in timespace, or 'space-time,' as it is referred to in the present. This is part of our destiny as beings that have mass and energy. Even as other mysteries began to appear after Einstein, notably first that of the behavior of quantum particles, scientists continued to consistently and persistently try to address all mysteries using the language of mathematics. This was not a bad thing, mind you. This exclusive approach to science just overlooks other fundamental things—other ways of seeing.

"Yesterday and the days just before, you all witnessed some things that lay outside the bounds of knowledge and even the bounds of language. You experienced your Presence. You saw things that you could not account for, such as water materializing from a ceiling, flashing lights, even me materializing in your bedroom, Jonathan. You heard sounds coming through a rock from another time. All of these events are impossible, mathematically speaking. All violate common sense. Yet, you witnessed them, did you not?"

Zjon did not wait for a response, but continued. "I invite you to consider the possibility that up until now human beings have been fixated on the problem of survival. This fixation has led to entire paradigms of globally and culturally accepted bodies of knowledge. These bodies of knowledge have all been constructed and preserved in globally accepted structures of language. *But all knowledge is the past.* You may see that where you will need to look may be outside of these structures. You may need to develop and employ other faculties beyond language and knowledge. You may need to develop a *relationship* with a rock."

With this last comment, everyone around the table smiled.

Zjon continued, "You can do this. In fact, each of you has latent, untapped capacities for lifting yourself far beyond super-survival. What you need to do is develop yourselves to interact directly with Intelligence. Samantha will talk with you about how to start tonight at dinner.

"Meanwhile, I will wrap up this session by saying a few simple things about space and time. Neither of them is what you think they are. Think of what you know to be space and time as subsets or versions of space and time. I will leave you with some things to ponder:

- Space is a happening.
- Whatever is happening is alive and in motion.

- Space is alive, and so is time.
- Time is the glue that allows for all things, including space.
- Space is the ultimate boundary of Infinity, not out there, but everywhere.
- It is in the space within you that everything happens.
- What is space? Space is the light of life.
- What is light? Light is love."

Samantha now added, "We always belong in a certain time. That is called 'living with the flow.' Living with the flow is living right now. When you are living right now, you do not have the past and the future to affect you. This is the true meaning of time itself."

With that last statement, Zjon stood up to leave. Looking at the faces of Jonathan, Edward, and Clare, he decided to say one more thing. "Please do not take these words and attempt to make them into some kind of religion or belief system. See if you can look behind them and feel something. Intelligence is in your body, in all your cells, as well as in all things around you. Time and space are gifts of Intelligence. Love them, and they will love you back."

CHAPTER 44

Las Vegas, Day Eight, 3:15 p.m.

"THANKS, DAVID. WE'LL RECONNECT AT SIX O'CLOCK." FEDERAL SPECIAL INVESTIGATOR Dan Hamilton wrapped up his three o'clock briefing call with Special Agent David Newman and turned to face the Chief. The two men were seated together in a private suite that David had previously arranged to serve as a meeting room on the top floor of the Wynn Las Vegas Hotel. "Well, Chief, I guess you heard the update."

The Chief (a.k.a., Wallace Wade) nodded his head and said, "Sounds like everything is still on track. Agent Newman seems to be getting the job done."

"I think so, sir. He's turned out to be a solid guy."

"Good. And how are you doing? You look pretty tired. You going to hold up through tomorrow's events?"

"I'm good. I've functioned on less sleep before. But it will be very good to get this meeting behind us and have our guests in custody."

Dan did not say it, but he was well aware that his fatigue was really coming from his efforts to juggle his official job on this case with the unofficial agenda of Mission Heart. The latter was a totally rejuvenating experience. The difficult part was the former, which felt to him like a burden. Deep down, he was not sure he would have a job after tomorrow. He was secretly worried that it could turn out to be worse, perhaps in the form of jail time. He had to keep putting that out of his mind. The whole thing was calling for an enormous amount of Heart Trust. He liked that term used by Zjon.

Wallace continued. "I agree. Are you confident that we can get them into custody? After all, from what you have reported, these people have an amazing capacity to escape."

"I believe so. What makes this different is two things. First, previously we were trying to entrap them. Second, and more importantly, they asked to have this meeting. We didn't. They came forward saying they wanted to meet with important people, specifically here in the United States. They have some things to tell us and to show us. They're acting like diplomats, as I see it. I think we should treat them that way. Yes, they do have remarkable capacities and technologies. That has convinced me they *are* from the future. The most important thing, I believe, is that we not threaten them in any way. I was relieved that the president chose not to bring in a big military presence. I genuinely think these people are on our side."

"Well, I trust your judgment. More importantly, the president also seems to see things the same way. You've done a fine job here, Dan, so far. I must say that if you are right, perhaps we may be at some kind of turning point in history. Don't tell anyone I said this."

"No worry, Chief. I would never let on myself, but one of my favorite things is poetry."

"No kidding?"

"No."

"Well, let me share another little secret. I actually knew that when I hired you."

"No kidding?"

"No kidding. Back to the topic at hand, though. I understand that Edward and Clare Hunter checked out of the Bellagio this morning. Do you know where they are?"

"No. I was tied up with David and did *not* see it happen." Dan knew he was walking the tightrope again and chose his words carefully.

"And you still have no idea where this Zjon and Samantha and the other man from the future are?"

"We have no idea where they've been staying. They have an ability to show up where they want to and when. The last couple of days they have chosen to contact Jonathan whenever they want to meet and have given him instructions as to the location. As of today, though, we haven't heard anything. Once you give me the go-ahead, I will let Jonathan know where the meeting will be held tomorrow, and Jonathan will pass it on to them."

"Very good, then. You and I should meet here tonight, in this room, at ten o'clock. Have David here with you. Also, bring Jonathan Elliot. I want to meet him in person."

"Yes, sir."

"Make no mistake about things, Dan."

"Yes, sir?"

"We *will* be taking these people into custody and back to Washington. Assuming, of course, that they prove to be who they claim to be. The president and I are considering this a matter of national security. Are you clear about this?"

"Very clear, Chief." Dan knew that this had to be the official government position. He hoped that things would go the way Zjon and Samantha and the others seemed confident they would go.

"What are you thinking, Dan?" The Chief was gazing intently at him.

Dan thought for a moment and then asked, "Can I ask you something?"

"Shoot."

"None of us who work for you know your real name. I understand you picked the name Wallace Wade for this mission. Where did that come from?"

The Chief chuckled and said, "Oh, that. He was a great college football coach, back in the Golden Age, long before my time. Actually, this name was not my choosing, but the president's."

"The president cares about football? I thought he was strictly a basketball man."

"Yes, well, the man has hidden depths."

The Chief's laughter that followed this last statement broke the tension that Dan had been feeling.

CHAPTER 45

Palms, Las Vegas, Day Eight, 7:00 p.m.

JONATHAN STEPPED OUT OF THE ELEVATOR ONTO THE TOP FLOOR OF THE FANTASY TOWER of the Palms Casino Resort. Accompanying him was Diana Chadwick, dressed in a stunning black evening gown and wearing a heavy Tiffany's gold-link necklace. His excitement at being with this gorgeous woman was heightened by the chance to introduce Diana to their guests from the forty-sixth century.

There to greet the couple was the hostess of the Nove Italiano restaurant, who escorted them to an upper deck used primarily for private parties. This room afforded one of the most stunning panoramic views of the Las Vegas Strip. At first Jonathan had questioned Edward for choosing this location for dinner. The Palms seemed to be off the beaten track in many ways, but Edward had told him that many celebrities choose the Palms for this very reason. One could dine away from the masses of tourists. Besides, Nove was renowned for its outstanding cuisine.

Immediately upon entering the room, Jonathan saw that most of his group had already arrived. Sitting around a large table were Zjon, Samantha, Clare, Edward, Neal, Sunanda, and Allison. The only person who appeared to be missing was Dan, although there were four empty chairs. Jonathan knew David was working and suspected that he was watching from a hidden vantage point, probably keeping an eye on the elevators from the casino level. As the couple approached the table, the three men stood to greet them.

"Allow me to introduce my fiancé," Jonathan announced. "Everyone, this is Diana Chadwick. She flew here this morning from New York. This afternoon, I asked her to marry me, and she accepted."

"Congratulations!" said Edward, and the others immediately started clapping.

"How do you do?" Diana said, beaming. "I am so pleased to meet you all at last."

Zjon shook Diana's hand and pulled out a chair for her, saying, "I believe we have met once, although probably only in your dreams."

"So, that was you!" Diana laughed. "You are the one who has brought my Jon into this web of intrigue and mystery. And are you the infamous Samantha?"

"Yes, indeed; here I am." The two shook hands across the table.

"Jonathan shared with me about his first encounter with you in London. I will say I was jealous for a little while. You are as beautiful as he described."

"Thank you, and so are you."

Everyone sat down. Jonathan introduced the rest of the group. "This is Clare Hunter and her husband Edward, both professors on sabbatical from UCSF. They have been Samantha's hosts and protectors for the past three years. To their left are two other compatriots from the future, Neal, and I assume, Sunanda." Sunanda nodded to him in the affirmative. "And last, to my far right is Allison Russell, esteemed professor of philosophy at NYU." Within seconds Diana found herself amazed at how quickly she felt like part of the family.

"Yes, you are indeed," Samantha said to Diana.

"Indeed what?"

"Part of our family."

Diana was shocked and did not try to hide it. "How did you do that?"

"Do what?" Samantha asked.

"You read my mind."

"Oh. I just listened; that is all."

Jonathan chuckled and said, "Don't worry, Diana, you'll get used to it."

Diana turned to him and said, "Well, I hope our friends from the future don't do this all the time. Some thoughts I would prefer not to have read." Turning to Jonathan, she said, "Especially tonight." Smiling mischievously, she picked up the two glasses of wine that Zjon had poured while she was being introduced, handed one to Jonathan, and said, "To my future husband!" Everyone at the table picked up their own glasses in a silent toast as Jonathan and Diana took their first sips.

"Diana, you are a fashion consultant, yes?" Allison asked. "I have just one question."

"What's that, Allison?"

"Would you consult with me? I need your look." Everyone laughed.

"I'd be happy to arrange it. Would you teach me some philosophy, so that I can hold my own with Jonathan?"

"You bet, although I suspect you don't need any more holding than you are clearly already getting." Again, there was laughter.

"Could we talk about something else, please?" Jonathan asked.

"No way, man, you asked for it this evening," Edward said.

"Okay, I surrender," Jonathan said, raising both hands.

Diana retorted, "Very smart, dear. And don't forget it. I like these people very much."

Jonathan tried to get out of the spotlight by asking, "Zjon, where's Dan? Isn't he coming?"

Before Zjon could respond, Dan's voice came from behind him across the room. "I'm right here, guys." Jonathan and Diana turned around to see Dan walking proudly across the room with a beautiful brunette on his left arm. "Everyone, this is my girlfriend, Emily. She flew into Las Vegas late last night. Thank you, Edward, for inviting us."

Edward nodded and announced, "Welcome, welcome. Everyone, dinner is on Clare and me tonight. I've taken the liberty of preordering family style—that is, Italian family style. Let the celebrations begin."

The next few minutes were spent in another round of introductions and more toasts, as Dan and Emily took the two remaining seats at the table. A quick flurry followed as waiters brought more rounds of drinks and opened two more bottles of wine. Zjon, Samantha, Neal, and Sunanda mostly watched in fascination as the twenty-first century social rituals unfolded and revealed themselves in front of their eyes. Jonathan and Dan caught each other's eyes for a moment and shared smiles of recognition. Life was indeed good, although bittersweet at this moment.

As things began to quiet down, Jonathan said to Zjon. "Well, I guess this is our last night together. If David could be here, we would have an even dozen."

"That would be a dirty dozen!" Dan put in.

Turning to Dan, Zjon inquired, "Dan, will David be able to join us, at least for dessert?"

"He's going to come by at nine o'clock. He can spend a half hour with us and then has to take me and Jonathan back to meet with my boss for a ten o'clock planning session. We will need to be careful not to drink too much, though. We need to be clear-headed for that meeting," Dan explained.

"Don't worry about that. Samantha will give each of you a special session before you leave, and you will be completely unimpaired."

"How can you do that?"

Samantha answered, "It's a special kind of signaling that will cause the alcohol to evaporate from your body. You both will be completely sober, alert, and awake."

Dan responded, "Well, that sounds good. You and Zjon keep talking about this 'signaling.' Just what the hell is it all about?"

"I will talk about that after we have had a chance to eat," Samantha answered.

On that note, Edward reached up and gestured to a waiter, indicating they were ready to begin their meal. "I hope you all like Italian."

CHAPTER 46

Signaling

"Signaling is the silent language of Intelligence." Samantha's out-of-the-blue words instantly brought everyone to attention.

The evening meal had begun to wind down. It was now eight forty-five. David had pulled up a chair to join them a few minutes before, in time to share dessert. Dan had noticed with satisfaction that David seemed to be more focused than he had been all week, as well as happier. David had clearly shifted something within himself and looked years younger in the process. Yes, he really was an altogether good guy. *Now we are a dirty dozen*, he thought. Dan smiled to himself as he sipped his after-dinner cappuccino and turned his full attention to Samantha.

"Would you please repeat that?" Allison requested. Dan noticed that something had changed about Allison, too. The Allison he had seen earlier in the week had been defensive, challenging, and almost hostile. Before him tonight sat a woman who was calm, poised, and at ease. *I actually think I like this person*, he realized.

"Signaling is the silent language of Intelligence."

Zjon stepped in. "As I mentioned, Samantha is an expert in sensing, tapping, and signaling. I wanted to wait until she had recovered her full memory for her to speak about this. Even in our time, Samantha is very advanced. Consider this conversation our final gift to you." Zjon looked back at Samantha for her to continue.

"Sensing, tapping, and signaling are all special faculties human beings have for interacting with Universal Intelligence. They are innate human capacities, carried by everyone in our cells through our genetics. It took thousands and thousands of years of evolution after the dawn of the human species for us to develop them. In your time, I can see and feel them latent in all of you. You really are no different from people in our time. You just never have had these faculties awakened in your body. It requires practice as well as awakening and awareness.

"Sensing is the capacity to feel something before it happens, like an earthquake or other natural event. Sensing is an emotional eruption of brilliance that you feel before something comes. It can be connected to the weather, an accident, an approaching friend, or so many other things. Even in the future, very few people have become expert in sensing because there are many other ways we can engage with the future without sensing. The universe will give clues all the time, if you are smart and awake enough to see them. When you are, you will go into the future more awake and aware. And you sometimes can even make a prediction and change an outcome. We all have the ability, deep down. It is really a matter of listening to Intelligence—listening to, from, and through the heart.

"Tapping is another very powerful faculty. The best way I can describe it is by analogy. Tapping is like tapping into a maple tree. The maple tree has the syrup, but unless you tap into it, you do not get the syrup. In a similar way, Intelligence lives in Silence. Right now in the world of the twenty-first century, people think that Silence is like sleep, an emptiness, or just an absence of sound. They do not realize that Silence is a powerful force you can tap into, if you attune yourself.

"A good way to start using this faculty is by taking a moment of pause. Create a moment of pause in whatever you are doing, especially in moments where you are feeling busy, frenzied, or caught up in your life. If you know how to tap into Intelligence, into Silence, then the Silence breaks, and what comes out of Silence are realizations, recognitions, appreciation, and acknowledgment. Things open up brilliantly, in your emotions, in your body, and in your thinking. But you have to know how to tap into Silence.

"This brings me to talk about signaling. Signaling is emotional overflow that comes out of deepest love and recognition. Most often it can take the form of motions with your hands and your fingers, or with your breath. You often signal unconsciously in the way you carry your body and the way you talk and think. For example, if you think hostile thoughts, Intelligence can hear them and respond in accordance with them. This can make your life miserable. On the other side, there are a number of forms of signaling you can do that can have amazing effects.

"Signaling is an ancient art. When you look at statues of the Buddha and the various ways the Buddha is shown holding his hands, you are seeing representations of signaling. The same is true of early paintings of Christ: for example, where Jesus is holding up one hand with his fingers in a blessing or holding his other hand down in this position." Samantha demonstrated hand positions as she spoke.

"Artists often depicted halos around Christ's head or beams of light coming from his hands in order to try to depict the manifestations of signaling. In representations of the Buddha and Hindu Sadhus, artists depicted expressions of the overflow of love. Hand positions of the Buddha and in Yoga were called 'mudras.' These gestures and postures were, in fact, forms of signaling. People have tried to imitate them without understanding what they actually do. One cannot use them mechanically. One has to feel it in one's heart, and then it is like a melody.

"Signaling is like playing the piano through your emotions. Tapping with your fingers or thumbs or doing various types of breathing will open various other spaces in your Heart Spectrum. The same can be true of certain sounds, which in the past were known as 'mantras.' People misunderstood those as well, and many have tried to use them mechanically.

"The other night, when you watched Zjon blow into my fingers and saw light coming out from my other hand, you were witnessing a powerful act of signaling. You saw the water fountains and the lights undergo a powerful change. That was Intelligence responding in a very playful way. Intelligence loves to play with us. You only need to ask it to. Intelligence is everywhere."

Samantha paused. Allison asked, "Samantha, can you teach us some forms of signaling before you leave us tomorrow?"

"We will see what time permits. But regardless, do not be afraid to experiment for yourselves. There are some basic kinds of motions you can do with your hands and fingers and with sounds and breathing, as well. You will need to try them to see what feels right. Your body naturally will attune itself, and you can trust your feelings and emotions.

"Before we leave for tonight, I wanted to show you some other things. These also have a special connection to the Universal Intelligence. Sunanda, would you get out the stones?"

Sunanda reached into a satchel she had brought with her to the table and extracted five objects. From where he was sitting, Jonathan thought they looked like deep blue, luminescent rocks or crystals. He could not tell for sure. Samantha laid them out where the group could see them. Everyone leaned in closer for a clearer view. Jonathan saw that each stone had been crafted into the shape of a heart. Each heart had a different kind of symbol carved into its face. The symbol was a pure white, which dazzled as it stood out from the radiant blue background of the stone. These were beautifully crafted pieces of art! As he looked at each one individually, Jonathan felt a different kind of feeling or emotion. He noticed that the entire group was mesmerized.

At last Jonathan asked, "What are these objects?"

Samantha replied by asking him, "Tell me, Jonathan, what do you see?"

"These look like heart-shaped, engraved stones."

"Yes, they are stones that were crafted by one of the great artists in our time, a man named Miller. As you look at each one individually, what do you see?"

"Well, looking from my left to right, the first one has an image like a circle. The second has a vertical line in the center. The third looks like the letter 'S.' The fourth looks like the letter 'X.' And the last one looks like the picture of an arrow. But what do they represent?"

Samantha answered, "I will try to explain, first what they are on the surface, and then what they mean below the surface. Throughout history, people have communicated about nature through various mathematical symbols and languages. These began with arithmetic and geometry, and then evolved into algebra, calculus, and other forms of mathematics. We developed special symbols. You should easily be able to recognize the first two symbols and their significance."

Edward spoke up in response. "Those are zero and one."

"Exactly. In what you have called the digital age, the age of computers and basic electronics, zero and one are the foundation for all understanding. Your technology is based on the binary system, the system of zero and one. The first two stones represent the zero-one elements—the elements Earth and Fire. The zero-one configurations are used for what we call horizontal communications and are, essentially, about survival.

"In our time, our symbology has expanded. As human awareness opened up and moved beyond the plane of survival, we developed other symbols to represent other dimensions—the other three elements. The people who introduced the other three symbols changed our evolution."

Edward asked, "How did they do that?"

"Think of it this way," Samantha responded. "Symbolically speaking, zero stands for the matrix, and one is the ascendant force. Zero (the circle) is the feminine; one (the straight line) is the masculine. The circle energetically represents the mother's womb and Mother Earth. It also evokes sensuous love and giving. The one, the straight line, is like a force. The force is the force of ascendance. The era of zero and one extended from the discovery of the wheel all the way through the computer era. But people did not know or recognize the symbolic functions of the S and the X and the Arrow. Those came into prominence about a thousand years in the future from today.

"Think of S as the natural form of your emotions. It is like a running current, like the river, like water. It is always running, always feeling, always flowing. S is also shaped in the form of a hook, meaning it is like a link. The S can hook into various things and hold onto them. So, S is symbolically the bridge between the circle and the straight line. In terms of the five elements, S represents the element Water.

"The next symbol is that of the X. The X means represents a 'vanishing point.' The X is analogous to a window. The window is at first closed. The form X can on the surface mean closure or blockage. But at its center is a hole—the vanishing point. At its center, you can symbolically go through the X. Thus, the X actually means 'crossings.' Crossings are emotional interactions. Another way of looking at X is as two horizons, not straight but tilted. When the horizons are tilted, there is a new space that is an opening. Einstein, Galileo, and others crossed the X when they encountered it in their thinking and then went through its center into a whole new dimension of thinking. Ultimately, the X symbolizes the connection to Infinity. The element associated with this symbol is Air.

"This brings us to the Arrow. You and I cannot actually experience Infinity, which is why we have the Arrow. The Arrow is something that is already in motion. The Arrow represents the continuum of infinities. Space, light, and all that exists in and after life all exist symbolically as the Arrow, which is associated with the element Space. To see the symbolism of the arrow requires the connection with Intelligence. Through the symbol of the Arrow comes the power of realization.

"The symbols in front of you represent the five elemental forces going through your bodies. The first two represent the horizontal plane. The other three symbolize the vertical, the vertical ascendance."

Samantha looked around the table and recognized that her friends had become mentally and emotionally saturated. She concluded, "With practice, you may gradually come to appreciate sensing, tapping, and signaling. We need to finish so that David and Dan can get to their meeting, and the four of us can get some sleep. Clare, if you will hand me that glass of water, I will charge it. Each of you should take a drink, and you will sleep very soundly tonight."

CHAPTER 47

Wynn Las Vegas, Day Eight, 10:25 p.m.

CHIEF WALLACE WADE WAS LOUNGING IN ONE OF THE CHAIRS OF THE SAME TOP FLOOR suite where he and Dan had met that afternoon. Seated across from him was Dan, and between them, sharing a sofa, were David and Jonathan. Wallace motioned to an aide to bring coffee refills for everyone. While he appeared totally relaxed, he had spent the past twenty-five minutes carefully scrutinizing David and Jonathan. This was the first time they had met, and he wanted to gain a firsthand sense of each man for himself. All three men seemed calm and at ease. He thought it unusual. Especially David, whom Dan had earlier characterized as being "histrionic."

David and Dan had just wrapped up the latest debriefing. The Chief turned his attention back to Jonathan. "I can see that you have provided a valuable service in this whole matter, Jonathan. Your connection to Samantha seems to have been key to bringing us to where we are now."

"Thank you, sir."

"Please call me Wallace, at least for now."

"Okay, Wallace."

"Just how did you come to the conclusion that these people were from the future?"

"In the end it was the simplest explanation. The existence of the Avalon Charged Field, the incident in New York, and what they later demonstrated to us personally, all showed that these people have technological capabilities far beyond our own. And there was another reason."

"What was that?"

"Who they say they are, their explanation. These people are unbelievably honest. Frankly, I trust them instinctively. And that wasn't just me, mind you. Dan and David have told me the same thing. Therefore, I conclude that the explanation that they come from the future makes the most sense."

"So both of you agree with Jonathan's assessment?"

"Absolutely," Dan affirmed. "I thought this had to be some kind of hoax, but I changed my mind when I met them face to face."

David concurred, "Me too, sir. In fact, meeting these people has changed my life."

"That's quite a claim, David."

"I know, but you will see what we are talking about firsthand tomorrow."

Wallace stirred some sugar into his coffee and nodded noncommittally. "I have a confession to make."

"A confession?" Jonathan asked.

"I had an ulterior motive in bringing you and David here tonight."

"What was that?" Jonathan felt some alarm.

Without answering the question, Wallace made another motion to his aide. The aide walked over and leaned in closely. Wallace whispered something to him. The aide turned around and went over to the bedroom door, knocked twice, and then entered the room, quietly closing the door behind him. Jonathan watched this and then shot a glance over to Dan, who merely shrugged his shoulders. Wallace picked up his coffee cup and took another sip, keeping his eyes intently focused on Jonathan, who remained intentionally unperturbed. He was not going to get sucked into some game of cat and mouse. Nevertheless, he was very glad that Samantha had charged that glass of water at the end of their dinner. His body continued to vibrate with a feeling of wellbeing and assuredness. After some time, they heard the sound of a latch being turned.

Without a word, Wallace set down his coffee cup and rose to his feet. Instinctively, the other three men stood as well. Into the room strode the president of the United States, who strode over to the other unoccupied couch and took a seat. Dan realized that the president had carefully staged this whole scene. The four men reseated themselves, turning their undivided attention toward him.

Wallace broke the silence with, "Good evening, Mister President."

"Good evening, Wallace."

The three others echoed in unison, "Good evening, Mister President." The president nodded to each in turn.

"Mister President, I understand that you already know Special Investigator Dan Hamilton and *The New York Times* Chief Science Editor Jonathan Elliot."

"Yes, indeed. Good to see you both, and thank you for coming."

"And I would like to introduce FBI Special Agent David Newman, serving as chief liaison from the western region."

"Pleasure to meet you, David, if I may call you David."

"By all means, Mister President. It's an honor to meet you."

The president then got down to business. "Wallace?"

The Chief nodded. "The president arrived here earlier today and insisted on meeting each of you personally. That is why I asked you both to join Dan for this evening's meeting. Incidentally, he heard all of the briefing that you just gave me through an intercom, so you do not need to review what you have already told me. He may have some questions for you."

The president stepped in. "Thank you, Wallace. And thank you, men, for your thoroughness, your clarity, and your good work this past week. Dan, I want to thank you especially for your stellar work in pursuing this situation—a situation that has turned out to be far from anything that any of us could have imagined. It has required me to stretch my thinking and my imagination to their limits. I am hoping that tomorrow's meetings will shed enough light for us all to be operating in the light, instead of in the shadows. I trust you are in agreement with me on that."

Dan answered, "Absolutely, Mister President. It took a hell of a lot of stretching for David, Jonathan, and me to reach the conclusions we have reached. We know that tomorrow will bear us out."

Wallace corrected him. "To say you 'know,' Dan, is a strong statement. I think it still would be best for you to say you 'believe,' or 'feel' confident."

"With all due respect, Chief, the three of us are confident enough at this point to say that we know this. They have demonstrated their claims with indisputable evidence, and we expect that tomorrow you will see the evidence for yourselves."

The president said, "I will accept that, Dan, not only because I am familiar with both you and Jonathan, but also for other reasons that I choose not to divulge at this moment." Everyone in the room found themselves wondering what the president meant by this. The president resumed. "But there is one thing that you seem to have omitted from your report."

The president was looking at Dan, who kept a poker face. "Yes, Mister President?"

The president turned his attention to Jonathan as he continued the conversation. "Perhaps you know what I am referring to, Jonathan?"

Jonathan forced himself to remain quiet.

The president continued. "No, Jonathan, I do not want you to answer me. I do not want to put you into a position of possibly lying. But I suspect that you know what I am thinking. My people tell me that an unusual number of high-level people from various news organizations have arrived in Las Vegas over the past two days. We checked and saw that there are no special conventions in town, so we found this quite a coincidence."

"It does sound that way, Mister President," said Jonathan, who had regained his voice.

"You, of all people, must realize the power of the press in such a sensitive matter."

"I fully understand, Mister President."

"Then, I trust that you might have some good ideas about how we can keep a leak of information from happening here."

"I think I do have an idea."

"Then please share it."

All eyes in the room had turned to Jonathan Elliot. Wallace now felt quite sure that Jonathan had been responsible for this situation. He thought to himself how he would have handled this conversation had he been in the president's shoes. He would have had Jonathan Elliot arrested on the spot. But then he was not the president.

Jonathan thought for a second and then proceeded. "Well, Mister President, I think we could allow hand-selected representatives of the press to attend the interview meeting, under strict instructions to just listen and not participate. Then they could release information that you have sanctioned, in the timing of your choosing. For national security purposes, naturally."

"And what about those who are not selected?"

"Well, we could make this a lottery, with the entry opportunity including signing an agreement of confidentiality where their jobs would be on the line. The agreement would also specify that none of the press representatives would have exclusive rights to the information."

"This idea has merit. What do you think, Wallace?"

"I think it could work, Mister President. Assuming that Jonathan actually can reach all parties, of course."

"I think I could, especially with the help of some of David's men and the president's people, who probably already know how to find them."

"Very well, Jonathan," the president said. "We will go with your idea. You design the lottery. Plan for three representatives of the press to be there. No TV cameras, though. Wallace, you draft the agreement and give it to me by six o'clock in the morning. Jonathan, you will be responsible for making the lottery selection, no later than nine o'clock. I will leave it to you to make sure everybody understands the consequences."

"Thank you, Mister President." Jonathan felt relieved.

Wallace Wade once again found himself impressed with the president's wisdom. The commander in chief had turned a potentially devastating situation to his own advantage and one that seemed to be perfectly aligned with the interests of the nation. At the same time, he had preserved the reputation of a loyal citizen.

Satisfied, the president said, "The other reason I wanted to talk to you three tonight concerns something personal."

"Anything, Mister President. How can we assist you?"

"As you know, we are going to be observing this meeting through closed-circuit cameras from a room nearby. But I have decided that I want to meet these people privately, either before or after the interview. Not just Samantha, but also the one called Zjon."

"Are you sure that is wise, Mister President?" Wallace asked. "I think this is very risky, both personally and politically."

"I am certain on this point. I know you can keep it secret. And I have my own reasons to think that I will be physically safe. Something happened some time back. This meeting far outweighs the theoretical risks."

"But Mister President, we cannot let you take such a risk, no matter how small."

"I am not asking here, Wallace."

"Yes, Mister President."

Turning to Dan, the president asked, "Will you arrange this for me?"

"I will, sir."

"Thank you. Anything else for you tonight, Wallace?"

"I believe that covers everything." Wallace now found himself facing a new set of worries. He hoped that the president was right about these people from the future. But it was not his call. "How do we handle your Secret Service detail?"

"They do not have to know, do they? I am sure that Dan and David can arrange this without stepping on any toes."

"We can handle it, Mister President."

"Thank you all, and good work. This meeting is adjourned."

All rose as the president stood up and left the room.

After he'd left, Dan asked Wallace. "Chief, just how did the president manage to get here without being seen by the whole world?"

"We flew into Nellis and caravanned from there."

"No, I mean into this hotel. How did he get here without being recognized?"

Wallace smiled and answered, "Ever hear of landing a helicopter on a roof?"

CHAPTER 48

Palms, Las Vegas, Day Eight, 11:30 p.m.

FOLLOWING THEIR DINNER, EDWARD AND CLARE HAD ADJOURNED WITH ALLISON TO their suite in the Fantasy Tower of Palms Casino Resort, leaving Zjon, Samantha, Neal, and Sunanda back in the restaurant. It had now been almost two hours since they had left the others, and Clare was getting worried.

"What do you think is keeping them so long?" she asked.

"Don't worry, honey. They can take care of themselves."

"But they should have been here by now. What if they were caught?"

"Caught? If something had happened, we would have heard a ruckus. You know Zjon and what he is capable of."

"Edward is right, Clare," Allison said reassuringly. "We would have heard some kind of explosion or seen some unusual lights."

"I know you're right. I just get worried about Samantha. It's a habit."

At that moment, they heard the sound of a key card being inserted in the lock of the front door, followed by a beep. The door latch turned, the door swung open, and in came Samantha, laughing. Following behind were Zjon, Sunanda, and Neal, all giggling like children.

"What's so funny?" Clare demanded.

"You should have been there!" Neal exclaimed. All four of them kept laughing, as Zjon clumsily closed the door behind him.

"You four look plastered!" Edward said. This observation caused only more laughter.

"Are you drunk?" Clare asked.

Samantha only nodded as she plopped down with Zjon onto the empty sofa. She picked up a pillow and covered her face, trying to bring herself under control. Neal and Sunanda staggered over near the window and sat down on the carpet.

Allison demanded, "Stop this now and tell us what happened!"

Zjon finally composed himself enough to speak. "After dinner we were getting ready to come back up to the suite. But Samantha asked if I would take her out dancing."

"Dancing!" Clare said. "Samantha, you've never gone to a nightclub since we've known you."

"I know, Clare, but I've wanted to see one for a long time now. I was curious, you know. So, I figured, since this is my last night here, why not?"

Neal said, "So I called a taxi, and the four of us went over to the Cosmopolitan."

"A taxi?" Edward was flabbergasted. "Why didn't you take Melissa?"

"We wanted to experience the true Las Vegas. You have to ride in a taxi at least once. So we gave Melissa the night off."

Edward chuckled. "Don't even tell me what Melissa did. I don't want to hear about it."

Allison said, "Anyway, what happened?"

Zjon continued. "We asked the taxi driver where he would go dancing if this were his last night in Las Vegas. So he took us to the Cosmopolitan. When we got there, we went into one of the clubs. I ordered a Scotch for me, red wine for Samantha, and martinis for Neal and Sunanda. They hadn't had any twenty-first-century liquor yet."

"We loved the olives!" Sunanda said. "We kept ordering martinis so we could have more olives. They really crept up on us!"

Zjon continued, "While we were drinking, Samantha and I were watching people on the dance floor. It was fascinating. The way people dance here seems like some sort of unbreakable code."

"Definitely not what we are used to," Samantha said.

"Definitely not," Zjon agreed. "Then all of a sudden, these two males walked up to Samantha and started making suggestions. They sounded like some form of sexual advances, perhaps a form of mating ritual from this time. I was not quite sure. Then they got physically closer and closer to her, and finally one of them tried to reach out, as if to grab her."

Clare said, "Oh no, Samantha. What happened?"

"Before they could continue, Samantha gave a quick signal with her thumb and forefinger, and the two men were propelled backward across the dance floor to the other side of the room."

"You should have seen their faces when they landed on their rear ends on a sofa against the wall," Samantha said. "They looked like they had no idea what had happened."

"They had no idea how to deal with a woman like Samantha," Zjon said.

"The best part was," Samantha resumed, "after that the bartender gave each of us another drink for free. She said he had never seen anything like that before, and could I teach her? I said maybe in twenty-five hundred years. She got a big kick out of that!"

Allison said, "I bet she did!"

With that everyone in the room joined into the laughter.

As the clock approached midnight, the room grew quieter. Allison looked around the room and suddenly recognized she was in the company of three distinct couples. Neal and Sunanda were sitting comfortably back against the windowsill, apparently lost in their own thoughts. Clare and Edward were on one couch and looked like they would soon be ready to doze off. And Zjon and Samantha were looking into each other's eyes. Now Allison completely understood why it was that Zjon was the one who had come to rescue Samantha. "I think it's time we all agree to call it an evening. Good night, everybody."

"Good night, Allison," Clare and Samantha said at the same time. "See you at breakfast."

"Before leaving, I just want to say thank you, Zjon and Samantha and Neal and Sunanda. You have awakened in me a fuller understanding of the wisdom of those who preceded us, and for that, as well, I will always be grateful."

Zjon replied, "You are most welcome, Allison. We all thank you for your friendship."

"I'll see you at breakfast, Clare." Allison then turned and left the suites.

Neal and Sunanda stood up and said to Zjon and Samantha, "We will go back to the ship and get some sleep. Sleep well, lovebirds." They followed Allison out of the room.

The two remaining couples rose and headed in opposite directions, after wishing each other good night.

Once inside their room, Zjon and Samantha quietly and with heightened anticipation undressed and slipped under the covers. Theirs was a long-awaited reunion. As they held each other, Samantha said, "Honey, I want to remember this forever. I feel so good here-now. Part of me wants to live in both times."

"You know that is impossible. You belong in our time."

"I know, my love. But this is such a great time too. There is something sweet about it."

"Of course, it is sweet. I feel that way too. But we have to go back to our own world."

"I know. Can I take one little thing from this time? Just for me to remember?"

"You know that is forbidden, Samantha. We cannot take objects from one time into another. It could throw everything out of equilibrium and balance. This has been tricky enough as it is. Take good pictures in your memory. You will always have these friends with you in that way."

"Make love to me, Zjon. I have missed you so badly."

"I love you, my Samantha." Zjon reached over and turned out the lights.

As they settled into their bed, Edward and Clare hugged each other without speaking. There were sharing a bittersweet feeling. This was the last night they would spend with their beloved daughter. She had become their daughter. Life was indeed a strange and grand mystery.

Edward reached over and turned out their lights. Surprisingly, after a moment, the dark room became illuminated. The atmosphere in the room took on a blue tint. "That's strange," Edward said. "Do you see that?"

"I do. What do you think it is?"

"I have no idea."

The two watched with surprise as flashing lights began to flit in and out of the space of the room. They looked like the lights were dancing.

As Edward watched in fascination, he suddenly realized he was becoming aroused. "Are you feeling what I'm feeling, Clare?"

"Shut up and make love to me."

CHAPTER 49

MSM-HRC, Day Nine, 11:00 a.m.

THE CAMPUS MAP OF THE UNIVERSITY OF NEVADA, LAS VEGAS, COMMONLY KNOWN AS UNLV, labeled the building complex "MSM-HRC." More formally, it was known as the Marjorie Barrick Museum/Harry Reid Center. David, having conferred with the proper officials, had arranged to rent the MSM-HRC for the day.

In a tour the day before, Dan and David together had concluded that the Barrick Museum housed a suitable auditorium for conducting the interview. It was not too big and not too small. Easy access was provided from the main front doors as well as from a back entrance. David's men could readily manage the foot traffic and necessary security, leaving traffic management to the campus police and Metro. At this time of year, the campus generally was not crowded. After all, it was summer.

The HRC was known primarily for its laboratory and research facilities and its electron microscope. All agreed that this venue was a good place to host a group of noteworthy scientists, and at the same time to surreptitiously handle the small group of American political leaders, all the while avoiding public exposure.

Samantha also liked the idea. She had spent much of the last year doing her own research in the UNLV's libraries and had grown quite fond of the campus. When she and Zjon had held their breakfast prep meeting with Dan and David a few hours before, she had made David promise that he would return two books she had borrowed weeks

ED STROUPE AND TILAK FERNANDO

ago. They were way past due. David cheerfully volunteered to pay her fine for her. He was not quite sure at this point whether he was more in love with Samantha or Melissa. Dan had been very surprised to see what a romantic David had turned out to be, and David had even surprised himself.

At 10:00 a.m. sharp, Dan and Jonathan heard footsteps coming down the hall toward the HRC conference room. "They're right on time," Dan commented to Jonathan. Leading the group down the hallway were David and the president's lead Secret Service team. Following closely behind were Wallace Wade and the president's chief of staff, followed in turn by the president and the first lady, much to Dan's and Jonathan's surprise. Trailing them were the Speaker of the House, senate majority and minority leaders, and finally the press secretary and the rest of the Secret Service team.

Once the contingent was completely inside the room, Jonathan followed Dan in. Directing the others to make themselves comfortable, the president walked over and shook Jonathan's hand, then Dan's. He whispered to the two men, "Are we all set?" Dan gave a discreet thumbs-up, and Jonathan nodded.

Jonathan then whispered to the president, "I am going over to wait in the auditorium for the others. They are set to arrive at eleven o'clock. I am saving you a seat in the back of the room, as well as a place in the front right corner, in case you choose to come down there. Dan will give me the signal either way." The president nodded, and Jonathan turned and left the room.

At that point, Wallace came over to join the president and Dan. Dan proceeded to brief them both on the setup: "The monitor over there on the wall is tied in by closed circuit to cameras in the auditorium, allowing you to observe everything that happens there until the end of the interview. Each camera has its own recorder so we will have an electronic record as well as a backup. We will bring that to your chief of staff when the meeting is over. In addition, we have a camera ready in this room should you choose to interact with our visitors at any time. This will be strictly your call. Any questions, Mister President?"

"Who won the lottery to be here?"

"Interestingly, representatives from *The Washington Post*, CNN, and Fox News."

"Very good. A perfect cross-section. And what will happen after the meeting?"

"Jonathan will escort Zjon and Samantha across the street to a secure location at McCarran. The airport is closed until midnight, and we have been guaranteed privacy by the TSA. Wallace and I will take you, the first lady, and anyone else whom you choose, over to meet them. Your Secret Service team is clearing the airport as we speak."

"Perfect. From there I will make the call to coordinate our return to Camp David. Last question—what is the status of the third man?"

"David has his team and the Metro Police out on the lookout. Without a photograph, it's tricky. Hopefully, though, Zjon and Samantha will call him in once you fully have their trust."

"Excellent. I will call upon my elite campaigning skills to make that happen. My secret weapon will be my wife. She can persuade anybody of anything!"

On the far side of the HRC building, three men were gathered in a video control room making final checks and rechecks of all the audio and video equipment.

"Cameras A and B are working fine," a grad student named Johnson called out.

His colleague, an undergraduate named Harrison, called back, "All good on the sound system as well."

"How's the HRC system checking out?" Johnson asked the third man, who was officially representing the government team.

"It appears that we are all set."

Johnson said, "Thanks for your help, Neal. I don't think we could have gotten all this done without you."

"No problem." Neal smiled. "I am happy to be of service."

"Where'd you say you were from?"

"Not far. A small town on the West Coast called Los Angeles. I just happened to be in the neighborhood."

"You in the movie business?"

"Not exactly. But something like that."

CHAPTER 50

MSM-HRC, Day Nine, Noon

ALL THE BUZZING OF VOICES AND SHUFFLING OF PAPERS BEGAN TO SUBSIDE IN THE Barrick Museum auditorium as four figures marched down the aisle toward the dais in the front of the room. This area was empty, except for two padded director's chairs. Behind them a blank screen was hanging from the ceiling. There were no chalkboards or flip chart stands. No doubt the audience of professors and scientists and scholars found this unusual. One would expect some sort of presentation. Just what kind of a meeting was this?

The four people, two men and two women, filed across the dais until they had placed themselves in front of the two chairs, facing the audience. Looking out at the group, Jonathan saw that their guests had almost entirely filled the seats in the center section, including the front row. This was unusual. Normally one would expect an audience to avoid the front row. He guessed that these people were expecting an exciting show.

In the HRC conference room at the other end of the building, the president and his entourage waited with more than a little concern. The expected guests had not yet appeared. David and his men had been combing the area around the complex, intending to intercept them. Dan reported to Wallace that thus far, they had been no-shows.

"Welcome, everyone, and thank you for coming." It was Clare who made the opening speech. "For those of you whom I have not met, my name is Dr. Clare Hunter, and I am professor of anthropology at UCSF. Standing to my left is my husband Edward, a professor of mathematics at UCSF. To my right is Jonathan Elliot, chief science editor of *The New York Times*. And to his right is Dr. Allison Russell, professor of philosophy at NYU. We are very glad you were able to make it on such short notice.

"We have with us today a first. I know that you have been told that we have guests who came here from a future time. One of these people has been living with Edward and me for three years. It was only recently that we learned her true identity. For those of you who also may have met her, you should know that her true identity came as much of a surprise to us as I am sure it did to you. I will let her tell her story. Suffice it to say that Samantha had lost her memory and had no recollection of who she was until she was joined by colleagues sent here to rescue her."

At this point the audience began to murmur. Many of them turned to look at their neighbors to see if this was some kind of joke. Hearing Clare's words being spoken aloud made everyone realize that they were risking their professional reputations just by being there. Clare immediately sensed that they needed to get things started. She turned and nodded to Jonathan.

"We know exactly how this sounds," Jonathan said. "Nine days ago, I would never have thought that this could be possible. But I promise you that it is. These people have brought a message that is well worth receiving—especially today, in our time, a time of deep unrest. We are grateful to have received support from the highest levels of our government. And you were the ones whom we hand-picked to be here today."

Clare stepped back in. "So, without further ado, I would like to introduce to you two of our new friends, Samantha and Zjon. Please welcome them." Everyone in the audience stood and began a polite round of applause. The four left the dais and began parading out. The applause continued for another thirty seconds and then began to dwindle. The mysterious guests were nowhere to be seen.

People turned toward their neighbors with questioning looks. In the HRC conference room Wallace Wade said, "Dammit! I think we've been stood up." The president continued to stare at the monitor and held up his hand for everybody to wait. Slowly a smile began to break on his face. Just wait, he motioned. Something is coming.

In the main auditorium, the sound of applause was turning to grumbling. An unidentified voice was heard to say, "We've been had, everybody." At last everyone was seated once again. Two people remained standing, however, a man and a woman in the rear. The two turned and moved toward the right aisle.

As the couple stepped into the aisle, several in the audience noticed that they began walking down the incline toward the front of the room. Within a few seconds, others in the room noticed these two unfamiliar people. They seemed to be very confident and at ease. They were also remarkable in appearance. There seemed to be a lightness emanating from their bodies. They moved with catlike gracefulness. Who were they?

Samantha and Zjon reached the front of the room and took their seats in the director's chairs. "Hello," the woman said, "my name is Samantha. This is Zjon. We have traveled here from the year 4544. Three years ago, I fell into 'now.'"

"It was *him*," the president whispered under his breath. Then aloud, "It *was* him!" All turned from the monitor to look at him.

"What, sir?" his chief of staff asked.

"I have seen that man. Three summers ago, I saw the face of that man in a dream. At least, I thought it was a dream." Abruptly the image returned to his memory, accompanied by three words: *Something is coming.* "This is extraordinary."

Stunned by the president's outburst, all faces turned back to look at the monitor.

CHAPTER 51

MSM-HRC, Day Nine, 12:10 p.m.

I N THE CONTROL ROOM ON THE OTHER SIDE OF THE BUILDING, NEAL WAS ENGAGED WHILE his two technical cohorts were watching their monitors. He quickly finished his manipulations and sat back with a smile. Internal cabling and electrical wiring were now synchronized with Sunanda's onboard systems back at the ship. Invisible signals were now beaming up to all of the telecommunications satellites in their geostationary orbits. Unbeknownst to the satellite television and cable owners, Neal had succeeded in performing the first global hack in history. What was appearing on television sets in living rooms throughout America and around the world, from Russia to China to Brazil, from Israel to Iceland to Kenya, were the faces and voices of Zjon and Samantha.

Back in the Barrick Auditorium, Samantha described to the audience—both inside the auditorium and around the globe—how she had "fallen into 'now.'" As she spoke, her Presence filled the room and radiated through the airwaves in the atmosphere. She spoke without doubt, conveying the assurance that her words were absolutely true. Even the most skeptical among the scientists believed every word. People lost themselves in a story that became as vivid to them as their own.

As she wrapped up her account, Jonathan glanced at his watch from the back row of the room and saw that she had been speaking for more than thirty minutes. He turned to his three colleagues from the press and saw that they were completely absorbed—even the man from Fox News. Jonathan knew at that moment that this was going to work. He had made the right decisions. The world was going to hear the whole story.

Zjon was next to speak. "We will now be happy to address any questions you may have."

Hands shot up from every row. Samantha pointed to the woman seated in the center of the front row. Jonathan turned to the three press members and whispered a reminder to them, "You will not be called on, so please keep your hands down." He noticed each of them had pulled out a smartphone and was recording the meeting. He whispered again, "I recommend you listen with your ears, hearts, and minds. Do not rely on recordings, or you will be disappointed."

The woman whom Samantha had called on stood and asked, "I am a professor of physics from Cal Tech. Can you explain the technology that allowed you to travel here?"

Zjon turned to Samantha. "Let me take that one. I am afraid that we cannot explain anything relating to the technology of the future. To begin with, our explanation would do you no good. Our knowledge is the product of more than two thousand years of investigation, experimentation, and learning, from where you are today. More importantly, we consider it a fundamental principle not to interfere. After Samantha's accident, our leaders searched their hearts deeply to determine whether to allow us to come here. There is a risk of our interfering in your society in such a way that could endanger future generations. Thus, we cannot divulge the very things that we know most of you came here to find out. You will have to forgive us."

Samantha put in, "We are happy to share many other things with you."

"Since you come from the future, what can you tell us that could help us?" This came from the same woman. She now sat down. The audience held its breath with hushed anticipation.

Samantha thought for several seconds before answering: "My time here living with you has made me appreciate how we human beings have succeeded in evolving. Most people in this time think evolution is some kind of mechanical thing involving just genetics. Yes, genetics is important and does lie at the foundation of human evolution, and all animal evolution. But genetics is not everything. There is another kind of evolution. I will call this 'intelligence of the human heart.' The heart is not just an organ that pumps blood, or a center of emotions. Heart is the synergistic totality of your organic cellular being. Heart resides in every cell of your body.

"Thus far in history, your evolution has served one purpose—your survival. Survival is necessary for life. Yet, it is limited. We have learned that, in truth, our lives are unlimited. When I say 'unlimited,' I mean that we have the access to all of life's energies and fascinations. This access is virtually unlimited. But because of our human unworthiness, we feel limited. We think we only have five senses and that we are here to just live and die. And we are trying to make the best of it. To do this, we have invented stories to live by. This is nothing new. It has been part of the fabric of humanity since the beginning of recorded history.

"When you look at it with your heart, you will see that we are so much more than animals trying to survive. The way we are built, our physical bodies are perfect for allowing the elemental forces to go through us. It is perfect for enabling us to ascend into vertical dimensions of living, beyond the horizontal world of animal survival. Our senses are capable of opening other dimensions of experience—other spaces and extensions that exist—to the very nature of what human beings have called 'infinity.'

"There are three fundamental principles of life: Imperfection, Unpredictability, and Impermanence. Even in my time, as you can see from my accident, life is unpredictable. Our technology, as highly developed as it has become, is imperfect. We human beings are imperfect. Finally, nothing is permanent. Everything and everyone has its time. It is unworthiness that most prevents us from experiencing our true nature. Unworthiness is the natural condition that sets in when we least expect it. Like these other principles, it is a necessary part of living. The next time you feel bad about yourself, see the unworthiness that lies underneath this feeling. You can allow it to dissolve in an instant by truing yourself up. This will allow you all to evolve."

"How can we true ourselves up?"

Zjon answered, "In the game of chess, there are five major pieces: the king, the queen, the knight, the bishop, and the castle. They are all like the energies within us. As an analogy, the castle is like the human body—a steady, grounding energy, the energy of the Earth. The knight has a special way that it can jump into unexpected places and go around other pieces. This represents the force of Water. The bishop can move diagonally great distances, explosively like the element Fire. The queen is really the most brilliant piece in the game, being able to move in any direction. She is the element Air. Finally, the king is the Space of the whole game. The objective is to capture the opponent's Space.

"All across the board there are also pawns. The pawns can only move very slowly, one square forward at a time. They are important and necessary for protection of the major pieces, in other words for survival. They represent thoughts. To win in chess, a player needs to be willing to sacrifice pawns. Similarly, to ascend in the game of life, we need to be willing to sacrifice our thoughts! Thoughts are not the same as thinking. For us to have true thinking, we must let go of what we think we already know. To unleash into inquiry means to listen, not just to question. Listening from the heart must provide the impulse for your questioning.

"No one time is better than any other time in human existence. Think about prehistoric people when they invented tools. Think about the ancient steppes of Asia, where people invented the wheel.

Ancient people could not have invented nuclear power. Yet, they had one thing they needed to do—to travel. They could not travel, and so they invented the wheel. Discovering the wheel was actually the greatest act of *intelligence of the human heart.* In every age, the intelligence of the human heart has found the way for humans to move to the next level and break time. In your age you have reached a point of super-survival. It is time for you to ask yourselves, 'What else is there?'"

A man in one of the middle rows asked the next question. "We have heard rumors that you have performed feats that I, as a scientist, would classify as miracles. In the past we have only heard stories of people performing miracles in religious books, like Jesus in the Bible. Is this true?"

"Samantha, I think this one is yours."

Samantha smiled. "We are not like Jesus, the Buddha, Mohammed, Confucius, Zoroaster, or Krishna, or any other of the great beings of the past. We are ordinary human beings, just like you in this room. I will answer this question briefly by saying that we have evolved to a place where we have developed capacities for sensing and tapping into the Universal Intelligence, and as part of that we can interact with Intelligence through the silent language of signaling. These capacities all of you share with us, but they are latent and undeveloped. In time you will come to discover these for yourselves."

"Can't you show us something?"

"Something is happening right now, all over the world. You will hear about it later."

At the other end of the building, everyone experienced a sudden shock.

"What the hell do you think she is talking about, Mister President?" It was the Speaker of the House.

"Damned if I know."

At that moment, there was a knock at the door. Dan opened it a crack and peered out. One of the Secret Service men handed him a note and said, "This is for the president. It's urgent." Dan closed the door and handed the president the note.

"My God!" the president exclaimed.

"What is it?" everyone asked.

"This meeting is being broadcast everywhere. On all the networks."

"How could that have happened?" Wallace Wade asked, suddenly furious. He looked over at Dan, who only shook his head in genuine bewilderment. "Find out, Dan, right now!"

The president intervened. "No, Wallace. I should have anticipated something like this. What they are trying to offer applies to all of humanity, not just our country. It was arrogant for me to think we could corner the market on this. We have just entered a whole new world. I think it is time for us to let go of the way things have always been and realize that this is a true game changer."

"I hope you are right. But what about China and Russia and the terrorist networks?"

"Do you think Americans are the only people in the world witnessing this? We need to expand our thinking here."

"Yes, Mister President." For once in his career, the president felt that the majority leader's last words were authentically spoken.

Jonathan again looked at his watch. Amazingly it read 1:25 p.m. He knew that they only had half an hour before Zjon and Samantha needed to leave for the airport. He raised his hand. As if on cue, Samantha pointed to him and said, "Yes, Jonathan?"

"I have a question to ask myself. I have been forced to acknowledge that what you say is true and that you are really here from the future. I am just wondering where you are from on the planet Earth in your time."

Samantha laughed. "Do you mean, are we Americans?"

"Yes, I guess that is another way of putting it," he said, chuckling.

Zjon said, "I can handle this one. I was originally born in the metropolis that used to be known as Chicago. Our two compatriots, who are not in this room, were both born in the successor to the city you call Denver. Samantha is the only one of us who was not born on this continent. She came from an island in Asia that I believe you call Serendip."

"Actually," Samantha corrected, "that is the ancient name. In this time, it is called Sri Lanka."

A woman raised her hand, and Samantha called on her. "What about government in your time. Do you still have countries?"

Zjon responded, "This is another question that we cannot answer. Human societies need to evolve, discover, and invent new ways of living together. Suffice it to say that there have been numerous experiments in government, and this is a constantly evolving and changing area. I will tell you that we have long ago succeeded in eliminating war, hunger, poverty, and most diseases. We have new kinds of problems that I will not go into."

"What kinds of problems?"

"The kinds of problems that arise naturally when people solve old problems. That is all. Just look at your own life experience."

"Are you two married?"

Samantha laughed. "Yes and no. In our time the nature of marriage has changed. We no longer have it as a type of legal status or a fixed religious idea. People are able to form long-lasting love relationships. Zjon and I chose such a relationship. We declared it and registered it, and next year may choose to renew it. This is the most common form of relationship, kind of like marriage. The most common convention people choose is three- or four-year terms.

Naturally people who choose to have children usually select much longer terms."

Another question came from the audience: "What about religion? Is there a universal world religion?"

Zjon took this one. "The difference between your time and our time can be characterized by one word: variety. The variety that exists in our time would probably drive you insane. However, what is universal is recognizing the mystery of being alive and letting go of a need to have the right answers. When people finally reached the point of letting go of rigid beliefs, it opened up their hearts to true exploration and the appreciation of life. All religious expression is characterized by the great teachings of the past masters. Foremost among these are Unconditional Love and Unconditional Compassion."

"It sounds like you live in a utopia."

"Truthfully speaking, it is exactly the opposite," Zjon said. "The word 'utopia' means 'not a place.' Utopias have always been fantasies, but the world we live in is not at all a kind of fantasy. I know that what we have described sounds like some kind of perfect life. But life is still subject to the principles of Unpredictability, Imperfection, and Impermanence. No one time or era is better than any other. You are in the right time for your lives. If you want to know how I can say that, it is because you are here-now and not there-then.

"Our time for this interview has reached its end, and we have to be going. Later today we will be returning to our time."

With that both the auditorium and the president's conference room erupted in a collective groan. A man from the audience shouted, "Why do you have to leave us so soon?"

Zjon said calmly, "Samantha came here through the grace of an accident in the fabric of timespace. We succeeded in following her here through the same kind of grace, the gift of Universal Intelligence. We cannot remain here; we belong in our own time. There is a precise timespace window that has remained open for nine days, but will be closing in a few hours. For us to stay could have devastating consequences."

Samantha ended the interview. "We will be leaving exactly at 3:33 p.m. this afternoon, from across the street at the airport. If you would like to see us off, come to Sunset Road. We will say our good-byes then."

As the room stirred to life, Zjon and Samantha quickly stood and walked out through the exit door in the corner of the room. Outside the building, David and Neal met them and briskly escorted them to a black limousine. Zjon and Samantha hopped into the backseat, while Neal and David jumped into front. "Welcome back, David." Melissa's voice once again was music to David's ears. Zjon clapped David on the back as the car pulled away.

At the other side of the building, the president and his contin-gent, shocked into sudden action by the latest revelation, spilled out of the building. The president and the first lady climbed into the first limousine, along with Wallace, who took the front passenger seat. The others clambered into the cars behind them. Dan left the group to go pick up Edward, Clare, Allison, and Jonathan. The president pointed to the departing limousine that held Zjon and Samantha, and ordered, "Follow that car!"

The first lady said, "You're such a ham."

He smiled and said, "I've always wanted to say that."

CHAPTER 52

McCarran Airport, Day Nine, 2:00 p.m.

THE CONVOY OF LIMOUSINES CARRYING THE PRESIDENT AND HIS ENTOURAGE PULLED UP the central drop-off area of Terminal 3. The Secret Service team hustled the presidential party into the terminal, then shepherded them through security and onto a waiting shuttle train. From there the group proceeded to the Centurion Lounge in central Concourse D. The concourse itself was set apart from the main airline terminal, and the lounge offered quiet surroundings with modern amenities, including a buffet.

Upon entering the lounge area, the chief of staff took the president aside and whispered to him, "Sir, we have quite a situation."

"Please fill me in."

"The car carrying our visitors seemed to disappear in the airport complex. Dan Hamilton and David Newman are with them."

"I believe they will honor the appointment."

"I hope so. Second, the charged field is apparently back, surrounding this airport complex. We are now inside of it. We may be cut off from the outside, with no one able to reach us. Should I contact the chairman of the joint chiefs?"

"Yes, but tell him for now not to try to breach the field. The best thing would be to come to help manage traffic control around the airport. It is predictable that there will be a lot of people coming to see the show, and I do not want anyone getting hurt."

"Done. And yes, I'm told that people are gathering on Sunset Road and Las Vegas Boulevard. Thousands so far."

"Keep the military on standby, and see that the Metro Police are supported. Anything else?"

"Yes. I've called for Air Force One to leave Nellis and arrive here at six o'clock. This will give us time to load up and leave before the FAA reopens the airport at midnight."

"Good."

"One last thing ..."

"What?"

"We have received messages from the president of Russia, the Chinese chairman, and the Indian, Israeli, and British prime ministers, as well as other leaders from every continent. They all saw the broadcast."

"Are they angry?"

"I would have thought so. What's mind-boggling is that they were blown away."

"Not surprising."

"This is the clincher: every one of them reported that the broadcast took place in their native language!"

"What? How?"

"Beats the hell out of me. They all expressed thanks that we included them with translations. They said that for once America was not trying to hide something."

"You're kidding! Zjon and Samantha actually make us look good. Any idea how they reacted to the announcement that our visitors are leaving?"

"Russia and China have both requested we ask them to stay and come on a tour to meet them. Alternatively, they would be happy to meet them at the United Nations."

"Let us see what our friends say when they get here."

"Speaking of which ..."

Just then, David escorted Zjon, Samantha, and Neal in through the Centurion Lounge entrance. Trailing shortly behind came Dan,

Jonathan, Edward, Clare, and Allison. "Well, well," Dan said jovially, "It looks like the gang's all here." This was more of a polite heads-up to alert the Secret Service than to make an announcement.

In a matter of seconds Dan's chief, Wallace Wade, approached with a pair of Secret Service agents from a hidden place at the back of the lounge. Once introductions and standard weapon searches were completed, Wallace led the group back to meet the president.

It had been the president's plan for Air Force One to fly from Nellis to pick up his group and then take him and his honored guests back to Washington. Now plans obviously had to change, as their presence had been leaked to the world. This was slightly more than a leak, the president mused. And there had been a *hell* of a change of plans.

The president and first lady stood as Zjon, Samantha, and Neal approached them. "It is an honor to meet you at last, in person," the president said, extending his hand.

"The pleasure is all ours, Mister President," Zjon said. "I am Commander Zjon III of the Global Federation Explorer *Jasmine Antares.* This is my partner Samantha, also a renowned 'Captain' in our time, and our chief navigator, Neal." All shook hands with the president, and then with the first lady.

The first lady escorted the three over to a makeshift buffet table. "Is there anything else we can offer you to drink?" she asked.

"Do you happen to have Oban Scotch?" Zjon asked. "Jonathan introduced me to it, and I have grown very fond of this drink. We have nothing quite like it back home."

"I'll see what I can find." She invited them to sit with the president and then stepped out of the room on a special Scotch search mission. At the same time the Speaker of the House and the senate majority and minority leaders filed into the room. The president introduced each and invited them all to sit down.

Then the president opened the conversation. "I was surprised and sorry to hear that you are leaving us. Your presence here has come as quite a shock, and it will be a long time before we will be able to digest this. Is there any way you can extend your visit with us? We think that you have much to offer to us in our time. Also, other world leaders are also clamoring to meet you."

Zjon responded, "I am afraid we cannot stay. As I indicated in the meeting, we are on a very delicate timeline."

"I had to ask. Rest assured we would not attempt to keep you here. Can you answer a few questions before you leave us?"

"I will do my best."

"Can I assume this young man, Neal, was responsible for the global broadcast?"

"Yes, that was me," Neal replied. "I replaced one of David's men, the one assigned to work with the university techs who were manning the audio-visual system. I placed him into a safe state of temporary unconsciousness, and then signaled for him to awaken after I was finished."

The president said, "It was very impressive. How did you manage to get translations into the broadcast? I am told that everyone heard you in their native languages."

"That was easier than you think," said Zjon. "We had no translators. As we spoke, everyone naturally heard us in his or her own language. Language manifests among human beings in many ways. What we speak is language itself, the language of language. In our time we have learned speaking and listening from inside the essence of language, transcending the strictures of particular languages. You see, language is a gift of Intelligence to the human heart. We speak human being to human being, heart to heart, if you will. That is the best way I can explain it. Someday this ability will come to human beings, in your future."

"Okay," the president acknowledged. "How about this charged field? What is it?"

"'The field,' as you call it, is a necessary manifestation of the timespace phase shift connecting tunnel. Suffice it for me to say that it activated for a temporary period as we originally homed in on Samantha nine days ago, and it has reactivated for our return.

The field will disappear within twenty-four hours after we have departed. Part of its function is to protect our space from contamination. Once we have left, it will remain as a residue and then dissipate. It will not interfere with your timespace or prevent your air traffic after four o'clock.

"Because we are from another time, we cannot take anything from this time with us when we leave. Nor can we leave anything that belongs to our time here in your time. In a sense Samantha has been on an extended loan between our times. Today your time will be paying our time back, so to speak. This is all part of the natural equilibrium. Incidentally, when the field dissipates tomorrow, any electronic records that people have made here will disappear with it. This includes memory sticks, broadcast tapes, and photographs. You can think of it this way. Our physical beings and systems all belong to the future and will return with us. Electromagnetic representations will necessarily disappear. We will live among you only as memory. For many it will all seem to have been a dream. Only in this way can Nature guarantee noninterference in human evolution."

"Excuse me for interrupting," said the first lady, who had reentered the room. Following her were Jonathan, Clare, Edward, Allison, Dan, and David. She carried a bottle of Scotch, as did Jonathan. Dan and David brought buckets of ice.

The president stood, and the entire room naturally did the same. Taking a glass in hand, after all had been served, he said, "Allow me to propose a final toast."

CHAPTER 53

Ascendance, Day Nine, 3:30 p.m.

THE AFTERNOON SKY ABOVE LAS VEGAS WAS BRIGHT BLUE AND TOTALLY CLEAR, WITH the exception of a single, small, cumulus cloud that was slowly drifting over the city. Directly below, the runways of McCarran International Airport were quiet and deserted. This was the first day since the 9/11 aftermath that all air traffic had been suspended.

Police had closed off traffic from Las Vegas Boulevard, Sunset Road, and Eastern and Tropicana Avenues, for one-quarter mile from the airport. These were the four streets that bracketed the airport. In addition, they had blocked all traffic that passed by the airport terminals and through the underpass below the runways.

In the aftermath of Zjon's announcement of their imminent departure, thousands of people had migrated to the airport to view the event. They wanted to see firsthand the "Earthlings from the Future." The cable and national networks had immediately latched onto this moniker as soon as the hijacking of the airwaves had ended.

Television stations had rushed their news vans from all over to the airport, parking most of them on Maule, which provided the closest unblocked access. Camera and sound people had hoofed their equipment up to Sunset to grab the most central vantage points outside the airport perimeter fence. In the sky could be seen armies of helicopters, each keeping a safe distance from the space directly above the airport.

This was "perhaps the fastest assembly of masses of people since the March on Washington," one newscaster touted. Indeed, all that anyone could see now was a carpet of human beings. Many people had found their way to the rooftops of the buildings that lined Sunset in order to get a better view. People even could be seen hanging out of the second-story windows of their homes.

The airport grounds remained deserted. A few people had tried to scale the perimeter fences, finding to their amazement that some unnatural kind of force was preventing them from gaining access. No one was hurt, but people learned very quickly to keep their distance. All in all, the crowd of people constituted a peaceful assembly. Indeed, this was the most amazing example of a flash mob in modern history. Today's gathering, however, was not coming for entertainment.

The nation's atomic clocks fed their time signals through the satellite network, the Internet, and the nation's mobile phone carriers, triggering every smartphone and tablet PC to display the time to be 3:30 p.m. Inside the Centurion Lounge on Concourse D, the air suddenly resonated with beeps, gongs, and other audible alarms, signaling that it was now the bottom of the hour. Heads ducked down while the owners of the offending devices fumbled and fiddled. The president shook his head and said to the first lady, "Now you know why I don't carry one of those."

Thirty minutes before, Samantha, Zjon, and Neal had bid their personal farewells to each of their friends and newfound allies. Samantha had spent several minutes hugging and kissing Clare and Edward, none wanting to let the other go. She had then hugged each of her other friends and finished by thanking the president.

After shaking hands with David and Dan, thanking each in turn for his courage of heart, Zjon had at last come over to Jonathan.

"This has truly been remarkable, Jonathan," he said. "You have provided two keys in my life. To begin with, you provided the genetic key that enabled me to exist in my time. And second, you provided the key to unlocking the mystery of our arrival in your time, the key for our connection. I could never sufficiently express to you the gratitude I have in my heart. I love you, my greatest grandfather." With tears in their eyes, the two men had hugged each other.

Their clocks announced that there were three minutes to go before the time of departure. The president's team scattered among the bank of windows overlooking the runway area where Zjon had indicated they would make their exit. Jonathan, Dan, and David stood together before one window. Clare, Edward, and Allison stationed themselves at the adjacent window. Everyone in the room waited in silent anticipation.

It was 3:30 p.m., and outside nothing was happening. People were beginning to fidget. The murmurs of the crowd were starting to grow. The feeling was beginning to turn from one of eager anticipation to restlessness edging toward agitation. Then suddenly from somewhere in the crowd a chant began to take shape. "We want Samantha; we want Zjon; we want Samantha; we want Zjon." The volume rose as the chanting rippled up and down the street.

At 3:31 p.m., a single, black limousine drove out from a hidden corner inside the airport complex. The car cruised along the concrete until it reached a central position on the east-west runway, a few hundred yards from the cameras on Sunset Road. There it came to a stop. The crowd spontaneously erupted into a cheer, with clapping and whistling. The cheering lasted for almost a minute before settling down. Then nothing happened.

It was now 3:32 p.m. People were looking at their watches and smartphones, counting down the time, holding their breath. There was no movement from the limousine. The only sounds that could be heard were the voices of the commentators as they tried to fill the airtime until something happened. Something was coming. Everybody felt this. Nobody knew what that something was.

At 3:33 p.m. the cloud that had earlier drifted over the airport descended to the ground, filling the entire grounds with mist and obscuring all views of the airport from the outside. The crowds on the street fell into a hushed silence. This mist formed a wall just inside the fence lines that extended vertically upward for hundreds of feet. Outside the mist, however, the air remained clear and the sky was totally blue.

After less than a minute, just as abruptly as it had appeared, the mist evaporated completely. The atmosphere in and around McCarran now shimmered with a sheen that created an almost surrealistic clarity. The feeling in the air was electric. Where the car had been only seconds before stood ...

Something?

Newscasters tried to describe the object they saw standing—or hovering—before them. It appeared to be about twenty or thirty feet across and seemed to extend perhaps forty, maybe fifty, feet above the ground, its width narrowing to reach a point at the top, like an upside-down toy top. Nobody could tell if it was spinning. It was perfectly symmetrical, and the surface had a sheen that seemed to shift in coloration—now grayish silver, now bluish green, now an almost reddish brown. While there were no discernible marks or openings, it gave off sparkles of colored light, dancing in and out of view along the surface in seemingly random patterns.

Inside the airport lounge, everyone's attention had been completely captured by the scene taking place outside their window.

"So that is their ship," Dan whispered to David and Jonathan.

"Oh my God!" the president exclaimed, momentarily breaking the spell in the room.

Allison ventured, "It's shaped perfectly like a leaf of the Bodhi tree, only spherical instead of flat. I have several such leaves at home that I collected in the Far East."

"You're right, Allison," Clare affirmed. "Those light patterns are not random, but are moving outward and upward from the base, just like the veins of a leaf. It's almost an optical illusion, but I can see it clearly now."

For what seemed like a very long time, but was actually only about twenty seconds, nothing happened. Then in a liquid-like motion a section of one side of the ship unfolded into an opening, and Neal and Sunanda appeared, holding hands. As they walked out, part of the ship's surface extended forward, forming a wide platform. The two released each other's hands and walked in opposite directions, stopping when they were about twenty feet apart. Following through the same opening, Zjon and Samantha emerged, also holding hands. They walked out along the platform and stood between the other two. The ship's surface resealed itself, leaving no trace of the doorway.

The crowd erupted into a tremendous cheer. Inside the terminal lounge the president and everyone in his entourage began to cheer, too, the first lady and the Speaker of the House applauding the loudest.

After allowing the sounds to subside, Zjon raised his right hand to wave to the crowd. Instantaneously, both his and Samantha's images were projected onto the side of the ship so everyone could have a clearer view. The projection technology made their images appear as if they were directly facing everyone, both inside and outside the airport. Jonathan thought to himself that somehow once again they had managed to defy the laws of physics. How can one image be projected in all directions at once? He felt an upwelling of pride in his body.

The cheers subsided into a respectful silence. Zjon lowered his hand and began speaking. As he spoke, his voice carried throughout the crowd and into the airport lounge, without the need for amplification.

"We are your brothers and sisters. We are your lovers and your children from the future. We are not here from another world. We are from this world. But we are from a different time. The greatest part about our appearance here is that I believe, in one way or another, it will accelerate evolution and will enable humankind to ascend to a much higher quality of living. Our deepest wish is that you will be inspired by our visit to end all suffering in your world. You have that capacity, each and every one of you.

"This is not the time to explain about the future. This is just a time to say that planet Earth ... well, there is no other planet like Earth in the whole universe. Stay here, in this 'now,' fully in your Presence on Earth. Your time is one of the best in the whole universe."

Zjon paused and looked at Samantha. Samantha spoke. "What is most important, most powerful for you to understand now, is that the Truth is in all of us. By 'Truth' I mean the Heart of Intelligence. By 'all of us' I mean each and every one of you. The Heart of Intelligence lies within you. Now, all I have to tell you is how grateful we are. We will never forget you and will carry you back with us in our hearts, forever."

Spreading her hands out in front of her, as if embracing the crowd, she concluded, "You are not this and not that. Out of the space of the nothing that you are arise all things. Let it rise!"

Without further words, the four raised their hands in salute. Then they turned around and briskly walked back toward the ship, which opened for them and then swallowed them as they disappeared into its interior.

As all the people watched, there arose a gentle sound of humming. Slowly and steadily the ship ascended to a height of about one thousand feet and then stopped. People watched in fascination as the surface began to emit light in every color. Then there was a sudden flash of white, and it disappeared. In its place people saw small specks of white suspended in the air where the ship had been. Thousands of specks started drifting down toward the crowd, descending like a soft blanket. Soon everyone realized they were flowers—jasmine flowers. Everyone reached their hands into the air to catch one. As the flowers drifted into their eagerly opened hands, the sweet scent of jasmine permeated the atmosphere.

Inside the Centurion Lounge the air carried the same fragrant scent, causing everyone to smile.

The president of the United States and the first lady kissed each other. "My dear," the first lady said, "I think a new day has dawned."

He answered, "I know there is work to do, but for the first time in a very long time, I truly feel hope that we can do this."

The Speaker of the House and the senate majority leader and minority leader walked over to the president. The Speaker said, "We are ready. Let's get on with it!" The three leaders shook each other's hands in turn.

Jonathan turned to Dan and asked, "Are you going to head home tonight?"

"Yes, with Wallace."

"Mind if Diana and I hitch a ride? You and Emily could be our guests in our home."

Dan looked over to Wallace, who nodded to him.

"Great! Let's go find them."

"Just one thing, Dan," Wallace interjected, speaking with authority. "I expect to see you in my office first thing Monday morning."

"Yes sir, Chief!"

"I'll fly back to Washington with the president. Take my plane to New York and drop it off in Washington tomorrow night. You're on your own from there."

David reached his hand into his pocket to retrieve his car keys. Feeling an unfamiliar lump in his pocket, he pulled it out to see what it was. It was one of the blue, heart-shaped stones from the night before, the one with the straight line—the Fire stone. He looked at the others. "Can you believe that?"

Dan rummaged around in his pocket and pulled out another stone—S, the Water stone. Allison and Clare eagerly followed right behind him. Allison had the X stone—the brilliance of Air. Clare, to no one's surprise, found the stone with the circle—the Mother Earth. All eyes turned to Jonathan. Jonathan searched for and located it in the side pocket of his jacket. Pulling out his hand, he found he was holding the Arrow stone—Space.

"That's my Samantha," Clare said with a laugh.

"I'll be damned," Jonathan said with a sigh, pondering the fact that these gifts seemed to contradict what Zjon had told them all earlier. Nevertheless, he knew that space had always been his true element.

CHAPTER 54

Camp David, Day Ten, Early Evening

EXACTLY TWENTY-FOUR HOURS AFTER THE EVENT THAT HAD BECOME KNOWN AS "THE Ascendance," telecommunications circuits lit up. News organizations, which since the evening before had continuously shown replays of the events from the previous afternoon, discovered that their video and audio recordings had vanished.

Shockwaves rippled around the world. Internet traffic reached its highest frenzy of activity in history. News organizations contacted each other in desperate attempts to locate some video footage, to no avail. The "Global Erasure Phenomenon," as it would come to be called, extended even to the footage from local surveillance cameras, personal video recorders, smartphone recordings, and still cameras, both digital and film. Every news organization frantically searched through their backups, including the backups of their news broadcasts from the evening before. Nothing was there!

Technically, it was not the recordings and data storage that had vanished. What had vanished were all the images and sounds of Zjon, Samantha, Neal, Sunanda, and the ship itself. Video recordings taken from Sunset Road showed nothing except for a monotonous view of empty runways and the airport buildings behind them. Audio recordings held nothing but the voices of the commentators, noises and clapping from the people in the streets, and the rotors of the helicopters hovering above. Recordings made of the interview showed two empty chairs in front of a group of people seated in rapt attention, with an occasional raised hand and question, followed by an eerie silence.

At Camp David the president was sitting in a dining room enjoying dinner with Wallace Wade and his contingent from the day before when the call came. He hung up the line and turned on the television. The room sat in stunned silence as they saw for themselves.

"Well, I'll be ..." the president said.

Wallace said, "Dan and Jonathan told us Zjon said this would happen. I just didn't really believe it."

The president said, "They were true to their word in everything they said. I guess we should have expected this as well."

After a few more minutes, the president turned off the television. "Ironic, isn't it? We are standing at the pivotal moment of freedom and choice, in the face of the possibility for the grandest of futures, but have no road map for how we are going to get there."

"I'm not sure I follow you, sir," Wallace Wade said.

"They knew all along how this all was going to turn out, and told us so. We, on the other hand, didn't believe them. We arrogantly figured they would give us all the answers. True to their word, they weren't going to interfere by giving us any answers."

Wallace Wade put in, "I guess that leaves it all up to us, sir."

"Yes, Wallace. It really is up to us now. But you know, Wallace, it was always up to us anyway. Nothing has changed; yet everything has."

With that last remark, the president smiled, sat back, and then began gently tapping his thumbs, forefingers, and middle fingers together.

EPILOGUE

New York City, Day Ten, 11:59 p.m.

Jonathan and Diana climbed up the staircase from the kitchen to their bedroom, having just said their good-byes to Dan and Emily. They walked into the bedroom, kicked their shoes off, and sat down on the bed.

"So, this is where it all started," Diana said.

"Yes, ten days ago in the middle of the night, here in our room. Seems like an eternity has passed."

"I am very proud of you."

"Thank you." He stood up, took her hand, bent down, and kissed her. She stood up, and the two embraced for a long time.

"I think we should go to bed now," she said.

"Yes, I'm exhausted."

The two undressed and walked around to opposite sides to get into bed. Once they had settled in, Jonathan started to reach over to turn off the lights, but stopped when he noticed the blue heartstone lying on his nightstand, where he had placed it earlier that day. Seeing it triggered a moment of sadness.

"You know," he said, "I miss them already."

Diana reached across and took his hand, saying nothing.

"Do you think we'll ever see our friends again?" he asked.

"You never know," she answered.

"No, I guess you don't." He leaned over and switched off the lights. "Good night, my dearest."

"Jonathan?"

"Yes?"

"I can see you. There's a light on somewhere, a blue one."

He sat up in bed and looked around to see its source. They both realized at the same time that the light was coming from the television. It was off but emanating a strange blue glow.

Fascinated, they watched as shapes began to appear on the screen. They saw a bright-blue dot appear in the center of the screen and then expand to fill the entire screen. Out of the blue appeared the images of Zjon, Samantha, Neal, and Sunanda, smiling as they peered out through the television toward Jonathan and Diana. The four raised their hands and waved. Jonathan and Diana raised their hands and waved back. The energy of love shot through both of their bodies as they sat in a stunned state of wonder. As quickly as the image had appeared, it dissolved once again into a blue dot and vanished into a flash, sending sparkles of light scattering through the air of the room.

Jonathan and Diana sat for several seconds, speechless. Jonathan's body was glowing inside. At last, he turned to his fiancé and said, "Honey, let's get started on that baby, right now. We have a destiny to fulfill."

THE END

Colorado and Las Vegas
March, 2015–December, 2016

ACKNOWLEDGMENTS

Publication of a novel never takes place in a vacuum. In our case, what started out literally beyond a dream a decade ago has now led to a new future. All of you who have contributed your support and encouragement are too many to count or name, but you know who you are, and know that we appreciate you. To the thousands who have ventured to be Tilak's students over more than three decades, we thank you. To our families and friends, for all your love, we thank you. Many of you have been true partners, and again, you know who you are. We hold you all in deep appreciation and gratitude.

A few names deserve special recognition. First, we want to thank Carol Angley, who held the vision with Tilak for all those years that this dream could become a reality. She also provided the unique gift of insight at key moments during the collaborative writing process. Ed especially wants to thank Barbara Miller, friend and editor extraordinaire, both for her guidance during the writing, and for her meticulous and patient teaching about the intricacies of style and story cohesion. ("Don't listen to what anybody tells you—just write!") Ed also wants to thank Elsa Dixon, another world class editor, for her fabulous refinements of language, and for loving the book. (Even though she chopped it by 20%, she kept our voice intact!) Thanks to Connie Sakrison for her generous listening and coaching over the past two years. She created a space of noninterference that helped allow the book to glide itself into existence with ease and grace. Thanks to Orion Fernando for early readings, questions, and helpful feedback. Finally, thanks to Mary Stroupe for being an undaunted, unwavering "yes" to this whole project.

49060544R00202

Made in the USA
San Bernardino, CA
11 May 2017